Ryker rubbed his eyes. "Nikki and I kept getting woken up by something big crashing around outside our window last night. I couldn't see anything, and even if I did, it would have been double. We'd go back to sleep and half an hour later, it would be back. Must have been a moose or something wandering around. Maybe it was attracted to the smell of the steaks we grilled up."

"That was probably it," Andrew said, feeling as if someone had just walked over his grave. "They were damn good steaks."

"Well, I vote we cook inside tonight. I need my beauty rest."

"That you do," Andrew said, the joke on his lips falling far short from his eyes. He turned away before Ryker could spot his concern.

He tiptoed past Kate in the bed, slipped on his running shoes, and went out the front door.

Running up the drive, he kept an eye on the ground, searching for any tyre tracks that didn't belong. If the townies were back, perhaps they had driven onto the property late last night with their headlights turned off.

The gravel made it impossible to see if a multi-ton garbage truck had come around. Getting to the main road, he turned and headed onto the trail. The makings of a headache throbbed at his temples, but that didn't stop him from pounding down the trail.

If they're back, maybe Ryker and I can set some kind of trap or catch them in the act. Kate would feel better with Nikki inside with her, and we can put an end to this nonsense.

He leaped over a gnarled root. *Or maybe it really was just a moose.*

No matter how much he wanted that to be the case, he just knew it wasn't going to be that simple.

Besides, he couldn't punch a moose.

But he could unload on their night visitor if it was a person.

Sure, he was supposed to call the deputy if they heard anything else, but by the time the deputy got out here, the mystery prowler would be long gone. Andrew would have to show the little asshole how much he appreciated the nightly shenanigans.

He pulled up, gripping a low-hanging tree branch, panting so hard he thought he was going to hyperventilate. He spat into the leaves, fighting the urge to get sick. He needed some time to cool down before heading back to the cottage.

Andrew looked around, the terrain unfamiliar to him. Lost in his little revenge fantasy, he must have gone farther than usual. The lake was nowhere to be seen.

"Must have taken the wrong fork," he said, the sound of his voice somewhat comforting. "Hope I didn't get myself lost."

His cell phone was attached to a band on his arm. Of course, there was no service out here.

Better that way. If I called Ryker, Kate would overhear and get upset.

He walked the rest of the way, anxious to come to the fork and backtrack his way home. The tree cover here was thicker, blocking most of the sun. The ground was still damp with dew and the remnants of the last storm. Rich, mouldy, earthy smells assailed his senses, making him feel even more isolated and alone.

When he saw the dead bird on the trail, its innards spilling from its open beak, body flattened in the contour of a sneaker, Andrew pulled back.

He checked the bottom of his running shoe and saw what looked a lot like a spatter of blood.

Disgusted, he rubbed his sneaker along the pine needles and leaf-covered ground, hoping to wipe the blood and any bird remnants off.

"Sorry, little guy. At least I didn't kill you." He gave a wide berth to the bird's body…this time.

It took five slow minutes to get to the fork, and he saw where he'd gone wrong. He normally stuck to the trail on the right. The berry bush he passed by every day was there, thick, glistening cobwebs woven between the leaves.

Part of him wanted to run the rest of the way, but his legs weren't having any of that. His thigh muscles were twitching like an overheated motor and his calves were starting to cramp up.

It was strange, walking the trail. When he ran, he noticed very little, living inside his head. Now, he took note of a crumbling log for the first time, wildflowers growing from its rotted trunk. There was an old licence plate partially buried under brittle pine needles, the yellow background faded, *Vacationland* in blue lettering still prominent. He'd taken Buttons out a few times, going at a sub-snail pace because Buttons was old and curious, but they'd never been out this far. Evidence of people in the woods was everywhere. He found a broken Budweiser nip bottle (when was the last time Bud made those?), a crushed, empty pack of Kool cigarettes, bottle caps, and a strip of cloth that looked to have come from a shirt.

Andrew remembered partying in the woods when he was a teen. It looked like it was no different up here. Teenage hormones and stolen beer were the calling card for woods everywhere.

What he was finding looked very, very old. The teens who'd left this stuff were most likely middle-aged now, recalling the good old days when a nip of Budweiser was all they needed to get rip-roaring drunk, the promise of copping a feel holding the same weight as winning the lottery.

He saw another dead bird, this one a robin, just on the edge of the rough path. Its tiny legs stuck straight up in the air. It wouldn't have been worth a second glance if its head hadn't been twisted completely around.

Maybe it died and some scavenger started poking at it.

If that were the case, wouldn't there be bite marks? There wasn't a single ruffled feather. It looked as if someone had snatched it from midflight, twisted its head around, and simply dropped it. It couldn't have been dead long because there weren't even any bugs around it.

Nudging it aside with his sneaker, Andrew moved it deeper into the foliage. Feeling its tiny weight against his shoe made his skin crawl.

Despite the fatigue and cramping in his legs, he broke into a slow but steady jog. He wanted to get the hell off the trail and back into the cottage.

As he hurried to the cottage, he spotted more birds along the path, birds that he had passed earlier but somehow missed. There were sparrows and blue jays, even a lone, crimson cardinal. Their tiny, stiff-as-a-board bodies had been scattered along the path like breadcrumbs.

Or birdseed.

The sweet stench of rot curled into Andrew's nose.

He saw the cottage between the trees and almost cried out in relief. Pushing harder, he kept his eyes riveted to the house, having had his fill of dead birds.

He spilled out of the trail, jogged to his car, and leaned against it, catching his breath.

There was one final bird placed in such a way, it was if the killer had anticipated his decision not to look down at the killing field.

A crow, its black feathers golden tipped from the sun, had been impaled on a broken branch on the tree opposite him. Something pink and wet stuck to the end of the jagged branch. He was no vet, but he'd bet it was its heart. Its cold, dead eyes seemed to stare at him, *into* him. Andrew refused to break its gaze, his legs gone numb.

*   *   *

"Seriously, Andy, what the fuck?"

Ryker and Andrew stood before the spiked crow, arms folded across their chests. He'd gotten his brother-in-law out of the house as quietly as possible. Nikki had been in the bathroom, Kate still asleep. Andrew didn't want the women to know what had been left for them.

Because no one could convince Andrew this wasn't a message.

"The cop we spoke to said he was pretty sure he knew who had been making noises and stuff around the cottage at night. He was going to find them and tell them to back off. I guess this is their way of telling me they don't like having the cops called into this."

"Well, you have to get the cops out here now. This is sick."

"That's not all. Follow me."

Before getting back on the trail, Andrew found a stick and pried the crow loose. It hit the ground with a hollow *thump*, rolling under a bush and mercifully out of sight.

While they walked, taking note of the various birds, all of their necks broken, Andrew told Ryker about buying the rifle and worrying that he'd shot someone. Ryker took it all in, letting Andrew unload everything.

When he was done, Ryker stopped and said, "What the fuck is this, *Deliverance*? I can see whooping it up and maybe tossing a few rocks, but killing animals? This is starting to skirt into satanic territory. Or serial killer stuff."

An iceberg was forged in Andrew's stomach.

Ryker gripped his arms. "Let's get back to the house and call the cops before all those birds get carried off by scavengers."

Andrew had never felt so torn in his life. He took a ragged breath. "I don't want Kate to know."

"Dude, she has to know. She's living in the middle of this crazy shit."

"You don't understand. What she hasn't told you is how bad her heart has gotten. The lupus has it enlarged, and there are issues with her valves. I had her in the emergency room with chest pains not too long ago. I'm really worried what this will do to her."

Ryker spun in a circle with his eyes closed. When he opened them, he said, "I'll take her and Nikki out. That way you'll have the place to yourself and the cops are free to roam around."

"It won't happen today."

"Why not?"

Andrew looked back at the cottage. "Kate's not going to be able to get up for more than going to the bathroom today…with help. A day like yesterday is a lot for her. I'll be surprised if she's even able to stay up for more than an hour at a stretch."

Both men stared down at a sparrow, its head pointed the wrong way.

"This is bad," Ryker said.

Andrew suddenly lashed out, punching a tree. His arm jerked back and he howled in pain, tucking his hand under his armpit. When he dared to look at his hand, all of his knuckles were bleeding. Ragged curlicues of flesh poked up, exposing welts of hot pink.

"Jesus, are you all right?"

Andrew hissed, shaking his hand as if he'd touched a hot stove.

"Can anything go fucking right? Do you know how much I put into this for Kate? Everything! This was her dream, *our* dream, and even though the circumstances are far from perfect, I thought maybe, just maybe, we could catch a break for a few months before we were thrown back in the shit storm. And now there's this. I can't keep her here. We're going to have to leave and she's going to be devastated. Motherfuckers!"

He kicked a bird carcass, watching it sail out of sight.

Ryker said, "You have to get ahold of yourself. Take a breath."

"Save it for your seminar, Ryker. I have a right to be pissed."

"I'm not disagreeing with you. But you gotta calm down. Let's think our way through this."

Andrew's hand throbbed. It felt as if he might have broken something. His knuckles were on fire.

"What's there to think through? The assholes win. I hope they're happy, breaking a sick woman's heart. If I ever get ahold of them, I'll…I'll…"

The knot of rage caught in his throat.

"Ryker? Andy? You guys out there?"

It was Nikki. Andrew could just make her out, standing on the front porch.

"We gotta get you inside and get that hand wrapped up," Ryker said.

"I'm not ready to go inside just yet."

"I'll stay out here with you."

He patted Ryker's shoulder with his good hand. "No, you go. Just tell Nikki I'm out running like a lunatic. When I come back, I'll say I fell or something."

"Okay. I'll play it any way you want. I still think you need to get the cops back while all the evidence is still here."

Andrew didn't respond. Should he tell him about the rabbit and squirrels? He turned away from Ryker, staring deep into the woods. He stayed that way for the better part of an hour, his anger still burning white hot. The sheriff and his deputies might handle this, but it would be very impersonal. He wanted the chance to meet these sick assholes face-to-face.

CHAPTER TWENTY-TWO

Kate tried to get up and join civilization. She really did. But every time she opened her eyes, it was like some invisible hand was forcing her eyelids back down. Those brief moments of wakefulness also came with a heightened awareness of pain, her muscles and joints incredibly sore, every nerve agitated and raw.

It was better to sleep.

Part of her felt it was weird, her curled on the bed, cradling her Mooshy, while Andrew, Ryker, and Nikki walked and talked around her. Another part found it comforting, making it easier for her to doze through a day that only promised to be miserable.

She caught snatches of conversation, but they were folded into her dreams until she was no longer sure what was real and what was her imagination.

*   *   *

Copper.

Her mouth was filled with the acrid tang of copper.

Kate opened her lips, expecting old pennies to pour out as if she were a slot machine.

Blood flowed between her shaking fingers. So much blood.

Kate gagged.

Something was caught in her throat.

Her back hitched, stomach convulsing, eager to push the thing in her throat out.

Sitting up, she vomited between her legs, blood and bile pooling in the sheet.

Within the obscene mess, she saw bones. Tiny bones bobbed on the waves of putrescence that spilled from her, and kept spilling until she felt her organs would implode.

Why won't it stop?

She struggled to breathe through the unending flood of offal. Quivering, purple blobs slid over her tongue, were punctured by her teeth, unleashing their foul contents into her lap.

It was everywhere, drowning her.

★　　★　　★

The sound of the closing sliding door woke her. She looked up to see Andrew, Ryker, and Nikki on the porch, steaming mugs of coffee on the rail.

Kate ran her tongue over the roof of her mouth and her teeth.

She stuck her fingers in her mouth, probing.

Her fingers were clean. No blood. No bones. No…Jesus, what was that?

Kate shook her head, making herself dizzy. Dizzy was better than that nightmare. The nightmare where she'd…she'd…

It's already gone, she thought. *Thank God.*

She looked back out at the porch.

Was that a bandage wrapped around Andrew's hand?

"Andrew?"

They continued talking, not hearing her. Kate cleared her throat. "Andrew."

Buttons, who had been on the bed with her, barked once, as if knowing her voice was too weak to make it across the short distance to the porch.

Three heads turned around.

For the briefest of moments, Kate swore Andrew wore a look of pained resignation. He caught her eye and his expression lightened. He smiled and said, "Hey, welcome to the world. You need anything?" He got up and came into the living room.

She pointed at the gauze wrapped around his hand. "What happened?"

He flicked his eyes at the bandage. "It finally happened. I got my feet tangled up in some roots and took a header."

A spot of blood had soaked through. "Does it hurt?"

"It doesn't tickle, but I'll be all right. How are you feeling?"

"Like I was put through a meat grinder."

There was that look again. And once again, it was gone in a flash. Kate wondered what was on his mind. Had he hurt his hand more than he was letting on?

He put on a smile that seemed a trifle too wide. "It's a good thing you woke up now. You're due for some meds. You hungry?"

She shook her head, the simple act sending arcs of pain from her shoulders to her temples. "I just need a little something to drink."

While he was fishing around in her mason jar, Ryker and Nikki popped in.

"You look worse than me, sis, and you didn't drink the house dry." Ryker chuckled, grabbing her toes underneath the sheet.

Kate attempted to sit up and adjust her hair. God, she must look a mess. "You always know what to say."

Nikki backslapped Ryker's chest. "You're such a prat."

Rubbing his chest, he said, "That's what little brothers are for, right, Katy?"

She rolled her eyes, unable to stop her smile. "That is true. So, what are you guys up to today?"

Andrew handed her a glass of soda. She washed her pills down.

"Once we feel like real live human beings again, I said we should take turns in the kayak. The lake is just lovely," Nikki said.

"I think Nikki is the only one kayaking today," Andrew said. "The boys will probably be homebodies. Too bad it's not the fall. Football would be a great excuse to miss a beautiful day and just veg on the couch."

Kate thought she saw Andrew give her brother a nervous glance.

What's with him today?

A jagged bolt of pain in her hip overwhelmed her thoughts. She dragged in a long, hissing breath, squeezing her eyes shut.

"Oh, dear, are you all right?" Nikki said. Kate felt pressure on the edge of the bed and Nikki's soft hand on hers.

When she felt she could finally speak, she said, "It's just my hip. That's the way it says good morning."

What she didn't tell Nikki was how her left wrist had popped out when she went rigid from the pain. She twisted her hand under the covers and felt it slide back in.

Nikki had a tissue in her hand and was wiping Kate's forehead. "Look, you just rest and we'll all take care of you."

"I'll be fine. Ask Andrew. This is just business as usual."

Ryker didn't even try to conceal the dread in his eyes. She could tell he was scared too. Scared for her. She wished she could tell him everything would be fine, but she wasn't up to starting the day with a lie.

The last thing she wanted was to have them standing over the bed with long faces.

"Guys, there's no sitting around the house today," she said. "Go out, get some sun at least. I'm going to chill with my But-But and sleep to old movies."

Andrew ran his fingers through her hair. "Are you sure? I'm happy to be at your beck and call."

She took his hand and kissed it. "Give me your boo-boo hand." She kissed that one too. "Now get out of here. I'm starting to feel like I'm on display."

"Your wish is our command," Ryker said. "We'll just get changed and grab some sunscreen."

Nikki gave her a finger wave, following Ryker to the bedroom.

Andrew sat next to her and found the oldie movie channel. "How's that?"

It was a Humphrey Bogart movie she'd never seen before. Too bad she wasn't going to be able to stay awake long enough to see how it ended.

"Perfect. I'm sorry I'm such a bum today."

"I knew you'd need to rest and recover. You just lay back and chillax."

"Chillax?"

"Yeah. It's what all the kids are saying."

"I really don't think so. Maybe kids from ten years ago."

He kissed her forehead. "You're not street like I am. I won't hold it against you."

When he shifted his weight to get off the bed, he winced.

"Maybe you should get your hand checked out."

"It'll be fine. Guess I'll just have to give it a rest for a while. Lay off the... you know."

He made a jerking motion, a lopsided grin on his face.

Kate could only muster a weak laugh. "Don't look at me to bail you out."

"Get some sleep. We'll be right outside if you need us."

Andrew went back onto the porch and took a sip from his coffee.

As Kate drifted off, she heard Ryker and Nikki walk past her, Nikki saying she had never been in a kayak before and Ryker telling her how easy it was to paddle. She heard the three of them clop down the wooden steps to the backyard, heading toward the dock.

Every part of her ached and her exhaustion was overwhelming, but that didn't keep her from wishing she was with them. They were out there having fun at the lake (*my lake!*) while she was once again glued to the damn bed. Times like this, she would gladly trade her incurable diseases for something like cancer. At least with cancer, there was hope. The only way she'd be rid of the dark things that plagued her was to die and leave this broken body for them to feast on until there were no longer enough vital nutrients left for them to survive.

How long will they live after my soul leaves my body?

She relished the thought of leaving them a rotting, putrid carcass. She hoped the errant cells that made her life so miserable choked on it.

Buttons nestled close to her and licked her face.

She couldn't keep her eyes open, Bogart's voice fading…fading…

Kate whispered as she tumbled into a troubled sleep, "Just…choke on it."

*   *   *

Andrew held the kayak steady while Nikki settled in. It really was a picture-perfect day. He could have enjoyed it if not for the avian mass murder around their cottage.

"Don't go out too far," Ryker said to his wife. "Since this is your first time, maybe it's best if you stay where I can see you."

Nikki rolled her eyes. "You swim like shite. It's not like you can come out and save me if I cock up and tip the boat."

"It's a kayak, not a boat," Ryker said good-naturedly.

"Whatever. Eat my waves, boys."

She dug her paddle into the water and shoved off, the kayak gliding to the dead centre of the lake.

Andrew watched her paddle away, her strokes strong and steady. It was hard to believe she'd never done it before. "At least someone's having fun today."

Ryker kept glancing back up at the cottage. "Man, you were right, there's no way Katy could leave today. She looks…well, she looks…"

"Terrible. I know. It used to scare me, how quickly things would turn for her. I hate to say that I'm used to it."

"Do you think she'll be all right by tomorrow?"

Andrew shrugged his shoulders. "It's impossible to say. A few years ago, I would have said yes, she can bounce back. But lately, it's been harder and harder for her. Plus she still has that stuff the doctor gave her in her system."

Ryker went into his pacing-by-spinning routine. Now that Nikki was out of sight, he no longer tried to hide the deep concern on his face. "I can see toughing out one more night if we have to, but man, it's going to be rough if it goes much longer."

Andrew picked up a rock and skipped it on the lake, throwing it so hard his shoulder popped. "You and Nikki fly home tomorrow. Don't worry. I'll get her out the second she's up to it."

Ryker stopped spinning, his hands balled into fists. "There's no way on God's green earth I'm leaving until I know you and Katy are in that car and heading south."

"Or we've had a chance to show these local yokels why you don't fuck with Jersey."

Ryker grinned. "Or that."

He might be a self-help guru now, but Andrew knew his brother-in-law had been in his fair share of dustups. He'd been banned from two diners for fighting when he was in high school.

Ditching the idea of skipping rocks, Andrew contented himself with simply chucking as many big ones as he could find. The bigger splash they made, the better.

"Whoever has been coming out here has stuck to keeping outside the house. As long as we're locked up tight, I'm sure there won't be much of anything for us to worry about or do. They're chickenshits who obviously know how weak and worthless they are, which is why they do what they do to small animals. What's unnerving are those sounds. They must have a recording of some animals or something."

Ryker lay down on the towel Nikki had left on the dock. He put his hands behind his head, face turned to the sun. "You and I should get some nap time in."

Andrew settled onto his ass at the water's edge. "And you're sure you don't want to tell Nikki?"

"Look, I'm hoping it's a quiet night and we don't need to bother. If things kick up again, well, she'll find out then. Best she carry on blissfully ignorant for now. Besides, I'm sure you and I, no matter how hard we try, are acting like something's not quite right. One of us has to look like it's just a normal day. We can just play off Nikki's vibe. Most of all, we don't let on to Katy that things have taken a turn."

"That may be very easy to do. I don't think she's going to be awake much today."

"All the better. And if she's good to go tomorrow, we'll help you pack."

The thought of leaving filled Andrew with equal parts relief and regret. Sure, he and Kate could savour the rest of the summer together on a kind of staycation back home. But it wouldn't be the same. He could easily picture the disappointment in her face, despite the nightly harassment. One thing they weren't were quitters. Going home now would be the biggest fail of their lives. But with Kate so sick, her heart so bad, he couldn't continue to allow the stress to build. *That* would be the ultimate fail.

"I need a drink," Ryker said.

"Hair of the dog?"

"Hair up my ass. If I don't unclench, I may pop."

Andrew got them each a beer. They both agreed it was important to only have a couple. They needed to be as clear-headed as possible. There was no telling what they were in for tonight.

*　　*　　*

Just as Andrew predicted, Kate slept through the day. She didn't even move a muscle while they were making dinner, plates and pots and pans clacking. Nikki had taken a shine to kayaking and pestered Ryker about buying a pair when they got home. She had obviously shaken off her hangover, a new bottle of wine three quarters done. The more she drank, the louder her voice got. Ryker kept throwing glances at Kate to see if Nikki had woken her. Andrew knew when it got like this, he could bring in a marching band and she wouldn't budge.

They sat around the dining room table, Nikki digging into her bag of off-colour jokes.

"Okay, stop me if you know this one," she said. "What's the difference between a bedpost and a dead baby?"

Ryker groaned. "This is one for the kids," he said, burying his face in his hands.

Andrew was glad they hadn't clued Nikki in to the stalker details.

She'd been doing a bang-up job keeping his mind off the coming of the night. "I have no idea where this could possibly go."

Waving her wineglass for emphasis, Nikki said, "You can't fuck a bedpost."

Despite its incredible crassness, Andrew couldn't help laughing. Nikki giggled between sips of wine. Ryker just shook his head.

"Wow. I didn't see that coming," Ryker said. "Though, being your husband, I should have known it would be disgusting."

"You Americans are so sensitive. And people think it's the Brits with a stick up our asses." She nodded at the soda cans in front of them. "Plus, you're lightweights."

"Yes, but a wimpy American with a normal sense of humour stole your heart, now didn't he?" Ryker said.

She leaned over and kissed him on the lips. "I'm not the first thing you American gits have stolen from the greatest nation on earth."

"And I'm not giving you back."

Nikki got up and hustled into the kitchen, wineglass in hand. "Let me check on dinner. Should be ready soon."

Pasta was boiling away, a pot of tomato sauce beside it. Nikki said she made an amazing spaghetti sauce. Andrew's stomach rumbled. He'd skipped breakfast and lunch, his mind lost in worry. The smell of Nikki's cooking had him ravenous.

He looked to Ryker, who was preoccupied with watching his wife stir the sauce, a small smile on his lips.

They were so happy, so *alive*.

He and Kate had been just like them what seemed a long, long time ago. Yes, they still loved each other very much. But were they happy? There were moments of happiness. It was hard to be cheerful when there was always something ready to piss in your picnic basket.

Watching Ryker and Nikki made him wistful, and Andrew was not prone to wistful thoughts. It made the weight of so many missed years that much heavier.

Anxious to derail his musings, Andrew blurted out, "What gets louder as it gets smaller?"

Nikki turned, one eyebrow arched. "No idea."

"A baby in a trash compactor."

Nikki spurted her wine onto the counter. Ryker even laughed.

"There's hope for you yet," Nikki said.

As she was wiping up the wine with a paper towel, she saw the small radio tucked next to the sugar bowl on the counter. "You think it's okay if I find some tunes as long as I keep it low?"

Andrew looked at Kate. She was on her side, her back to them. Buttons slept on the floor beside the bed as usual. Andrew stared hard at her, waiting to see the gentle rise and fall of her side. He couldn't count the number of times he'd done that, waiting with held breath for his wife to take one, worst-case scenarios playing through his head. Only when he saw the sheet move oh-so-slightly did he resume his own breathing. She wasn't as bad as she had been at times in the past, especially that year in the hospital when they were told numerous times she wouldn't make it out. But with a bad heart, things could take a turn for the worse on a dime.

"Sure, it'll be fine. I'm going to wake her up soon to see if she can eat anyway."

Nikki found a station playing eighties hits and started an awkward dance while she cooked. Ryker asked Andrew about his job (had he ever had a job? Absence did not make the heart grow fonder) and they fell into easy conversation. The impaled crow drifted further and further from his mind as the sun grew paler, the shadows starting to creep along the back deck.

*   *   *

Kate was aware that Andrew, Ryker, and Nikki were in the house, making dinner. At one point, she lay still, listening, wanting to get up and join them, but her body wasn't going to allow it. She drifted in and out of sleep, unsure what was real or imagined. If the pain started to really creep in, she'd know she'd been awake for a spell, allowing her mind to float back into the darkness.

Sliding between microwave feels (her body stiffening when her back went nuclear, but only for a few moments), bad feels, and the comfort of having her family around, Kate felt like a woman at the edge of a cliff, grasping for a handhold, but none was to be found.

At one point, she was running through the woods, the air sharp as razor blades against her flesh (bad feels).

Then she was in the kitchen, listening to Nikki order Ryker and Andrew around to get dinner ready (comfort).

A bolt of flame shot from the base of her spine to the top of her head, waking her instantly (microwave feels).

Something watched her from the window, whispering to her in an alien language. She knew it wanted her to come outside. It had a secret to tell her. The sound of its voice turned her bowels to water. She shit the bed, preferring to sit in the acidic stink than take one step toward the window (bad feels).

Eyes closed, she felt Andrew's hand press down on her forehead. He caressed her cheek with the back of his fingers. His lips kissed the tip of her nose (comfort).

Her ear was itchy. She scratched it. When she pulled her finger away, a giant, green walking stick bug clung to her. It had the face of a man – a small, distorted, diseased man, a circus freak, a burn victim, an abomination. The walking stick leered at her and said, "I live inside your ear, you know." Kate writhed in horror as the chimeric bug made its slow entrance back to its warm home (bad feels).

Kate forced herself to wake up. She was too weak, too tired to call for Andrew, much less get off the bed. The endless flip-flopping had sapped her strength.

Her family, the ones she held most dear, were in the kitchen. That, at least, hadn't been a dream.

She might not be able to fully comprehend what they were saying, but she knew they were enjoying themselves. The cottage was filled with their laughter and contentment. Part of her was glad just to be able to bask in it, even from her prone position on the bed, one part removed.

Happy to be away from the bad feels, she was still upset that she and Andrew could never have this easy alliance with bliss. Even when they had their fun, it was always knowing that bad times were at their backs, closer than even their own shadows.

She should be with Nikki in the kitchen drinking wine, dancing with Andrew when 'Careless Whisper' played on the radio. She'd danced with Jerry Deevey to that song at a school dance.

For now, she'd have to dance alone in the uneasy state between dreams and wakefulness, always present but not quite there. Never existing wholly anywhere.

CHAPTER TWENTY-THREE

A nightmare scared Kate awake. The second her eyes opened, the terrifying images faded, shattering like safety glass under a sledgehammer. Her heart was racing, causing pain to ripple out from the centre of her chest. She felt the sweat at the back of her neck, her legs tangled in the sheet as if she'd been twisting and turning to get away from something…or someone. Her back ached, heat emanating from between her shoulder blades.

The meds and fevers were wreaking havoc with her dreams. She couldn't remember the last time she hadn't had at least one nightmare. Images so strange they were impossible to fully convey to Andrew had become commonplace.

She recalled watching a bizarre beast made of mouths, the lips shredded from too many sharp teeth. It was crouched over something, all of the mouths opening and closing with horrid clacking and slurping wetness. Kate kept moving closer and closer against her will. She wanted nothing to do with this creature, but every time she stopped, her feet were dragged along the harsh pavement, like a metal filing drawn toward the magnetised monster.

When she was close enough to peer over its shoulder, purple tongues darting between the masticating teeth, the tips severing and falling at her feet, still twitching like bruised maggots, she saw what had drawn its horrid attention.

It hovered over a boy and a girl, twins from what she could tell, because it hadn't eaten their faces…yet.

Kate screamed and screamed, unable to break away from the grisly feast.

The creature stopped, turned to her and—

Kate took a deep, rattling breath, wiping her face with a corner of the pillowcase.

She couldn't remember what came next, nor did she want to.

The TV was on but muted. The blinds were drawn but the lights were on. Andrew wasn't in bed with her.

She picked up her tablet and checked the time. It was a little after nine. Maybe Andrew had gotten the fire pit going.

Even Buttons was MIA.

The remote had somehow made its way under her pillow. She needed the sound of human voices to calm down. On the screen, Joel McCrea passed himself off as Captain McGlue in a madcap effort to reunite with his wife. A comedy was just what she needed.

Andrew was really what she needed, but he was with Ryker and Nikki, getting what he needed – a break from her.

Several minutes later, the pain in her chest faded just like the nightmare. She was thirsty. Getting up took some doing (*now I know how Grandma used to feel when the arthritis got real bad toward the end*), but she managed to zombie-walk to the kitchen and get a cold can of soda. The entire cottage still smelled like Italian food.

That was when she remembered Andrew trying to wake her up to eat. She'd been too tired. She hadn't even been hungry. She still wasn't, despite the pleasant aroma.

Leaning against the counter, taking a sip, her hand trembling from the insignificant heft of the can, she heard voices. They were coming from inside the house.

She put the can down and slowly made her way to the bedroom, her hips and shoulders vying for gold medals in the chronic pain Olympics. Someone tried to muffle a laugh. Nikki.

Ryker, Nikki, and Andrew were sitting on the floor of the bedroom. There was an empty bottle of wine between them, but only Nikki had a glass. She must have said something witty, because Andrew was laughing too.

They hadn't noticed that she was peeking in on them.

Ryker leaned against the wall, sitting cross-legged. Andrew lay on his side, head propped up by his hand, all of his attention on Nikki, who was quite tipsy and still beautiful despite her messy hair and dress-down clothes.

Andrew looked so happy.

When was the last time he'd laughed with Kate like that, just the two of them?

Did he look at Kate the way he looked at Nikki? Was he even now thinking about what it would be like to be with Nikki? Of course he wanted to fuck her. It was obvious. How could her brother not see it?

Her spine cracked from the sudden ignition of flames. The agony almost made her cry out, knees buckling. She felt heat at the back of her eyes.

Get him out of here, Ryker! Don't you know what he wants to do to your wife?

Kate bit down on her cheek.

The burning sensation flared and died just as quickly. She rested her forehead against the wall.

Where was this coming from?

Andrew had never shown the slightest romantic interest in Nikki.

Their sex life might have been running on empty, but that didn't mean Andrew was suddenly lusting after Nikki. When she looked at them again, Andrew was talking to Ryker, his eyes off Nikki.

You're being ridiculous.

Yes, she was, but screw anyone who would fault her for having moments of jealousy. Sometimes it got bad when she knew he was out and at work or at the store, surrounded by pretty, healthy women, many of whom would jump at the chance to be with a successful, caring man (who still had all his hair and looked years younger than most guys his age). He was a man, no matter how many times their friends and family called him a saint. A saint simply because he didn't run from her when things got bad. That wasn't a reason to canonise someone. You were supposed to honour your marriage vows. If the sickness part came earlier than expected, that didn't give you permission to jump ship.

Andrew hated it when people called him that. He was no saint.

Kate's head reeled. She lashed out to grip the doorway's edge.

"Kate!" Ryker said.

Andrew leaped to his feet, curling his arm around her waist before she fell.

"Hey, little crip. Did we wake you?" he asked. "I'm so sorry. We were trying to keep it to a dull roar."

With all eyes on her now, her knees wobbling, Kate felt stupid for allowing even the most minor thread of jealousy to creep in. Nikki took her other side, fingering her wet hair from her face.

"It was just another one of my nightmares," she said, knowing she had to sit down before she collapsed.

"Oh, honey, you're burning up again," Andrew said, leading her – practically carrying her – back to the living room.

"I'll get some Tylenol," Ryker said from somewhere at her back.

"One cold washcloth coming up," Nikki said, disappearing into the bathroom.

When Andrew settled her into the bed, she said, "I'm fine. You all go back to having fun."

He tucked Mooshy behind her head so she could sit up and take her pills. "We were just sitting around bullshitting."

"You should be outside. I think I hear the fire pit calling."

Buttons lay watching them from the opposite chair. He looked back at the window and uttered a low howl.

"See, even the dog knows you should be out there."

A strange look passed over Andrew's face. It was gone before she could grasp it.

"Here you go, sis." Ryker handed her two pills and a glass of water. "Now that you're up, are you hungry? I could make you a meatball parm like I used to when we were kids."

"You mean the ones I forced you to make if you wanted to hang around with me and Carol?" She smiled and even that hurt.

Crouching beside the bed so they were eye to eye, Ryker said, "I still remember how you liked them. Toast an English muffin partway while heating up three meatballs in the microwave. I had to smoosh a meatball and a half onto each side of the muffin, cover them in cheese, garlic, and oregano, then pop them in the toaster oven. When the cheese was melted, I cut them in fours."

"With a pizza cutter," she said.

"Right. That time I used a knife and made the muffin all ragged, you told me I couldn't come with you guys to the movies."

She patted his hand and could see by the look on his face that hers was red-hot. "It sounds great, but I couldn't eat a thing if I tried."

"Aren't you supposed to feed a fever?"

Nikki arrived with a folded, cold washcloth. She wiped Kate's face down and then settled it on her forehead.

"I think that's for a cold," Nikki said.

Andrew covered her with the sheet. She was on fire, but she'd started to shiver. Her back throbbed, devoid of the initial burst of heat that now broiled the rest of her body.

"It's just a fever. It'll go away," she said. "Really, I'm fine. Thank you, everyone."

She wasn't fine, but she suddenly wanted them to go away. The more they doted on her, the worse she felt. She was the sick, crippled child surrounded by cloying adults. It made her feel helpless and angry. So, so angry.

Andrew ushered Nikki and Ryker away. "I bought a deck of cards. Who's up for some gin rummy?"

They were mercifully sliding their attention away from Kate when the most inhuman of all screams echoed through the woods, turning everyone inside the cottage to stone.

CHAPTER TWENTY-FOUR

Nikki stopped in midstride, her eyes gone wide as softballs.

"What in the holy fuck was that?"

Ryker and Andrew exchanged nervous glances.

"Sounds like our local fox is whooping it up again," Andrew said unconvincingly. He looked back at Kate in the bed. She struggled to sit up, eyes on the blinds over the sliding doors as if whatever had made the sound was standing on the porch, waiting for someone to let it in.

It.

Andrew shivered.

What was out there wasn't an it. No, it was a pair of stoner dropouts (his assumption all along, because who else would have the time or inclination to do this?) playing some recording they had ripped from the audio track on a horror movie.

"That is not a fox," Nikki said.

"We thought the same thing, but we looked it up. Kate can show you some videos we found that'll give you goose bumps."

"No, I can't," Kate said softly. When Andrew caught her eye, she looked guilty, as if she hadn't meant to speak it out loud.

"If that's a fucking fox, I'm Lady Gaga," Nikki said. She still hadn't moved from her spot.

Ryker tried to lighten the mood by saying, "You do sing pretty good in the shower."

The scream came again, a ragged, throat-searing screech that morphed into a strangled howl before tapering to a dull, repetitive chuffing. Every hair on Andrew's body stood on end. He backed into the bed and sat next to Kate, gripping her hand.

This was nothing like before. At least on the other nights, they had found correlations to the strange sounds lurking around the cottage.

Not this time. What was out there sounded neither like man nor beast.

Nikki flew into Ryker's arms. Andrew knew it was impossible, but the temperature in the cottage seemed to plummet twenty degrees.

"The doors!" Andrew exclaimed, bolting from the bed to lock the front and back doors.

"Do the windows have locks?" Ryker asked. Nikki had her face buried in his chest.

Andrew shook his head. Of course they didn't. Why the fuck would you need window locks out here in the middle of the sticks?

To keep the monsters out, he thought, sending a fresh wave of shivers up his back.

Kate caught his eye and he was more alarmed by what he saw. She'd gone white as the sheet, fat beads of sweat pouring down her face.

"Kate?"

She was still staring at the sliding glass doors.

The flimsy sliding glass doors.

Suddenly, Andrew was finding weaknesses everywhere. They wouldn't be able to stop a determined child from breaking in, much less a…a…

"Shhh," Kate said, eerily calm.

"What?" Ryker whispered. Nikki wiped her eyes and did her best to compose herself.

Kate pointed at the doors. "It's out there."

The cabin was preternaturally silent. Andrew breathed slowly through his mouth, straining to listen.

"Is it on the porch?" he said, wondering if Kate had heard the creak of the wooden steps, if there was something (no…someone) standing still just on the other side of the blinds, waiting patiently.

"No," she said. "But it's close, and coming closer."

"How do you know that?" Ryker said.

They all stared at the doors, not daring to move, to make any noise that would mask the approach of whatever was in those woods and making those hideous sounds.

"Wait, I hear it," Nikki said.

Andrew and Ryker stepped toward the glass doors. The floor popped under their feet and Nikki gave a startled gasp.

Hand clasped over her mouth, she muttered, "Sorry."

Andrew stopped a couple of feet from the doors and leaned as close as his crawling gooseflesh would allow.

He heard it.

The soft crunch of leaves.

Someone was walking out there, close to the fire pit from the sound of it, and they didn't care who heard them. His heart beat in his throat as he tracked the footsteps, fading to the right, now circling past the bedroom.

"Stay right here," he said to Ryker.

Kate's face had gone blank. If he hadn't known better, he would have sworn she was hypnotised.

"Are you okay?" he said, touching her forehead. His hand came away hot and soaked. "How's your chest?"

Being scared like this was dangerous for her. He was far more afraid of her having a heart attack out here, miles from the nearest hospital (and something in the woods separating them from the car) than he was of their returning stalker.

His wife's breathing was slow and steady, which was at least one good sign.

"It's fine," she said, her voice far away, lost in a dream – or in this case, a waking nightmare.

"Nikki," he said. His sister-in-law grabbed the washcloth and wiped Kate's face and neck down.

Andrew skidded in his socks, nearly crashing into the front door. He rested his ear on the sturdy door, hands clenching and unclenching, waiting.

He didn't have to wait long. The footsteps grew louder as whoever was outside passed by the front of the house. He followed their progression as they went by the kitchen, then around again to the back.

"He's circling us," he hushed across the cottage.

"I hear him," Ryker answered. He looked like his bones wanted to leap from his skin.

They waited in silence for a minute or two, the footfalls sounding closer. Ryker pointed toward the bedroom. "He's coming your way again."

"What the fuck is he doing? And who the fuck is he?" Nikki said. She sat beside Kate, holding her hand.

"I don't know," Andrew said.

Nikki grew suspicious. "I thought you said it was an animal."

Andrew didn't want to talk. He wanted to keep his ears zeroed in on their stalker. "Not now," he hissed, motioning for her to quiet down.

The footsteps came toward the front again. Yes, they were definitely closer this time around. He moved his ear from the door, feeling that the wood wasn't thick enough to protect him any longer.

But protect him from what?

One thing he was sure of – whoever or whatever was out there, there was only one. With him and Ryker covering both ends of the cottage, they would have heard if there were more than that.

One against the two of us, he thought. *I have the rifle. Maybe Ryker and I should run out there and put the fear of God and gunpowder in him.*

You're not going to kill someone.

Just give him a damn good scare.

Yeah, like the one you thought you gave him before? All that seemed to do was piss him off and scare myself.

Piss it *off.*

Not an it. It's someone walking on two legs. Two legs and one damaged brain.

Through everything, he hadn't taken notice of Buttons. The dog had been nonchalant about their visitor in the past, and tonight was no different. He was in the kitchen now, slurping from his water bowl.

Andrew watched his tail wag lazily, a dog without a care in the world.

Should we be taking our cues from Buttons? If he's not worried, why are we?

Dogs had far keener senses than people. While Andrew could only hear the stalker, Buttons could smell him, scent out the man's intentions. Andrew remembered the day he'd taken Buttons to the new dog park a mile from their house. It was just after dinner and the place was mostly empty. Buttons did a little butt-sniffing on a Pomeranian while Andrew talked to the couple walking the yapping little dog. It turned out the woman had gone to the same school where Andrew's mother had worked as a secretary. They'd been chatting for a while, the dogs getting along nicely, when a man walked by, wearing a suit and carrying a briefcase. There was a townhouse development at one end of the park and several glass office buildings at the other. Andrew had assumed the man was simply walking home after a long day at work.

Buttons took one look at the man and went berserk. He tugged on the leash so hard, Andrew nearly fell trying to keep him heeled. The man jumped away from the snarling beagle, holding his briefcase in front of him like a shield. Andrew apologised profusely, all while his normally amiable dog did everything in his power to get at the man.

"Dogs usually like me," the man said, casting furtive looks behind him as he walked away.

Two weeks later, Andrew saw the man again.

This time, he was on the news, accused of molesting the two preteen girls he and his wife were fostering. In fact, both adults were taking turns with the girls, and there was speculation they had been doing it to at least a dozen other children they had fostered over the past decade.

Buttons had known. There was nothing about the man's appearance that screamed *child molester!* Andrew didn't know how the beagle had known, but he was positive Buttons had sniffed out the man's dark soul as easily as he could his treats.

So why wasn't he going bananas now?

Because it's just a kid and Buttons knows stupid when he smells it. You can't get mad at stupid. Only feel pity.

The footsteps stopped.

Andrew waved his hand for Ryker to come over. He pointed at the dog.

"See how chill he is?"

"Yeah," Ryker said.

"I think that's his way of telling us to settle down."

"Or he's just too nice for his own good. Or too old."

Andrew didn't have time to go into the molester story.

Whoever was out there wasn't far from the front door.

"I'm going out with Buttons," Andrew said.

"Not without me, you aren't."

"Hold on a sec."

Andrew went to the supply closet and dug into the back, where he'd hidden the rifle. When Nikki saw it, she screamed, "Have you lost the plot? A gun?"

Kate didn't turn around to look or utter a word. That worried Andrew deeply. He needed to get rid of this moron and focus all of his attention on her instead.

"Seriously?" Ryker said, eyeing the rifle.

"I promise I won't shoot anyone."

"Oh, well, then that makes me feel better." Ryker mopped his brow with his forearm.

"I'm calling the police before you end up in jail," Nikki said. She ran to the bedroom to look for her phone.

"Buttons, come here," Andrew said. The beagle looked up from his bowl, water trickling off his snout, and padded over.

Andrew grabbed the doorknob and was about to twist it when he stopped, suddenly unsure. He took a deep, steadying breath and tried again, heart thudding, skin crawling, at war with himself but knowing deep down he had to see. More than anything, *he had to see* what was out there.

"He's right outside. It's now or never."

Ryker grimaced, balled his fists, and said, "Fine. Let's scare him away, not blow him away."

All Andrew could do was nod. His teeth were clamped so hard, it felt as if his jaw had locked.

Buttons stayed between them, sniffing at the door but still not raising his hackles.

So why am I so freaked out?

He had just started to turn the knob when the house shook on its foundation. Andrew jumped back as if the knob were a screaming-hot oven, the rifle slipping from his tenuous grasp.

Next came a dreadful howl that was so loud, so close, it sounded as if it were coming from within the cottage.

Nikki let loose with a terrified screech.

Buttons started barking furiously, paws scratching at the door.

And then the power went out.

CHAPTER TWENTY-FIVE

The bed shook seconds before the lights went out. The sudden plunge into darkness whipped Kate from her paralysis.

Andrew, Ryker, and Nikki were all yelling, but she couldn't make out a single word. It was like being trapped in a dream, her brain fuzzy, disconnected, unable to grasp what was going on around her. Utterly blind in the total darkness, she tried calling out for Andrew, but only a strangled gasp spilled from her mouth.

What had happened?

It felt like an earthquake.

Kate had never been in one before (though she remembered reading the little card about what to do in case of an earthquake at the hotel she and Andrew stayed in when they went to San Francisco), but what else could rattle an entire house like that?

Unless a car or truck had lost control and plowed into them.

She would have heard a car barreling down the narrow drive.

Aaaaaaaahhhhhuuuuuuugggghhhhhhh!

The beastly wail stopped her heart.

"An...Andrew!"

The scream broke from her locked throat.

"Kate!"

She heard heavy footsteps, then felt her husband's body press against her. She smelled his aftershave and pulled him close, her face pressed to his neck.

"Andrew, what's happening?"

"I don't know."

"Nikki!" Ryker shouted.

"I'm all right."

Kate twisted within Andrew's embrace to look behind her. A white glow, almost like a ghost floating into the room, found Ryker in the kitchen, his back against the sink, both hands gripping the counter. She could just make out Nikki, the cell phone held out in front of her like a candle.

"What the fuck was that?" Nikki said. She sounded on the verge of tears.

"It's like something tried to lift the house," Ryker said. He used the cell phone's light to locate the block of knives, extracted the big chef's knife, and pulled Nikki close.

Kate's hand drifted to Andrew's chest. She could feel his heart pounding madly. "Hand me my tablet," she said.

He passed it to her and she turned it on, adding a little more light to the cottage.

It cast weird shadows on Andrew's face, making him look like a ghoul from an old silent horror movie.

Lon Chaney from Phantom of the Opera, she thought. *That's exactly what he looks like.*

Had those bags and dark circles always been there?

She shifted the tablet away from him.

"Do you have any candles?" Ryker said.

"Yes," Andrew said. "There's a whole drawer of them."

He got up, his fingers lingering in her hair before he left her side, and started roughly opening drawers in the kitchen. "Get me some saucers," he said. Nikki and Ryker found the few saucers they had in the cabinet.

Andrew lit a match. The sulfur smell permeated the cottage. He lit the wick on a long, thin candle and let the wax drip onto the saucer. He pushed the end of the candle into the wax, holding it until it set. Nikki took over, lighting the rest.

Outside, the howling had stopped.

The flickering glow of candlelight revealed Buttons scratching at the door, letting out the occasional wary growl.

Andrew picked up the rifle.

Kate was too jittery to just lie in bed. With a little effort, she managed to get to her feet. Her fever had lessened, but it still had her on a low boil. Even the soft kiss of displaced air felt like needle pricks on her skin. Every joint in her body felt as if it had been spackled with grains of glass. She walked unsteadily and looped several fingers under the dog's collar, pulling him from the door. He didn't fight her, but he also didn't shift his attention a single inch. His stubby legs remained locked and rigid, sliding backward on the bare floor.

Keeping the barrel of the rifle pointed at the ground, Andrew put his index finger to his lips. Everyone went silent, including Buttons.

The only noise in the cottage was the crackling of a candlewick.

There were no more howls, no crunching footsteps circling the house. It was so deathly quiet, Kate was sure if they opened a window, the crickets would even be lying low.

"I think he's gone," Ryker said.

Kate felt the tension coiled within Buttons' collar.

No, Buttons sure doesn't think he's gone.

"Shite, I have no bars," Nikki moaned. "Do any of your phones work?"

"Not without the Wi-Fi," Andrew said. "You'd have to get to the main road and drive about a mile before you got decent cell service."

"What about a landline? This is an old-fashioned little place. Surely they have one."

Andrew shook his head. "Nope."

"Well, then we're good and properly screwed. Are we supposed to call the police by smoke signal?"

Nikki had gone from scared to angry, and Kate thought that might be a good thing. Anything was better than cowering in fright.

"Kate, can I borrow your tablet?" Andrew asked. She handed it over, happy to be rid of the excess weight. The tablet and its case were heavier than her damaged shoulders could stand for much longer.

He disappeared, but she could hear him open the metal door to the circuit breakers, the clicking sound of flipping switches giving her hope, then dashing it when the lights refused to go on.

When he came back, he was sweating profusely.

"I'm gonna check outside and see, make sure the foundation of the house is still in one piece. We might have to abandon the place," Andrew said, though he didn't make a move toward the door.

"Let's go," Ryker said. "I'll open the door and you go out first, show them you're armed...if anyone's bothered to stick around. I think the damage is done and he scattered."

"He?" Nikki huffed. "You think a single person could do this to a house? That's utter nonsense."

The men ignored her. Andrew lifted the rifle. Ryker twisted the doorknob and pulled the door open.

Buttons broke free, scampering out the door, barking the way he did when he chased squirrels in the yard back home.

"Buttons!" Kate squealed.

She ran after him, or her version of running, brushing past Andrew and Ryker, heedless of Nikki's cries to get back inside.

The beagle bounded down the couple of steps and disappeared into the pitch.

"Buttons, get back here!"

"Kate, get inside," Andrew blurted. She took a quick glance over her shoulder and saw him reaching for her. She just avoided his grasping fingers.

The dog barked and yipped, but she couldn't see him. He sounded close, but that was little comfort.

"Buttons!"

An arm wrapped around her waist, making her jump. Andrew put his lips close to her ear. "I'll get him. I need you to get back in the cottage, now."

She couldn't believe how incredibly dark it was out here. With no lights and a thumbnail of moon, it was like being locked in a closet. There wasn't even a lick of wind, so it felt just as stuffy.

"I have to find him," she insisted.

He tightened his grip on her. "I'll carry you inside if I have to."

"We both will," a voice said behind her. Ryker was holding his cellphone, the meagre light made all the smaller in comparison to the deep, dark woods around them.

"Let me have that," she said, plucking it from his hand.

"I'm serious, Kate, you have to get inside. We don't...we don't know who's out here."

She wanted to say, *I don't give a good goddamn*, but that would have been a lie. The spreading pain in her chest urged her to listen to her husband and brother. They had enough to contend with without having to worry about rushing her to the hospital. The speck of rational thought she allowed to creep in knew she had to head inside, sit or lie down, and take a pill to calm down. Because if she didn't....

Nikki called out from the open front door, "Where are the keys to the car? We might as well get the hell out of here while we can!"

"Not without Buttons," Kate snapped. "But–But, come to Momma."

He yapped, but sounded farther away.

Kate sprang free from Andrew, using the cellphone's light to scan the front yard, or at least the miniscule swath it was able to illuminate. Staggering toward the tree line, calling for her dog, she'd forgotten all about the terrifying noises and the house shuddering. Her baby was out there, and she wasn't going anywhere without him.

"But–But! Come here, But–But!"

The beagle barked in reply, this time coming from the side of the house. She followed the sound.

"Kate!"

She turned the corner, keeping the light pointed at the dirt so she could see where she was going and not get tripped up. She had a hard enough time navigating paved ground.

Something huffed to her left.

She froze.

Skin crawling, she lifted the phone, slowly turning.

The feeble light quivered, moving higher, higher, higher.

When it lit upon the terrifying face, Kate tumbled into a silent scream.

*   *   *

The moose had been split open, ribs pulled back, meat and organs steaming in the dirt.

Kate crouched on her hands and knees, peering into the dead animal. She sniffed the rotted contents of its perforated intestines.

"Come inside," the moose said.

Its eyes were human, sky blue and clear as a cloudless day. Those eyes captivated her, daring her to look away.

"Don't be afraid," it said, though its mouth never moved. No, its mouth, black, parted lips buzzing with flies, would never move again. "It's safe in here. I promise."

Without hesitation, she crawled into the hot, putrid cavity.

"Welcome home," the moose said.

She nestled deeper into its chest.

Ribs closed down on her like an iron maiden.

Kate wasn't afraid.

She was home.

She stretched her legs, slipping into its legs as if they were comfy socks. With little effort, the Kate/moose stood.

There was a light in the woods.

She would go to it.

In her home.

*　　*　　*

Andrew heard Kate cry out and for a terrifying moment found himself unable to move. Eyes furtively searching the darkness, he spotted the soft glow of Ryker's cell phone. The only problem was, it was on the ground.

"Kate!"

Andrew shoved the rifle into Ryker's chest and ran toward the light. He found her on her side, unconscious. After scooping her into his arms, he headed back inside the cottage, bumping into Ryker.

"Honey. Wake up. Kate, can you hear me?"

"What happened to her?" Ryker said.

"I don't know. It looks like she fell. She might have hit her head."

They hustled to the lambent light spilling from the open front door. When Nikki saw them, she backed out of the doorway, hand to her open mouth.

"Is she okay?"

Andrew carried Kate to the bed, gently laying her down. Twigs and leaves were caught up in her clothes, falling onto the sheets. Kate's flesh was hot and clammy, a pungent, oaty smell coming off her in waves. He realised she'd peed herself and quickly covered her up so Ryker and Nikki couldn't see the triangle of wetness.

Grabbing the washcloth, he dabbed the perspiration from her face. She was out, but her brows were knit as if she were concentrating or angry.

"Kate? Come on, little crip, come back to me."

Her breathing was steady, but he was very concerned about the fever that had come roaring back.

He heard Nikki say to Ryker, "What happened to her?"

"I don't know. She screamed and Andy found her passed out."

Andrew whispered her name over and over, hoping the sound of his voice would be a beacon, luring her back to them. While he did that, he checked her head for lumps, plucking detritus of the woods from her hair and tossing it onto the floor.

"Did you find the dog?" Nikki asked.

"No. He's still out there."

Andrew hadn't heard Buttons barking, but he also hadn't been listening for the pooch since he found Kate passed out.

"Kate, honey, if you can hear me, please wake up," he said softly by her ear. He kept squeezing her hand, hoping for her to clutch him back.

Nikki and Ryker lingered behind him.

"Come on, sis, this is no time to take a nap."

"Katy, sweetie, please wake up."

Kate took a deep, ragged breath. Her mouth pulled tight and her eyes flashed open. She looked absolutely terrified.

Struggling to get out from under the sheet and Andrew's grasp, she twisted around in the bed.

"Oh my God! Close the door! You have to close the door! Andrew, Ryker, close the fucking door!"

CHAPTER TWENTY-SIX

Kate had never been so scared in her life.

She'd also never seen anything like the creature outside the cottage.

Andrew tried to hold her down, but she had to get out of the bed. Her nerves were too frazzled.

"Please, Andrew, let me up."

"Kate, you were just unconscious a few seconds ago."

Ryker had slammed the door and locked it.

It wouldn't be enough.

Pushing Andrew away, she got to her feet, the interior of the cottage going hazy for a moment. She felt the wetness at her crotch but didn't care. She parted the blinds over the sliding doors and peered into the darkness.

It was out there.

If it wanted to come in, glass doors and meagre locks wouldn't stop it.

Shivering so hard her teeth clacked painfully, Kate wrapped her arms around herself. A sliver of fiery pain flared in her back, bending her over. She caught her breath, wishing the microwave feels away.

"Katy, why don't you at least sit down," Nikki said, reaching out to guide her to the chair.

"Leave me alone!" she snapped. "You didn't see it. None of you saw it. You don't know."

Andrew approached her but was wise enough to give her some space.

If he saw what I saw... Kate thought.

He said, "Kate, what's going on?"

Just thinking about it made her want to sink back to sweet oblivion.

"It...it's not human."

"What do you mean? Was it an animal?"

She shook her head, her back to the door, feeling all too vulnerable.

"It's a monster."

Ryker tried to hand her a glass of water. "It's all right, Katy. You just need some time to settle down."

She smacked the glass out of his hand. It shattered at her feet, water splashing her bare ankles.

"What the hell?" Ryker said, staring at the glass bits.

"I'll get it," Nikki said, rushing to get the broom.

Andrew didn't say a word, but the expression on his face spoke volumes.

He thinks I imagined it. The sick girl with the fever and on enough meds to knock out a rhino is just having a hallucination. It's not just Andrew. They all think it!

"Don't you dare look at me like that," she snarled, pointing at Andrew specifically.

Her eyes started to sting from the sweat pouring into them. She blinked hard, stomach quivering, legs wobbly, but she refused to be treated like an invalid.

"I saw it! I didn't imagine it."

Andrew held his hands up, palms out. "Why don't you tell me what you saw and we'll take it from there."

Nikki was on all fours, sweeping up glass and mopping the water with a dishtowel. The broom knocked into Kate several times but she refused to move. She was going to stand there for as long as she wanted. They couldn't make her lie down like some maiden with the vapours. They couldn't!

"Why should I bother?" Kate said. "It's not like you'll believe me."

"Don't say that," Andrew said, keeping his voice calm when it was plain he wanted to yell at her. Ryker stood to her side with his hands in his pockets, unsure what to do.

She grabbed the cord and ripped the blinds open. Beyond the window was pure onyx. Nothing was standing on the porch, waiting to be revealed.

But it was out there. Kate was sure of it.

"You want to know? Fine. But if you say one word about me having a fever or try to tell me what I saw wasn't real, I'll…I'll punch you in the freaking throat."

Where was this coming from? Kate had never been a violent person.

Because I'm scared and it's real and they won't believe me and it's going to come in here and they won't be able to stop it and even if we try to get to the car I know it will be waiting for us and oh sweet fucking Jesus what are we going to do?

And Buttons is out there with it.

Everyone was taken aback by her outburst. Nikki looked like she was about to say something, but instead she turned away and dumped the glass shards in the kitchen garbage.

When no one said anything to stop her – or piss her off – Kate took a breath and decided there was no going back now. Funny, the moment she started to speak, she began to feel uneasy, as if putting it in words made it less real. She had to keep telling herself it was real, and they were all in danger.

"It was big, really tall. I'm not good with judging height, but I'd say it was around seven feet. Maybe more." She'd once met Patrick Ewing, who had played for the New York Knicks. If she remembered his bio correctly, he was seven feet tall. The thing outside was definitely taller.

Andrew, Ryker, and Nikki stood in a row opposite her, faces grim but mouths closed. She continued.

"It had a wide face, like in a cartoon when someone gets run over by a car and just kinda flattens out. But it wasn't flat at all. Just wide, almost human looking but with exaggerated features. And it was scarred, like someone had slashed it at one time. It also had deep pock marks and gouges taken from its flesh. It looked hurt...diseased. I couldn't see much of its body, but I think it was covered in hair.

"And I don't know if it was the reflection from the phone, but it had yellow eyes, just solid and almost glowing. Those eyes, I couldn't look away. They were terrifying. I was looking in its eyes and then I was in here." She swallowed hard, her stomach coiled in a painful knot. "I can still see them, staring into me. It was like being stabbed. Those eyes. Those eyes..."

A wave of exhaustion threatened to pull her under. She wanted to throw up. She felt like passing out. Her mouth was dry as dust, all of the moisture in her body expended in running rivulets of sweat. The building microwave feels nuked whatever fluids were left in her. Kate shuddered as a strange, pulsating wave swept through her. It left her spineless, her muscles turned to jelly.

She looked at Andrew, her gaze sliding up toward the ceiling. She heard shuffling feet and found herself in her husband's arms.

"I'll get her legs," Ryker said from the next town over.

"Nikki, I need a fresh, cold washcloth," Andrew said, setting her on the bed.

"You don't believe me," she croaked. Her throat made clicking noises when she tried to swallow.

He pushed the covers aside. "I do, honey. Right now, I'm more concerned about you. Can you put this under your tongue?"

She turned away, the thermometer hovering inches from her mouth. Andrew's hand was trembling.

"No, you don't believe me," she said. "But you're going to."

Kate recoiled when Nikki wiped her head with the washcloth. It forced her to open her mouth, and Andrew was quick to insert the thermometer. He took her pulse and waited, the candlelight making her feel as if they'd tumbled back in time. They were early settlers cowering in their cabin, terrified of the unknown animals crying and grumbling in the pitch.

"Your heart's racing," Andrew said.

"For a very good reason," she mumbled around the fragile thermometer. She was both boiling hot and ice cold. It took all of her strength to keep her teeth from chattering and breaking the thermometer. She didn't need to add mercury poisoning to the list of her ills.

She'd been struck by the mother of all bad feels. That thing out there, that horrid, monstrous thing, was the living, breathing embodiment of all her darkest fears. One look from its cancerous eyes and she'd been turned to dust.

Andrew read the thermometer by the light of his phone. "Just under a hundred and four. I need you to take two more Tylenol. If this goes up any higher, I may have to get you in a cold bath."

"No."

He'd had to do it twice before during their marriage, and both times she'd nearly hit the ceiling, the icy water propelling her from her delirium.

The big difference this time was that she wasn't delirious, despite what Andrew, Ryker, and Nikki might think. Something was wrong with her; that she knew. She regretted not telling Andrew about the strange microwave feels all this time. They might have been burning her to a cinder and infecting her dreams, but she hadn't been dreaming outside. It was real, and it was out there, waiting for them.

Out there with Buttons.

"I want my dog," she said.

"I'll go out and find him," Andrew said.

She lashed out and grabbed his arm. "You can't! It will get you if you do. Promise me you won't go out there!"

He patted her hand condescendingly, but she could tell he wasn't all that anxious to go back outside. He couldn't deny the strange noises and the cottage being shaken from its foundation. Something was definitely out there, but he wasn't buying her monster theory. It infuriated her to no end, and she knew the more she insisted, the more they'd resist, especially given her high fever.

I must look and sound like a crazy person to them. So what? I'm not lying to them. I'm not!

Why couldn't she be dealing with this and *not* have a raging fever clouding their opinion of her? Did it always have to be a total shit storm?

Ryker had gone to the dining room window and opened it a crack. "I don't hear him," he said. Buttons had either run clear from the cottage or was cowering somewhere, too afraid to make a sound. Kate's heart broke thinking about him out there. Even if he didn't see the creature, his dog senses would know it was out there.

Run, Buttons, and don't come back until light, she silently pleaded.

At least they had the cottage walls between them and the thing in the woods. Her baby was all alone, exposed, with only his old stumpy legs to save him. She started to cry.

"In fact, I don't hear anything," Ryker added. He was now in possession of the rifle. It was so strange, seeing her pacifist brother with a rifle. She wondered how the people who paid for his positive life enhancement seminars would feel if they could see him now. Ryker preached that with the proper frame of mind, anything was possible. The universe would open itself to you, enfolding you within the slipstream of intention and reward.

Have a monster stalking your house? Affirmations that it would go away, if you believed them in your heart, were all you needed to rid yourself of the beast.

Kate made a low chuckle, covering her mouth.

I guess they don't cover monsters in his seminars.

She laughed louder, this time catching Nikki's attention, her brows knit, looking with pity at the sweating, sick girl in the bed.

Maybe I am losing my mind.

Ryker held his hand out. "Wait!" His voice got lower. "Something's moving around out there. I think it's at the back of the house."

Andrew strode across the room and took the rifle from him, leaning into the window to listen.

"Footsteps," he whispered.

Kate couldn't hear them from across the room. Nikki crouched down and held her hand. Both women turned to look at the sliding glass doors, the blinds still pulled away.

It was right there!

Kate's palm dripped with sweat but Nikki didn't let go.

"Ryker, the blinds," Nikki said. "Whoever's out there can see us."

Kate wanted to grab her by the shoulder and shout, "*It's not a who! It's a goddamn monster!*"

Andrew and Ryker ran to the back door. Ryker fumbled for the pull string to close them, unable to find it in the flickering light.

Kate saw the eyes before anyone else.

Appearing from within the impenetrable gloom, a pair of golden, luminous eyes hovered between the rails of the back porch. They were looking right at her. Kate's entire body was engulfed in flame. She was Joan of Arc at the stake, the pain too great for words or wailing. The convulsions started right when Nikki screamed.

CHAPTER TWENTY-SEVEN

Nikki's shriek caused Ryker to pull the blind cord so hard, it broke off in his hands. Andrew nearly dropped the rifle.

"It's out there!" Nikki shouted, pointing out the glass door.

Andrew looked and felt his balls draw up.

What looked to be two mini yellow suns floated in the air. Based on their position through the slats, they had to be almost eight feet from the ground. For a second, he thought he was staring at some kind of bug, like fireflies on steroids.

Until they blinked.

He brought the rifle up, aiming at what could only be eyes, despite the impossibility of the height and colour.

Dear God, they were glowing!

There wasn't enough light coming from the house to make that kind of reflection.

Don't shoot, he reminded himself. If he did, he'd shatter the glass and there would be nothing between them and…and…

It could also be kids who had rigged up a pair of lights. He did not want to be responsible for killing someone, no matter how stupid and misguided they were.

But something in that malevolent, fiery gaze told him these were no lights and there were no foolish youths out there.

Kate was right.

She'd seen the face that held those eyes.

"Katy!"

Ryker was the first to notice that Kate had gone into a seizure, her arms and legs locked at her sides, back arched, bucking up and down on the bed.

As terrifying as it was to turn his back on those eyes, Andrew set the rifle down, grabbed one of his used paperbacks from the end table, and inserted it in her mouth to keep her from biting her tongue. Nikki held on to the arm and leg on her left side, Ryker doing the same on her right. Though they had all shifted their attention from the fiend staring in at them from just several feet away, Andrew could feel its alien stare rippling his flesh.

"It's the fever," Andrew said. "Kate, honey, I'm right here. I'm right here."

Unfortunately, he'd been with Kate when she had convulsions before, and knew that as scary as it was, they just had to ride it out. It shouldn't last more than a minute or so, but each second stretched to an eternity.

Her wide eyes were glued to the ceiling. He wasn't sure if she could hear him, but he kept talking to her, reassuring her that she would be all right.

"Should we get her in a cold bath?" Nikki said.

"Not while she's having a seizure," he said. "It won't last long."

He noticed Ryker kept stealing peeks at the window. If they'd had more light, he was sure he would have seen his brother-in-law's complexion growing paler with each look.

Kate writhed under them, her seizure seeming to be getting stronger, not weaker. Her teeth bit into the paperback, piercing the cover and yellowed pages underneath. Andrew's gut tightened, wondering if he should chance it and run with her to the car and get her to the hospital. With no cell service, they couldn't even call for an ambulance…or the cops.

"*Hyaaaaaaahhhhhhhhhhh!*"

The monstrous roar made all of them lose their grip on Kate. Andrew looked out the doors. The eyes were gone.

"Where the hell is it?" Ryker said.

Andrew peeled his attention back to his wife, reasserting his hold on the book. She was tearing it to shreds. For such a frail woman, she bounded with the strength of a full-grown man. Her arm flew up, sending Nikki's hand into her own face with a loud slap.

Thump!

Something heavy crashed on the roof above them.

"What was that?" Nikki screamed. Even in the wild light, Andrew could see a red welt forming where she'd hit herself.

"Rocks," Andrew said.

There were loud thuds as whatever was outside found bigger and bigger rocks to toss. Each impact made them jump, Kate practically juddering free of them.

Andrew felt so exposed with the blinds open. It could see them clear as day, whereas they could only guess where it was going from moment to moment.

Unless it bore down on them with those gleaming, demonic eyes.

Andrew desperately wanted to pull the blinds closed, but he didn't dare leave Kate.

More and more rocks peppered the roof. Nikki started to hyperventilate. To her credit, she held on to Kate, Ryker doing what he could to calm her down despite the growing panic in his own voice.

The cottage was under assault. So many rocks were hitting the structure, it seemed impossible they could all be coming from one source.

That thought sent a deep chill down Andrew's spine.

What if there's more than one of them?

He couldn't think about that now, though it was hard to ignore as stones battered the sides of the house. Any second now, a rock – or a boulder from the sound of some of them – would come crashing through one of the windows.

"Katy's seizure isn't stopping," Ryker said.

"Don't you think I know that?" Andrew blurted.

Each tossed stone frayed their nerves more and more until Andrew's entire body felt like a drilled tooth awaiting a root canal.

Nikki was openly weeping, flinching every time a rock hit the house.

Andrew wiped Kate's forehead, his hand coming up dripping with sweat. Her skin sizzled. He could only imagine what her fever was now. If something didn't break soon, she would be in serious trouble. It was getting to the point where he didn't care what was outside. If he needed to rush her to the hospital, he'd just have to take a chance.

The monster – Kate had called it a monster, hadn't she? – bellowed as it unleashed volley after volley of heavy stones. Andrew trembled when he heard the window in the bedroom crack. It wasn't followed by the sound of glass tinkling on the floor, so there was hope it hadn't given way completely.

The power of Kate's convulsions had finally started to dissipate, but she was far from being out of the woods. Her eyelids fluttered as her hands opened and balled into fists over and over.

"Is there anything else we can do?" Ryker said.

Andrew shook his head, white-knuckling the paperback.

Christ, when would the seizure end? He remembered one of her doctors telling him that any seizure over ten minutes required immediate medical attention.

How long had it been? Two minutes? Ten? Twenty?

He hadn't thought to check the time when it started. The wild beast attacking the house hadn't made his perception of time any sharper.

"Katy, please stop. Please, Katy," Nikki sobbed. Andrew had never seen her upset before, much less broken like this. She was near hysterics, which wouldn't do them any good.

When the rocks stopped, the silence was almost more disturbing.

Nikki and Ryker were able to let Kate go, her muscles still twitching but without the same power as before. Andrew removed the book from between her relaxing jaws, feeling terrible that it had left deep lines at the corners of her mouth. The pungent staleness wafting from her pores virtually smacked him in the face.

Andrew put Kate's head in his lap. Her eyes were closed, but her breathing was steady. He kept repeating her name softly, hands caressing her face. He couldn't tell whether she was asleep or had passed out. It seemed a narrow distinction, but he knew it was quite the opposite.

"Do you think it's gone?" Nikki said. She was on her feet now, Ryker embracing her.

Andrew nodded at the blinds. Ryker caught his intention, keeping one hand around his wife while he used the other to shut the blinds.

"I don't know," Andrew said.

"Maybe it just ran out of rocks," Nikki said, sniffling, getting herself under control.

"I want to know what the hell *it* is," Ryker said.

"We all do," Andrew said. Kate's skin felt a bit cooler, her sweat beginning to dry.

"I'll tell you what I think it is," Nikki said. "And you might think I'm a world-class prat for saying it, but you both know Katy described a bigfoot. Don't fucking pretend it didn't occur to you."

In actuality, the insane notion that it was a bigfoot had never entered Andrew's mind. And he wasn't going to start entertaining the thought now.

"That's ridiculous," he said, watching Kate sleep.

"Unlike those terrible screams, the yellow eyes, and the stones crashing around the house, right? That's all quite normal for Maine, is it?" Nikki said.

"Baby, just calm down," Ryker said.

She broke away from him. "Are you both so daft that you don't see it? I'm no bigfoot expert, but I've seen enough specials on the telly to know that everything fits perfectly."

"There are no bigfoots in Maine," Ryker said, peering out from between the blinds.

"And how do you know that?" she replied, hands on her hips, the dark streaks of her makeup running down her face.

He whirled around. "Because there's no such thing as a bigfoot, that's why!"

He was suddenly very glad they hadn't told her about the dead birds. That would only fuel her ridiculous speculation.

She turned away from him in disgust.

Andrew sighed. "Look, Nikki, I'm with Ryker on this. I don't know what the hell is out there, but I'm pretty sure it's not Sasquatch."

Nikki went to the kitchen and lit another candle. She did her best to avoid looking at them.

Andrew tapped the inside of Kate's wrist. "Kate. Can you hear me? I just need you to wake up for a second and make sure you're okay." He said her name louder, his tapping more insistent. Kate's eyes didn't so much as flicker.

He looked to Ryker. "I'm starting to get worried."

"What do you mean? She's not seizing anymore. That's a good thing, right?"

"It would be if she were conscious. But not if I can't get her up. It could be a sign that something else is very wrong. I think I need to get her to the hospital."

They slowly turned to the front door.

"What time is it?" Ryker said.

Nikki checked her phone. "Half past one."

He punched the top of the chair. "I was hoping it would be closer to dawn. It feels like we've been up for days."

Andrew pulled the sheet up to Kate's neck. The fever had definitely broken, but at what cost?

"It doesn't matter. This can't wait until light. Look, I'll take her to the car. You two can stay in here and keep everything locked."

"Not a fucking chance," Nikki said. "I don't want to stay here with that thing."

Ryker said, "Nikki's right. We'll all go. It's not safe here."

"It's sure not safe out there," Nikki said, eyes on the kitchen window, the blinds and white curtains protecting her from seeing the glowing, jaundiced eyes if the beast happened to be on the front porch.

"You carry Katy," Ryker said to Andrew. "I'll go out first with the gun. We should find something for Nikki, any kind of weapon."

"There's an axe handle in the closet. It's thick and sturdy."

"You couldn't spring for the whole fucking axe?" Nikki said. Andrew couldn't tell whether she was serious or making a joke. The expression of bubbling terror hadn't changed on her face.

Ryker got the axe handle and handed it to her. She banged it against the counter a couple of times as if to make sure it wasn't made of brittle timber. A candle on the counter fell over on its saucer.

And still Kate slept. Andrew's growing concern was fixed less and less on the unknown creature outside.

"Let me get the car keys," Andrew said, fishing them from the cereal bowl on the pedestal by the door. He wished they had an honest-to-God flashlight. The one he'd bought in town had been cheap, the bulb burning out one night when he wanted to sit on the dock with a beer after Kate had gone to sleep. It was now in the trash can. Candles would be useless outside in the breeze, and the cellphone flashlights weren't all that powerful. If Ryker was going to cover them while he got Kate in the car and started it up, Andrew would need as much light as he could get.

Andrew wrapped Kate in the sheet the way a mother would swaddle her baby. She didn't so much as make a sound as he shifted her around and lifted her from the bed.

"You guys ready?"

"No," Nikki said, both hands on the axe handle.

"You open the door, and I'll see what we're dealing with," Ryker said to his wife. He turned on his phone's light, but Andrew could see it was difficult juggling the phone and rifle. Nikki did the same with her phone, a cone of light illuminating her feet. Andrew's hands were full, the key ring looped around his index finger.

They would have to move fast. He had no idea what they were rushing into, but he had a sinking feeling things weren't suddenly going to go their way. He stood behind Ryker, shifting Kate in his arms to get a better grip. She looked so peaceful. In a way, he was glad she was someplace else at the moment. She'd experienced enough terror as it was. Sooner or later, her heart was going to send up the white flag. If what Kate had seen was truly out there, he wasn't sure she could endure another encounter.

"Let's just go straight to the car," Andrew said. "Watch my back while I get Kate inside. Nikki, you go in next to her while I start the car. Ryker, the second you jump in, I'm punching the gas whether you have the door closed or not."

Ryker nodded. "I'll ride on the roof if I have to."

Andrew's muscles tensed and he took a deep, warm breath. He nodded at Nikki. She ripped open the door.

They peered into a darkness thicker than lead.

Ryker sprang onto the porch, rifle raised, the light from the phone giving him several feet of visibility. Andrew scanned the night, sure he'd see those saffron eyes rushing toward them. He followed his brother-in-law, the door slamming behind them, Nikki bumping into his back as they descended the two steps to the walkway.

He couldn't even see the car.

But he could hear the pounding rush of footsteps getting closer.

Closer.

Closer.

He ran in the direction of the car, Kate clutched tightly to his chest.

"Where is it?" Nikki shouted.

Ryker twirled in circles as he shuffled to the car, pointing the rifle at Andrew and Nikki over and over as he searched for the source of the footsteps. It sounded like they were coming from every direction.

Andrew spotted the car as Andrew's light flashed across it and sped past his brother-in-law. With a flick of his wrist, the key fob flipped up so he could depress the door button with his thumb. The car's lights flashed twice as it beeped, the locks opening with a loud *click*.

Nikki grabbed his collar, her nails raking the back of his neck.

He could hear the creature's laboured breathing as it pounded the uneven terrain. It was heading straight for them.

"To your right! To your right!" he shouted.

Ryker turned.

There was a sharp and terrifying growl.

The rifle cracked, a brief flash of light blinding Andrew.

Ryker screamed.

CHAPTER TWENTY-EIGHT

Nikki pulled on Andrew's collar with such force, he was yanked back from the car door, his fingers grazing the handle. His ankle rolled and he staggered, hip smacking the front fender. Kate started to slip from his embrace, at least until his elbow struck the hood of the car. He used the hood to rest for just a second, giving him time to readjust his hold on his unconscious wife.

Nikki's unsteady light wavered on Ryker. He was on his knees, the rifle hanging limply from one hand. His phone was nowhere to be seen.

Ryker sobbed in obvious pain. When he looked up at them, Andrew saw why.

Three long, ragged gouges ran from the top of his forehead down to his chin. It looked as if he'd been clawed by a lion.

"Ryker!" Nikki bleated, rushing for him.

"Get him in the car!"

Nikki dropped her phone, the light shining into the impermeable sky. There was just enough dull radiance for Andrew to make out Nikki helping Ryker to his feet.

"My face is on fire," Ryker moaned.

Andrew felt something at his back.

He took a quick glance but could see nothing but infinite black.

It's there, he thought, restless panic clawing at his chest. *It's intentionally keeping quiet, but I know it's right behind me.*

Andrew froze, the flesh of his back tingling.

Nikki was having trouble with Ryker, and the phone was still on the ground. Ryker couldn't stop screaming about the burning wounds on his face.

The car was so close, but the monster was closer.

A soft night breeze flitted over Andrew's shoulders. An animal musk sailed on the wind, affirming that they were not alone.

Andrew knew with dreadful certainty that they were not going to be able to get in the car. The obstacle between them and escape was waiting patiently for them to make the unfortunate move of stepping right into its clutches.

He could see the open front door to the cottage, the lit candles spilling dancing light onto the porch.

"Nikki," he said.

"I've got him. We're coming."

"I need you to run back to the cottage."

He kept his voice as calm as possible, considering the rapid pattering of his heart. The monster surely couldn't understand his words, but it might be able to read his tone. Let it think he was calm and unsuspecting. Andrew was not going to fall into its trap.

"Andy, the car's right there," Nikki said, her voice tinged by tears. Ryker had settled down, but his breathing was wet, as if blood were pooling in his mouth and nostrils.

"Just do what I say and go."

"Ryker needs a doctor too. Just let me get my phone."

He saw the light rise from the forest floor.

"No!"

The crunch of rending metal and shattering glass set Andrew's feet in motion. The beast roared at his back as it assaulted the car. Nikki screamed.

Andrew ran, Kate bobbing in his arms, his eyes locked on the front door.

Whup! Whup! Whup!

It sounded like the monster was hammering the car with its fists.

Taking the steps in one bound, he raced into the house. Nikki staggered close behind with Ryker's arm draped over her shoulder.

There came a tremendous crash, and Andrew knew the car had been flipped over.

Once Nikki and Ryker were inside, he kicked the door closed and leaned his back into it. As he sank to the floor, Kate's dead weight settled onto his lap.

Ryker slumped into a dining room chair, blood from his face spattering the table. Nikki collapsed on the floor next to him, panting hard, doubled over, her hand on her chest.

Andrew reached up and locked the door, not that it would do any good. Whatever was out there had demolished his car with its bare hands. If it wanted to come into the cottage, it could easily punch the door right off its hinges.

First things first. He got up and carried Kate back to the bed. The fact that she hadn't woken up through all of the running, screaming, and mayhem worried him deeply. Could a seizure that went on too long lead to brain damage? Had her lungs constricted enough to cut the flow of oxygen to her brain? He was no doctor, though he'd been around enough to have a good working knowledge of the profession, but at the moment, his thoughts were too scattered to coalesce into rational thought.

"Oh God, I'm bleeding," Ryker said. He'd been so obsessed with the burning, he must not have realised that his face had been flayed open. Andrew balled paper towels around his hand and ran the wad under the water. He took the chair next to Ryker and dabbed at his face. The towel instantly turned red. Nikki got to her feet and took the towel from him.

Neither Andrew nor Nikki spoke aloud what they were thinking.

The wounds were bad. The only positive thing was that Ryker's eyes had been spared. The trio of jagged lacerations started at his hairline, the one above his right eye so deep, Andrew could see the dull white sheen of his skull through pulped flesh. They ran down his face, bisecting his eyebrows, skipping past his eyes and resuming on his cheeks.

The one in the centre of his face was the worst. It had sliced his nose in two, sickeningly reminding Andrew of a split hot dog on a flat-top grill. It had also torn his lips apart. Blood ran into his mouth and poured from the chasm between the two halves of his bottom lip.

He needed stitches. A ton of them, and soon, before he bled to death.

"A sewing kit. Where did Kate pack the sewing kit?" he muttered to himself.

The crunch of rending metal had ceased. All was silent in the woods…for the moment.

Andrew raced to the closet in the bedroom and dug until he found his and Kate's luggage. His wife loved to pack (or grossly overpack, as Andrew had lamented more times than he could count), preparing for every eventuality. She collected the little sewing kits sometimes found in hotels, always making sure to stow one in a pocket of her suitcase just in case a button needed to be sewn back on or Andrew once again ripped the seat of his pants, which he hoped had been a one-time thing.

Digging through the plethora of little storage compartments in her bag, his fingers seized a small plastic case.

Yes, he had the kit, but who was going to sew up Ryker's face? He wasn't sure he would be able to do it.

If Nikki can't, you'll just have to.

He'd had to do some pretty unpleasant things the year the surgeon had left an open gash in Kate's stomach so the infection could seep from her body. Andrew remembered the smell, and the bubbling sounds he and Kate had called her baby volcano, signaling that the thick gauze padding would need to be changed. At the time, he just did what needed to be done. It was only later, when that crisis was over, that he'd get weak in the knees with the recollection of the sight and smell of the seeping wound and how often he'd had to tend to it.

Please, Nikki, be stronger than me, he thought as he rushed to give her the packet. It had several tiny spools of thread, a few needles, and a thimble so small, he wondered whose finger it could possibly fit.

Ryker saw the kit and his eyes bulged. "What's that for?"

Nikki was doing her best to stem the tide of blood pouring from his face, but it was a losing battle.

"We have to stitch you up, bud," Andrew said, feeling light-headed. Ryker's face was unsettling to look at.

"Oh no you won't." Ryker tried to get up, but Nikki grabbed him by the shoulders and eased him back into the chair. He had a hard time pronouncing words correctly through his split lips.

"Andy's right," she said, a tear dangling from the end of her chin.

"If anyone's giving me stitches, it's going to be a doctor!"

Andrew pulled a chair over and sat in front of his brother-in-law. "In a perfect world, that's exactly what would happen. But that thing is out there, and it demolished the car. We have to do this now before you lose any more blood."

Ryker looked at Nikki, who simply nodded while she bit her bottom lip.

"It's going to hurt like hell. Do you have anything to kill the pain?" Ryker said nervously.

Before Andrew could tell him about the bottle of whisky, Ryker's eyelids fluttered and his eyes rolled up and out of sight. His body slumped forward, but Andrew caught him before he fell over.

Andrew checked his pulse, which was still strong.

"We should do it fast while he's still out," he said.

Nikki unzipped the kit and immediately started threading a needle, her hands trembling so much it took her numerous attempts. She looked ready to crumble. If she passed out, Andrew would be the only one left who was conscious.

"If you want, I can do it," he offered.

She took a shaky breath. "He's my husband and my responsibility. If anyone's going to stab him repeatedly, it should be me."

The corner of her mouth turned up just slightly. Andrew felt a brief burst of relief, then remembered Kate and the monster waiting for them outside.

"Just hold him still while I try to channel my mum. She could have been a seamstress."

When the needle pierced the skin at the bridge of Ryker's nose, Andrew faltered. Nikki pinched two meaty flaps of skin together and did her best to reconnect them. Ryker's body shifted and Nikki huffed. Shaking his head to clear the fuzziness that wanted to creep in and take over, Andrew steeled himself. Nikki worked slowly yet methodically, her hands stained and slick with her husband's blood. She tackled his lips next. They bled less, but it looked like she was stabbing squirming slugs. Andrew looked away in the interest of self-preservation.

If there was one thing to be thankful for, it was that Ryker remained out of it the entire time. After she was finished with his nose, Nikki went about connecting the folds of skin on his forehead, then his cheeks. When she was done, she was pale as milk but seemed more in control of herself.

"He'll need a plastic surgeon," she said. "But at least he won't bleed to death."

Together, they got Ryker to a more comfortable chair and covered him with a blanket. The area where they'd worked on him in the dining room was covered in blood spatters and crimson towels.

Andrew checked on Kate. Her forehead was cool to the touch. The fever was gone. Why wasn't she waking up?

"I don't think I've ever been this knackered," Nikki said. She sat on the floor by Ryker's feet. "And yet I know there's no way I could close my eyes for even an instant."

"You and me both. You did an amazing job, you know."

"I wouldn't go that far." She stared at Ryker's patchwork face.

"Not many people could do what you did. He's lucky to have you."

"I tell him that all the time." She kissed his knee, resting her head on his lap.

Andrew couldn't stop looking at the glass doors to the back porch. They were no protection whatsoever. The beast could come crashing through at any second.

As if it could hear his thoughts, the creature ripped off a bladder-quaking howl.

Andrew and Nikki bolted to their feet, looking all around the cottage.

"Why won't it leave us the fuck alone?" Nikki said, fingers enmeshed in her hair as if she were going to tear it out by the roots.

Andrew spotted the rifle and silently thanked God that Ryker had managed to hang on to it. It felt heavier than before, or was that just exhaustion settling in? How many bursts of adrenaline could he endure before he simply burned out?

"There!" Nikki exclaimed, pointing to the back of the house.

Sure enough, he heard its lumbering footsteps.

He needed more light by the glass doors. If the thing decided to enter through the path of least resistance, Andrew wanted to see it as well as possible so he could shoot it in the face. Carrying a candle over and placing it on the floor to the side of the door, he turned and saw Nikki grabbing another. Next, he pulled Ryker's chair into the centre of the cottage so he wouldn't be hit by flying glass. Then he gripped the bed frame and looked to Nikki.

"We'll put the bed next to him," he said.

Nikki nodded. The legs of the bed made a terrible racket as they dragged it away from the window. Kate slept on, worrying Andrew further.

The sound must have caught the monster's attention, because it stopped moving. Andrew crept toward the doors, hearing its laboured breathing. His finger curled around the trigger as he backed up.

Andrew's thoughts wavered. Should he wait for it to come crashing inside? Or should he take it by surprise? He could have Nikki throw open the door and just start shooting.

Don't wait until it's in here. Once it gets inside, Kate and Ryker are vulnerable.

"Do you hear that?" Nikki whispered.

Andrew could barely hear *her* over the thrumming of his blood.

"It…it sounds like someone's talking," she said, fresh terror creeping into her eyes.

He needed to take a couple of steadying breaths to calm himself. When he did, he heard it.

It was a dull, continuous mumbling, a string of nonsense sounds. The more he listened, the more it sounded like a kind of Native American chanting. There were no words, or words as he understood them, just a low, guttural monotone. It was far more chilling than the ear-piercing screams and howls.

"What the fuck is it saying?"

Andrew shook his head. "I don't have a clue. It's definitely not English."

The sound of its voice terrified him more than anything else that had taken place. What was it saying? Was it speaking to them? To another creature? To itself?

It was still muttering when they heard one of the back porch steps creak.

Go out there now when you know exactly where it is!

It was the right thing to do, but he couldn't force his legs to move. The strange chanting of the creature was almost hypnotic.

Another groan of wood as it took the next step.

Nikki touched his back and he nearly screamed.

When it reached the third step (just three more to go!), Andrew broke from his stupor. He saw his hand reach for the door handle, but he was so numb with dread he couldn't feel it.

Just pull and shoot. Even you can't miss from this range.

His vision blurred. He rubbed his eyes with a knuckle. He'd never been so scared in his life.

The world outside the paper-thin glass doors was suddenly filled with the sound of incessant barking. The creature stopped talking to itself.

Nikki said, "Is that Buttons?"

Andrew's heart turned to ice.

It was.

Buttons advanced on the monster, growling in between angry barks. The creature answered with its own roar.

"Buttons!"

Andrew spun to see Kate sitting up in bed. She threw the covers off and jumped to her feet, nudging him aside as she went to open the door.

"Kate, no!" Nikki and Andrew screamed in unison.

They were too late.

CHAPTER TWENTY-NINE

Kate instantly knew that she was, as her colourful father would say, out where the buses don't run. Propelled from the warm comfort of the darkness (the only place where she could truly be pain-free, both physically and mentally) by the distressed barking of her beloved Buttons, she wasn't even exactly sure where she was. She only knew that her dog was beyond the door and she needed to get to him.

People shouted at her, but all she cared about was finding Buttons.

She briefly wondered why it was so dark and who would put candles on the floor. Next thing she knew, she was jerking the door open and stepping outside, the wood chilly on her bare feet. A hand clutched her shoulder, stopping her.

"Buttons!"

The beagle was growling in a way she'd never heard him growl before.

A rush of displaced air smacked her in the face.

Very little light penetrated the pitch outside, but there was just enough to see what had Buttons in a frenzy. One look at the horrid face brought reality crashing down around her.

The monster had turned to glare at her with its cold, glowing eyes.

She felt stark terror, trapped by its gaze. Those flaming eyes penetrated her like laser beams, raping her soul, leaving her empty and hopeless.

Nikki wrapped her arms around Kate, dragging her back.

Andrew knocked into them, rifle raised.

He could have pulled the trigger.

The creature let loose with a bone-rattling bellow. Andrew froze.

Buttons scampered past the beast, positioning himself between Kate and the monstrosity.

It was huge, its barrel chest almost taking up the width of the stairway. Getting a longer look, Kate saw she been right earlier. It *was* covered in short, bristly hairs, with exposed patches of corrupted flesh. The mephitic stench rolling off it in waves made her gorge rise. Its face looked slightly different than before, its complexion gone sallow.

A long, heavily muscled arm lashed out, reducing the railing to splinters. Andrew regained his senses, but it was too late. The beast bounded off the stairs and ran, its thunderous footfalls heading toward the water.

Andrew fired, but there was no subsequent cry of pain.

It kept running and running until it faded into the distance.

"Get back inside," he said, ushering them in the door. Nikki still had Kate in her arms, the pressure tightening as they crab-walked into the cottage. Andrew slammed the door shut, chest heaving.

Nikki pulled Kate to the bed. As they were about to sit down (Kate's legs had suddenly gone numb and her sagging weight must have been more than Nikki could handle), Andrew blurted, "Not there! Use the chair over there."

Buttons had stopped barking, staying close to Kate and Nikki.

They turned as one and Kate saw her brother.

"Oh my God! Ryker!"

His face was covered in thread and blood. Was he dead? What had happened to him?

The commotion of Andrew lifting the mattress and jamming it against the glass doors stopped her from voicing the multitude of questions circling her brain like agitated gnats. Nikki settled her into a chair next to Ryker. Kate reached out to touch his arm, relieved to see he was breathing.

"Help me move the table," Andrew said to Nikki.

They piled the heaviest furniture they could find against the mattress, scoring the floor with deep gouges.

The owners are going to be pissed, Kate thought, immediately wondering why that would even enter her head. *Because maybe it's better to think regular thoughts than face the fact that there's a crazed creature that wants to kill us.*

She couldn't stop her heart from racing, and her chest was getting tight. In the throes of her fright, it seemed that every joint in her body had swelled to twice its normal size and was screaming in agony. Her wrist started to slip out of place and she had to pull her hand away from Ryker, resting it in her lap, feeling the bones slide back in place.

Even if the pain in her chest got worse, she wasn't going to tell Andrew. What was the point? There was nothing they could do about it now.

When he and Nikki were done reinforcing the front and back doors with every stick of furniture that would move, they collapsed onto the floor beside Kate and Ryker.

Andrew was sweating profusely and having a hard time catching his breath. Nikki was just the same.

"Did…did you see that?" Nikki said.

Andrew stared at the wall, through the wall, into the woods where the beast waited to make its return. "I still can't believe it. I mean, what the hell can it be?"

"It's sick," Kate said.

Two heads turned to her.

Andrew gingerly rested his hand on her knee. "What?"

"Something's wrong with it. I've seen it twice now and it looks worse than before."

"For all we know, that's the way it always looks," Nikki said, wiping a tear from her eye.

"No. It's infected. With what, I don't know."

"Honey, you can't know that," Andrew said.

"I know I can't, but I do. I can't explain it."

Buttons licked her ankle. She patted his head, her shoulder aching from the simple act, and he rose on his hind legs to put his head in her lap. He was covered in brambles and dirt. It looked as if he'd gone rolling through the woods the way little kids tumbled down dandelion-filled hills, laughing with the joy of total innocence.

"I was so worried about you." She kissed him over and over.

"I'm just glad he didn't try to attack that thing," Andrew said. "There's no telling what it would have done to him." He cringed when he looked to Ryker.

"Did it do that to Ryker?" Kate said.

Nikki nodded, fresh tears springing to her eyes.

Kate's stomach felt as if it were filled with hot lead.

"Who sewed him up?"

The flesh between the stitches was puffy and raw.

"I did. It's a shite job, but I had to stop the bleeding. I'm just worried about infection now, especially after what you said."

Kate looked at everything piled against the doors. "Maybe when it's light out, we can get him to the hospital."

Andrew got back on his feet, the rifle in his hands. "We tried that earlier after you had a seizure. That's when we were attacked. The...the thing destroyed the car too."

A wave of crushing guilt pounded Kate square in her constricted chest.

"Ryker's hurt because of me?"

Nikki was quick to hold her hand. "No, Katy. It's not your fault. It's that monster's fault. It was more than just going to hospital. We wanted to get the hell out of here."

Andrew caressed her shoulder. She refused to let the pain show on her face. "She's right. You can't pin the blame on yourself. We'll get Ryker help. I promise."

Without a car, electricity, or cell service, Kate wasn't sure how exactly they were going to do that. Setting out to walk in those woods would be the same as committing suicide. If they took her along, all she would do was hold them back. In her condition, she couldn't go faster than a slow walk. If that beast came for them, their only chance was to leave her and save themselves – but she knew they'd never do that. They would all die because of her.

She buried her face in her hands and cried.

Andrew said, "Someone has to have heard it. I mean, some of those screams were loud enough to have been heard for miles. And when I shot it. Jesus, the noise it made when it attacked the car. We're remote but not that remote. Help will come. I know it will."

No one had the strength to speak for the rest of the night, the silence creeping into the first golden rays of dawn.

Help never came.

CHAPTER THIRTY

Andrew and Nikki had fallen asleep on the hard floor. Buttons lay by the back door like a prostrate guardian, one ear flopped over his eyes.

Ryker was still out in the chair, a blanket pulled up to his chest. Kate inspected the wounds on his face. They appeared to be getting redder, the swelling increasing. There was no telling what diseases lurked in the nails of the monster. She had a feeling that even if they were able to get him to a hospital right now, doctors wouldn't know how to heal him.

Even though the creature was flesh and blood, it didn't feel as if it were part of this world. The infected cells it deposited in her brother's torn face would be beyond medical science. Weeping quietly, she stroked her brother's arm, wishing with all her might that he'd wake up and somehow start to get better all on his own. Just like the classes he taught: if he could think it, it would become reality.

"Oh, Ryker," she whispered, leaning over to kiss the one spot on his head that hadn't been ravaged or crusted with dried blood.

For once, she was the only one awake. The pain wouldn't allow her to close her eyes, even for a second. She had intentionally skipped her medication because she didn't want to be in a narcotic fog. She couldn't afford to be. Yes, she still had her fentanyl patch on her arm, but it was due to be changed later today and most of the drug had already been absorbed into her system. She'd had more than her share of misery over the years, but the absence of the pain-dulling meds had brought her to a whole new level of hell. Every nerve, muscle, and joint was on fire. Her stomach felt necrotic, her lungs constricted because breathing hurt too much.

Worst of all were the steady knife-lunges to her heart. They were almost like a pregnant woman's contractions. If Kate could have reached her tablet and set the timer, she'd bet they were coming closer and closer together with each passing hour. Only she didn't have a beautiful new life to look forward to holding in her arms. These pains would give birth to something dark and final.

Sunlight sneaked past the blinds and curtains, giving her enough light to walk about the cottage without tripping herself. The candles had burned out long ago, trapping her in the predawn darkness, ears straining for a hint of the creature's return.

But it had stayed away, and there was a glimmer of hope that Andrew had shot it, a stroke of blind luck that was due them.

Kate struggled out of the chair, knees popping, her left hip warning her that if she didn't adjust her position fast, it was going to slip free from its socket. Careful to avoid making a noise or bumping into Andrew or Nikki, she crept to the kitchen. She was so parched, her tongue kept sticking to the roof of her mouth. The refrigerator was still cold, but meat and dairy would start to go bad by the afternoon. She found a can of soda and draped a dishtowel over the top to muffle the sound of the tab when she pulled it open. As she drank half the can in one pull, her throat burned from the carbonation.

Just what I need, more pain.

It would be so easy to just curl into a ball and cry, waking Andrew and begging for Percocet and her nerve blockers. A fresh fentanyl patch would be welcome as well.

No! If I take them, I'll eventually go under, and I'm not leaving Andrew to face this without me. I have to face reality, no matter how unreal it seems.

This cottage, Ryker's infected face, the warnings from her heart – *this* was her reality. And like always, it fucking sucked.

Drinking the rest of the soda, she pulled the blinds over the kitchen sink open with her fingers.

The can tumbled out of her hand, rolling on the floor.

The car looked as if it had been hit by a semi, then run through a compactor. The wheels faced the sky, the rubber frayed, every window blown out, bits of glass sparkling in the morning sun. The forest floor looked as if it were covered in diamonds.

One of the doors had been bent over on itself and cast into the flower bed. The bulk of the car was covered in muddy dents, as if the monster had beaten it like a drum with feet and fists. It wasn't even fit for a junkyard, much less driving.

"Are you okay?"

Andrew's voice startled her. She jerked her hand back, the blinds clapping closed.

"The car," she said.

He slipped a hand around her waist and leaned over to look for himself. "Holy cow. How did it do that?" he said.

She looked at the junk stacked against the doors, then back out at the car. A realisation hit her more forcefully than the hammer blows to her chest.

"It doesn't want to come in here."

He tore his gaze away from their demolished car. "What?"

They kept their voices down so as not to wake Ryker and Nikki.

"If it wanted to get us, it could," she said. The resigned look on his face told her he'd thought the same thing. "I think it wants to keep us *in* here. It wants us afraid."

Andrew looked so tired. He'd aged five years overnight. The dark circles under his eyes looked as if they were in competition with her own. He ran a hand over his face, the bristles of his beard scratching like sandpaper. "Well, if it wants us afraid, it's working. The question is, why does it want to keep us trapped? I saw that thing. It doesn't look all that capable of complex thought. Maybe there's something in here that it's afraid of."

Kate looked around the cottage. "I think we all know it's not us. And I can't see anything here that would scare any animal that could turn a car into a pile of broken metal and glass with its bare hands."

He reached into the refrigerator and grabbed a bottle of beer. "This is all insane. I'd hoped when I woke up that everything would be back to normal. You know? Like maybe I'd had way too much to drink with your brother and Nikki and just had the nightmare of a lifetime."

She hugged him, loving the strength of his body and the musk of his neck and hair.

When he suddenly pulled away, she had to flail for the counter's edge to keep from falling.

"What time is it?" he said.

"I don't know."

He hurried to get his phone from the floor. He'd left it next to the rifle.

"Crap."

"What's wrong?"

"It's almost time for their morning kayak on the lake."

"What? Who?"

With haunted eyes, he hissed, "Henry and Ida. They'll be here any minute!"

* * *

Andrew tore at the furniture and mattress plastered against the back doors, startling Nikki and Ryker awake.

"What on earth are you doing?" Nikki cried, pulling herself up by the arm of Ryker's chair. His eyes were open but he was silent. His lips looked far too swollen for speech.

"The old couple will be coming by," Andrew said frantically. "We have to tell them to call the cops and send an ambulance."

"What are you going on about?"

"Just help me, please!"

"And let that thing inside? Andy, just stop and think."

Kate stood beside her brother. He looked up at her with glassy, uncomprehending eyes. "There's an old couple that kayaks by the house every morning," she told Nikki. "They may be our only chance to get outside help."

"But if we expose the door..."

Nikki had her hands on her hips, adamant that they needed to keep the door barricaded.

"It won't come in," Kate said.

"Is everyone taking the piss?" Nikki said. "You've all lost your fucking minds, and you're going to get us killed."

"Just trust us," Kate said.

She could see Nikki wavering. "We have to try so we can get Ryker to the hospital."

Nikki turned and helped Ryker with the mattress. They flung it behind them, crashing into the detritus that he'd scattered around the room. Buttons started barking from the burst of excitement.

"Come here, But-But," Kate said. He wedged himself between her legs.

Ryker surprised her by reaching for her hand. His own was hot with fever. Again, she worried that even a hospital couldn't help him now, hating herself more and more, no matter Andrew and Nikki's assurances that she wasn't responsible. She loved her brother more than anyone in her family. The thought of losing him brought a painful twist to her already taxed heart.

Andrew pulled the blinds so hard, they broke free from the brackets, clattering on the floor. He kicked them aside and slid the door open. The cool morning air exploded into the stuffy cottage. The scent of dew and pine contrasted sickeningly with the stench of blood and sweat that they'd grown used to over the past five hours. He stepped outside recklessly. The monster could have been waiting for just this moment. Kate held her breath, reluctantly leaving Ryker to join Nikki at the doorway.

"Is it out there?" Nikki said, sounding like a little girl asking about the boogeyman.

Andrew looked around. "No, not that I can see."

Nikki swiped his rifle off the floor and brought it to him. "Just in case."

"Thanks."

"Do you see Ida and Henry?" Kate asked. The thought that help from the pair of nonagenarians might only be moments away upped her anxiety.

When Andrew headed for the stairs, she cried out, "Don't! Stay close."

He turned back to her, his expression grim but his eyes sparkling with optimism. "I won't go far. They're old. I'm not sure they'd be able to see or hear me from this distance."

She could see the dock and the lake that was smooth as glass. She hated to admit he might be right. Henry and Ida might be healthy enough to go for a slow paddle every day, but their senses must have been dulled by time. At least in the light of day, they would be able to spot the creature if it came for them.

"Just be careful. Don't get fixated on the lake. It could be anywhere."

Knowing in her gut they were all safe as long as they stayed in the house, and that it wouldn't dare even walk in an open door, she was also sure that Andrew had just waltzed into the lion's den. With each step he took, she calculated how long it would take him to run back inside when the creature appeared.

It was close. She could feel it watching them. The hairs at the back of her neck prickled.

Andrew cautiously stepped into the yard, head swiveling back and forth, rifle at the ready. By the time he made it to the path leading to the dock, Kate knew with icy dread that he'd gone too far to make it back safely.

The microwave feels bubbled up and down her back. She doubled over when a sword went through the middle of her chest.

"Are you okay?" Nikki said, one hand on her back, the other gripping her upper arm.

"I'm fine. Just…just my stomach," Kate lied.

That was a rough one. Any more like that and I won't be able to fake my way through it.

She straightened up and searched for her husband. He was still walking slowly down the path. He'd never seemed so far away from her, not even that time he traveled to Italy for work for two weeks.

He stopped and held up his free hand. "I think I see them."

Kate staggered to the porch, Nikki still holding on to her, straining to see if she could spot the couple past the tree line by the shore. Andrew broke into a run, heading for the dock.

"Andrew! No!"

CHAPTER THIRTY-ONE

Andrew thought he saw the tip of a yellow kayak and couldn't restrain himself. They were too close for him to wait.

He started shouting, "Henry...Ida...we need help! Can you hear me? We need you to call the police!"

A family of ducks floated around the dock. Sometimes he fed them crackers while he sat reading and sipping on a beer. In the weeks they'd been here, the babies had grown noticeably. To them, this was just another day and another chance to get some soggy crackers. He never thought he'd wish to be a duck.

Keeping his ear tuned for the monster's heavy footsteps, he ran with his typical madman gusto to the shore.

Once he got past the stand of trees to his left, he confirmed that these were Henry's and Ida's kayaks.

"Henry! Ida!"

He waved both arms as he ran, not once thinking that he might scare them off with the rifle.

When the first kayak came into full view, he fell to his knees, acidic vomit splattering the ground, splashing up into his face.

The kayaks floated lazily past him.

Henry and Ida were in them, but they'd been torn in half. Wisps of steam curled from their cracked chest cavities. Their heads had been torn from their necks and placed in their laps.

"No, no, no, no!"

Andrew punched the dirt, spinning away from the grisly tableau.

He heard Nikki and Kate scream as the kayaks entered their sight line.

Eyes stinging with tears, he pushed away from the pool of vomit and got to his feet, his legs feeling like lead.

It knew I would come out here. Their bodies are still warm, which means it just killed them. I have to get back inside the cottage!

His knees refused to bend, but he pushed on, stumble-running as fast as he could.

He didn't hear the approaching footsteps until it was too late.

The beast leaped out from behind a tree, as if this were all some kind of game. Andrew pulled back, suddenly unable to figure out how to use the rifle.

Kate was right.

It *was* diseased.

In the full light of day, he could see how deformed, how sickly the creature truly was. The bones under its hideous face were knobbed and twisted. He thought of the movie *The Thing*, and how the alien tried to assimilate men and dogs, the underlying skeleton a mélange of impossible bony structures. This creature could have stepped right out of one of the frames of that movie.

There seemed to be less hair on its body than last night, though it was impossible to be sure. If it had mange, it was in the final death throes of the sickness. Open sores leaked various colours of pus.

Yet it still looked strong, bulging muscles flexing as it blocked his path to the cottage. The women were shouting something at him, but in his panic, he'd gone deaf.

Shoot it! Shoot it!

He couldn't feel his hands. His arms registered the weight of the rifle, but it might as well have been held by someone else. Raising the barrel toward the creature was akin to trying to lift a car. He had to look down to see if his finger was on the trigger, bolts of terror racing through his body because he'd taken his eyes off the monster for even that one second.

The monster was close enough to swipe at him with one of its sharply taloned, massive hands, yet it simply stared at him, as if amused by the weakling who had the means of salvation in his hands and couldn't do something as simple as point and pull a trigger.

It smiled, wet brown lips pulling back to reveal cracked yellow teeth, its gums black as oil, spotted with red, infected pustules.

Andrew pissed himself, resigned with the awareness that this monstrosity would be the last thing he'd ever see on this earth, its ungodly touch his final contact with a warm, living creature.

Who will take care of Kate?
In the end, that was all he really cared about.

* * *

The moment the monster erupted from the woods to stand in Andrew's way of escape, Kate went wild with panic. Words spewed from her mouth that had no form, no true meaning, except for one – *Andrew*.

She tried to run to him, but Nikki held her fast, struggling to drag her back into the safety of the cottage. Kate fought Nikki like a madwoman, punching her arms, kicking at her legs, and jerking her head back to smash her sister-in-law's face. Her husband was going to die, and she wanted to die with him.

"You can't! You can't! You can't!" Nikki bleated like a mantra, unsuccessful in her attempts to gain control over Kate.

What Nikki couldn't know was that when there was nothing left to lose, there was no reason to hold back. Kate didn't need to save her strength to see another day. A miracle cure could wipe away all of her pain and afflictions, and she would still be as good as dead. She knew there was nothing she could do to stop the beast, but it owed her a quick death beside her husband. It had robbed them of their dreams, but maybe she could use it to deliver herself to the oblivion she belonged to, because living in this broken body without her true love was a hell unfit for even the worst of humanity.

Buttons cowered behind them, whining pitiably. She couldn't tell if he was scared of the creature or already mourning the loss of one of his masters.

"Let me go!"

She writhed within Nikki's surprisingly strong arms, feeling and hearing a loud *crunch* when Kate's flailing elbow clipped her nose.

Suddenly, she was free.

Nikki had fallen to her knees, both hands cupping her nose, blood trickling between her fingers.

Kate wanted to say she was sorry, to console her, to help her, but she had to face the creature before it did its terrible deed and disappeared. Her foot touched the first step, her heart racing, Andrew and the monster frozen in a stare-down, when she was yanked off her feet.

"No way, sis."

Ryker looked like a cadaver risen from the autopsy table. His skin was chalky and grey, the damaged and dead flesh within the stitches puffing up like poison mushrooms. How he was conscious, much less had the fortitude to lift her up, was beyond comprehension.

"Stay with Nikki."

Her sister-in-law reached up and snatched her hand, though her grip wasn't quite as strong as it had been moments before. In that touch, Kate felt her begging not to go – to let Ryker, who would most likely not see the end of the day, at least have a final moment of heroism.

Kate broke apart.

All of the pain and despair she fought against every minute of every day came rushing to the fore.

Buttons howled, as if giving voice to the wellspring of emotions that had broken free. His tail was tucked under him, snout pointed at the sky, whimpering to the heavens.

Once again, molten lead poured down Kate's back. Her brain erupted in wildfire. The agony that engulfed her was immeasurable. She was going to watch her husband and brother die, and her very being would shatter into a million hurtful pieces. Her and Andrew's jokes about reincarnation and how she must have been one awful son of a bitch in her previous life seemed prescient.

Please, dear God, end this! I feel like I'm going to explode!

Her heart went into a stuttering rhythm, causing her periphery to go wonky and dark. It was so hard to breathe. But she didn't dare take her eyes from the men she loved. She wanted Andrew to see her. She wanted them to look into one another's eyes one last time and know they had done their penance. The next life would have to be better.

Ryker stalked toward the beast with only the axe handle to protect himself.

"Hey!" he shouted to get its attention.

It whirled around, claws outstretched, its demented face curled into a mask of animal hate.

"No, Ryker, don't," she huffed, but she was too weak for the words to span the distance between them.

When the creature moved, Andrew finally looked toward the porch. Nikki was still on the ground, bleeding profusely, while Kate's mouth made O-rings like a fish gasping for air. Both hands now clutched her chest.

Ryker never broke stride, the axe handle raised behind his head. "Run, Andy, run!"

Shoot it, Andrew! Kate begged, her voice lost to the searing torment in her chest, radiating down her legs, through her arms, and exploding in the base of her skull.

Her heart made a loud, distressing *thump*, as if it were trying to break her rib cage and escape its confinement. It sent Kate sprawling onto the floor. She lay on her side, able to see through the slats as Ryker attacked the monster.

The creature howled loud enough to send every bird in the copious trees around them on a mad dash for safer limbs.

It tottered for a moment and then doubled over, sinking to one knee.

Ryker's swing whooshed over its head and he lost his footing, spinning away and struggling to keep his grip on the axe handle.

Andrew stood over the fallen behemoth, the barrel of the rifle inches from its head.

Before he could pull the trigger, Ryker charged it, crashing the handle down on its shoulder with a *crunch* that echoed across the lake. The monster wailed in agony.

And so did Kate.

CHAPTER THIRTY-TWO

When Andrew saw Kate's face scrunched up in agony, her skin was so pale, it took him back to the night his mother had passed away from ovarian cancer, the family beside her at hospice. Seconds before she'd drawn her final breath, her face had gone a waxy white that had troubled him ever since. One moment she was alive, though unable to open her eyes and rambling about a joke that someone name Johnny the Gambler had told her; the next she'd become something that no longer seemed real. He'd always felt that was the moment her soul left her body, her heart beating on for a few more rounds. She was dead yet not dead.

That was exactly how Kate looked now.

Her hands were on her chest, and he knew everything had been too much for her.

But there was something else.

The shape of her shoulder was off. There was a dip in her clavicle that shouldn't be there. It looked as if something very heavy had been dropped on her, shattering bone and her already damaged muscle. Buttons had his snout buried in her hair, whimpering, as if he were trying to wake her up.

All of this he saw and thought in the blink of an eye, his finger just needing one more ounce of pressure to pull back on the trigger and take off the top of the killer beast's skull.

Ryker had the axe handle raised for another blow when Andrew shouted, "Stop!"

He was a fraction too late to stop him completely. Ryker shifted his feet and the handle glanced off the side of the monster's thick skull. Its head whipped around to face Andrew, blood already springing from the laceration above its eye.

Andrew jumped back, worried it would lash out at him.

Instead it went onto its hands and knees, emitting a wheezing gasp like a busted accordion.

When he glanced again at Kate, he saw a rivulet of blood snaking down her face.

Ryker, who looked all the part of a horror himself, reared back to deliver a kick to the creature's ribs. Andrew hopped over it, tackling Ryker to the ground. The impact burst many of the stitches on his face. Andrew was showered with blood and foul-smelling ooze.

Through his split lips, Ryker shouted, "What the fuck is the matter with you? We have to kill it!"

The odour boiling off Ryker's face was enough to make Andrew woozy. Just like his mother and very possibly Kate, his brother-in-law was dead yet still waiting to die.

He had to roll off him before he threw up.

"You can't," he said, sucking in cleaner air. "Or you'll kill her."

Ryker staggered to his feet, searching for the axe handle. The beast remained on all fours, shuddering.

"Her. Him. I don't care what it is. It has to die."

Andrew grabbed ahold of his jeans, stopping him short from being able to pluck the handle from the ground. "You don't understand. I think it's connected to Kate."

"You're out of your mind. Stop being a pussy and shoot it so we can all get the hell out of here."

"Look!"

He pointed at the blood on the creature's face, pattering the crisp leaves beneath it. He then turned Ryker toward the porch. Kate was no longer moving, but they could see the blood on her own face.

Ryker pulled away from him and tried to wrest the rifle from his hands. "So? She fell and she's bleeding. Jesus Christ, have you lost your mind?"

"No. Come with me."

It was too easy to pull Ryker along. He could feel the man's strength ebbing away. The only thing keeping him alive was his hatred of the beast and his anger at Andrew for stopping him.

Nikki ran down the steps, enveloping Ryker, her blood smearing his shoulder as she held him up.

"I thought I was going to lose you," she sobbed.

Andrew ran up the steps and knelt beside his wife. His relief almost made him black out when he saw she was still breathing. When he touched her shoulder, he recoiled. There was nothing there. At least nothing whole.

"You hit it in the shoulder with the bat," he said.

More and more of the whites of Ryker's eyes were beginning to show. He swayed next to Nikki. "What are you talking about?"

"You bashed its shoulder. Now look at Kate's."

He tugged the collar of her shirt down, confident she was beyond feeling anything at the moment. What lay beneath was a purple, ruined mess. Buttons saw it and barked, frightened by the damage to his best friend and mother.

Nikki gasped.

Ryker huffed, "No."

"It stopped right when Kate grabbed her chest. When you hit it the first time, both she and it screamed in pain. The second time, they both bled from the same spot."

He looked at the beagle, who hadn't once taken his rheumy eyes off Kate. As far as Buttons was concerned, the demon in their yard wasn't even there.

"I think that's why Buttons wasn't reacting to it like he should. He knows. He's not afraid of it. He might not understand what it's doing, but he hasn't feared it, not once."

As if to tell him that his assumptions were correct, Buttons nudged Andrew's hand, wanting to be petted.

Grabbing the rail for extra support, Ryker said, "But that's not possible. How?"

Andrew shook his head, lost for words.

It wasn't possible, yet the evidence was right before their eyes, daring them to accept it.

"I can't fucking believe it," Nikki said. "How can Kate have anything to do with that...that monster?"

Andrew said, "That thing is undeniably real when we all know it shouldn't be. I don't think we're in any position to say something is out of the realm of possibility."

Ryker lurched up the stairs to touch his sister. He didn't make it all the way, sprawling across the porch, the tips of his fingers brushing against her hair.

"I would never hurt you," he whispered, his tears falling into the angry red gashes in his face.

Andrew held on to Ryker's back as it heaved with deep,

heartbreaking sobs. "She knows that. She loves you more than you can ever know."

"I wanted to save her. All of us. I didn't know. I didn't know."

Andrew knew there was nothing he could say to console him. Nikki melded herself on top of him like a tortoise shell, murmuring softly in his ear.

He needed to get Kate inside. If she was going to die, he wouldn't allow it to happen on a dirty porch. He took a quick glance at the creature and saw it was still down. In fact, it had collapsed onto its side, its ghastly face angled toward them, eyes half-closed and staring at Kate.

Andrew shivered at the thought that Kate and the monstrosity were somehow bonded to one another. The how and why would have to wait.

"We have to get the hell out of here," Ryker said, his voice thready and weak. "While it's down, we have to go. This could be our only chance. We have to go, now!"

The odds of them getting far with Ryker and Kate in their conditions were slim to less than none. If Andrew could have one wish, it would be for a helicopter to land on the back lawn, armed guards escorting them inside with doctors in wait.

That helicopter wasn't coming, and they weren't going to be able to simply make a run for it. He stormed into the living room. The thing, so far, wouldn't come into the house. It was the only safe place for them for miles.

The mattress was on its side, resting against the upturned bedframe. He laid it back down on the floor and found a sheet and the pillows scattered about the room.

As he stepped back onto the porch to lift Kate, his eyes flicked toward the yard and his throat closed up.

The monster was gone!

"Nikki, we have to get them inside now."

She looked up, her eyes red and puffy. Ryker reached out for Kate as Andrew slipped his arms under her and hoisted her up. His face had gotten worse, more stitches giving way, the meat on his skull turning odd colours. Yet he was still alive, desperate to be near Kate, grunting with the effort to get up and follow them into the house.

Andrew was walking through the doorway when the porch rattled, wood snapping, and the entire world shifted out from under his feet.

The monster had somehow gotten onto the roof, bounding off it and landing between them. Andrew held a shaky certainty that it wouldn't do anything to him as long as he held Kate. That was probably why its back was to them.

Instead, it was focused on Ryker and Nikki.

"I won't hurt her again," Ryker said, blood bubbling from his bisected lips. "You can kill me if you want, but I won't hurt her."

Ryker pushed Nikki behind him. "If you're connected to Katy, go the fuck away so we can get her out of here and to a hospital before she dies."

The creature stared at him for a moment, its massive head tilted as if considering his request. Andrew felt the tremendous heat coming off Kate, wondering if the same fever was eating the monster alive. If so, how long before it collapsed just as she had?

Ryker held up his hands to show the creature he meant no harm. "Please, just let us take care of her. She can't stay here."

With a swipe of its hand, Ryker's head was separated from his neck, spinning end over end until it landed by the fire pit, bouncing several times and rolling under a bush.

Arterial spray showered the creature and Nikki as she screeched.

Buttons again wailed, his cry chilling Andrew's spine, but he refused to attack the beast.

Andrew kicked the monster in the small of its back. Kate, though still unconscious, arched in his arms. It fell down the stairs, knocking Nikki into the rail. She somehow managed to keep her footing, rushing up the stairs and following Andrew into the cottage. He slammed the door closed with his foot and set Kate on the mattress.

Nikki was in hysterics. Her husband's blood stained her face, dripped from her hair, splattered her clothes. She screamed and screamed, hands balled into fists, running around the cottage and knocking into everything in her path. Andrew tore himself from Kate's side and had to practically tackle his sister-in-law. She shouted in his ear so loudly, he could only hear a high-pitched ringing immediately after.

There was nothing to say. He could only hold her to keep her from hurting herself and wait to see if she could calm down. He wasn't sure he would if the same had happened to Kate, if he were wearing her blood, still warm to the touch.

When he saw them in the mirror, they looked like they'd just emerged from a swim in the runoff tank at a slaughterhouse. They had become the face of madness.

We are mad. How can we not be? How can any of this even be real?

It took a long time for Nikki to wear herself out, to mercifully shut down. He guided her to a chair, the chair Ryker had slept in the night before, rapidly decaying from the fatal damage to his face.

"I'm going to check on Kate; then I'm going to help get you cleaned up."

Her eyes flicked over his shoulder and went wide.

He turned back.

The creature stood on the other side of the glass door, glowering at them. More of its fur had fallen out, revealing rotting flesh. He couldn't see the top of its head, and its width took up the entire doorway.

Buttons sat, staring at the monster. His tail wagged a few times. Then he turned away to join Kate on the bed.

Andrew spied the curtains in a mangled heap on the floor.

He couldn't function with that thing looking at them. That way lay ruination.

"Just look away," he said to Nikki. She shut her eyes, covering her face with her crimson hands for good measure.

Andrew grabbed the box spring and pushed it across the floor toward the door. The creature watched him, its jaundiced eyes and broken face unreadable. As he covered one of the doors, he saw the rifle on the ground outside. He'd completely forgotten it.

Ryker's head is somewhere near there too.

He covered his mouth with his fist as an acidic burp promised more bile to come.

"Fuckfuckfuckfuckfuckfuckfuck." Nikki rocked in her seat, hands covering everything but her mouth.

He used a blanket to cover the other glass door, blocking their view of the creature and vice versa.

It doesn't need to see us to know exactly what's going on, he thought, staring at Kate. *Its eyes and ears have always been with us.*

CHAPTER THIRTY-THREE

Kate awoke gasping for air.

Something was in her throat. Something large and wet and matted with hair and tasting as foul as old sewage in the hot sun. She didn't dare swallow. If she did, it would slide further within her.

But she needed to breathe. Each attempt to snatch a lungful of air pushed the grisly lump deeper and deeper down.

Oh God, kill me!

As she floundered on the mattress, her violent actions startled Buttons, who jumped up, barking. She got tangled in the sheet, wondering if and when she was going to get her next breath.

A pair of rough hands latched on to her arm.

"Just calm down and breathe. That's right, honey, let yourself breathe."

Seeing Andrew's face centred her, allowed her waking panic to subside. She was breathing, but it hurt like hell. It felt as if someone had taken a wrecking ball to her chest and ribs. Something was wrong with her left arm. All she could feel was a dull tingling in her fingers. Her arm was in a sling (she always took a sling with her because she never knew when a shoulder dislocation would be especially bad). It was secured by a bathrobe tie around her midsection. The more she came to, the greater the pain in her shoulder. She didn't need to see or touch it to know that it was in a very, very bad way.

Once she had settled down, wondering how she'd gotten inside, her husband lay next to her, pulling her close. He smelled terrible – a mix of body odour and rust. It reminded her partly of her grandfather's cramped workspace in the basement: old tools, open tubes of grease and oil, paint cans, and bits of projects to be done filling every corner.

Inching away, she saw all the blood. His clothes were covered in it.

"Is it…?"

He cupped her face in his hand. "No."

"Then whose blood is it?"

"Let's focus on you first. How are you feeling? You're way overdue for your medication. I'll get it for you."

She snagged his shirt, preventing him from getting off the mattress. Her body might crave her medication (He didn't know just how overdue she was. Years of being on opioids had made her an addict by the dictionary definition. She was feeling strange and jittery, a desperate clawing *need* tearing her guts to ribbons), but she wouldn't take a thing until she got some answers.

Looking around the empty room, she said, "What happened to my shoulder? Where are Ryker and Nikki?"

Andrew paled, his mouth opening but no words coming out. His eyes glimmered with tears.

Impossibly, the pain in Kate's chest got worse. "No. They're both... gone?"

Before he could answer, she heard footsteps, then Nikki's voice. "Only your brother."

"Nikki!"

Kate felt the room spin out of control. Not Ryker. Not her dear, good-hearted brother.

Her sister-in-law was a walking nightmare. The only things not red with dried blood were the whites of her eyes. Her hair had clumped together like dreadlocks.

When she saw Kate's eyes roving over her body, she said, "This is all I have left of him. Well, in here at least. His body is on the steps out back. At least I think it is. Not sure where his head went. I was too busy getting showered in his blood as it cascaded from where his head had been. Funny thing, that. When it happens, you tend not to notice the big things...or the little things. Did you know blood burns when you get it in your eyes? Maybe not a drop or two, but when you take a liter to the face, it fucking burns. It burns like hell, Katy."

"Nikki," Andrew said.

"She wanted to know, Andy. Didn't you, Katy? I may have lost a lot today, but not my hearing."

Andrew flashed a warning look Nikki's way. Something had been going on between them while Kate was out, and it obviously wasn't pleasant. Why was Nikki being like this? With Ryker dead, Nikki should have been leaning on Andrew, not being angry and aggressive.

"Not now, Nikki. Let me get her what she needs."

Nikki's arm had been behind her back the entire time. She swung it forward so they could see Kate's mason jar of pills in her palm. "Are you looking for this?"

Buttons gave a low warning growl. Even he could sense the change in Nikki.

"Yes," Andrew said, his tone level, empty. "Can I please have it?"

Kate was afraid to speak.

"Anything to help our dear Katy," Nikki said, her voice dripping with sarcasm.

As Andrew got up to take the jar from her, she cocked her arm back and threw it against the wall. It shattered into hundreds of pieces, pills flying everywhere.

Buttons skittered away from the rain of glass and pills, yapping.

"Come here, Buttons," Kate said, hooking her fingers under his collar. The act of moving sent waves of fire rippling from her damaged shoulder down her left arm. Kate bit her lip until it bled, fighting through the agony. She didn't want Buttons walking around and getting glass stuck in his paws. She'd lost her brother (and all the good parts of her sister-in-law...the poor woman had lost it). She wasn't going to see her beloved dog hurt if she could help it.

"Why the hell did you do that?" Andrew screamed, running up to Nikki and stopping just short of bumping chests.

Nikki snarled. "Because she killed him! She killed Ryker and she won't stop there!"

"You don't know what you're talking about."

"Oh, I think I do. That thing is a part of her. You're the one who showed us that. She didn't even try to stop it. She just did her fainting act and let it tear Ryker's fucking head off!"

It was like a punch to her already roiling stomach. Kate wrapped her arms around a squirming Buttons. What was Nikki talking about?

"How could she have done anything if she wasn't even conscious? Tell me that?" Andrew was shouting now, his shoulders heaving.

"I don't fucking know! But I do know that whatever they have between them must work both ways." Nikki wasn't backing down. In fact, she inched even closer. They were practically nose to nose.

"What is everyone talking about?" Kate said. "What's a part of me? How...how could I possibly have killed Ryker? Or stopped it? Please, somebody tell me."

If she had been on the edge of madness before, she felt she was dangerously close to stepping right into the maelstrom and never coming back. How could Nikki blame her for Ryker's death? It was insane. Impossible! No one loved him more than Kate. Not even Nikki.

"Tell her," Nikki said, her voice eerily calm. "Go on, Andy."

He turned to her, looking more worried and exhausted than any human being had ever been. It was a wonder he even had the strength to argue with her.

"Please," Kate said, unsuccessfully trying to hold back her tears.

Andrew sank to his knees beside the mattress, reaching out for her good hand.

"Your shoulder," he said in a rasp.

She glanced at the white sling and the odd angle of her shoulder.

"Did I break it when I fell?"

"No." He looked to be on the verge of tears. "It happened when your brother attacked the monster. He...he hit it in the shoulder with the axe handle. You and it screamed at the same time, and then your shoulder was...was caved in."

Kate's skin started to crawl. "But...how?"

"We don't know. Before that happened, you grabbed your chest. That's when the creature stopped as well and doubled over. It's what allowed Ryker the chance to hit it and for me to get away. He was going to smash it in the head when I stopped him. The handle only grazed it. And...and at that moment, a wound opened up on your head."

Nikki grabbed a dining room chair and sat. "Ryker could have killed it then. He could be with us right now."

Andrew didn't take his eyes off Kate. "Ryker was sick. When that thing tore him up, it infected him. There was nothing we could have done to save him. Ryker knew it too. But if I'd allowed him to finish what he started, you'd both be gone now." He held up his hand, shushing her. "I know how inconceivable it sounds, but in my heart, I know it's true."

Kate didn't know how to process this. It was hard enough thinking straight through the thickening fog of pain. This...this was just too much.

"Have you noticed how Buttons doesn't give a fig about your

monster?" Nikki said. She crossed her right leg over her left, the caked-on blood crackling. "It's because he's known all along that beast is you."

"I can't believe that," Kate said.

Had Andrew and Nikki utterly lost their minds? It was very plausible, considering what they'd been through.

"It's not up for debate," Nikki said. "I bet your friend is still out there. I'm sure it would be happy to see you." She got up from the chair, knocking it backward.

"Nikki, don't!" Andrew said.

She ran to the back door and ripped the blanket down.

Kate shrieked, backpedaling in the bed to get as far away as possible.

The creature's sick eyes grew wide when it saw her.

"Get the gun, Andrew!" she shouted.

Instead of scrambling for the rifle, Andrew laid his arm over her chest. Her destroyed shoulder brushed against his arm and she saw stars.

"Kate, it's not going to come in," he said, his tone not quite matching the words. It was plain to her that he was nervous he could be wrong. Oh, how she wanted him to be wrong.

"Then kill it!"

"I can't, Kate. I can't."

Nikki stepped away from the door. "Take a look at its shoulder, Katy."

She had turned away, unable to face the grisly vision in the doorway. It was beyond horrible in the light of day. Monsters were only for the night. They were never supposed to walk during the daytime.

Monsters aren't supposed to be real no matter what time of day, she reminded herself.

"Katy, I said look!"

She did.

The creature's left shoulder was in the shape of a U, the impression of the axe handle impossible to miss. She looked at her own matching indentation on her left shoulder. The pain suddenly seemed worse than ever.

Why wasn't it breaking through the glass? Why was it staring at them like that?

"You see?" Nikki said. "Twinsies." A cruel smile curled her lips.

The gore-covered woman had endured what no person should ever suffer, and there was no coming back.

"What the hell is the matter with you?" Andrew said, getting up and retrieving the blanket. He tried to put it back over the door, but Nikki just wrenched it back down.

"I want her to see."

"Why? Aren't things bad enough?"

She slowly shook her head. "I don't think Katy's fully convinced."

Kate barely had time to scream when Nikki lunged onto the mattress. Her sister-in-law grabbed the middle finger of Kate's hand that was in the sling and bent it back until it made the sound of a walnut cracking.

Kate wailed in pain, her body gone painfully stiff, as if she'd just grabbed a live wire. Andrew grabbed Nikki and flung her across the room.

"Why did you do that?" he shouted.

Kate's cries devolved into a silent, racking sob.

Nikki lay on the floor, staring at the door, laughing. Andrew hurled every curse he could at her, but the smile grew wider and wider.

Kate stared in horror at her finger. It was bent all the way back, lying flat against the back of her hand.

When her eyes rose to meet those of the creature outside, she understood.

She saw pain in those eyes.

And the middle finger on its left hand was snapped back.

*   *   *

As Andrew yelled at Nikki, Buttons stood beside him, barking at her continuously, thick ropes of spittle splashing on the floor. The beagle's lips curled back, teeth clacking.

Andrew had never been so mad at another human being before. Even though she was obviously out of her head, he still wanted to choke her to stop her laughter. Or at the very least, slap the lopsided grin off her face.

"It's true," Kate said.

He spun around and saw her gaping at the diseased abomination. Its finger was also broken. He'd hoped he had misinterpreted the situation all along (because to fully accept it would pull the rug out from under all of his beliefs), but there was no second-guessing now.

Perhaps Nikki had done exactly what needed to be done so there were no more doubts for any of them.

No! She hurt Kate and thinks it's a fucking joke!

"Welcome to the real world, Katy," Nikki said between her sputtering laughter. "Now, why don't you tell it to take a nice little swim so we can get the hell out of here?"

Kate cowered on the bed. "I...I...I..."

She shivered uncontrollably. Andrew covered her with his body. Her fever was back. Sweat leaked from every pore.

"How?" she muttered over and over. He wished he had an answer. Maybe if he knew, he could figure out how to disentangle them.

He looked over to see Buttons standing guard over Nikki, still barking, still mad as hell at her for attacking Kate.

"I don't know what that is. You have to believe me. I didn't make it come here," she said, blubbering.

"I know you didn't, honey. There's no way you could have."

"I would never do anything to hurt my brother."

Andrew recalled Ryker saying the same thing about his sister outside, when he had a chance to take the creature down.

When Kate attempted to shift her body, she leaned against her ruined shoulder. She howled, Buttons matching her cry. Andrew was so close to helpless panic, he feared he'd be just as lost as Nikki soon.

"Let me at least get you something for the pain," he said, slipping into caregiver mode. It had oddly become his comfort zone over the years. Caring for Kate's needs gave him purpose. Being able to provide the small things – feeding her in bed, making sure she took her medication on time, helping her shower, changing her sheets and propping her pillows – they were the only things he could control, making him feel less impotent when he thought of the larger issues that were well out of his hands.

She couldn't answer him through her tears and pain.

He searched the floor for the right pills. He palmed three and wobbled to the kitchen on anesthetised legs.

"I'll get you a soda. You want a soda?"

The unreality of their reality was overwhelming.

Just keep your shit together and focus on Kate.

How many times had he said that when things got bad at work or when he looked at their medical bills and wondered how in the name of God they were ever going to pay them. It was always *focus on Kate*. The rest was never as important as it seemed. Bills were not life or death. What Kate faced on a daily basis was. There were less shitty ways of gaining perspective, but it was the only way he knew.

The horror outside their door followed him with its impenetrable yellow eyes.

It was coupled with Kate, and even though he knew she loved him, this monstrosity did not. It would tear him in two the second he stepped outside. Of that he was sure. It glared at him, daring him to slide that door open.

When he tried to give Kate her pills, she knocked them out of his hand, as well as the can of soda. It spilled all over the mattress.

"Kate, it's going to help you," he said, sopping up the mess with a throw pillow.

"Nothing's going to help me," she said, her eyes closed tight, her face a rictus of agony.

"She's right about that," Nikki murmured.

"Shut your fucking mouth," Andrew snapped. "Or I'll throw you outside with that thing!"

She arched an eyebrow, the wicked smile returning. "Oh, finish what the wife started, eh? Brilliant."

When he jumped to his feet, Kate said, "Stop. Leave her be. She's... she's not right."

Andrew was seething, but he had to fight his impulses.

"I'm not right, she's not right, you're not right," Nikki said. She looked fixedly at the beast. "Ryker sure as hell isn't right. I think the only one that has any sense left is the dog. And he's not about to tell us what to do, are you, you little mongrel?"

"Shut your mouth."

She glanced at him defiantly. "Or you'll throw me to the big bad wolf? Stop being such a sodding wanker and lie down with your wife, Andy. Feed her her pills and pretend that you'll make it all go away. That's what you want to do, isn't it? Well, you could never save her, and you sure as shite can't save her now."

Andrew saw red.

Kate attempted to grab his pants leg but he pulled away.

"Face it. We're never getting out of here. That's what it wants us to know. That's why it's standing there like some kind of fucking gargoyle. We...can never...leave. Not me, not you, and especially not Katy."

"I need you to cut it out now," he said.

"Or what? Are you going to hit a grieving widow?"

"Andrew, just leave her be," Kate said. She sounded so lost and afraid, it only fueled his anger at his sister-in-law.

Nikki looked at them with disgust and turned away from the doors and the abomination that had killed her husband. She walked to the kitchen, where he hoped she would at least attempt to wash the blood from her face.

Instead, she pulled the cork from a bottle of wine and drank it straight from the bottle.

Adding drunkenness to madness would not be an ideal combination, but her momentary silence was more than golden to Andrew – it was platinum. If she had kept going on, he wasn't sure how much longer he would have been able to control himself. Widow or not, family or not, he'd had enough.

Focus on Kate.

Her face was buried in Buttons' side.

"Can you please cover it?" she asked.

When he turned to hook the blanket over the doors, the monster was gone.

Where the hell is it now?

She hadn't seen that it had left, so he quickly reaffixed the blanket, blotting out the yard and lake that looked so normal, so pristine, if only he didn't look down and see the bloodstains on the porch. He wondered if the old couple's bodies were still floating on the lake or if someone had found them by now.

If they had been discovered, he would hear sirens.

It was as if everyone around the lake had left them to the wild demon, only returning once it finished them off.

"Is it covered?" Kate said.

Her voice pulled him back.

"Yes. You can't see it now."

He threw a quick look at Nikki, who was too busy drinking to say something cruel or upsetting.

"Can you please hold me? I'm so scared."

Andrew had to nudge Buttons aside so he could enfold his wife in his arms. She felt as fragile as a newly hatched egg and as hot as an omelet.

"What am I supposed to do?" she said, sniffing back tears.

He caressed her back, rocking her on his lap. "You don't have to do anything, honey. There's nothing you can do."

"But what if there is? If we can feel each other's pain, why won't it read my thoughts? I keep telling it to go away, but it can't hear me."

"You've been telling it to go away?"

"Yes. In my mind. I keep thinking it over and over, picturing it walking into the lake and never coming up."

Looking at the covered door, Andrew asked, "Can you sense what it's thinking?"

She shook her head against his chest.

But had it heard her? It was no longer at the back door. Had Kate managed to open up a way to control it?

"Just keep thinking about it going away," he said. "Meditate on that. I want you to change one thing, though. Instead of imagining it drowning in the lake, just have it disappear. Or find a hole or cave and crawl inside, never to come out again."

"What if that's not enough?"

"Think to yourself that it will be enough."

"I…I don't know."

If Kate was in charge of the horror now, the last thing he wanted was for it to drown itself. When it took its last breath, wouldn't Kate as well? How far would their physical connection go? Would it stretch into the final throes of death, snapping only when both were gone?

He couldn't take that chance.

"You can do it, honey," he said. "Promise me you'll keep thinking it, but stay away from the lake."

When she tilted her face to him, the yellowing of her eyes stunned him. They were starting to look like—

"Put your big girl panties on and just fucking do what he says," Nikki blurted. She slammed the wine bottle on the counter, blood-red liquid sloshing on her arm. "Do it! Do it!"

Kate shivered, closing her eyes.

"Do you think shouting at her is going to help?" Andrew said.

"Piss off, Dandy Andy."

He forced himself to turn away from her. Kate trembled in his arms like a newborn kitten. She seemed lighter than ever, as if the thread between her and the beast was taking bits of her along with it, tug by tug, until there'd be nothing left.

CHAPTER THIRTY-FOUR

Even though Nikki wouldn't stop shouting at her, Kate was able to push her unhinged sister-on-law's voice away until it was a dull thrum of white noise. The heavy, unstable pounding of her heart filled her ears instead, its erratic rhythm making it hard to breathe. She felt Andrew's hand on her back, smelled the fear-tinged sweat of his body, and tried to send out a steady wave of thoughts for the beast to leave them forever. Andrew had told her not to picture it drowning in the lake, but where else could it go where she'd know they'd be safe?

No, it had to drown.

Her body felt as if she'd been thrown off a tall building into a vat of boiling oil. Every bone had shattered like spun sugar, her skin melting. And through it all, her heart and lungs laboured to keep her alive, to keep her wishing the nightmare monster into her dream lake, a dream that she'd been permitted to see but never truly enjoy.

If she and the monstrosity died together, it would be a mercy.

She would miss Andrew. She worried so much about him.

In the cold light of day, she believed in an afterlife, her spirit moving on but still able to love and check in on her husband from time to time.

Some nights, when death seemed to be lurking in the shadows, waiting, there were doubts.

Either way – heaven or eternal nothing – her suffering would be over. At least with the former, she would once again be with Andrew. If she was wrong, he would be left alone for the splinter of time left him, and that was always what made her scratch and claw her way back to him.

You're not going to have much choice in the matter this time around.

A starburst of pain exploded from her chest, cascading outward. She stiffened like a board as her heart went on a drunken stumble.

Concentrate! You can fight through this. You always have.

Andrew tightened his grip on her, the tone of his voice soothing. Did he know he was losing her? In the end, would it be a relief for him?

If she could convince herself of that, it would be easier to go.

Stop thinking about yourself and tell that thing to die!

Go!

Leave us!

Head to the lake. Step in the cool water. Keep walking until you can't breathe. Suck in the water. Let it fill your diseased lungs. Let the water embrace you, you goddamn devil! Die.

Die!

She opened one eye when Andrew's hand brushed against her face.

He was crying.

In that moment, Kate's will wavered.

"Don't...cry," she sputtered.

He leaned close to her ear. "I'm not crying," he whispered. "I'm just chopping onions."

A smile quivered on his lips, one of his tears falling onto her own, the salt of him burning her parched tongue.

She couldn't leave him.

"I love you," she rasped. "Thank you for giving me more than I ever deserved."

The cold reality hit him hard and his eyes shimmered. "I love you, my little crip. Always have, always will."

"No!" Nikki screamed. "You stupid fucking cunt! Can't you do anything right? You have only one thing to do – tell it to go away. Not get all mushy in the head with Andy. Jesus fuck!"

Andrew didn't even react to her outburst. His eyes wouldn't leave Kate's.

There was so much she wanted to tell him, but Nikki was right. Her infirmities might have kept her from doing much of anything this past decade to help her husband, but this she could do. This she *had* to do.

"Promise me," she said.

He choked back a sob.

"Promise you what?"

"Oh, enough of this," Nikki snapped.

Kate heard the knife slide out of the butcher block. The blade caught a harsh slat of light creeping through the blinds.

Nikki charged them.

"Andrew!" Kate screamed.

He turned but it was too late. Nikki brought the knife down, aiming for Kate's face. Andrew's shifting body made her miss. The blade sliced a clean, vicious line down his arm.

Nikki jumped back before he could grab her.

"If she dies, *it* dies," she said. "The sooner the better. I want to get out of here and collect my husband. Both parts of him. Damn you both for bringing us here!"

She wrapped both hands around the knife handle, raising it high over her head, lunacy swirling in her eyes.

Andrew blocked Kate with his body, nothing to defend them save his bare hands.

Nikki screeched, looking the part of an avenging demon.

Before she could plunge the knife into Andrew, the house exploded.

*   *   *

It was as if a grenade had gone off.

The front of the house blasted inward.

Nikki was thrown off her feet

Wood and shrapnel flew across the room, a heavy board crashing through the glass doors. The air was choked with dust and debris.

Andrew froze, his ears ringing from the impact.

What the hell had just happened?

Nikki lay unconscious by the mattress, a jagged shard of wood stuck in the side of her neck, blood bubbling from the wound.

He spun to check on Kate.

She was unhurt, eyes wide with terror and confusion, mouth open, collecting the grey dust that was everywhere. She had hold of his arm, knuckles white, but he couldn't feel the pressure.

His face stung but he had no desire to see what had happened to it.

Had the boiler exploded? Was there even a boiler in the cottage? Or was it a gas line? It was so hard to think.

Nikki.

She was hurt. He was about to pull the piece of wood out of her neck and stopped himself. What if it was like pulling your finger from a dike? Would she immediately start to bleed out?

In movies, when people have knives stuck in them, they always say to leave it in until they get to the hospital. This isn't a damn movie, but in this case, I think they got it right.

He almost felt guilty at the relief of Nikki being knocked out. But this was beyond knocked out. She could die, and that was what drove a dagger of guilt into his heart.

That hadn't been Nikki before. If they made it out of here alive, he wondered if the Nikki they all knew could ever return.

Most likely not. That Nikki had died right alongside Ryker.

Kate gasped, pulling on his arm.

Emerging from within the swirling dust came the creature.

It was in the cottage!

What remained of its mangy coat was covered in dust. It turned to Andrew with pus-coloured eyes. It seemed bigger than before, if such a thing were even possible. Bigger and stronger, despite looking as if it had contracted a flesh-eating bacteria.

It swatted Andrew off the bed, sending him through the broken doors and onto the porch with the ease of flicking a crumb off the table. Andrew couldn't catch his breath, his diaphragm hitching.

He watched in helpless horror as it lifted Kate off the bed and draped her over its shoulder like a rag doll. She was too weak to even slap it with her fists. Andrew's mouth bobbed open and closed, trying feebly to call her name.

Buttons, who had disappeared when the front of the house caved in, padded out from behind a pile of rubble. He growled at the creature. It slowly turned to look at him. Buttons gave a sharp yap, and then whimpered. The beagle kept his distance from the monster, but he also didn't seem afraid.

Because he has nothing to fear from Kate, Andrew thought. *Neither did Ryker or Nikki. But look what it's done to them. Why?*

The creature settled its yellow eyes on Nikki, knowing the dog was no threat. It straddled her, rust-coloured drool splattering on her face. It saw the knife she'd meant to kill Kate with, and its lips pulled back in a depraved sneer.

Andrew fought for each breath, straining to get his legs back under him.

It reached down to run a clawed finger across Nikki's body, prodding the wood sticking out of her neck. A spurt of blood stained its finger.

"Kate," Andrew wheezed.

She lifted her head but was unable to hold his gaze for long. She collapsed against the beast's back, arms dangling.

He didn't know how he was going to get it to let her go, but he had to do something.

It sniffed its bloody finger and grunted. Then it looked at the knife again.

With lightning reflexes, it grabbed hold of Nikki's head, lifting it from the floor, and bashed it so hard, it exploded. Nikki's skull cracked open, brains and blood gushing from the jagged cavity, squirting across the floor like spilled stew.

Andrew gagged when he saw a glob of grey matter on his chest.

Still holding the remains of her skull, the creature flung her body across the room. She hit the dining room wall and tumbled out of Andrew's sight.

Turning its back to him, the monster walked through the debris that had once been a charming cottage, stepping out of the gaping hole it had created when it came charging in. Kate's body swayed from side to side with each massive step. Buttons looked to Andrew with his dark, sad eyes and chose to follow the beast, to stay beside Kate.

Andrew shook the black spots from his vision and followed. His feet went out from under him when he stepped in Nikki's gore. Sliding in blood and grey matter, he hurried to his feet, leaving bloody footprints leading to the chasm that was the front of the house.

By the time he made it outside, his decimated car still there, a portent of what was to come, the monster, Kate, and Buttons were gone.

But he could hear it stalking away. With each footfall, there came a deep, laboured wheeze.

Andrew entered the dark canopy of trees, following his ears and nose – for it smelled more vile than ever – guiding him to Kate and, most likely, his own death.

*   *   *

Kate had never fully understood the phrase *making your skin crawl* until now.

The thing reeked of suppurating disease.

Is this what I'm like inside? she thought. *Is this the smell of the diseases that have ruined my life?*

Her face brushed against a purple boil on its back. If the boil popped, she knew she would lose her mind for good. This close to its body, she could hear the churning of its lungs and all of the mucus and sludge roiling around its bellows.

A fleeting sense of calm washed over her. For the briefest of moments, she could see into the creature's mind. What stared back at her was very much herself, though the parts she strove so hard to avoid. She saw the pain and frustration, the longing and dread, all of her fear and anger at the injustice of it all. A raging storm of all the negativity she'd harboured as she lay like an invalid, just struggling to stay alive, formed the soul of this horrid beast. The feelings she'd worked so hard to ignore were darker, more cancerous than the diseases that had been trying to kill her all these years. And then she'd come up here, a last chance at happiness, and her body and the treatment had stolen even that from her.

The treatment. The microwave feels.

Somehow that, combined with her frustration and Ryker's instructions to manifest her thoughts into reality, had birthed a monster. It was the living embodiment of everything she hated about herself and her life. It was finally free, and it was happy here. How many times had she told Andrew she never wanted to leave the cottage? Now the creature wouldn't let them leave. It couldn't. Without her near, it would fade away and die.

Kate should have felt a sliver of kinship with it, but all she felt was a hollow space where all of those negative emotions had lived. She'd managed to exorcise the worst parts of herself. If she could only eliminate them entirely.

Just as quickly, the connection was severed. Her vision was filled with the suppurating sores on the creature's back, her anger welling up as bursting boils on its flesh.

The cottage was well behind them. She wondered if it was finally listening to her and planned to take them both to the lake.

She had a strong feeling her mental commands earlier had been working. But when Nikki attacked her, its sense of self-preservation brought it roaring back. Kate might have accepted her fate at Nikki's hands, but this creature wasn't wholly her own. It might have been at one point, but it had changed...grown...since it had been birthed into the world. It wanted to live, and it knew it couldn't if Nikki snuffed the life from its…its what? Was she a host? A power source? How could she, who could barely stand, be the source of energy for such a massive beast?

Kate tried to find a way back into its mind – her *outer mind* – but it either wouldn't let her back in or the bridge between them was crumbling. The longer it lived in the real world, the less it relied on her, growing into its own poisonous persona.

I brought this on us. Please forgive me, God. I killed Ryker and Nikki.

A dog barked close behind them. She strained to move her neck, to lift her face from the creature's vile back.

"Buttons."

Her beagle, her baby, followed them. When he saw her, his tail wagged, though he was whining – wishing, she gathered, that she would stop moving away and let him cuddle her.

He won't attack it because he knows we're one and the same.

"Go back to Daddy," she said. It was a chore to speak with her midsection draped over the beast's massive shoulder. "Go on. Go to Daddy."

Buttons didn't pause or break his stride. He was going with her no matter where this ended. In a way, she was grateful. If these were her final moments, she wanted to pass in the presence of unconditional love. As much as she craved Andrew's touch, she hoped he stayed away. If the creature hurt or killed him, she would die a tortured soul. She couldn't think of a worse way to leave this world.

A fresh, lancing pain radiated from the centre of her chest.

The beast stumbled, smashing its shoulder against a tree, forcing it to slow down.

Not sure how many more of these I can take. Not sure how many more I want to.

When she couldn't draw a breath, the creature stopped, its own lungs seized.

If I die, will it die too? Or will I take my diseases with me, leaving it to heal and grow?

It fell to its knees. Kate slipped off its shoulder, her face in the mulch. Buttons yapped, sniffing around her head.

"I'm all right, But-But. Mommy's all right," she said without conviction. Buttons knew she was lying. He whined, pawing at her back, willing her to get up. She wasn't sure she had the strength to do something as simple as roll over. If she didn't soon, she would suffocate on mouldy leaves and dirt.

I'll be in the dirt soon enough.

She planted her palm on the ground and pushed herself up, her ruined shoulder a fireworks display of agony. It must have been really bad for it to steal the spotlight from the pangs in her heart and all of the other burning pains in her body.

Every muscle trembled, both from exhaustion and from going cold turkey off her meds. Her pain doctor had once told her that with all of the highly addictive opioids she was on, the thought of going cold turkey should never enter her mind. The shock to her fragile system would kill her. This he had said the day she'd lamented about the treatments for her conditions and a wish for a future without need for pills or patches. He'd said he had many patients who felt the same way, and some simply decided to stop taking them. It always ended in disaster.

"If this isn't a disaster, I don't know what is," she said to Buttons, who wagged his tail excitedly, using his body to help prop her up.

She looked over at the panting creature. A weeping scab the size of her fist took up the entire left side of its head. Strands of stained fur fell like dirty snowflakes onto the ground.

It turned a jaundiced eye toward her, and she saw hate.

"You are becoming your own...thing, aren't you?" she said.

It grunted in reply, a bloody line of drool spilling over its bottom lip.

"You hate what you've inherited from me, don't you?"

It turned away from her and she could see the knobs of its spine, flesh mottled and grey, so much of its hair sloughing off.

"The doctors told me that if I'd ever been able to have children, they would more than likely have come down with some of the same diseases I have. In a way, that made me glad I couldn't conceive." The fact that she was talking to the monster as if they were chatting over dinner didn't faze her. Maybe she was out of her mind, but a dying woman had every right to do and say anything she wanted without fear of judgment. "But now that I did – and believe me, I'd love to know how the hell you came out of me, so to speak – I'm glad you got it all and then some. It hurts, doesn't it? That never-ending burning. The way your bones feel like shattered glass. How every muscle feels as if it's being torn and sewn back, only to be torn again seconds later. Did you get mad and desperate when I stopped taking my meds? Did the pain suddenly seem like it was too much to bear? Are you scared?" She put her good hand to her chest. "I know I'm scared. I hope you choke on that fear."

It swiped a paw at her, knocking her onto her side. Buttons went into a barking frenzy.

Kate saw down the path. Pearls of sunshine sparkled on the swath of lake visible through the trees. Oh, how she'd envisioned herself and Andrew spending hour after hour on that lake. In a just world, they would be there now, enjoying an afternoon swim before lying on their towels at the shore, feeling the sun kiss their dripping bodies and reveling in one another's company.

The world had never been just, and the lake was a constant reminder of the life denied them.

She was so tired.

The sound of Buttons barking began to fade.

Rough hands tugged her off the ground.

The awful smell covered her nose and mouth like a rag of chloroform.

There was the faint impression of movement, but all she could hear was the lunatic thrum of her heart, all rhythm lost.

Take me now. For the love of God, take me now so I can drag this thing with me.

CHAPTER THIRTY-FIVE

Andrew sensed he was getting close. He no longer felt helpless and exhausted and scared.

He only felt rage.

He and Kate had been through too much just to have her snatched away by an impossible monster, left to die far from him in the woods. It wasn't going to happen.

So he ran, each passing second, each burst of fury in his blood strengthening his legs. He ran with his trademark abandon – except this time, he knew he couldn't stop when his body cried uncle.

A lyric from a Rage Against the Machine song from long ago, back before he and Kate had ever met, repeated over and over in his head as he ran.

Anger is a gift.

It was one of his all-time favourite lines, fittingly for a man with unsurprising anger issues. Kate hated it, and detested whenever he used it to justify things done by others in anger's name.

"You don't understand," he'd tell her. "When someone is truly angry, when all they see and smell and feel is uncontrollable rage, anything is possible. There are no limitations. That voice in the back of your head telling you that you can't or shouldn't do something gets burned to a cinder. Nothing can hold you back. Now, you may not always do the right thing, but if you can find a way to channel that power, to use it for something good – Christ, we could all be superheroes."

His theory had gone over like a lead balloon every time.

Right now, he was going to give his theory a field test.

You can't hurt it, he reminded himself as he plodded with feverish urgency. *You just need to take her away from it.*

This time I have the advantage.

I'm not afraid.

He heard Buttons barking in the not-too-far distance.

"Buttons!" he shouted.

Keep on barking, bud! Show me the way.

Andrew hurdled over a branch that had been thrown over the trail. He was once again able to smell the horrid redolence coming off the beast. He was close.

I'm not afraid.

With every step, he repeated the words, his confidence building.

I'm not afraid.

I'm not afraid.

There was a bend in the path. Andrew almost missed it, a pricker bush gouging his legs as he corrected his trajectory.

The barking beagle sounded so close.

"Buttons!"

Leaping over a rotting log, he spotted them.

The creature's back was an open wound.

It held Kate in its arms now, only her head and legs visible.

Buttons was right on its heels. Andrew assumed he was barking to wake Kate up. He couldn't tell if she was alive or dead, if he was on time or too late.

It didn't matter. Even if she had passed, he was not leaving her body to that thing.

Finding a reserve of energy, he ran faster, closing the gap between them. The monster didn't even glance back at him. Maybe the beagle's barking had masked his approach. If Buttons had somehow been smart enough to do such a thing, Andrew was going to make sure he lived the rest of his days like a beagle king.

When he was close enough to almost touch the monstrosity, he left his feet and wrapped his arms around its hips, letting his body morph to dead weight to bring it down.

The beast trudged on for ten feet, twenty feet, not slowing down nor trying to dislodge him. Andrew locked his hands, refusing to let go.

Without considering the horridness of its exposed, bilious flesh, he bit into the top of its buttock, his jaw clenching until his mouth was filled with a vile chunk of severed flesh.

The creature finally stopped, howling in agony.

Kate's eyes burst open. She let out a sharp cry.

Kate's alive! Andrew's heart swelled with hope.

Vile, nightmarish tastes assaulted his tongue. Andrew gagged when the infected blood hit the back of his throat. He spit it out, and the gelatinous effluvium quivered atop the fallen leaves.

Still, he refused to let go.

When the creature tried to resume its escape, Andrew thrust his legs between its own, like tossing a stick into the spokes of a bicycle's wheel.

This time, it went down, pitching Kate forward. She tumbled into the brush.

Buttons ran to her.

So did Andrew.

He nimbly avoided the creature's hand when it tried to grab him by the ankle. Sidestepping the fallen demon, he dropped beside Kate. Her eyes were closed but he could see them moving rapidly back and forth beneath her fragile lids. Blood blossomed on the seat of her pants. There was no time to regret what he'd done. Getting her in a fireman's hold, he turned and headed back toward the cottage. Again, the creature tried to stop him, but it was weak, worn down, and cupping the wound on its buttock. Its face was a patchwork of putrescence. Green pus leaked from a gash in its forehead that opened on its own, as if an invisible scalpel had parted its flesh. Its lips curled back in a sneer, a brown tooth spiraling from its exposed, gangrenous gums.

It's literally falling apart at the seams.

He wanted to stay and watch it die a slow, agonizing death.

Then a cold realization put him in motion.

That means Kate is as well. Please, Kate, don't leave me. Not yet. Not here.

The dying monster uttered a dull, low growl that sounded more pathetic than terrifying.

Buttons snapped at it, but not close enough to bite it. He ran ahead of them, leading the way.

Andrew ran, his own heart feeling as if it was going to burst.

Shut the fuck up, he said to his heart and any other part of his body that even thought of protesting or giving up. He had Kate back, and he was taking her home.

*　　*　　*

For a while, he could actually feel the tremendous footfalls of the beast as it followed him. Andrew plowed on, determined to outrun it.

He couldn't believe it had been able to get on its feet, much less chase him.

No matter. It couldn't match his speed. Sooner rather than later, it would fall. If there was any shred of luck left in this world for them, it would collapse and melt into the earth, food for the insects and critters.

Did that also mean that Kate would die as well?

Not if he could help it.

There was a canoe tied to a dock on the next parcel of land over. He'd seen it during his trips around the lake. It wouldn't take him very long to kayak there and bring it back. He'd get Kate and Buttons in the canoe and paddle to the end of the lake. It would be close to a three-mile trip. Round Lake might as well have been called Long Lake from the sheer size of it. No matter, he'd make it. At the mouth of the lake was the Bridge Mills Park and boat slip. There would be people there. People who could get them to a hospital, fast.

The key to Kate's survival, he had convinced himself, was distance. The farther he got her away from that thing, the more tenuous the connection between them. Distance would snap their tether, leaving the creature to die in the woods while he got Kate the medical attention she desperately needed.

"Just hold on for me, honey," he said between ragged breaths. It was so hard to talk, but he needed her to know he wasn't ready to let her go. "Remember that time the doctor told us you had a week to live? That the infection wasn't responding to the medication and they were out of options?" Buttons was moving faster than he'd seen the old dog run in years. Even he could sense they were close to emerging from this nightmare. "The doctor, I can't remember his name, he asked if you wanted to speak to a priest. And you, you were so out of it, but when you heard him, you said, 'I've already tried last rites. It didn't work. Tell him to find someone who's really sick instead.' I knew at that moment you were going to beat it, Kate. I need you to hear me now. I'm not calling any priests. You hear me? If I so much as see one, I'll tell him to hit the road."

He hadn't realised he was crying until he blinked and everything got gauzy.

A life with Kate was a life in which the darkest dreads were always lurking, waiting for their moment to steal their dreams, their future.

It was also a life of unbridled love and surprising strength, of second, third, even tenth chances, of an exploration of the limits of human endurance and the will of one's spirit.

Kate and Andrew knew what they had had survived made them different from most people. Sometimes, those differences made them feel like aliens on a strange planet, outsiders, the kids who were punished during the block party, forced to hear all of the fun happening outside their window but never allowed to join in it.

No matter what they missed out on, they had each other. Learning to live in the small moments, to lean into the good and the bad, to appreciate the simple joy of sitting next to one another, watching an old movie – that's what made life special. That they had found one another and shared those moments was miracle enough.

It's time for another miracle, Andrew thought when he saw the cottage.

The gaping hole in the front of the house called to him. Even though there was no actual safety in going inside, it was an escape from the wild, the domain of the creature.

If he could find a place to hide Kate just for the time it would take him to get the canoe and come back, that would be the sign that things were turning in their favour.

Can you hide her from it? Won't it know exactly where she is? Can it see what she sees?

There was no time for questions or contemplation. He had to keep pushing.

Focus on Kate.

For the first time, he saw Nikki's body. Her crushed head was mercifully hidden under her folded body. The impact must have snapped her spine in half. Settling dust had coated the pool of blood around her.

"Where should I put her?" he said to the dog. Buttons wagged his tail, panting like mad. The poor guy's legs trembled. "Better yet, where should I put the both of you?"

He looked outside. There was no sign of the creature.

Unfortunately, the cottage had neither a basement nor an attic. The only other rooms were the bedroom and bathroom.

The closet.

He'd settle her in the bedroom closet with Buttons. It wouldn't stop the creature from taking her again, but it might buy Andrew time to get the canoe. He'd lock the bedroom door and pile some junk against it, just to make it even more difficult to get to her.

With no time to waste, he carried her to the bedroom, yanking the clothes from the hangers to make a comfortable place to lay her down.

He smoothed her hair back. Her skin was cold, alarmingly so.

But she was breathing. Andrew covered her with the ugly sweater his mother had bought her for Christmas last year. It had the silhouette of a reindeer on it. She'd packed it because she said it kind of looked like a moose. What better place to wear a moose sweater than Maine?

"I love you, Kate. I'm going to be right back. I'm getting us a canoe, not a priest. You hear me? You just sit tight. Buttons will be right here with you, won't you, buddy?" The dog's heavy panting filled the small closet. "You're going to be okay, honey. I promise."

He kissed her cheeks, and then her cool, dry lips.

"Don't you dare leave me, Kate. There's a Jeff Chandler movie marathon on next weekend. I know you don't want to miss that."

It broke his heart to leave her. She looked worse than he'd ever seen her.

Should I just stay here with her and hold her hand until...until...

No. She never gave up. And neither will I.

He patted Buttons. "You watch her. If that thing comes back, it's not her. Don't let it take her."

The dog whined and lay next to Kate.

Andrew closed the door, doubting himself with each step.

The door to the bedroom had a push-button lock on the inside. He closed it, knowing he'd have to kick it in when he got back, which wouldn't be a problem. He gathered armfuls of wood and lathing, tossing them against the door to create an extra barrier. It wasn't much, but it was all he could do at the moment.

Taking one last glance out the front – the creature was still nowhere to be seen – he headed out the back, running to the dock, his gait markedly slower than before. The rifle was right where he'd left it. There was no sense picking it up, knowing he could never fire it. He willed himself not to look at Ryker's body nor give a cursory search for his head. If Ryker were alive, he'd want Andrew to do everything in his power to save his sister.

He wasn't going to let him down.

He untied the kayak, grabbed the paddle, and hopped inside.

The sun had softened with the dying of the day. A cool breeze whispered along the preternaturally still lake.

He thought of Kate lying in the closet, looking so close to death.

The canoe.

Concentrate on the canoe.

He paddled, his muscles' protests falling on deaf ears.

CHAPTER THIRTY-SIX

The sound of a room being torn asunder propelled Kate from the darkness.

She couldn't see a thing, but she felt something moving against her.

Then Buttons started barking.

Where the hell was she?

Great crashes and floor-rattling thumps quickened her heartbeat.

She managed to sit up, reaching out to feel her way around her black tomb. Her hand found a doorknob. She gave it a sharp turn, the meagre light in the next room enough to temporarily blind her.

Once her eyes adjusted, she realised she was back in the cottage, in the bedroom. Kate crawled out of the closet, fearing she hadn't the strength to stand.

"Andrew?" she whispered.

Buttons cowered beside her.

A stabbing pain in her chest made her go rigid as a steel girder.

There followed a mad howling, and something crashed against the wall, knocking the painting of two men out for a day of fishing onto the floor.

That wasn't Andrew.

Kate put her arm around Buttons' pliant neck. "It's okay, But-But. It's okay. Mommy's here."

That seemed to calm him down.

The noise in the next room also ceased.

Where was Andrew? Surely the beast hadn't brought her back here and tucked her in a closet.

Oh God, did it follow us here and kill him?

The sudden blast of guilt made her swoon.

"No. Please, not Andrew."

She wept, her body almost too broken, too dehydrated for tears.

What leaked from her eyes burned like acid.

Her legs trembling, she tried to open the bedroom door. When it didn't budge, she looked down and saw it had been locked. She pushed the button, but the door still wouldn't open. The noise of her trying to get out had caught the creature's attention. She heard it move around the living room and the sick, wet sucking of its lungs.

She realised that even if it hadn't already killed Andrew, it eventually would.

Andrew, if he was alive, was going to do everything he could to get her out of here and find a hospital.

The thing in the next room had been born not just from her anger and frustration, but also her desire to stay here forever. Anyone who wanted to remove her was bad and needed to be eliminated.

She closed her eyes, trying to delve once again into its mind. The unyielding pain wouldn't let her do it.

No matter. She couldn't let it live on.

Maybe it was a good thing it had found her.

She wanted it close so she could see.

With Buttons brushing against her leg, she struggled to open the dresser drawer with one hand. After some jiggling, it finally gave way.

Pushing aside her socks, she found what she needed.

Her box of fentanyl patches.

Her prescription called for the highest dose they had. She'd hoped to one day step down to a lower dosage and move to a newer, safer medication. The patches had always scared the hell out of her.

She pounded on the wall.

"I'm in here! I'm in..."

Her chest felt as if it had been kicked by a mule. But still her heart marched on.

It won't take much to stop it, she thought. *Not much at all.*

There was more crashing just outside the door.

Kate opened a patch.

The door shook on its hinges as the beast bashed it with its fist.

She found a pen on the dresser.

Whump!

Another blow to the door.

Kate jabbed the pen into the centre of the jelly-filled patch.

She slapped it on her arm.

Wham!

A giant crack zigzagged on the door.

She opened another patch, poked a hole, and stuck it on her chest.

A hand shot through the door, pulling the wood apart. She saw its yellow eyes first, run riot with bursting red veins.

The rush of fentanyl set her on her ass.

Her pain, her ever-present pain, began to ebb.

The creature yanked the door off, but was too weak to step into the room. It collapsed on the threshold, staring at her with bewilderment.

"I'm so sorry," she said, not to the beast, but to the spirits of the people she loved most.

She hoped they could hear her as she closed her eyes.

*   *   *

Andrew couldn't believe how much he hurt.

He'd found the canoe on the shore of the house hidden in the trees.

He'd also found the bodies of an older woman and a small child, both ripped in half and left to rot on the dock.

He'd had to step over the girl to get to the canoe. Her glazed eyes had looked up at him. If the bottom half of her body hadn't been several feet away, he would almost have thought she was gazing at the clouds.

Unable to find the canoe paddle, he'd used the kayak paddle to get back to the cottage.

It was difficult, but he laboured on.

After leaping out of the canoe the instant it touched the shore, he sprinted up to the house.

His heart nearly stopped when he saw the additional carnage.

He was too late.

"Kate!"

Buttons barked in the next room.

He saw the creature lying on its stomach, blocking the doorway to the bedroom. Andrew jumped over it.

Kate was on her side, several feet away from its outstretched hand.

Buttons ran in circles, yipping excitedly, almost mournfully.

"Kate."

He dropped beside her, lifting her onto his lap.

She was so, so cold. Her lips had turned a light shade of blue.

He was terrified to check for a pulse.

Fingers fluttering, he pushed them against her neck. He couldn't feel anything. He was also numb with shock and exhaustion and refused to trust his senses.

"Kate, can you hear me? Kate?"

He kissed her blue lips, crushing her against his chest.

"An...drew?"

Her eyes slowly opened. They were starting to grey, but he saw recognition in them.

"Yes, I'm here, baby," he said.

She reached up and touched his face.

"Priest...or canoe?"

Despite the sorrow threatening to swallow him whole, Andrew smiled.

"Just like I promised. Canoe. Good to know you were listening."

"Your voice...always breaks through. Always."

He finally saw the patches and knew what she had done.

"Why?" he said, touching the patch on her chest.

Her smile shattered him into a million pieces.

"To protect you. To...avenge you. I wasn't sure. I couldn't... couldn't lose either way. You want to hear the good...the good news?"

"Yes, honey. I could use some good news about now."

"I don't feel any pain. I actually feel...good."

His tears splashed against her face.

"That's good, honey. I'm so happy for you."

"I love you. Will you always remember that?"

"Always."

"Good. I promise I will...too."

Kate's mouth went slack. A long, thready sigh hissed from her parted lips, and she left Andrew, unafraid, free from pain, and filled with love.

*   *   *

Andrew cried for hours, refusing to put Kate down. Buttons cried in his own way as well, eventually resting his snout on her stomach. The three of them sat on the floor until dusk began to settle.

The monster beside them was forgotten.

It, too, had taken its last breath.

When Andrew felt sure he could walk without falling down, he lifted himself with Kate in his arms and walked atop the dead creature. Glass and detritus crunched under his feet as he stumbled to the living room.

The last thing he saw before he left the cottage forever was the upturned bag of his remaining used paperbacks that had scattered all over the floor, most of their pages stained with blood and dust.

Buttons followed him to the canoe.

He had to stop after settling Kate onto the floor of the boat, his body racked with painful sobs. It was full dark by the time he eased the canoe into the water.

There was no need to push himself. He could take his time. The town would be there, waiting for him.

He no longer needed to focus on Kate.

What the hell was he supposed to do with the rest of his life?

At the moment, he didn't know or care.

He stopped at the dock where he'd gotten the canoe. Buttons came with him as he made his way to the house. The back door had been demolished. Inside he found a man on the floor of the kitchen, his bowels ripped free and ripe with flies. There were also twin boys who could have been no older than twelve, stacked in a corner, their necks broken so their heads hung at nauseating angles.

He returned to the canoe, kissed Kate once again, and paddled on.

All through the night, he stopped at dock after dock, wandering to the pretty houses. What he found was just what Henry and Ida had told him – mostly old people, but all of them dead, their bodies savaged.

It was why no one had come to their aid, responding to their cries, the gunshots, or the roaring howls from the beast.

The creature had done everything in its power to keep them for itself.

The sun had just started to come up, bathing Kate's face in a soft, orange glow, when he made it to the Bridge Mills Park.

Beyond exhausted, he gently removed her from the canoe, laying her on the sandy beach.

He collapsed next to her, Buttons settling on her other side.

They finally had their moment to watch the sunrise on the beach.

AFTERWORD

After writing about ghosts and monsters, killers and demons for the past decade, this one proved a challenge I wasn't sure I could handle. The whole thing hit a little close to home. You see, my wife has a host of autoimmune diseases, just like Kate, and what we've gone through is the very definition of horror. You name it, we've faced it – surgeries, life support, radiation, doctor and prescription merry-go-rounds, last rites, second chances, experimental treatments, third, fourth, and fifth chances, and on and on. The creature lives in her cells, has slipped into my skin and devoured my soul at times, has loomed over us at our darkest moments and continues to lie in wait as we take life one moment at a time.

Never one to shy from a challenge, I explained my idea for the story to my editor and friend, Don D'Auria, over cocktails one night in a dark bar. He asked me several times if I really wanted to put myself through this. I never hesitated. I'd already lived it. Writing it within the confines of a fictional horror tale would be a snap.

Well, as my wife will be quick to tell you, I've been wrong before. *Creature* was a labour of love and hate, of bad memories and worst fears. I wrote it while my wife was bedridden with a bout of pneumonia that defied everything the docs had thrown at it. She started an experimental treatment just as I was editing *Creature*. Talk about art imitating life and vice versa. Sometimes I get confused between what is real and what fresh hell has sprung from the black pit of my mind.

Anyone faced with a physical trial will tell you it only makes you stronger. Yes and no. It hardens your will. But it can weaken your body. Sometimes it can break your spirit, and once that happens, the rest can come down like a house of cards. We've learned that, above all, you need to be stubborn. Defy everything life can throw at you. Tell whatever horror that may befall you to kiss your ass. Keep on trucking, just to show it and everyone around you that you're too damn stubborn to fall. Be *Cool Hand Luke*. Eat fifty eggs, dig that hole, fill it up, and dig it again. Smile when everyone else is crying. Spit in the eye of fate. Live an unconventional life and leave this world with plenty of scars.

Thank you, Don D'Auria, for letting me tell this story, and most of all, for bringing me aboard the Flame Tree Press express. There's no one on earth I'd rather work with than Don. Butch and Sundance ride again!

And to my wife, Amy, you have my eternal love and gratitude for all of the experiences we've shared, no matter how terrifying. We've never given up, and we never will. Bring it on.

A huge thank-you to you, the reader, for coming along on this journey. Take my hand and let's explore the darkness together. Follow my travails, get the latest horror news, reviews, and more, and even sign up for my Dark Hunter Newsletter to get free books and stories at www.huntershea.com

HUNTER SHEA

CREATURE

This is a **FLAME TREE PRESS** book

Text copyright © 2018 Hunter Shea

FLAME TREE PRESS
6 Melbray Mews, London, SW6 3NS, UK
flametreepress.com

Distribution and warehouse:
Marston Book Services Ltd
160 Eastern Avenue, Milton Park, Abingdon, Oxon, OX14 4SB
www.marston.co.uk

Thanks to the Flame Tree Press team, including:
Taylor Bentley, Frances Bodiam, Federica Ciaravella, Don D'Auria,
Chris Herbert, Matteo Middlemiss, Josie Mitchell, Mike Spender,
Cat Taylor, Maria Tissot, Nick Wells, Gillian Whitaker.

The cover is created by Flame Tree Studio with
thanks to Nik Keevil and Shutterstock.com.
The font families in this book are Avenir and Bembo.

Flame Tree Press is an imprint of Flame Tree Publishing Ltd
flametreepublishing.com

A copy of the CIP data for this book is available from the British Library.

HB ISBN: 978-1-78758-023-7
PB ISBN: 978-1-78758-022-0
ebook ISBN: 978-1-78758-025-1
Also available in FLAME TREE AUDIO

Printed in the UK at Clays, Suffolk

HUNTER SHEA

CREATURE

FLAME TREE PRESS
London & New York

For Tim Stanton.
I wish to hell you were here to read this.
The Dude does not abide.

'Normality is a paved road. It's comfortable to walk,
but no flowers grow on it.'
Vincent van Gogh

'How can I be substantial if I do not cast a shadow?
I must have a dark side also if I am to be whole.'
C.G. Jung

CHAPTER ONE

Kate Woodson was dying, and her executioner was her own body.

Her doctors hadn't said as much the past few visits, but even she knew there was a limit to what a body could take. She had been in worse shape before. Much worse. Last rites and funeral arrangements kind of shape. Kate had come out of it like a modern-day Lazarus.

But she was tired. And hurting. And sick. Always so, so sick. She'd forgotten what it was like to wake up and not be in agony, muscles weak as a newborn's. She couldn't even remember the last time she'd just gone out of the house to go to a store or a movie with Andrew.

Though she wasn't dying today (*fat chance, Grim Reaper!*), Kate was still wallowing in the deep end of the misery pool. What made it worse was the shadow watching her from the kitchen. It moved out of sight every time she turned her head.

"I see you," she said from the daybed in the living room, her voice deep and scratchy.

She chuckled at the thought that the shadow was scared of her. Then she shivered with the realization that she was scared shitless of *it*.

"Call the cable stations that do all the ghost shows. We have a haunting in Sayreville, New Jersey." Andrew wasn't home to ask her what she was talking about. He was at work, in a job he hated, because of her. That job came with great benefits. Benefits they couldn't afford to lose.

Not that Kate would have told him about the shadow. He was already worried enough about her. She didn't need him thinking she was losing it mentally as well. Or worse yet, he'd blame it on the meds, making her feel like some kind of delusional addict. The few times he'd ascribed her behaviour or thoughts to the pills had angered her so much, she'd worried she'd give herself a stroke over it. It was an extreme reaction, for sure. Kate was never one to hold things in.

Though she did hold back the fear that he might be right.

Besides, wasn't it better that the shadow was a hallucination, a construct of her *bad feels*, rather than an actual, lurking apparition?

She scratched the back of her shoulder, her wrist popping out just enough to make her see stars for a moment.

Yep, better it was a figment of her imagination, a bit of spoiled gruel.

If the shadow wanted to stay in the kitchen, let it. She had other things to worry about. Like getting her wrist back in place. She grabbed it with her good hand and gave a slight twist. There came a tiny, muted *crack*, and all the bones were back where they belonged.

"That's better," she said to Buttons, her old rescue dog and constant companion. He lay beside the daybed, wheezing doggie snores. She let her hand slip over the daybed, fingertips grazing his head. At least with Buttons, she was never alone. A weak smile curled Kate's lips. She stared at the ceiling, consciously avoiding the kitchen.

She'd never even known what an autoimmune disease was until she was told she had one. Thinking she'd passed the ability to be shocked, she was both flabbergasted and devastated when she was diagnosed several years later with a second, more damaging disease. The rare Ehlers-Danlos syndrome and more common but terrifying lupus were a hell of a one-two punch. The old Kate who didn't suffer from unbearable fatigue, swelling, degenerating eyesight, digestive system breakdowns, heart problems, and a host of other horridness was a distant and ever-fading memory. Most days, it felt like she'd always been this way — broken, hurting, and scared.

Nothing in the vast array of pills on Kate's nightstand would make it all go away. With Ehlers and lupus, there were no cures. At best, the pills dulled the pain, controlled flare-ups, and in some cases made her feel even worse.

Kate checked the pill schedule she'd created on her tablet. It was time for one of her nerve blockers. There was her whole home pharmacy in all its bullet-pointed glory: fentanyl (an uber dangerous patch that she changed every three days and was killing people with alarming frequency), Neurontin, gabapentin, Percocet, Ultram, prednisone, and Tagamet for her stomach, which had been utterly demolished by the pills themselves. Monthly checkups were required to measure the damage the pills were doing to her liver and kidneys, heart and pancreas.

One pill over the line…

Andrew kept trying to get her to migrate her pills into one of those big plastic holders, the ones with a day of the week printed on each slot. But the only one that would be large enough to support her cache of pharmaceuticals could double as an end table if you attached some legs to it. The sheer size of it depressed the hell out of her. And it made her feel like a feeble, old lady.

Instead, she dumped her assortment of pills in a mason jar. She'd even tied a red-and-white checkered bow around the rim to make it pretty. Martha Stewart would have approved.

She dry-swallowed the yellow pill, screwed the lid back on the jar, and shifted her attention to the television. Turner Classics was having a Joseph Cotten marathon. Kate was partial to Joseph Cotten. She especially loved him in *Portrait of Jennie*. Her mother used to tell her she looked like Jennifer Jones, the mysterious woman who captures struggling artist Cotten's imagination…and heart. What Kate saw in the mirror now was a far cry from Jennifer Jones. Her long, chestnut hair had gotten brittle, her eyes perpetually ringed by dark circles and puffy bags. It was hard to maintain her weight, so her cheeks had sunk, kind of the way she'd wished they would when she was a kid and thought Kate Moss was the most beautiful woman in the world. *I was a stupid kid*, she reminded herself. She'd give anything for some cellulite right about now.

Checking the channel guide, she was disappointed they weren't playing *Portrait of Jennie* today. Oh, but *Niagara* was going to be on after dinner. No one had ever told Kate she looked like Marilyn Monroe. Then again, who did? Maybe that poor girl Anna Nicole Smith, and look what happened to her.

Kate had to pee, but her ankles, knees, and hips felt like they were on fire, the swelling pushing the limits of her reddened skin. She could see the bathroom just down the short hall, but it might as well have been in another state.

"Too bad you're not bigger," she said to the dog. "Like one of those Scottish deerhounds. I could saddle you up and ride you to the potty." Buttons looked up at her with his sad, moist eyes. "But no, I had to fall in love with a beagle."

He licked her hand and snuggled his head back between his paws.

"Can you at least pee for me? You're very good at peeing."

His tail wagged but his eyes remained closed. He was tired and she was disturbing him.

The pill should take effect soon. Once it took the harsh edge off the pain, she could finally sleep. She'd worry about peeing later. The shadow would go right back where it belonged. Into the ether.

If she fell asleep now, she'd only miss *Peking Express*, not one of her favourites. A nice two-hour nap, or what she preferred to call a controlled coma, would have her waking up right around the time Andrew came home. Maybe she could get dinner started before he dropped his keys in the bowl by the door, which meant ordering up some grub on one of the many apps on her phone.

"But-But, you wanna veg out with Mommy?" she said, patting the daybed. Buttons jumped right up, taking his spot between her legs and the back cushion, always careful not to rest his weight on her.

Kate cut her gaze to the window, grateful she'd asked Andrew to keep the blinds shut before he left that morning. The sun was out in force today, or at least that's what the weatherman had said during the morning news. Kate hated sleeping with the sun on her face. It wasn't so much trying to nap under the sharp glare. She never had problems zonking out at the beach.

It was just a reminder of what she was missing.

Kate closed her eyes, visualizing the rebellious microorganisms in her body dying a slow, terrible death. Her brother, the motivational speaker, had told her that if she meditated on attacking the disease, she could cure herself without the need for medicine or surgery. He'd guided her through countless meditations. Yet she was still on a boatload of medications and had had over a dozen surgeries in the past five years. Still, she loved her brother and believed in him, so she kept trying. Maybe someday it would all come together and she'd rise from her sick bed and go skydiving. Or at least out to a nice restaurant with Andrew.

"Thoughts are physical, sis," her brother had said over and over. "If you concentrate on your intentions with a pure heart and clear mind, you can manifest anything."

"If the answer to life's woes is so easy, how come so many people are sick?"

"Who said it was easy? The Buddhists say it can take many, many lifetimes to even come close to mastering this."

"So you're saying I have no chance. I mean, it's not like I have a clear mind," Kate had said.

There was Ryker with his perpetual smile. "Maybe in previous lives, you've been working toward kicking some serious booty in this one. For all you know, this is your final exam."

"I flunked my finals in school."

"That's because you were always goofing around instead of studying."

"Well, I have plenty of time to study now, don't I?"

"That you do."

Part of her felt it was all a load of crap, and perhaps that's why it didn't work as well as it should. She sabotaged herself.

Thoughts destroying diseased cells in your body? Yeah, right. But she had to admit, the meditation part was relaxing. And she wasn't beyond admitting that it might have helped her a few years earlier when she'd gotten that terrible virus that had almost spelled the end for her. When she was at her sickest and barely able to open her eyes, much less talk, Ryker had sat beside her bed, talking her through a visualization of the virus. She'd grown up a huge *Star Wars* fan (yes, she'd had her tomboy phase). Ryker told her to picture the virus as the Empire's TIE fighters. She chased the TIE fighters in her own X-wing fighter, her trusty droid riding behind her, both of them blasting the viral spaceships to smithereens.

She remembered the day Ryker had whispered to her, bringing her back to the big battle, and there were no TIE fighters left to blast. Within hours, she was up and asking for a cheeseburger, which she was promptly told she couldn't have.

Of course, the virus could have just run its course, but Ryker swore that she had defeated it through the power of her thoughts.

I'm thinking of one of those bamboo huts on the water in Bora Bora.

Even if she couldn't make one appear in her living room, it was nice to just visit. She was too tired to be pissed at Ehlers-Danlos and lupus today.

Settling into her pile of pillows, she thought she saw a grey shape flit from right to left out of the corner of her eye. She turned and stared at the spot in the kitchen where she thought it had disappeared.

It's not really there. Stop thinking about it and it'll go away.

Kate pulled the sheet up to her neck, reflexively snuggling closer to Buttons.

She shut her eyes, turning the volume on the television up so she didn't feel so alone. Voices. She needed voices.

"Keep an eye on me, But-But. I'm going under."

Buttons whimpered in his sleep.

★   ★   ★

"Wake up, sleepy peepy."

Kate felt something pressing against her head. She opened one eye, saw Andrew leaning over her, traces of his cologne on his neck.

"What time is it?"

"Almost seven," he said.

She painfully pushed herself up into a sitting position. *Grandmas move quicker and more gracefully than me*, she thought. "What time did you get home?"

He sat on the edge of the daybed. He'd changed out of his suit and into a Notre Dame T-shirt and jeans. Kate rested her hand on his chest, felt his strong, healthy heart pumping away.

"A little after five."

"Why didn't you wake me?"

He smiled. "I tried. You were out cold. I even checked to make sure you were breathing."

It was impossible to count the number of times her husband had had to fearfully hover over her and make sure she was, indeed, still among the living. According to Andrew, she was no Sleeping Beauty. When she slumbered, she either looked like she was in excruciating pain or stone-cold dead. She hadn't believed him until he took pictures and video to show her — mouth hanging open, cheeks hollowed, arm hanging over the side of the bed, her chest taking an interminable amount of time to inhale and exhale.

God, what she put him through.

She truly believed she'd survived everything and he'd never left her side because they were more stubborn than any ten mules combined. When things got bad, they took turns looking at the sky and saying, "Nice try, but it's not gonna work. You can't break me!" They refused to give up or split up. If her illnesses had given them one thing, it was stark awareness of just how tough they were, and how much they loved one another.

"You don't fuck with Jersey," Andrew had said many, many times, always with a wry smile.

She was so glad to wake up to him. Just his presence made the house… lighter.

Rubbing crud from her eyes, she said, "I was going to order Chinese."

"Already taken care of. I got a pie from Milano's. And a salad, if we want to pretend we're eating healthy."

Her mouth instantly watered. After a dozen surgeries on her digestive tract, food was not her friend.

However, a thin-crust pizza from Milano's was something she could handle and a true slice of heaven. She and Andrew joked that she lived on their pizza, but they weren't far off.

Kate kissed him on the lips and quickly turned away, covering her mouth.

"You're the best," she said.

"Anything for my little crip."

People cringed when he called her that, but they could never understand. Everyone walked on eggshells around her. Andrew couldn't afford to do that, so they indulged in their fair share of gallows humour. If you didn't laugh, well, she'd done enough crying to fill a reservoir.

"Is my breath bad?"

He kissed her again. "Yep."

She swatted at the back of his legs when he got up – and missed.

Andrew wasn't wearing socks or shoes. Buttons trailed behind him, sensing food was coming. Andrew flipped the pizza box open.

"You want me to warm you up a slice?"

"I'll take it like that."

"Salad?"

"Sure. But not too much."

"You can have my cucumbers," he said, grabbing the dressing from the refrigerator.

"Don't I always?"

He prepared her dinner on a folding wooden tray and placed it across her lap. Buttons sat looking up at her.

"No people food, buddy," Andrew said. He opened a can of dog food. Buttons didn't budge.

The dog loved Milano's as much as Kate.

Sighing, Andrew plucked a slice from the box. "Buttons. You want some pizza?"

The old dog bounded into the kitchen, nails skittering on the tile. He couldn't pull up fast enough and skidded into a cabinet. Kate nearly choked on her Pepsi.

"We couldn't have had a child that would end up being more like you," Andrew said.

"Lucky for that unborn child."

Not being able to have children had long since ceased being a sore spot for them. They'd gone from disappointment to sadness, grim acceptance to now, where it was just a simple fact of life. No sense bemoaning and gnashing teeth over what could have been. Besides, Kate couldn't imagine what it would be like taking care of a child now when she could barely take care of herself. That would have been just one more very big thing on Andrew's already full plate.

Andrew plopped next to her, holding pizza and a beer. He hit the Mute button on the TV remote. There was a commercial for a Jean Arthur retrospective.

Kate wanted to wolf down the slice, but forced herself to nibble. Her internal mechanisms did not take kindly to massive food intake.

"How was work?" she asked.

He popped open the beer. Foam ran down the sides of the can onto his lap. He just shook his head, sucking up as much as he could.

"I came, I saw, I left," he said. "It was a meeting kind of day, which means I got nothing done."

"Can't you just tell them you have real work to do and blow off those meetings?"

"I'm not sure if you're aware of this, honey, but in corporate America, accomplishing nothing due to a solid slate of meetings is classified as a job well done."

She snatched a stray cucumber from his salad and popped it in her mouth. "I'd go crazy in a place like that. There's no way I'd be able to keep my mouth shut."

"Which is why Fate glimpsed your future and said, 'Hmm, I better give this chick something that'll keep her from ever trying to work with people. I know, I'll strike her down with anything I can scrounge up that's incurable, therefore maintaining the careful balance between progress and stagnancy we've worked so hard to imbue in this thing we call business.'"

Kate chuckled. "Then I thank Fate for saving us both," she said.

When Andrew shifted to put his beer on the coffee table, she winced.

"What hurts most?" he asked.

He'd long ago learned never to simply ask what hurt. Everything hurt, all the time. It was easier to explain which body part had taken the spotlight for the moment.

"My knees are killing me."

He pulled the blanket away to inspect the swollen melons she called *knees*. "I can get some frozen peas."

"After dinner. Maybe. What's it going to do other than make me cold?"

He gingerly touched her knees. "Believe it or not, it will help with the swelling."

"So I can forget all these doctors and meds and cover myself with frozen peas?"

"Absolutely! Well, we don't want to put all our eggs in the pea basket. We should mix it up with some frozen broccoli, corn, and carrots. Maybe even a bag of Tater Tots."

"What about ice cream?"

"Too messy. Besides, Buttons will devour it before it's had a chance to do its thing."

She looked over at Buttons, pizza sauce stains on his muzzle. "He does love ice cream."

"And like any child, he hates his veggies. So how about I go to ShopRite, raid the frozen food aisle, and we can flush these meds? It'll save us a lot of dough. And we can eat the treatment. Two birds with one stone."

Kate took a bite of her cold pizza.

"Can we reinvest that dough into pizza dough at Milano's?" she asked.

He raised an eyebrow. "Absolutely. You and Buttons will reek of cheese and pepperoni."

"I'd love that."

"You would."

She nearly dropped her pizza when a sharp pain blossomed in the centre of her chest. She hissed, eyes slamming shut. The pain passed quickly.

"You okay?"

All traces of humour blanched from Andrew's face.

She nodded, taking a moment to catch her breath. Because her lupus had gone undetected for so long, it'd had plenty of time to do a number on her heart. Nothing save a heart transplant would erase the years of damage, and no one would put a healthy heart in someone in her condition.

"You know, if you wanted me to shut up, you could have just told me to zip it," Andrew said, rubbing her back. She didn't even notice that he'd taken her plate from her hands and moved the tray onto the table.

When she felt like she could breathe again, she said. "Yeah, like you ever stop talking."

"I never talk during movies."

"And I appreciate that. Now, can I have my pizza back?"

"You sure it's passed?"

Keeping one hand on her chest, she nodded. "I'm sure."

But she wasn't sure at all. She could only be hopeful.

*   *   *

After dinner, they sat and watched a couple of sitcom reruns until she fell asleep. Sometime around midnight, Andrew roused her and slowly walked her into bed. He had no sooner tucked her in, given her her medicine, and gotten a cold bottle of water from the fridge than he was asleep, sawing logs.

She used to envy his ability to shut down like a robot who'd had its power pack removed, like the one in the old *Lost in Space* TV show. And unlike her, he slept like a beatific child, curled in a semifoetal position, hands tucked under his head and just the trace of a smile on his lips.

Sure, she could nod off at the drop of a hat, but her sleep was a combination of narcotics and her immune system wearing her down to a nub, even if she'd done nothing more than sit up during the day.

And of course, now that he was asleep, she was wide awake.

Worse, it was one of those nights when death seemed so close, she was afraid to close her eyes. A big part of her knew it was irrational, but she was still tethered to those times in the past when the possibility of never waking up again was a reality. Experience had taught her that no matter what she did, she couldn't shake the feeling. All she could do was stay awake and ride it out until exhaustion finally pulled her under.

It was a bona fide bad feels night. Sitting up in the bed, she peered into the corners of the room, expecting to spot her shadowy voyeur.

Kate's hands twisted the covers.

Something huffed in the dark.

Buttons lay by her feet, unmoving.

She quickly fumbled for the remote, turned on the TV and found a channel that played shows from the seventies. Light. She needed light in the room, even if it was flickering images of *Mannix*.

Kate reached across the sheets and laid her hand on Andrew's back, feeling the gentle rhythm of his slumber. She'd scared herself and wanted him to be awake with her, assuring her that there was no shadow in the room, no wraith waiting for her to let her guard down.

Let him sleep, she thought. *Put your big-girl panties on and deal with it. You're freaking yourself out like a big dummy.*

Mannix gave way to *Hawaii Five-O*, then *Hazel* and *The Flying Nun*. She was bored and bleary-eyed, but the bad feels wouldn't leave her.

Sleep didn't reclaim her until dawn. By the time she awoke, Andrew was long gone.

CHAPTER TWO

Buttons stood with his front paws on the front of the washing machine, sniffing at the detergent. Kate closed the lid and leaned against it, petting the dog. She'd opened the blinds today, low grey clouds promising rain in the early afternoon. A mail truck ambled down the empty street. There weren't many stay-at-home moms or retirees in their neighbourhood. By nine a.m. on weekdays, Kate pretty much had the entire street to herself.

Which was no comfort.

Kate's tablet chirped. It was time to change her pain patch.

"Come on, But-But."

She had a cane and a walker, but by and large, she refused to use them. She knew it was foolish and just this side of stupid, especially since no one would see her shuffling around, but it was important she prove to herself she could still walk on her own, no matter how much it hurt and how often she teetered or fell.

Sooner or later, the day would come when it was no longer an option. Then, she'd grin and bear it. But until that day…

The fentanyl box was on the table beside the daybed. She pulled the old patch off her arm and folded it over and over like origami, the remaining glue holding the tiny parcel together. She'd wait to throw it in the garbage with the remains of the wet dog food that Buttons didn't finish. The abuse of fentanyl had hit epidemic proportions. Addicts went through garbage cans looking for used patches, sucking out whatever foul-tasting drug remained.

Kate didn't want to be responsible for someone overdosing. So she mixed her used patches with the worst trash she could muster and hoped that kept any garbage picking junkies out. The dosage she received was the highest one could get. After three days, it might be time for her to slap on a new patch because the efficacy had worn out, but that didn't mean there wasn't still too much for some desperate addict to handle.

Normally, Andrew was there when she changed her patch, watching over her to make sure there were no problems and she wasn't about to accidentally overdose. But the pain was really bad and she couldn't wait until he got home.

Buttons watched the entire process, barking once after she'd adhered the new patch to her upper arm.

"I'm glad you approve."

She shuffled back to the kitchen, picked up his dog dish, and stuck the old patch in the middle of the ground meat in jellied gravy. She tipped the remains into the garbage under the sink and took a few moments to collect herself.

The washer timer said the load she'd put in would be done in twenty minutes. She'd keep herself busy until then so she was awake to throw the clothes in the dryer. With any luck, she'd even get them out and folded before Andrew came home.

Buttons scratched at the back door, whimpering.

"Of course you wait until I get all the way to this side of the house to want to go out."

Her hip popped but mercifully didn't dislocate, and Buttons ambled out the open door. Hip dislocations were a bitch. They hurt like red, white, and blue blazes and were not easy to pop back in. Sometimes she needed Andrew to pull on her leg, the dull, wet *thup* it made assuring her it was back where it was supposed to be.

Rubbing at her hip, she watched Buttons sniff around the forsythia until he found his favourite spot back by what she and Andrew called their penis tree. It looked like a ten-foot green dildo, helped along by Andrew's careful trimming to keep it a conversation piece.

By the time Buttons slipped back inside, her phone had started ringing. She looked at the display before answering.

"Hey, Mom," she said, settling onto the daybed and flipping through channels with the sound down low. There went Jerry Springer giving his final thought, another judge show awarding a guy who looked like a gangbanger five hundred dollars for his damaged piano, commercials for credit unions and ambulance-chasing lawyers, a gaggle of yentas carping about some celebrity she didn't recognise, and a slew of Spanish telenovelas starring busty women in low-cut dresses and guys with bristly mustaches.

It was no wonder she stuck to classic movies.

"Did your brother call you?"

Kate massaged her temples.

"No, but neither have you for three weeks."

If her mother wasn't going to play nice, she wasn't either. The woman lived ten miles away and only came to see Kate once every six months or so, keeping her well out of the running for mother of the year.

"Well, he said he was going to."

"I haven't heard from Ryker since he and Nikki went to Aruba. But hey, thanks for asking how I am."

There was a long pause.

Finally, her mother said, "They've been back since Sunday, you know."

"Good for them."

"Aren't you curious as to why he wants to speak with you?"

Kate balled her fist. Buttons, sensing her aggravation, jumped up and put his head on her lap. "I didn't even know he wanted to call me until ten seconds ago. And it's not that crazy, considering Ryker and I actually talk all the time. You know, just like regular families."

"Okay, I was just checking."

"That's it? The last time we spoke, I had pneumonia. Don't you even want to know how that's going?" Kate felt her blood pressure rise. She'd grown up with a mother who doted on her brother to the exclusion of everything and everyone else, including her father, who had puttered around the house like a forgotten visitor. Ryker was going to be the big, shining star in the family, his light so bright, dear old mom was blind to the rest of the world.

And Ryker had become just that, his success casting Kate into an ever-widening shadow, at least as far as her myopic mother was concerned. Kate used to tell herself that her mother just couldn't handle what her daughter was going through, so it was easier to bury her head in the sand. Mom avoided her like a plague blanket. But the truth was, it had always been like this. Hope for a change in their relationship was a waste of time and energy, neither of which she had in great supply.

"I assumed you'd be fine by now," her mother said, an edge to her voice.

"I was in the hospital for five days because my lungs filled with fluid."

"But you're not there now."

Kate pulled the phone away from her ear and gave a silent scream. She took a deep breath. "My doctor says the pneumonia set my timetable back to the fall to get my hip replacements. The don't want me anywhere near anesthesia until my lungs have repaired themselves."

"I don't understand why he says you need new hips. You can walk."

That got Kate's blood boiling. "Sure, I walk like a cripple who gets lapped by geriatrics. I kinda would like to be a little more stable."

Her mother sighed into the phone. "Why risk it with surgery? It's not like you go out all that often."

That was the breaking point. Instead of yelling, Kate said, "Just be thankful all this crap skipped you and went into me, Mom. Not everyone gets to live their lives with blinders on."

Silence.

It was her mother's ultimate defence. When met with resistance, it was better to just sit there, mute as a fish.

"Thanks for calling. I'll be sure to alert the news when Ryker gets in touch with me."

"There's no reason to take that tone, Kate."

"I'm sure you think that."

"Don't get all huffy with me. It's not like you call me, either."

Grinding her molars, Kate replied, "I was so sick, I could barely breathe, much less talk. And you knew that because Andrew called and left a message, which you never returned."

And here came the silence again.

"Look, Mom, I gotta get my clothes out of the washer."

"Oh good, you're feeling up to doing the laundry. See, I knew you were fine."

Kate disconnected the call before she could say something she would regret…or relish. Throwing the phone at a pillow, she struggled to get up, Buttons now at her heels. It was one thing to be chronically ill. It was another not to have the caring, sympathy, and attention of your own mother. She didn't wish it on her worst enemy.

Something crashed in the kitchen. Kate's heart fluttered, and she got dizzy and thumped back onto the daybed. Buttons barked at the kitchen, his tail tucked between his legs.

Reaching down to stroke his back, she said, "We are a pair of scaredy-cats. Take it easy, But-But, and let's see what fell."

Together they crept toward the kitchen. The blue vase she kept on the shelf above the counter was in pieces. It had come with the get-well flowers Andrew had given her during her recent hospital stint.

"Must have put it too close to the edge, you big goof," she said to the beagle, who had calmed down. "See what Grandma does? Just the sound of her voice makes bad things happen."

The last thing she wanted to do was sweep up glass, but she couldn't leave it for Andrew. Plus, she didn't want Buttons stepping on it. After shooing him back to the living room, she got out the broom and dustpan. The washer dinged just as she was emptying the pan into the garbage pail.

Her shoulders and wrists were aching something fierce by the time she collapsed onto the daybed, just in time for an Audrey Hepburn movie. She tried meditating, and when that didn't work, it was time to take a pill anyway. That did the trick.

*　　*　　*

Andrew looked at his schedule for the next week, checking it against the two doctors appointments Kate had. The pain management office understood that people had to maintain jobs to pay the bills, so they offered late appointments on Thursdays. He could get Kate there easily after work. The cardiologist on Tuesday morning would be an issue.

His boss had told him time and again that he could work from home any time, knowing what he and Kate were going through. But on his last review, he'd gotten dinged for team engagement, which was a veiled way of saying he hadn't been around the team enough. The fact that he got more done from home and never lost touch with the team – thanks to their video presence system – was beside the point.

"You coming out for drinks tonight?" James asked, his head popping over Andrew's cubicle wall.

"What's it for this time?" Andrew closed his planner.

"Brandi landed that whale account late yesterday. She said she's buying, and who am I to turn down free drinks?"

James tapped his fingers on the cubicle's edge. The man was a ball of nervous energy.

"I'd love to but I have to head home," Andrew said.

"Come on. You missed out on Drew's going-away shindig and Cara's promotion. And word on the street is you're not going to the team-building weekend next month."

Pushing away from his desk, the chair rolling into the file cabinet, Andrew said, "I can't do three days away from home, Jim. You know that."

Not to mention he had no desire to go rock climbing while listening to some career coach spout inspirational quotes all along the way. What moron decided this was a thing?

"Yeah, yeah, but what about tonight? We'll only be at Johnny's East Side for a couple of hours."

"Look, have a drink for me. I'll go to the next one."

"I'm gonna hold you to that," James said, giving him the gunfighter salute with his long index fingers. James headed for the bathroom, or the back parking lot to smoke. Probably both.

Andrew really could go for a drink.

Maybe the ding about being with the team was because he missed stuff like this – fun stuff, but important in any sales organisation. Well, if they were going to take money out of his pocket because he couldn't get hammered every week, sometimes twice, so be it. Yes, he missed out on a lot of good times and team bonding, but he had responsibilities. If they didn't want to cut him some slack, that was their problem. Life goes on, or so the Beatles told him.

"Ob-la-di, ob-la-da," he muttered.

There was a big conference call in fifteen minutes. After that was a Skype meeting with their team in Portland. Then he had yet another group meeting about the new database the developers were creating for the sales team. Those meetings went on for hours and he barely knew what the hell they were talking about half the time. Somewhere in there, he had to finish his proposal for a rate hike for his second-biggest client. That was going to require some major tap-dancing.

Stomach rumbling, Andrew thought of popping out to grab a sandwich from the deli up the block.

Better not, he thought. *If I leave this place today, I might not come back.*

Instead, he bought a premade wrap from the cafeteria downstairs and wolfed it down while he called to check on Kate.

The phone rang and went to voice mail.

He hung up.

It always worried him when she didn't answer. Any call could be the one where she was too incapacitated to answer...or worse. The worst part was what had taken years off his life, never knowing what he would come home to find.

"She's fine."

Andrew considered calling again.

"She's fine," he repeated. If he said it enough, he just might believe it.

It was time for the conference call anyway. He shot her a quick text and put his headset on.

I need a break before I break.

He smiled at Brandi and Luke as they passed by his cubicle, giving her a thumbs-up. But inside, he was a fucking mess.

CHAPTER THREE

Kate always hated this part.

Doctors telling you to meet them in their offices out of the blue was never a good thing. Good news could be easily conveyed over the phone. They saved the bad news for the office.

Dr. Kendricks came in looking very much like a pudgy Einstein, his grey mustache peppered with crumbs. He slipped his glasses into the tangle of hair on his large head and sat across from her.

"How are you feeling?" he said, opening a file folder.

"Much better," she said. She knew he meant the pneumonia. "I cough a little at night, but nothing like it was before. It doesn't feel like someone's sitting on my chest anymore."

"Good, good," he said, smiling. She'd been going to Dr. Kendricks since she was twenty. He was a nice man, a little scattered at times, but an excellent quarterback when it came to dealing with all of the specialists in her life. "You still have enough puffs in that inhaler?"

She nodded. "More than enough."

"Good." He closed the folder. "Look, what I'm going to say shouldn't come as a shock. The pneumonia took a lot out of you. Putting aside the fact that you've been undernourished and dehydrated, this one really walloped your system. Your lupus levels, well, they're off the charts. That's the problem with your condition. You're open to just about any virus or bacteria that comes your way which then weakens you enough to make your lupus flare up. And the worse it flares up, the more susceptible you are to illness and infection."

He was right: this was about as shocking as learning that reality television had nothing to do with reality. Or that the earth was round.

Kate's stomach still cramped up. "How bad is it?"

His elbow on the desk, the doctor rested his chin in his hand. He looked at her the way any father would a sick child. "We're almost at the point where chemo is our best option."

Nothing instilled cold fear in Kate quicker than the word *chemo*. Chemo meant losing her hair. It was vomit and cramps and utter exhaustion. It was taking her illness to a brand-new circle of hell, without any guarantees it would work. And if it didn't – well, my dear, lupus didn't give a damn. It was just dumb enough to knock off its own host.

"I don't want chemo," she said, sitting straighter in her chair. What she wanted was to bolt right out of there and pretend she hadn't heard him.

"I know. And I don't want to have to go that route. In fact, I'm going to do everything I can to avoid it. But you're going to have to go through some pretty unpleasant treatments."

"Fine. I don't care. Whatever it is, I'll just have to suck it up. When would they start?"

He rubbed his chin. "Today."

"Today?" She felt her resolve quiver. "What's the treatment?"

The doctor got up and sat on the edge of his desk, his hand on her arm. "I'm going to administer a cocktail of immunosuppressants and anti-inflammatory drugs. A couple of them are a bit experimental, at least for people in your condition."

"I've been down that road before," she lamented.

"Which means you know that this can work."

"Just as much as it can't."

He hesitated. "That is true. But I've thought long and hard about it and consulted several of my peers, and I think this is the best option available to you right now."

She knew that meant it was her only option, aside from the C word.

Sighing with resignation, Kate asked, "So are we talking some time hooked up to an IV, pills, or do I have to go inside some weird machine that drives claustrophobics insane?"

"It will consist of eight injections at the base of your spine."

He looked pained to even say it.

Her hand went reflexively to her back. "Will I be numb?"

"I can numb the surface, but I'm afraid you're still going to feel it. I promise we'll do it as quickly as possible. I'll finish with a painkiller that will keep you groggy for the rest of the day. You'll be sore for a few days, and you might experience a persistent burning sensation, but that will eventually fade."

Kate swallowed hard. She was used to pain. Burning, not so much.

"How long do you mean by *eventually fade?*"

He shrugged. "It's different for everyone. It could be two, three weeks."

"And when do I have to get my next treatment?"

"A month from today."

"So I'll be feeling better just in time to feel like crap again."

He didn't have to say it out loud, and to his credit, he didn't. "There's a gown for you in room one. Once you're ready, Mary will bring you to the suite. I'll be assisted by Dr. Martin. If you want to take a breather, gather yourself, talk to Andrew, that won't be a problem."

Digging her thumbnail as hard as she could into her palm, she said, "Might as well get it over with. Like pulling off a Band-Aid, right?"

He patted her shoulder. "You'll get two lollipops for this one."

"Promise?"

"Maybe even three. We'll see how well you behave."

Dr. Kendricks showed her to the examination room, an ugly hospital dressing gown wrapped in plastic waiting for her. She tore open the bag and stripped down to her underwear. She'd worn her lounging-around panties and bra, not expecting a paper gown kind of day. Kate was sure once she left the room, everyone would be able to hear her heart thumping in her throat.

She'd had two spinal taps in the past, and the pain had nearly driven her mad.

Now she was going to get eight needles, and she was sure they were long as an aardvark's nose, jabbed into the base of her spine.

Ryker's voice said, *Find a happy place and hide there until it's done.*

Except there was no such thing as a happy place when you were being stabbed.

The first injection felt like she was being run through with a lance. Tendrils of white-hot fire sped up her spine, exploding in her brain. Her fingers and toes curled. Her lungs constricted. Before she could expel her held breath, the next needle slid deep into her.

Again and again and again, the two doctors stuck her.

But she did not cry. No matter what any doctor had done,

violating her in more ways than she could ever have imagined, she refused to shed a tear in front of them. Her body might be weak, but her will could break a football lineman in half.

★   ★   ★

Andrew dropped his magazine on the floor the second he saw Kate walk into the waiting room. Her lips were pulled tight, her eyes glazed. She saw him rise and turned her attention to Kelly, the receptionist, telling Kelly in a strained voice that she needed to make an appointment for the following month. Kate took her appointment card, slipped it in her pocket, and headed for the door. He went to touch her back to give her support, and she hissed.

He didn't ask why. Not in front of everyone in the waiting room, all eyes glued to the woman who looked like she was about to break apart.

Careful helping her into the car, he buckled her in and raced to the driver's side.

What did they do to her now? he thought.

When he started the engine, Kate said, "Go slow. And watch for bumps. Please."

She closed her eyes and settled her head against the seat. A lone tear trickled down her cheek.

It was a twenty-mile drive back to the house. He'd take it at a snail's pace if he had to and ignore the bevy of honking motorists behind him. Jersey drivers were not known for their patience.

Merging onto the Garden State Parkway as smoothly and slowly as possible, he said, "Honey, what happened in there?"

She opened her mouth to answer, then stopped, waving him off. A small sob escaped her lips.

"It hurts so bad," she said, whimpering.

Every muscle in Andrew's body tensed.

He felt helpless, impotent, shut out. A million questions bubbled inside him, but he couldn't give voice to them. Not while Kate was in this kind of pain. He'd have to go against every emotion he was feeling and wait for her to explain everything.

As they got off onto Route 9, Kate said, "I think I can breathe now."

Andrew's grip on the steering wheel relaxed slightly.

"Where's the pain?" he asked.

She shifted in her seat. "My back. Man, they gave me the shots in my lower back, but my whole spine feels like it's crumbling."

"What kind of shots?"

They passed by a supermarket. Andrew had been planning to grab some food on the way home to make for dinner. That would have to wait.

"Lots of stuff with names I can't remember."

Kate opened the window, face tilted up toward the incoming breeze.

"How many shots?"

She'd had shots for her lupus before. Because her stomach had such a hard time metabolizing medication, especially the types of meds designed to treat lupus, she was often given an entire month's dosage in a couple of injections.

But never in her back.

"Dr. K said eight, but it felt like a hundred."

He opened his mouth but found he couldn't find the right words to say.

She cried for a moment, turning away from the car next to them when they stopped at a light. "The best part is, he said it's going to hurt for weeks. He gave me something to knock me out today, but after that, it's just ice packs and pray for it to end."

Andrew desperately wanted to take the pain away, even if it meant doubling it for himself. He never got used to seeing her like this. A sympathetic twinge in his back forced him to move up in his seat. He could only imagine what it was like for her.

"You at least feeling a little groggy now?" he asked.

She nodded, wiping away her tears.

"I'll get you all set up when we get home. You want to be in the living room or the bedroom?"

"Living room."

"You got it. I'll make a bag of ice for your back."

"Not now. I just want to sleep while I can."

"Okay."

"But have that ice ready. I think I'm going to need it when I wake up."

They turned off Route 9, leaving the endless array of strip malls behind.

Andrew saw that she was getting very sleepy. Her eyelids drooped, her head rolling liquidly with each turn. Before she went out entirely, he asked, "Why did they give you eight shots in the back?"

Staring straight ahead, she said, "It was that or chemo. I'm beginning to wonder if I made the right choice."

With that, she closed her eyes and fell silent.

Chemo.

Christ.

*   *   *

Four hours later and Kate was still asleep. That was a good thing. Let her sleep through the worst of it…if today was indeed the worst of it. Andrew had a sinking feeling it wasn't.

The moment they'd walked in the door, it was as if Buttons knew exactly what had happened. Instead of excitedly tangling himself up in their legs, he kept his distance, whimpering as he watched Andrew help Kate onto the daybed. The beagle waited for Andrew to get her pillows set, cover her with a blanket, and turn Turner Classics on low. Once she was tucked in, Buttons sat beside the bed with his head propped on the mattress, his wet nose half a foot from her back. Kate went back to sleep in seconds, but Buttons stayed right there, his canine senses zeroed in on the source of her pain.

"You want to go for a walk?"

The beagle didn't budge.

There was no sense trying to pry him from her side, either. Kate had her guardian angel.

Carrying Kate's things to the bedroom, Andrew saw that there was a voice mail from her brother, Ryker. There was also a text. Not wanting to pry but curious as to why the double whammy, he opened the text.

Hey sis — just checking up on you. Back from our latest adventure and have lots of funny stories. Had a weird dream about you on the plane. Just let me know you're all right.

Knowing Kate might be out of it for the rest of the day, Andrew shot a quick text to his brother-in-law, letting him know she'd had a new lupus treatment and he'd have her call him tomorrow. Andrew placed no value in dream messages, but Ryker was new agey enough to get all worked up if someone didn't tell him all was well.

Okay, Kate-kinda-well, which wasn't well, but it was better than the alternative.

Falling down the forbidden-thoughts rabbit hole, he recalled the day Kate's surgeon had told him the abdominal surgery they needed to perform only had a ten percent success rate. The infection in her digestive tract had turned gangrenous. It was basically a Hail Mary pass. Ten percent was better than the one hundred percent prognosis that she would die within a week. He'd given the doctor the go-ahead and stepped into Kate's room. She'd been surrounded by her mother and brother. Things had been so bad, even his mother-in-law sat vigil.

"Are you crying?" Kate had said, her eyes barely open, voice so soft and weak, it was like talking to a ghost.

He hadn't realised she was awake, much less that he had tears in his eyes.

"Nah, just cutting onions," he'd said, bending down to kiss her forehead.

"Are we home? What's for dinner?" she'd said, fading before he could answer.

He'd never told anyone the chances of her surviving the surgery. What was the point? Unburdening himself wouldn't have made him feel any better; it would just upset her family.

Yes, she had survived the fourteen-hour surgery, and that was a memory to celebrate.

Don't you have work to do?

Yes, he did, and it would take his mind off things.

Andrew sat at the kitchen table with his laptop, filling out his sales reports, all the while keeping an eye on Kate. The sense of helplessness only fueled his stress. He decided a little day drinking was in order. It took the edge off and made dealing with the slew of insipid emails a tad easier. Every little thing was a crisis. *These assholes don't know what a real crisis is*, he thought. He was on his fourth Lone Star when he realised it was dark out and the work day could officially be put to bed.

After he fed Buttons, the dog reluctantly taking a few bites before going back to his spot beside Kate, Andrew heated up leftover pasta and ate it over the sink.

He had energy – nervous energy – to burn. The thought of sitting and watching TV or reading a book seemed impossible. He needed to move, to sweat the alcohol from his system, to discharge the electric tension running through his body.

After writing a note and placing it on the coffee table, he changed into his sweats and headed out for a quick run.

The whole concept of running was ridiculous to him. Running in circles was what chickens did to kill time. He didn't run to stay healthy. Yes, he needed to take care of himself so he could take care of Kate, but that wasn't why he punished his legs, back, and lungs.

Before running, Andrew had denied to everyone, including himself, that he was stressed and overwhelmed with being a caregiver. Confessing his anxiety would be tantamount to admitting that he wasn't fit to provide for Kate and nurse her back to health. Denial was a hell of a coping mechanism. He assumed if he didn't speak or think his darkest thoughts, well, then they'd never be made real.

It came as no shock that that was not the way to go about things.

Andrew quietly closed the door and headed toward Locust Street. He wasn't so much a jogger as he was a mad sprinter. His worn sneakers pounded the sidewalk slabs, while his heart rate accelerated.

You can't outrun chemo, man.

Mr. Hanson waved at him from his car.

Oh yeah? Watch me.

All of the apprehension and stress had burst out of Andrew one day when he was out with friends at a Chinese restaurant. Kate was in the hospital for her third week, and there was no sign of her coming home. Despite everyone asking how they could help, Andrew said he had everything in hand. He ordered one of those fruity drinks that had a dozen different types of booze in them, and practically chugged it before their appetisers arrived. He thought he was having fun, a pleasant distraction with friends during a particularly trying time. It was nice to be away from the hospital, far from the beeping machines and antiseptic smells, and with that sense of relief came guilt. How dare he enjoy himself when Kate was trapped in that hospital bed? Beneath his smile and jokes, he began to simmer.

Then the man at the table next to them asked him to keep his voice down.

Andrew snapped.

The next few moments were still a blacked-out blur, but everyone who was there had filled him in on the embarrassing details. Without saying a word, he got up, grabbed the table next to them, and flipped it over. Plates, food, drinks, and cutlery flew in every direction. The man who had politely asked him to chill out ended up on the floor. Andrew attempted to stomp his head and thankfully missed. Before he could try again, he was wrapped up by his friends, Brent and Mitchell. They dragged him out of the restaurant, Andrew screaming all the way that he was going to rip the man's head off – in front of his terrified family, no less.

An automatic sprinkler popped up from a lawn, dousing him in cold water. Andrew veered into the street, running hard, breathing harder, the soles of his feet starting to ache.

No chemo. No chemo. No chemo.

With every heavy footfall, he repeated the mantra.

Envision it and make it your reality. Wasn't that the stuff Ryker babbled on about all the time? A lot of people paid for that babble.

He'd been envisioning Kate's health finally taking a turn for the better for ten years now.

No chemo. No chemo. No chemo.

No better, either.

The incident at the Chinese restaurant had been like popping the cork from a shaken champagne bottle. All of Andrew's fear and sadness and hate for a Creator who could do this to his wife had finally found an outlet – rage.

For the next year, he'd flown into a rage at the drop of a hat, always with strangers, and always in public places. The demon within him craved public spectacle but cowered from unleashing itself on those closest to him. The why of it all never came out, even during his years of therapy. Truth be told, he didn't care. He was just glad he never hurt his family or friends. He could live with breaking a strange man's nose. At least he'd never have to see him sitting across the Christmas dinner table.

He'd scrapped with people for little to no reason in bars, a bowling alley, parked at a stop sign, and even a supermarket one morning. The arrest didn't come until his fourth outburst, when no one was around to explain his situation and hope the other person would let it slide.

Luckily for him, the charges on his first and only arrest were dropped, but not until he agreed to anger management and counseling. The man whom he'd doubled over with a jab to the solar plexus – all for having the misfortune to have given a short tap on his horn when Andrew spaced out at a stop sign – had lost his wife to cancer several years earlier. He understood Andrew's fury and wished him and Kate the best. At the time, Andrew wanted to wipe that condescending look right off his face. Hell, he wanted to wipe every look off everyone's face.

A dog barked in the dark. Andrew listened out for running paws. He'd been chased more than once by a shepherd mix on Bentley Road. Tonight, he was looking forward to beating it in a footrace again.

The dog in the dark was all bark, no chase.

No chemo. No chemo. No chemo.

Therapy was a waste. The damn shrink kept asking about his relationship with his father, as if that had anything to do with what was going on with Kate. Andrew knew damn well what his issues were. The medication he was prescribed made him too drowsy to function, so there went that.

Anger management seemed an equal waste of time, until he met up with one of his fellow hotheads (that's what they liked to call themselves) at a diner after their weekly meeting. Her name was Sharon, and this was her third round of anger management. She was in it this time for throwing a chair into an aquarium at a pet store because one of the workers had called her ma'am. She had been only thirty-five at the time, and in her opinion, the furthest fucking thing from a ma'am. She hadn't intended to hit the bewildered pet store worker in his blue smock. She just wanted to see him struggle to save all the fish, knees crunching the pebbled glass.

"I think I'm finally done with all this craziness this time," she said over a coffee and BLT.

"You counting backwards from a hundred, or using affirmations?" he said with a roll of his eyes.

She smirked. "I'm running. I run like my ass is on fire. I don't wait until someone's pissed me off. I just do it, every day. I do it until that broken part of my brain is too tired to wind me up."

"And it works?"

"Ask the fish."

So he took her advice and he ran. Sprinting around the block after work, and before heading to the hospital to see Kate, took the edge off. He ran like his ass was on fire, and in doing so, he quelled the flames that had been simmering just under the surface twenty-four hours a day.

Turning down Texas Drive, he spotted his house in the distance. His chest burned; his knees protested.

No chemo.

Andrew collapsed onto his back on his front lawn. Ambient light obliterated most of the stars. He lay with his hands on his chest, steadying his breath. The muscles in his legs quivered and clicked like a hot car engine after a long run on a dark highway.

Letting the endorphins rush through him, Andrew's mind went blank and silent. Once his breathing and heartbeat settled down, he shakily got to his feet and went inside.

Kate was still asleep. Buttons looked up for a moment before settling again onto his front paws, ears splayed out at his sides.

Andrew wanted to touch her, to feel his skin on her skin, but he worried about waking her up. Wherever she was right now, she wasn't in pain. Best to leave her there.

He stripped off his clothes and tossed them in the washer. Then he headed for the shower.

Time, he felt, was closing in, gaining weight, incorporating into something that would take up more and more space. Like a child throwing a temper tantrum, it refused to be ignored. Time was both coming for them and running out. It had become a living, breathing entity, daring Andrew to look in its depthless eyes.

It crowded the shower, so close he could feel its cold, indifferent breath on his bare back. Drying quickly, he grabbed a pillow and sat in the easy chair next to Kate.

Sleep came suddenly and mercifully, time no longer mattering, at least for one more night.

CHAPTER FOUR

Dr. K had been right. The pain from the treatment was beyond excruciating. It was like being injected with time-released acid, the poison sizzling away at her spine, turning her organs to balls of flame. With pain came rage.

She was already maxed out on pain meds, so there was nothing to do but take it. For three weeks, she couldn't concentrate on anything longer than a minute. Food tasted worse than ever. Movies gave her no comfort. Sleep was hard to come by. Even Buttons was irritating with his constant, sad-eyed presence. Andrew absorbed her complaints, her irrational screaming to be left alone, or her demands for him to be with her seconds later. She knew she sounded crazy, but there was nothing she could do about it. She was, in fact, crazy, and she refused to be apologetic about it. Only once did Andrew raise his voice, telling her to calm the hell down after she had blabbered incoherently in a river of tears until she could barely catch her breath. It was either that or an old-fashioned smack to the face.

Every day had become a bad feels day.

And the shadow watched her.

As irrational as it seemed, Kate knew it was feeding on her agony – not just taking delight, but becoming more powerful.

Criiiiicccckkkk.

She startled on the daybed. The tension in her shoulders sent ripples of misery down her back, shooting out to her limbs like balls of light from a Roman candle.

Buttons perked up his ears.

"You heard that too, didn't you?"

She hooked her finger under his collar, keeping him close.

For the past two weeks, she'd been hearing odd sounds when Andrew was at work. Doors inching open, objects shifting inside closed cabinets, things falling on the floor. Except whenever she went to investigate, she could find nothing.

This time, it sounded as if someone had closed the bathroom door down the hall.

"I'm losing my fucking mind."

She cried out in both pain and fear. Not fear of the shadow closing the door. It was fear that the pain and sleep deprivation were making her unhinged.

Unless the shadow was real.

And if it was real...

"Come here," she said to the dog. She wiped the tears on her cheeks into his fur. Buttons made for a world-class hankie.

She stared down the hallway, knowing she'd see nothing. At least directly. The shadow only lived in her periphery. If she concentrated on something, in this case the corner of hers and Andrew's bed beyond the open bedroom door, consciously aware to be mindful of the edges of her vision, it might reveal itself.

And then what?

Lie here cowering like a child until Andrew came home?

Kate was well aware that if she let herself get worked up, she wouldn't even be able to sleep it away. There were times over the past few weeks when she was sure that the moment she closed her eyes, the strange, dark shape would steal her breath and drag her to whatever black pit had birthed the expectant spectre. She didn't dare tell Andrew, because doing so would let *it* know she was aware of it. Maybe, just maybe, if she pretended she never saw it, the wraith would move on.

She reached out to the coffee table, grabbed the cold mason jar of pills, and rested it against her forehead.

"This is all your fault," she said to the pills. The sound of the refrigerator clicking on almost made her drop the mason jar. "At least I hope it is."

*   *   *

Andrew left work an hour early to get Kate to her appointment with Dr. K. It might have been his imagination, but he thought his boss flashed a disapproving look his way as he passed by his office.

He had to wrestle the urge to go back and tell him to go screw himself. Or maybe he could invite him to go outside and tell him to his face what that look really meant.

Calm the hell down. He's probably just looking over some report that's not promising to pad his pockets come bonus time.

He stuffed his fists in his pocket and went straight to his car.

The state Kate was in had put him in a dour mood. Kate's anger had only inflated his own. Except he had to stow that shit real deep. There was no letting that pissed-off genie out of the bottle. Kicking the shit out of his boss would not make things better for them, even though he would feel a blessed release for a short time.

All the way home, he fantasised about being let go and signing his release papers. The first thing he'd do, after celebrating with some champagne – okay, a lot of champagne – was sleep in. He and Kate would sleep whole days away, getting up only for the bare essentials. She loved having him in bed with her, especially when she was feeling sicker than usual. It gave her comfort. Andrew had been bouncing around so much the past few years, making sure every plate was still spinning on its pole, that it would be nice to just let them crash. Even if Kate slept twenty hours a day, he'd lie next to her, stroking her hair or resting his hand on her belly, feeling the soft, warm comfort of her body. She always felt better, slept better, when he was beside her. Maybe his getting fired could be the key to her finally leaving all this misery behind them.

Could it be that his struggle to maintain the status quo was what was holding her back? If that was the case, he'd have to do something pretty damn quick to rectify that.

* * *

"Did you get a raise or something?" Kate said when he walked in the front door. She was dressed and waiting for him. The abysmal aftereffects of the treatment had finally run their course a couple of days ago. And now here she was, dressed and ready for more.

"Why do you say that?"

"You've got a smile on your face like someone just gave you the winning lottery numbers."

"I, my dear crip, have put myself in a positive frame of mind for your doctor visit today."

He extended his hand to help her off the daybed. "That makes one of us," she said.

"Hence the big ol' smile. I have to be positive for two."

As he helped her into the car, she said, "You haven't been drinking, have you?"

He blew into her face. "What does that smell like to you?"

She waved at her nose. "Like you've been to that deli that makes those meatball parm sandwiches that give you indigestion."

"I can't help it. They're addictive."

"Even Buttons can't stand to be around you when you eat those things. I mean, it's like something dies in your stomach."

Andrew laughed, keying the ignition. "Buttons licks his own butthole. I wouldn't use him as an arbiter of what smells bad or not."

Kate chuckled. She was pale today – paler than usual – but there was a tiny spark in her eyes. He knew she was terrified, so he did his best to keep her mind off things, blabbing the whole ride about dumb things he overheard people say at work. Because Kate hadn't been well enough to work for so long, she yearned to hear about office life. What he found to be mundane, she couldn't get enough of. It should have made him appreciate what he had when it came to his career, but it didn't. It only made him sad for her.

The doctor saw Kate right away.

Sitting under the television, Andrew tried reading a magazine, but his mind kept wandering to fantasies of being freed from his job. The thing he feared losing second most after Kate, it turned out, was nothing to fear at all. They would persevere. He would find another job. Medical insurance was a disaster for everyone, so it wasn't like his current plan was irreplaceable. Their medical bills would be paid off right around when he turned nine hundred and seventy. What difference did a few years make?

"Andy?"

He hadn't realised he'd dozed off.

Kate waited for him by the receptionist's desk. She didn't look to be in agony. In fact, she was smiling.

"I need the co-pay," she said.

"Oh, yeah."

He handed his credit card over, slipping an arm across her shoulders.

"You okay?" he said.

"Yep."

He waited until they were in the car to press her for more.

"I take it no needles? Or maybe just a couple?"

Kate tucked her hair behind her ears. "Last month's treatment put a dent in my lupus. He's also worried about the overall effect another one so close to the first will have on my body. So, he's giving me a break. I don't get another one like it until the fall."

He gave her a high five. "That's great news."

"It's nice to know that I won't spend the summer rolling around in agony. Just the fall."

"Maybe by then things will be even better, so long as we take extra special care of you."

"And how do you propose to do that?" Her smile lit up the car. She had left the house a condemned woman, and she'd just gotten a reprieve. He didn't know who was feeling happier at the moment.

"I have my ways. First thing we're going to do is step up your nutrition game. I'll get you those health shakes. You know, the ones they feed old people in rest homes."

"No way. I hate those things. They taste like chemicals."

He shook his head. "Sorry. You're not going to be able to fight lupus and every other germ that floats your way on leftover Milano's. We have to make you strong, like bull." He tapped his chest with a fist.

Kate giggled. "Fine. But I can only suffer one of those shakes a day."

"I'll take it."

She cranked up the radio, filling the car with Katy Perry's latest bombastic ballad.

This was the first good news they'd had all year. Even though darkness was on the horizon, they were being given a small break, one they needed to take advantage of. They'd have to celebrate properly.

By the time he got her changed and comfortable in the living room, Andrew knew exactly what he was going to do.

CHAPTER FIVE

Meditation wasn't working. Nothing she did could get her to sleep. Even the new fentanyl patch, which usually got her head all soupy, limbs soft as cooked spaghetti, had failed.

The doctor had said there would be lingering effects from the treatment. Kind of like acid flashbacks. Right now, she pictured some toxic green goo running through her veins instead of blood. She felt both powerful and powerless. If someone put a gun to her head, demanding to know exactly what she was feeling and why, she'd be eating a bullet.

One moment, she was restless and breathless, her heart trip-hammering. The next, she was dizzy and weak, her body feeling as if she were about to spontaneously combust.

There were no lurking shadows. This hadn't been a bad feels day.

No, this was new.

It was a feel without a name...for now.

It was like waiting for something to happen, except she didn't know whether that something was good or bad. She was simply... expectant.

Before heading for bed tonight, she and Andrew had watched a horror double feature from back in their dating days: *The Faculty* and *Blade*. They used to devour scary movies like buttered popcorn, but somewhere along the line, real life got scary enough. Kate moved on to the old black and whites, while Andrew became a documentary junkie. It was fun going back to the days of monsters and gore, at least for a night.

Now, Andrew was all curled up and snoring, and she was ready to jump out of her skin.

Turner Classics was playing a silent film. Not her number one choice. The absence of sound was making her ears ring. She opted for an infomercial about a magic frying pan. It was dumb, but it was also loud and over the top and busy.

"Who the hell orders these things?" she said to Buttons. The beagle gave a single thump of his tail on the bed as if to show her he heard and was equally perplexed.

She was about to get up and go to the bathroom, just to burn off some of this nervous energy, when the TV turned itself off. Their bedroom was cloaked in total darkness. Andrew had forgotten to turn on the little night-light in the bathroom down the hall. The room-darkening blinds refused to let in even the tiniest sliver of moonlight.

Kate fumbled for the remote and found it wedged under her thigh. She hit buttons at random, but nothing happened. The time display on the cable box was out too.

She reached out to the light by the bed and flicked the switch.

Nothing.

They'd either blown a fuse or the whole block was out.

Before she woke Andrew to check the fuse box, she thought it would be better to go to the front of the house and look outside, see if the streetlights were on or not.

Sliding her feet into her slippers, Kate patted Buttons on the head and whispered, "Come on, But-But. Keep Mommy company."

The beagle reluctantly padded off the bed, sneezing onto her feet.

"Ewww. Thanks a lot, buddy."

Buttons went ahead of her, presumably toward his dish in the kitchen. If he was going to be forced to be awake, he might as well have a post-midnight snack.

The house was eerily quiet. The dull hum of their central air system had gone silent. Out of habit and comfort, Kate always had the TV on. Without that background noise, it was like walking through a deserted graveyard.

Now you're being dramatic.

There was some light illuminating the floor of the living room, but not the usual pasting of yellow from the streetlight. This was more subdued – the blue/black of the moon forcing its way into their home.

Buttons stopped at the entrance to the living room.

His tail dropped.

A low growl rumbled in his throat.

Kate stopped.

Buttons never growled. Ever.

Shit. What if this was one of those home invasions where the thieves cut the power to the house? Was someone in her living room at this very moment, standing still as a statue, careful not to make a sound, not to breathe too hard, waiting to clobber anyone who stumbled into him?

She thought of Audrey Hepburn in *Wait Until Dark,* a terrified blind woman turning the tables on the criminals who had broken into her home.

You're not Audrey Hepburn and this isn't a movie.

Normally, she'd think it was just her paranoia, the meds, or that strange treatment aftereffect playing tricks with her mind, like it had been all night. She hadn't told Andrew half the things she saw and felt over the years, knowing (after the fact) that they were just phantom images culled from a brain that was awash in chemicals. Kate once saw a baby with one arm hopping on their bed, singing a song in Spanish as it leered at her with a mouthful of razor-sharp teeth. The rational part of her brain had known there was no evil baby, but as it leapt over her feet and up toward Andrew's pillow, it took all of her strength not to grab the lamp and try to smash it.

She cast a quick glance back to the bedroom.

Andrew.

Her legs were suddenly trapped in quicksand, afraid to go forward and unable to retreat to the bedroom.

One hand resting on the wall, she parted her lips and breathed through her mouth, in case air whistling in her nose would give her away. She felt for the vibration of any movement through the soles of her feet and palm of her hand. Her ears strained so hard, a tiny buzz of tinnitus rose from the silence. Her hips and shoulders ached from the creeping tension that stiffened her back.

Who was in her house?

Buttons also hadn't moved, looking into the living room at something…or someone…she couldn't see. Trapped in the moonlight, his lips pulled back, slobber splattering the floor.

Oh God, oh God, oh God!

Kate wanted to scream. She wanted to cry. Most of all, she wanted to run and get Andrew. But her body, as always, refused to listen to her.

What had Buttons so riled up?

Please bark! If he got to barking, that would definitely wake Andrew up. And maybe, just maybe, it would scare off whoever was in her living room.

She swallowed hard, her stomach growing nauseated. She didn't know how much longer she could stay like this.

Buttons suddenly sat, gave a short whine, and started to wag his tail.

He looked back at her, as if to say, *Are you coming or not? This was all your idea.*

Whatever had spooked him was gone. He turned away and waddled out of sight and toward the kitchen.

Kate nearly collapsed as she let out the breath she'd been holding.

Her paralysis broke and she was able to creep down the hall, encouraged by the slobbering sounds of Buttons attacking his bowl, crunching the dry food with abandon.

The apprehension that had been steadily crushing her like a soda can was gone. She peeked into the living room. Of course it was empty. Daring herself to look out the window, she parted the blinds and jumped back.

A bird had been perched on the window. Startled when she touched the blinds, it tore off into the night. With a hand over her own shocked heart, Kate spluttered with nervous laughter, despite her chest hurting.

She'd nearly pissed herself over a bird.

Buttons hated birds. She and Andrew wondered if he'd been a cat in a previous life. She wasn't going to be much of a fan after this, either.

It probably didn't help that they'd spent the night watching horror movies.

Buttons nudged his cold, wet nose against her calf.

"Thanks for freaking me out."

To top it all off, it looked like the power was out everywhere.

Kate's head spun.

Whoa.

"Okay, now I think I'm ready to sleep."

Exhaustion hit her like a cold fist to the temple.

Before she walked back to the bedroom, she took one more look at the window where the bird had been. A cold realization made her stomach churn.

Buttons hadn't been growling in that direction.

★   ★   ★

Andrew had been exceedingly busy over the past two weeks, but few of his endeavours had anything to do with actual work. There was a lot of research going on.

He had to pull the trigger now, and even though everything was rushed – and kept secret from Kate – it was all going to be for the better.

The meeting with HR and his boss was nerve-wracking. Not so much because he was afraid to talk to them. His main concern was that they would say no and delay things so much that he'd miss his opportunity. At one point, as he was basically spilling his guts all over the conference room table, he started to cry. He was embarrassed as hell, but to his surprise, it changed the atmosphere in the room. Suddenly they were more than happy to work with him and grant his request. Noella from HR had tears in her own eyes when she handed him the papers to sign.

Andrew pulled into Milano's parking lot, opened the folder on the passenger seat, and scanned the printed sheets for the hundredth time. He couldn't remember the last time he'd felt this light, this happy.

After picking up two pies, he stopped to get a six-pack, Kate's favourite soda, and the few snacks she still liked to eat. There was also a pit stop at the florist, where he purchased three dozen yellow carnations.

Needless to say, she was shocked to see him home early on a Tuesday, his arms laden with all of the booty he'd picked up on his drive home.

"What is all of this?" she said, groggily rubbing her eyes. Her hair was sticking out every which way and the bags under her eyes were heavy and dark. He knew she'd been having trouble sleeping lately, but so far she hadn't broached the subject with him.

"This, my dear, is a celebration."

"You got me carnations!"

"I sure did."

Buttons barked his approval when Andrew placed them on her lap. She bent close and sniffed them.

"I don't know why I love yellow carnations so much," she said.

"At least when it comes to flowers, you're easy to please. It kind of makes up for everything else. Kinda," he said with a wink.

"And please tell me that's Milano's."

"It is."

She set the flowers on the coffee table. "Okay, spill it. Did you get a promotion? Did you find out you have a long-lost rich uncle that just died and left you his mansion in Saddle River?"

"I wish." He handed her the file folder. "Check it out."

She flipped it open. The front page showed a house on a lake nestled underneath a thick canopy of evergreens. "What is this?"

"Would you be shocked if I told you it's our home for the next three months?"

Her eyes grew wide, the fatigue washed away instantly.

"What? Three months? Where?"

He put his arm around her. "You know how we've always talked about moving to a lake house in Maine?"

"Yes."

"Well, I rented one for the entire summer. It has everything we ever wanted – a deck overlooking the lake, dock, and privacy, all surrounded by two acres of nothing but trees and walking trails."

She went through page after page, reading the specs on the house and looking at the dozen pictures Andrew had printed. Her eyes shimmered.

"But how can we do this? Your job isn't going to allow you to work remotely for months."

Hugging her, he said, "I know, which is why I've taken a three-month leave of absence. No leaving you during the day, no having to hit the hay early because I have to get up in the morning. You've got me twenty-four-seven, if you can stand me that long."

"And they're okay with this?"

"Yep. It's all part of the Family Medical Leave Act. The leave is unpaid, of course, but we can afford it."

She threw her arms around his neck, scattering the pages. Buttons howled.

"Oh...my...God! This is incredible!"

"I know," Andrew said in a high falsetto.

"Where is it in Maine?" she asked.

"In Bridge Mills, in the lakes region. The house is right on Round Lake."

"But…how did you get a gorgeous place like this on such short notice?"

"Call it fate, but it just became available the day I had decided to do everything. The realtor said a couple had rented it into the fall, but the husband passed away suddenly."

Kate's excitement dulled. "That's horrible."

"It is. But we shouldn't look a gift horse in the mouth."

She took a deep breath and nodded. "You're right. You're right. The big question is, when do we go?"

"You think we have enough time to pack for Saturday?"

"Hell yeah." She hugged him again. "I love you so much, you know that?"

"I love you too."

"Now, where's my pizza?"

CHAPTER SIX

Kate wasn't the least surprised when she came down with a stomach virus on Thursday. It always happened. Give her something to look forward to, and her body would find a way to crap all over it. In this case, literally.

That meant Andrew had to do all the packing while she made lists in the bathroom. He'd become very adept at running the entire house, but he was starting to gripe at the slew of errands she'd mapped out for him to pick up all the stuff they needed.

He said, "You know, they do have stores in Maine that sell things to people who possess this thing called money. If I keep buying stuff here, we won't have enough room in the car to carry it all."

Scrolling through her tablet in the bathroom, she said, "Ha-ha. It's just a few things."

"It was just a few things two days ago. Now it's bordering on comical."

"We don't know the kinds of stores they have and if they carry the stuff I need and like."

Her stomach cramped and she squeezed her eyes shut. She hated stomach viruses most of all because of how quickly they depleted her already fragile system. Andrew kept trying to force those damned shakes on her, but she couldn't bring herself to taking the slightest sip.

"We're going to Maine, not Azerbaijan," he said through the door. "I'm pretty sure we can find cortisone cream and Mike and Ike candy there."

Of all the pleasures she'd lost, her sweet tooth wasn't one of them. Candy soothed her stomach. Andrew swore she was part insect, happy to live in a bag of sugar. Some days, it didn't sound like such a bad idea. If insects couldn't get autoimmune diseases, she'd sign right up. She'd already looked up the longest-living insects and decided she'd want to be a queen termite. They could live up to fifty years. If she turned into one now, that would take her to eighty-eight. She had far better prospects as an insect than a human. Plus, bonus, she'd be a queen!

"You don't know that for sure," she said.

"Pretty sure I do."

"Can you please just get what's on my list?"

"Which list? You've made about a hundred of them in the past two days. I'll need to hire someone just to go shop for all the things you want," he said irritably.

A stomach cramp made Kate's eyes water.

Why was he standing outside the door like that? The last thing she wanted was for him to hear her pooping.

"Just go," she said, holding back what was desperate to come out.

"I guess I'll see you in three days. If I'm lucky."

"Three days without you mumbling and cranky would be nice."

There was a thump on the door and she heard him walk away. Or stalk away might have been more appropriate. He was a stickler about packing the car, and she was a little fuzzy when it came to spatial awareness, so getting prepared for trips always brought moments of tension. She wasn't angry at Andrew (well, she was now, but she hadn't been before this). Mostly, she was upset with herself and the inevitable illness that robbed her of what should be a fun, exciting time.

He returned later that night, his arms laden with bags, the expression on his face telling her he had only gotten more upset as the day wore on. They argued, as usual when things bubbled up like this, Kate taking the daybed for the night, both of them fuming. Kate was both angry at him for making such a big production of things, and herself for not being able to help. Did he think she liked making all these lists? She'd give anything to be able to go all over town and get everything herself.

The next day, Andrew extended the olive branch first, saying he was sorry and offering to make her breakfast. She accepted the apology and gave her own, but turned down the food. The thought of something even as bland as toast made her cringe. As the time drew near to journey to Maine, they both worried that she wouldn't be able to make the trip.

By Saturday, there was nothing left inside Kate, so she gave him the official okay to hit the road.

"You sure you'll be fine?" he said, adjusting the straps on the vinyl cap he'd had to buy and install on the roof of the car to carry all their stuff.

She reclined her seat as far as it would go, cradling her favourite pillow, which she'd named Mooshy when she was a little girl. Mooshy came everywhere with her. It was a soft, amorphous blob that had ceased being an actual pillow fifteen years earlier. Now it was just something comfortable for her to cradle.

"Trust me, the tank is empty. How long did you say the trip will be?"

He checked the GPS on his phone. "Ah, seven hours, give or take. I'm sure we'll hit a traffic snarl around Boston that'll make things interesting. Then there's walking Buttons. And your bladder that's about the size of a thimble."

"Good, that'll be a nice seven-hour nap."

The car rocked when he got in and closed his door.

"I'm going to wake you from time to time to make sure you drink," he said. "If you won't eat, you at least have to rehydrate yourself."

"I'm not thirsty."

"Not a concern. Sometimes you have to do things just because. I bought a few of those little baby drinks that amp up your electrolytes. They're in the cooler behind you."

She smiled. "Aw, I really am your baby."

Kate was tempted to crack one open now. Her heartbeat was ragged from time to time, making her dizzy. But at the moment, she just wanted to nod off.

"If putting it in a bottle helps, I'll stop at the supermarket and pick one up," he joked. However, she knew if she told him yes, she would drink a lot more if it was in a baby bottle, he'd run out and buy a gross of them.

"Drive on, my good man. We're burning daylight."

As he backed out of the driveway, she waved goodbye to their house, a house that doubled as a hospital and prison. She wouldn't have gone so far as to say it felt haunted lately, but it no longer brought her the same comfort it had in the past.

Buttons in his crate in the backseat gave it a farewell bark.

They were off to their dream house for a wonderful summer. Kate tried not to fixate on how shitty she felt, hoping Maine would somehow infuse her with the health, both physical and mental, that had been slipping from her grasp like fine sand.

* * *

Seven hours turned into almost ten, thanks to the Boston traffic Andrew had predicted, Kate and Buttons needing several pee breaks, stops for lunch and dinner (for Andrew and the dog), and getting lost for a spell down winding one-lane roads in Maine. Andrew woke her up when they passed through the small town of Bridge Mills, but by the time she was awake enough to take in the scenery, the shank of the town was behind them.

"That was small," she said, peering at the fading row of shops in the side view mirror.

"Hey, it was four whole blocks. Looked like something out of a movie from the fifties. You missed the drive-in."

"A drive-in? They still have those? Was it even operational?"

"Oh yeah. It looks like they have oldies Wednesdays, though not as old as you like them. We're talking *Caddyshack* and *Meatballs*. Guess someone's a Bill Murray fan."

"Can we go?"

He stroked her hair. "As many times as you want."

She was glad he didn't say *as many times as you can*, which was the truth of it all. Right now, she wanted to live in a fantasy where everything was possible.

It was still light when they spotted the sign for Highland Road a split-second before passing it by for the fourth time.

"All righty, we now know our little house is so far off the grid, even Google can't find it," Andrew said.

"I don't have any bars on my phone."

"I'm not surprised."

They passed a roadside mailbox shaped like a birdhouse. Andrew consulted the chicken scrawl of directions he'd made. "I think this is it." The narrow dirt and gravel road meandered through a thick umbrella of trees, plunging them into near-total darkness. Kate rolled down the window, took a long, deep breath, and started coughing.

"Smells great," she said.

Andrew laughed. "You've been cooped up so long, you can't handle nature."

The aroma of pine cones, old leaves, and the mineral tang of the nearby lake was intoxicating. She hung her arm out of the window. It was a lot colder up here, or maybe that was just because they were under such dense shade. Buttons twanged the bars of his crate with his tail. He was up and looking out the window with her.

"Look at all that territory you get to mark, But–But," she said.

He gave a few quick, happy yips.

"You can pee and poop anywhere you like, but you'll still need your leash, buddy," she said, slipping her fingers into the crate to touch his wet nose.

"A leash? He'll be fine," Andrew said.

"With my luck, he'll get eaten by a bear. He's a city dog. He has no country sense."

"That makes three of us."

They turned a bend and the world suddenly opened up to them. Kate gasped. Andrew hit the brakes. Even Buttons whined to get out of the crate.

"It's beautiful."

"I think the old shack will do," Andrew said, smiling wider than she'd seen him do in years.

The house, described by the realtor as a dreamy lakeside cottage retreat, was more than she could have hoped for. A break in the trees allowed sunlight to bathe the blond wood cottage as if it were spotlit by God himself. The small but immaculate front lawn was bordered by perennials. There were only two steps to get onto the porch, a pair of Adirondack chairs flanking the door. A wind chime that looked to have been made by a local crafter, burnished metal cut and pounded into spirals, tinkled in the soft, cool breeze. Behind the humble house was the lake, the pink rays of the sun stippling its serene surface. It was like stepping into a dream, or a Thomas Kinkade painting. Kate wanted to wrap her arms around the cottage and hug it.

"Hold on a sec," Andrew said, jumping out of the car and running to open the front door.

He came back and lifted Kate out.

"What are you doing?" she said, giggling.

"I'm going to carry you over the threshold like a proper gentleman."

"You know, guys carry their brides over thresholds so they can be very improper later."

Andrew wriggled his eyebrows.

She could tell the instant they went inside that the house had been cleaned just that day. The scent of lemon and pine cleaner, along with a fresh bowl of potpourri on the shelf by the door, instantly put her at ease. She'd secretly worried all week that it was too good to be true. The pictures were a lie and the place would be a roach motel.

Nothing could be further from the truth.

With the kitchen on their left, the open living room was spread out before them, sliding doors leading to a raised porch with a stunning view of Round Lake. The furniture looked comfortable and relatively new. Everywhere she looked there was blond wood, accentuating the fading light of day.

Andrew set her down on the couch and kissed her.

"So, what do you think?"

"I think the owners are going to have a hard time getting me to leave."

He propped Mooshy behind her back. "Now, you just sit back while Buttons and I unpack the car."

"I'm sure he'll be a big help."

"He's good with the little things. At least I hope."

Even though she'd slept most of the ride, Kate was exhausted. Her body ached more than she was going to let on, a dull throb in her chest. And her stomach felt as if it had folded in on itself. She knew whatever she ate was going to come right back up. Still, she was, for a change, hungry.

A few minutes in the country and I'm already on the mend, she thought with a smile.

While Andrew made round trip after round trip, Buttons at his heels, Kate got up to explore the house. She poked her head into the bedroom, the floor covered in their luggage. The room seemed small because it was filled with two double beds. The wood paneling shone like glass. A lone window had a nice view of the lake.

Just across the hall was the bathroom.

Kate was a stickler for bathrooms – she often had made them switch hotel rooms back when they could pick up and get away at will – if she spotted the slightest smudge of mould or grime. Bathrooms were a big make or break for her. She needn't have worried today. The recently refurbished bathroom was nicer than their own in Jersey, with a brass claw-foot tub and a shower with a built-in bench that was a huge plus. All of the moulding and grout work was spotless.

Kate felt the ground shift under her feet and grabbed the sink. After steadying herself for a couple of minutes, she ran cold water on her wrists, dried off, and went back to the couch. Her hip popped along the way but stayed in the socket. Andrew was in the kitchen, unloading some of the groceries she'd made him bring along.

"I'm almost afraid to ask about the bathroom," he said, reading the label on a bottle of wine.

"I give it a gold star."

"No kidding?"

"It's cleaner than ours."

"I guess technically, at least until after Labor Day, it *is* ours."

She craned her neck and stared at the slatted ceiling. "I love the sound of that."

Kate pulled a chair out from under the dining room table and sat down. Everything about the cottage screamed *quaint*. It was perfect, a thousand times better than she'd imagined. The maid service had done a hell of a job. She couldn't even find a speck of dust.

"Promise me we can stay here forever?"

"You might change your mind after being cooped up with me for a whole summer," Andrew said, checking the kitchen cabinets and finding a pair of glasses.

"I seriously doubt it."

Buttons jumped up beside her and buried his nose in her armpit, his tail whacking her thigh. Andrew asked her if she wanted something to drink.

When she answered him, it was in a dream, the day's excitement shifting into fragments, her body painless, weightless, flirting with bliss.

★   ★   ★

Kate awoke in the middle of the night, enshrouded in darkness so complete that for a moment, she panicked.

Am I dead?

Her arm flailed out and she cracked her hand on something hard and unyielding.

Guess not. Unless you can still feel pain in the afterlife. That would suck.

As her eyes adjusted to the darkness and her heart went from a gallop to a trot, she saw that she was in a strange room. Sitting up and looking around, she realised the bed wasn't her bed. This wasn't her house. This wasn't her room.

She was about to scream when she glanced next to her and saw Andrew fast asleep.

Wait.

"Where the hell am I?" she whispered.

Buttons was at his spot by her feet. He groaned, one ear perking up.

Think, Kate, think. Where were you before you fell asleep?

Thinking was easier said than done. Her brain was dimmer and foggier than a London alley at night. Her mouth was so dry, her tongue stuck to her palate. Andrew had placed a bottle of water beside the bed. She struggled to unscrew the cap and took a big swig.

Her stomach gurgled as reality hit her. She was in the lake house in Maine. Moonlight trickled through the blinds covering the sliding doors.

The lake house.

It was no wonder she was confused. Sometimes she woke up in her own house disoriented and afraid.

But wait. She was in a bed. Hadn't she fallen asleep on the couch, watching TV with Andrew?

She turned on her phone's flashlight, waving it around the room. Now that she could remember settling into the house, she recalled the layout of the living room. It appeared Andrew had rearranged everything so the bedroom furniture was now in the living room, the bed facing the back porch and lake beyond.

And he'd done all of it while she slept, including changing her into pyjamas and putting her to bed.

Sometimes it frightened her how deeply she slept. It was no wonder she worried about dying in her sleep, considering how close she must be to the diaphanous veil every time she drifted off.

She leaned over and tenderly kissed the top of Andrew's bare shoulder. After driving all day and unloading the car, he'd still found the strength to rearrange the house so she had a prime spot to rest her head every day and night.

It was easy to feel guilty for trapping him in this existence of pain and doctors and illness. This was no picnic for either of them, but at least he was strong and healthy enough to walk away and start a new, normal life. She'd said just that to him on more than one occasion, offering him a heartfelt 'get out of jail free' card to run and never look back.

Of course, he'd told her every time she was crazy and the offer was this side of insulting. He'd say, "Wait until you see what I saddle you with someday. You'll wish you were the one who left," always with a wry smile.

He must really love her, because it wasn't like he was in it for the sex. She couldn't remember the last time she'd been well enough to even contemplate getting busy under the sheets. She'd have to rectify that this summer. Maybe some good, clean air would do what doctors and meds couldn't.

Doctors and meds and treatments and surgeries.

It was a toss-up whether they were doing more harm than good.

This summer, she'd find a way to feel somewhat better. Not just for her, but for Andrew.

And yes, she'd drink those miserable shakes by the gallon if Andrew insisted.

After everything, she owed that to him.

Buttons shifted on the bed, lying across her lower legs, his warmth making her sleepy.

At least there were no bad feels and lurking shadows up here. The cottage would replace them with good feels. She'd left her shadow peeper in Jersey.

Her stomach fluttered and she felt a stabbing pain in her back where Dr. K had stuck her over a month ago. The flare of agony was fleeting, but it left her strangely hot and weak.

It's like walking through a ghost, she thought, wiping a fresh sheen of sweat from her forehead. *Only ghosts are cold. This is…different. What the hell is it now? I can't even catch a break for a full day?* Shivering yet burning under the covers, she closed her eyes and rode it out, doing her best to ignore the unsettling sensation of being on a rotating dish in a microwave.

CHAPTER SEVEN

Andrew woke up a little after nine. He was normally an early riser, even on weekends, but yesterday had worn him out. He'd wanted to surprise Kate by setting everything up for her in the living room so the lake and evergreens were her constant companions.

She stirred a little when he got out of bed. Her skin was fish-belly pale, her hair plastered to her head. She had a nice fever going. He woke her to take something for the fever. She swallowed the pills and went right back out. He wondered if she was even aware she was in the bed in the living room.

He drank his coffee on the back porch, no shoes on his feet, the morning chill numbing his toes. An older couple of kayakers drifted past the dock – *his dock*, for the summer at least – and waved when they spotted him.

"You don't see that in Jersey."

It was way too cold to swim. The realtor told him the lake warmed up right around July Fourth. That was less than a month away.

He changed, attached the leash to Buttons' collar, and headed out for a walk. Normally, he'd go for one of his punishing runs on Sunday mornings, but he was feeling far too content and relaxed to abuse himself.

Stacks of firewood were lined up under a small lean-to on the side of the house. He checked it to see if any was dry enough for a fire tonight. He was no campfire expert, but the wood seemed fireplace ready.

"Come on, buddy."

Buttons went on a sniffing spree, the old dog's dulled senses coming alive in the new environment. This was definitely going to be a slow amble. The beagle stopped every two feet to sniff around a tree or bush, lifting his leg to mark his territory They followed a slender trail, going deeper into the woods and away from the lake.

Was this a walking/hiking trail or a game trail? Andrew wasn't sure. He knew that one was made by people and the other by passing animals.

He did know he didn't want to run into a moose. They were big and nasty and best avoided. He'd watched enough nature shows to understand that if he saw a moose, it was in his interest of self-preservation to skedaddle. He was pretty sure Buttons would have no problem beating a hasty retreat as well. The dog was no hero. Or maybe he was just old and wise.

Andrew recalled that their nearest neighbour was supposed to be a couple of acres away. Of course, he had no concept of how big an acre was, not in any real-world sense, but he assumed it was a lot.

Round Lake wasn't large, nor was it deep, which discouraged most boaters and Jet Ski lunatics. The realtor said there were only about twenty houses built on the perimeter of Round Lake, the owners preferring the privacy and quiet that you didn't find at most other lakes in the region.

He'd expected it to be too quiet to sleep last night, but the woods around the house had been alive with a riot of sound. The crickets up here must be the size of poodles for all the racket they made.

In the half hour he and Buttons were outside, they never strayed far from the house. Andrew could always spot at least a corner of it through the trees. Buttons barked, his signal that he was done, and padded back home.

"You sure you don't want to explore a little further?"

Buttons barked again.

Nope.

A half hour away from Kate must have seemed an eternity to him. Andrew was happy they'd found the skinny, shivering dog in the shelter. Leaving Kate to go to work always left him feeling uneasy. At least with Buttons, he knew she had a companion to keep her company. Now if he could only teach the beagle to text or make a phone call in case of an emergency.

Kate was still asleep, but at least her fever felt like it had gone down. Buttons claimed his spot beside the bed. Andrew went out back, saw the fire pit had been cleaned and was ready to go. By the time he was done here, he'd be a true fire starter.

There was a mossy path leading to the small dock. The dock was just big enough for the two of them to lay a towel down and get some sun. There was also a tiny sandy beach, perfect for a few people to lie out. He saw that the sand extended into the water. At least they wouldn't have to squish their way through the dark, damp muck that made up most lake beds. The realtor had told him it was the last of the sandy beaches in Round Lake. Importing sand had been banned a couple years after this one was laid down. Something about harming the ecosystem. He was just happy they had one.

Maybe I should find a place to rent a canoe or kayak, he thought. He loved being out on the water. Maybe some hard rowing would replace his pounding sprints. His back and legs would sure appreciate it.

He took off his shoes, rolled up his jeans, and sat on the end of the dock, feet dangling in the water. It wasn't as cold as he thought it would be. A wandering breeze rippled the lake's surface. There wasn't another soul he could see on or near the lake. The old kayakers were probably home now, having their coffee and reading the paper. They'd make plans to go into town for a late lunch, maybe take a flyer for one of the bean suppers that were advertised everywhere. After an afternoon nap, they'd have a light supper, watch some TV, and turn in early so they could be up for an early morning jaunt around the lake.

It sounded corny and routine and boring…and it was everything Andrew hoped for his and Kate's future. Even something as mundane as that seemed so out of reach.

He walked to the reedy shoreline, found some rocks, and tried his hand at skipping them. It was like riding a bike, something he also had never been very good at. After sinking a dozen stones, he went back to the house, found the Robert Parker book he'd brought, and read on the porch, looking through the glass doors at Kate every ten pages to see if she was awake.

He should have been relaxed, but the ever-present knot of tension between his shoulder blades was still there, hunching his shoulders up and making him grind his teeth.

It's not like flicking a switch, he thought. *It's gonna take time to unclench your ass.*

As soon as the clock struck high noon, he went to the fridge and cracked open a beer.

When all else failed, a few beers would get him to exhale.

*　　*　　*

Kate saw the note on Andrew's pillow.

> *Hey sleepy crippy – I went out to get some groceries. Be back soon. Love you. —A*

A champagne flute filled with her favourite candy had been placed next to her mason jar of pills.

There was also a cold can of Pepsi ensconced in a maroon Koozie with a MAINE – THE WAY LIFE SHOULD BE logo on it. She wondered when he'd picked that up. Probably at that rest stop and visitor centre back on I-95. Kate had opted to stay in the car with Buttons, the both of them woken from their naps when Andrew pulled in.

As she tried to sit up, her head spun and she settled back down. Under the can of Pepsi was another note, this one on a square Post-it. *By the way, you have a nice fever going. Take two more pills at 2:00.*

She had a fever?

Of course she did.

Why allow her a day to walk around the house, check out the lake, and absorb her surroundings? No, it was much better to be stuck inside… again, just like always.

She balled her fists in frustration, the tension bringing bolts of pain to her wrists, elbows, and shoulders.

"I can't even get mad without hurting myself, But-But."

The dog whined at the sound of her voice. He looked up at her from the floor, tongue lolling from his mouth.

"But you know what, I'm not going to let it get me down. I mean, look at that view."

Sunlight speckled the lake, the tops of the trees swaying in the wind.

A huge bird – was that an eagle? – circled overhead. No, it couldn't be an eagle. She had just enough strength to get up and open one of the doors a crack. The cool, fresh air that wafted in was as delicious as fresh cinnamon toast.

She couldn't find the remote to the TV, or her tablet, so she had to get out of her comfort zone and enjoy the silence. A leaf skittered into the cottage. Buttons gave it a sniff before settling back down. By one o'clock, she started to feel achy and hot. Andrew was right. She washed down the Tylenol, along with her Percocet and two nerve blockers.

Once her fever went back down, she'd take a much-needed shower. Maybe she could even surprise Andrew by wearing that lacy red bra he loved. She might not be able to do much, but she could work out some way to thank him. The first of many thank-yous to come, she hoped.

If she wanted them to have some fun, she needed to get better.

An image of her smiling brother popped into her head. He was sitting on the porch, looking in at her, the door open and letting in the fresh, piney air.

"Hey sis. If you can't meditate here, I mean really meditate, you might as well give it up altogether."

He was right. Or more accurately, *she* was right. Kate couldn't imagine more peaceful surroundings.

It can't hurt to meditate on this fever taking a hike.

She fluffed her pillows at her back, sat up, put her hands on her lap, closed her eyes, and took three deep, cleansing breaths. Focusing on her breathing, she felt the tension in various parts of her body and released it. Her mind was a jumble of thoughts, her excitement at being here filling her with lists of things she wanted to see and do. It took a long time to quiet her mind, always dragging herself back to her breath.

Unaware of the passage of time, her mind eventually quieted down.

It was only then that she thought of the word *fever*. It was lit up in bright lights against the black backdrop of her still mind: FEVER.

Breathing in. Breathing out.

FEVER.

With each inhalation, she repeated the word.

With each exhalation, she pictured another piece being broken off the lighted FEVER in her imagination. Bit by bit, breath by breath, the word crumbled.

It was down to its last remnants when Kate felt an intense pain in the small of her back. A spark whooshed into an inferno, the flames engulfing first her back, then her entire body.

What remained of FEVER shattered into tiny projectiles.

Kate gasped.

A ball of flame roared in her core. The pain was excruciating.

No!

Her eyes flew open, fingers knotted, her back arched to the point of breaking.

Opening her mouth to scream, she slipped down the pillows, her body covered in acrid sweat.

In an instant, the fireball rocketed from her body, leaving her cold and empty and shivering. It took her several minutes to catch her breath, using the sheet to wipe her face.

"What the hell was that?" she said to Buttons. The beagle opened one eye but offered no advice. He rarely did.

Kate massaged her back. It felt as if she'd been kicked, and then burned with a lit cigar. She couldn't stop shivering.

She wrapped the sheet around her and padded to the bathroom to find the thermometer. She took her temperature while she sat on the closed toilet, the soreness and cold dissipating. After two minutes, she checked the thermometer and smiled.

"It worked."

Her temp was back to normal.

And now she was exhausted.

She went back to bed in the living room, thinking she'd take a quick nap before Andrew came home. She couldn't wait to tell him her fever had broken.

That was one powerful meditation, she thought, snuggling in the bed. *I won't tell him that part. He thinks it's all a crock of shit anyway. He'll say it was the Tylenol he left for me. Who knows, maybe he's right. But what the hell was up with that session?*

When the door opened, startling her, she was shocked to see that it was almost four o'clock.

"Hey, you're awake," Andrew said, both hands filled with multiple plastic bags.

"I guess I am." She didn't remember falling asleep, but it also didn't feel like she'd just been lying there thinking about what had happened for three hours. She was more tired now than she'd been before she'd come back to bed.

"Sorry it took so long. I did a little exploring, not that there's a whole lot to see. Then I found this used bookstore and got really lost. Hold on."

Her knees popped when she got up to walk to the kitchen. She had to settle into a chair before she fell.

He came back with a paper sack full of books and put it on the counter in front of her.

"Guess how much these cost?"

She looked inside the bag, turning the mildewed paperback books over to look at the covers. Most of them were old crime novels, with some science fiction and courtroom dramas thrown in.

"I don't know," she said. "Twenty bucks?"

"Try five."

"But there have to be at least thirty books in here."

He started unpacking the bags, canned food, bread, and boxes of macaroni filling the counter space.

"I know. You buy the bag for five bucks and fill it to the brim. I have enough reading material to keep me going for the summer."

Kate sneezed again and again until she was gasping for air.

"I think they're a little too mouldy for my taste," she said.

He took the bag away from her and stowed it in the bedroom. "I'll have to find a place that sells new books for you, my fragile flower. Boy, I remember when I used to brag to my friends that I was dating this super low-maintenance chick."

"Oh? And what do you say to them now?"

He chuckled as he filled the fridge with soda, water, and beer. "That I was deceived, tricked, and bamboozled."

She smiled. "That's right. Boys are suckers."

Once he had everything put away, he ushered her back to the bed and found the remote that had been underneath Buttons.

"I really need to take a shower," she said, feeling her body melt into the bed.

"You'll live without one for now. I can tell you're beat."

He poured himself a scotch and added some ice. "I got you a nice protein shake."

"I'd rather that than scotch. At least it doesn't burn."

"There are good burns and bad burns." He held up the glass, tinkling the ice. "This is a good burn."

Andrew sat in the chair opposite her, taking a long sip.

"I didn't realise how much I needed this until we got here," he said.

"A drink? You could have one anytime."

"No, all of this. And some scotch. I still feel all bunched up inside, but I know it's going to loosen up soon. It's weird how you don't know how wired you are until you take a step back."

Kate was surprised to hear him talking so candidly. Normally he told her he was just fine, no worries, everything was under control. Not that she believed a word of it. He'd have to be a robot or sociopath not to be deeply affected by their situation.

His words hurt her more than she could tell him. It was her turn to put on a happy, brave face. She knew he didn't mean to make her feel bad, but she did just the same. She was the reason he was so balled up and stressed, and there was nothing she could do to make it better.

"Well, you have three whole months to unstress yourself," she said.

He raised an eyebrow. "Unstress?"

Kate blushed. "Isn't that what people say?"

"Not any people I know." His laughter was infectious.

She drank her shake and he had two more scotches. They played cards until eight, when her eyes started to roll up in her head. At one point she came to with cards still in her hand. Andrew's attention was on the TV.

There would be no red bra tonight. She couldn't even cut through the fog in her brain to tell him she loved him.

*   *   *

Kate dreamed she was in the woods, rocks and sticks pressing into her palms and knees as she crawled through the brush. She sniffed the air, filling herself with pine and mould smells. Something skittered to her left, dashing under the carpet of dead leaves.

Lashing out, she reached under the crunchy leaves, casting them aside, blowing the tiny critter's house down. A chipmunk cowered before her, trembling, furry chest pulsing with fevered breaths.

"I'm sorry, little guy. I didn't mean to scare you."

She wanted to offer him some food, but she had no pockets to check. She was startled to realise she was naked. A cool breeze danced across the lake, raising goose bumps on her exposed flesh.

The chipmunk chittered.

Then hissed.

Chipmunks didn't hiss.

Its eyes swirled, the blackness dissipating until they were red as fresh blood. Kate cringed at the sound of its tiny bones popping. A yellowed ridge of bone ripped through the fur on its back, twisting it into an L shape. The chipmunk's jaw opened wide, wider, until it was large enough to swallow her fist.

Oh, but she wouldn't put her hand near that thing. Its gums separated as rows of jagged teeth pushed through like shards of glacial ice.

"Get the fuck away from me," the woodland creature spat.

Kate scampered back, a sharp rock slicing her knee.

"You don't belong here," the chipmunk said, its body continuing to morph, distorting into a mass of bone and teeth, its crimson eyes holding her in place, even though she desperately wanted to run. "Don't belong here. Don't belong anywhere. Don't belongdon'tbelongdon'tbelongdon'tbelong."

"Stop it!" she screamed.

The eyes disappeared, replaced by shields of cancerous bone.

Kate opened her mouth to scream.

The bone chipmunk sprang from the mouldy earth and leaped down her throat.

She flipped onto her back, hands wrapped around her throat, squeezing, trying to stop it from plummeting into her stomach.

Echoing in her mouth as she struggled was the chipmunk's chant…

"Don'tbelongdon'tbelongdon'tbelong."

*   *   *

Kate woke up with a sore throat, tangled up in the sheets. Somehow, Andrew had slept through her flailing about. The scotch must have helped.

She looked around the cottage for the shadow. Beyond the glare of the television, everything was in utter darkness.

There was no shadow. Or none she could perceive.

What had her all worked up wasn't exactly the bad feels.

Her hands were cold, but she felt hot inside, as if someone had poured molten lead down her throat. It was just like the other night.

First, she checked her fentanyl patch to make sure it hadn't split and she wasn't on the verge of overdosing, her brain and body misfiring as the drug raced through her system.

It was fine.

It was also time for her nerve blocker. A Percocet wouldn't be a bad idea either. Anything to put her back to sleep, where she'd stop feeling like this.

She just hoped that evil chipmunk wasn't waiting for her.

CHAPTER EIGHT

Things settled into a pleasant routine by the end of their first week. Kate was still fighting off the strange 'microwave' feelings. Andrew thought she had a cold, but she knew better. The fever stopped, but it left her weak as a kitten. She'd had some wicked nightmares, waking him up several times in a panic, but that was to be expected. The meds made her imagine things that would send Stephen King running for his blankie and momma's breast. Add a fever to the mix and there was no way she could rest easy. This only added to her frustration, because, as naive as it sounded, she'd really thought things would be different up here.

In a way, they were. The bad feels had been replaced by the microwave feels, and her shadow visitor had morphed into nightmares about the wildlife outside the cottage. Just lovely.

* * *

Kate had yet to venture outside. Andrew really wanted to get her down to the dock so they could do some proper lake gazing. The temperature had almost hit eighty a couple of days, warming the lake up a notch.

"Maybe we could light the old fire pit tonight," Andrew said, slipping on his running shoes.

Kate was on her side, clutching Mooshy to her chest.

"Maybe. That would be nice."

The tone of her response told him it wasn't going to happen. He deflated a bit but hid it from her. He'd been dying to light a fire outside and just stare into the flames for an hour, the heat keeping the night's chill at bay. So far, the pit remained cold and empty.

"Where are you going?" she said. Her eyes were closed, her hair tied in a ponytail.

"Out for a quick run. You need anything? Pine cones? Crusty leaves? A gnarly walking stick?"

"If you see a spare, healthy body lying around, I'll take it."

"If I see any bodies in the woods, I'm hauling ass the other way and calling the cops."

"You know what I'd really like?" she said.

"What's that?"

"To get my butt well enough for us to lie on our little beach and watch a sunrise."

"Sounds romantic."

Her eyes closed and she pulled the sheet around her. "Mmmm. Very. Like something out of a Cary Grant movie."

"Pretty soon the mornings will be warm enough to do just that."

"I hope so. For some reason, that's what I want more than anything."

He was pretty sure she'd fallen back to sleep by the time he walked out the door. Taking a long, deep breath, he jumped off the short porch and hit the trail, his quick, steady stomping scattering any small critters in his way.

Before embarking on the path in the woods, he ran down to the dock to say hello to the lake. As usual at this time of day, it was empty and quiet. He pictured him and Kate down here, beach towels laid out next to one another, holding hands while they watch the sun come up. He had never been accused of being a hopeless romantic, but he really looked forward to doing that with Kate. After what she'd been through, she deserved anything she asked for, especially something so pure and simple.

Turning to head to the trail, he tripped on a thick tree branch. Looking to see what had nearly sent him sprawling, he noticed the gash of fresh, exposed wood in the centre of the branch. He crouched down to get a better look at it.

Looks like something took a bite out of it, he mused. His fingers traced the grooves of what looked like teeth marks around the outer rim of the oval of fresh, pale wood. *What the hell kind of animal likes to eat trees?*

He picked up the branch to get a closer look.

Now he wasn't so sure those were bite marks. It was probably just the way the bark had fallen off. What did he know about the great outdoors anyway?

No matter. He tossed the branch in the lake and went running.

*   *   *

Kate heard the door close and started to cry.

God, she wanted to be able to be out there with him. Her frustration mounted more and more every day. It was bad enough that the treatment flashbacks were making her feel like the Hulk boiling under a shower of gamma rays. Her growing irritation with her broken, truly fucked and out-of-luck body was burning her twice as much.

It wasn't easy only being able to watch people slip by on their boats, listen to the warble of the loons at night, or see Andrew on the porch, reading one of his mouldy books, a beer on the short table beside him, almost as confined to the house as she was. He said he loved every minute of it, this learning how to relax. How long would that initial fascination last?

Even Buttons was sitting by the glass doors, looking wistfully outside.

She felt like a failure, and that was one thing she had never told anyone. She'd failed herself, her husband, her family, her friends, everyone. What good was she to them when she could offer them nothing but a litany of complaints? How could she be a part of their lives when she couldn't even partake of her own?

Crying in her beer – or protein shake – was repugnant to her, but some days, she just couldn't help it. Especially days when she was too weak to keep the bad feels at bay.

Thwack!

Kate flinched at the sound of something smacking against the glass doors. Andrew had pulled the blinds open so she could see the lake. Leaning forward on the bed, she couldn't see anything on the porch that could have hit the door. But she did spot a tiny crack in the glass.

"I wonder if a bird tried to fly in here," she said to Buttons. "I hope he's okay."

The porch was bathed in late morning sun. Andrew's book was on the arm of the chair, its cover wagging in the breeze.

Swinging her legs off the bed, she said, "Hey, But-But, come help your momma."

Buttons trotted to her side, nuzzling her leg. As soon as she stood up, he backed away, giving her space. It was amazing how he knew not to trip up his unsteady master.

Kate was several steps away from the door when her knee popped, the entire joint dislocating. Bright sparks exploded in her brain and she cried out, tipping, falling. Her spine burst into a great wall of flame. The blast of heat baked her core, flashing to her extremities.

Did the house just rumble, or was that her nerves jittering from the instant explosion of agony?

Buttons barked as she toppled to the floor. Her hip hit the hardwood with a dull thump, also dislocating. She was powerless to stop the tide of tears as she rocked on her good hip, blubbering incoherently.

Gritting her teeth, she willed the pain to leave her body, but it was no use. Until she could get her joints back in place, there was only white-hot, incoherent agony.

And anger.

The anger made her spine go nuclear, the burning intensifying until she worried that something far more horrible, perhaps irreversible, had occurred from the fall.

She tried to call for Andrew, but his name was mangled by the ragged scream that shredded her throat.

*   *   *

It was his first run since they'd settled into the cottage. Andrew had started out with his usual reckless abandon, but after nearly catching his feet among the countless raised roots and forest detritus, he'd settled into a much calmer, steadier pace. The last thing he wanted to do was break a leg out here in the middle of nowhere. He'd left the cottage behind twenty minutes ago. He knew they had neighbours, distant as they were, but somehow the path kept him well clear of the nearby homes. He'd heard that Mainers were private people, and this path was proof of it.

Forget worrying about breaking his leg. He just hoped he could find his way back. At one point, the path had veered to a three-pronged fork. He forgot which fork would take him back.

If all else fails, just follow your nose and find the lake. You can stick to the shore until you come across the cottage.

Round Lake had a very definitive odour, a hard-to-classify tang that smelled like childhood summers, fishing with his grandfather, and clear yet simple possibilities. He'd been soaking it up like a bloodhound on the back porch every day while he read. Three books, short police procedurals, were already on his 'done' pile. Sitting outside with an afternoon cocktail and a book, glancing over at the lake between chapters, had become his favourite pastime.

Well, his only pastime to this point.

Running around a wide tree that looked to have been standing since the dawn of the Industrial Revolution, Andrew headed for home. His legs were getting tired, not used to this style of running. The ground was uneven and hard on his ankles.

He needed to run today because he was starting to feel discouraged. Yes, he'd finally felt the stick fall from his ass two days earlier. He'd stopped thinking about work, stopped checking his phone for messages. But Kate was still bedridden, unable to even join him on the porch.

What really bothered him was the source of his frustration. Was it her illness, or Kate herself?

Sometimes, he just wanted her to slough off what was squashing her down at the moment and *fucking live*. Use whatever incredible willpower had pushed her through a dozen surgeries, a year on life support, and that night she'd been given last rites by a sombre Nigerian priest, to get up and *just do something*. How hard would it be to walk out that door and sit on a dock? She knew he'd carry her if she needed, and she still didn't try.

What the hell was the sense of all this fighting if she wouldn't even try to really, really live? Being trapped in a house with old movies and an old dog wasn't life. At best, it was purgatory.

Stop it!

Andrew felt sick to his stomach even thinking it. So he ran, picking up his pace, pushing those forbidden thoughts away, deep into the dark corners of his subconscious where they belonged. It was evil to even contemplate such things. This wasn't her fault. Why blame her? She was the victim, not him.

Shut...the fuck...up!

He didn't see the tree branch that had been bent into a mini St. Louis Arch over the narrow path until it was too late.

CHAPTER NINE

The one good thing about pain was that it could only hit certain heights before your nerves started to dull and your brain shut down. Kate was still very conscious, but had started to lose feeling on her left side. Her spine had cooled down (which was an odd thing to say, even to herself), but attempting to move was out of the question.

The door banged open and Andrew came rushing inside.

"Oh my God!"

Andrew knelt over her, sporting a considerable knot on his forehead, blood smeared up into his hairline. "What happened?"

"I fell," she said, trying to hide any sarcasm in her voice. Buttons had his face inches from her own, his hot dog-breath washing over her.

"Here, let me help you up."

Her husband slipped one hand under her thighs and the other under the middle of her back. When he tried to lift her, she screamed.

"Stop! Stop!" she begged. "No. Don't pick me up."

He licked his lips, eyes anxious. "You have to tell me what's wrong."

"My knee. It came out," she said tightly. Her body had gone so stiff, it felt as if all of her bones were going to splinter. "My hip too."

Andrew muttered something, bouncing on the balls of his feet, unsure what to do.

"Help me put them back in," she said, dreading it as much as every fibre of her being craved it.

"Okay. Okay. Where should I start?"

Unfortunately for Andrew, he'd become as adept as any orthopedist at slipping joints back into place. It was fortunate for Kate, because she didn't have to run to a hospital every time it happened. Without Andrew, she'd be in emergency rooms daily.

After hundreds of subluxations, the tendons and ligaments around her knees, shoulders, hips, and wrists had become soft and pliant. It meant bones could and did pop out at will with the slightest provocation. It also meant they could go back in just as easily – though never painlessly – with some assistance.

"I don't know," Kate said. "They both hurt like hell."

So did her chest, but there was nothing he could do about that. Kate willed her heart to settle down, but it wasn't listening. It rarely did.

"Which knee, which hip?" he asked, his tone high and nervous. This was the first time both had ever gone out simultaneously.

"The left," she said, fresh tears springing.

His warm hands circled her ankle and calf.

"I'm going to pull slowly, and we'll see which one goes back home first."

She almost laughed at the thought of her kneecap being a little piggy crying wee-wee-wee all the way to its damaged home. Almost.

The instant Andrew pulled on her leg, fresh waves of agony pierced her nerves from head to toe. She must have cried out, because he stopped and said, "Okay, I'll try something else."

"No," she urged him. "Just do it. Keep going, no matter what."

Andrew wiped the sweat from his brow and took her leg again. This time, he tilted her leg slightly to the left as he pulled down. She felt her kneecap shift.

It was hard not to let fly with every curse in her arsenal, but she had to keep quiet or risk Andrew stopping again. No matter the pain, he couldn't stop until they were both in.

Every pore on Kate's body leaked hot, pungent perspiration. It was the smell of pain and fear. It made Buttons back away, though his dark, sombre eyes never left her.

Something clicked in her hip. It was still dislocated, but not as bad as it had been seconds before. Her kneecap continued to slide.

Kate bit her tongue, copper flooding her mouth. She reached up and grabbed Andrew's sleeve, twisting it in a knot. He looked pale, on the verge of panic.

"Don't...stop," she said. "Almost...almost there."

Her knee slipped into place with a wet *thunk*. There was no relief, because her hip still had a ways to go. Her hips were always the hardest. She'd been known to projectile vomit a time or two when a hip had been jammed back in place, pain and adrenaline and endorphins pooling in her core.

"Just the hip to go, honey," she said, her voice tremulous in her ears.

He moved both hands to her thigh. She grabbed the leg of the chair and tried to help him by pulling her body back.

Her hip bone made a sickening *crack* that startled them both. This time, she couldn't hold back her scream. At the exact same time, an animal outside the cottage let loose with a high-pitched screech. The strange cry stopped her own peal of agony. Andrew looked at her as if to say, *I don't have a freaking clue.*

There was no time to worry about the animal.

Kate thought her hip bone had broken.

But the sudden dulling of the searing agony told her the cursed joint was back where it belonged. With so little cushion left, the bone-on-bone shift was like tectonic plates in a dry boogie.

"It's in!" she cried, the back of her head thumping on the floor. Buttons leaned forward and licked her face, knowing it was time to celebrate.

"You want me to get you back in bed?"

She waved him off. "No. I just need to lie here for a while."

Andrew put a pillow behind her head, patted her with a wet washcloth, and gave her a painkiller and anti-inflammatory, his movements fast and sure.

"You feeling better?"

"Just give me five minutes and we can go dancing."

A small, nervous smile played on his face as he sat on the floor beside her. "You don't dance on a good day."

She laid one hand on his leg, the other on Buttons, the most important men in her life. "That doesn't mean I can't start."

"We have video from our wedding that says otherwise."

"Hey, at least I tried."

He smoothed her damp hair from her forehead.

"What happened to you?" she said, fingers grazing the bump on his head.

"I wasn't watching where I was running. Someone must have bent this tree over the path. I smacked right into it, like a dummy."

"Does it hurt?"

"Not as much as your knee and hip."

"Go put ice on it. You're starting to look like a unicorn."

Andrew kissed the tip of her nose and took the washcloth he'd used to cool her down and filled it with ice from the freezer. He slumped into a chair, holding it to his forehead.

"If someone peeked inside right now, they'd call the cops, thinking we just beat each other up," Kate said.

"We'd be fine. We have Buttons as a witness."

The beagle wagged his tail at the sound of his name.

"That is true." She finally felt good enough to sit up, resting her back against the chair. "I thought a bird had flown into the doors, and I wanted to check on it. Serves me right for trying to be nice."

Andrew checked the porch and said, "If it was a bird, it's flown off since then."

She didn't mention the house quaking a bit. Kate was pretty sure she'd been the one shaking, not the cottage.

He palmed the side of her face and she tilted into him, loving how strong he felt. "Feeling any better?"

"Anything is better than the way I was before you came in."

Without warning, he scooped Kate up, slid the door open with his foot, and settled her into an Adirondack chair on the porch. Buttons came out with them, poking his nose between the slats of the railing.

"Thirsty?"

"Very," she replied, her hip and knee throbbing.

He went inside and returned with a can of Pepsi for her and a beer for himself. She looked at the beer, then back at the clock on the kitchen wall.

"It's noon somewhere," he said, popping the tab.

"Times like this, I wish I drank beer."

They tapped cans. "Hey, you have stuff in that mason jar way better than beer."

"Yeah, but not as much fun."

They looked across the lake, watching a loon dive under the water, searching for fish, popping up fifty yards away. Andrew held her hand.

Despite what had just happened and her being sick in a new way she hadn't been before, Kate should have been happy.

Should have.

Something just wasn't right, and she didn't have the heart to rain on Andrew's parade.

★   ★   ★

"Look what I got."

Andrew dropped a plastic bag on the bed. It was an unseasonably hot day for late June. Kate had made a note to look for a fan somewhere in the house. She was watching a Myrna Loy movie, drifting in and out.

"What is it?" she said, taking a loop of cable out of the bag.

"It's a USB cable. A long one. Since the Wi-Fi in this place is so iffy, we're going to have to go old school for your tablet. I found it three towns over at this little computer repair shop. The guy who ran it smelled straight up like onions. You owe me for this one."

It had been hard living without her tablet. As much as she hated to admit it, the device was her window to the world. Andrew had been looking for a way to reconnect her with it for days now. It was a small miracle that the cottage even had a router. They'd both been expecting to be cast back into the Stone Age. At least the spotty Wi-Fi sometimes made it possible to get enough bars to make a phone call, not that they'd needed to call anyone yet.

"Oh yay," she said, clapping. She'd been feeling a little better today. No microwave feels or bad feels. Or shadows or rumbling houses. "Can you set it up?"

"Nah. I just got it to tease you."

"Jerk."

"Cripple."

She tossed a pillow at him.

"I will after lunch. I also found a place that makes pizza."

He went to the kitchen, bags rustling.

"I thought you said there weren't any pizza parlors around," she said.

"There aren't. However, there is a deli that has a pizza oven. It actually looks good."

Andrew handed her a paper plate with a slice of greasy pizza. Her stomach rumbled.

She took a bite and smiled.

"I know it's not Milano's," he said, tucking into his own messy slice.

"It'll do. What the heck kind of pizza is that?" she said, pointing at his plate.

"They call it a Big Mac pizza. It has all the ingredients of a Big Mac, minus the sesame seed bun. They went a little extreme on the Thousand Island dressing."

"It looks disgusting."

"Wanna try?"

"Ew, get that away from me."

A dollop of hot dressing spilled on Mooshy. Kate gave him the stink eye.

"Looks like I'm doing some laundry today," Andrew said. "What are you watching?"

She fed Buttons a corner of crust. "It's an old comedy with Myrna Loy and William Powell."

"Sometimes I feel like I married an old lady. I've never even heard of these people."

"You did marry an old lady, or at least a young woman with an old lady's body. Alfalfa from *The Little Rascals* is in it too."

"Now him I know."

"Watch it with me and expand your horizons."

They watched the movie together, and then Andrew washed the pillowcase and some clothes. Afterward, she slowly and carefully walked with him to the dock, her virgin trip to the back forty, as Andrew called it.

She asked him to take her shoes off so she could feel the sand between her toes. Maybe tomorrow could be the day they sat here and watched the sunrise.

A cluster of bulging white clouds approached lazily from the other side of the lake. The sun was strong but the humidity low, especially with the wind blowing off the cool lake. On the dock, Kate dipped a bare foot in the water and quickly pulled it back.

"Check to see how many fish are in there," she said.

Andrew laughed. "In the whole lake?"

"No, just around the dock."

"You can see for yourself. The water's clear as can be."

She peered over the side and saw the sandy bottom. Most lakes she knew were murky because the bottom was a bed of black, mouldy vegetation.

This was even nicer than the beach at Cape May. There were a few large stones and a couple of small branches, but no fish.

"It's not like there's anything big enough down there to eat you," Andrew said. He took a pull from his beer, one hand playing with her hair.

"Fish skeeve me. I just don't want them brushing up against me."

"I'm pretty sure they're going to do everything in their power to avoid that. We are a little bit bigger and more intimidating than them."

Kate leaned into his chest. Her knee and hip still ached, but the pain had dulled. Andrew had found a sturdy stick during one of his runs and had presented it to her as a cane. She used it sparingly around the house – just when he was looking.

"It's really beautiful out here," she said.

A seaplane circled overhead before disappearing south.

"More so now that you're out here to enjoy it with me. I vote we eat on the deck tonight. It should be plenty warm enough."

"I second that. I'm not that hungry, though."

He rubbed her shoulder. "You rarely are. How about grilled cheese sandwiches?"

"Half."

"Okay, half."

They stayed down at the lake for an hour, the water calm and empty save for a family of ducks bobbing about and a goose that flapped overhead.

Leaning on Andrew's arm as they walked back up to the house, she said, "I'm serious, I never want to leave here."

"I feel the same way. I'm getting very used to a life of leisure."

"It's kinda like the lake belongs to us and us alone," Kate said. "It should make me feel lonely, but I don't."

As he helped her onto the bed – she was tired and in need of a nap so they could have fun outside later – he said, "I'd love to see where everyone lives. That path I take to run steers clear of any sign of civilization. It's as if it was cut intentionally to avoid people."

Kate's head melted into the soft folds of her Mooshy. "I'm sure it was. Take Buttons for company."

The beagle was asleep on a chair, not even flinching when they'd opened the sliding door.

"He can't keep up with me."

"Neither can I, but you keep me around."

He covered her with a sheet and turned the television on. "That's because I'm locked in with you. I don't have time, money, or energy for another wife. But getting another dog is a simple trip to the animal shelter."

She slapped his hand. "So you're saying if you had time, money, or energy, you'd be ready for wife number two?"

"I'd need all three, and I don't see that happening in my lifetime." He smiled as he kissed her forehead, nose, and lips. "Now, take a nice long nap. I'll get the fire pit ready for tonight."

Kate settled in, the fresh air making her drowsy in a good way, not the usual pull of sleep because she was hurt or sick. She looked forward to dinner on the patio and sitting beside the fire. Andrew seemed so excited when he talked about it, like a kid going over plans for his birthday.

She drifted off to the soundtrack of a Western on the television, the brass section blaring away as the cavalry came storming in.

*　　*　　*

"Care to stay a while?"

The bear beside her bed smiled, its coal-black eyes crusted yellow.

Kate hurriedly gathered the sheet and blanket to her chest, pushing away from the wild creature in her room.

"You don't belong here," she said. "Shoo! Get out of my house."

"But you invited me in," the bear said, resting his muzzle on the bed, his dripping nose nudging her side.

"I...I did no such thing."

The bear yawned, but she knew it was simply to show off its massive teeth. The roof of its mouth was black as cancer, its gums raw and red. It said, "Then why am I here?"

Kate turned to wake up Andrew. His side of the bed was empty.

"He's out there," the bear said, craning its massive head toward the front door. "Running. Always running. Running from you."

"I don't want you here."

"Yes, you do."

"You're a liar and you're not wanted. Besides, we're not allowed to have bears in the cottage."

When the bear sighed, the gust of hot breath blew the covers off the bed. Kate looked down to see she was naked. But something was wrong. The body below her neck was not her body. It was the rail-thin body of someone in the cold, deathly grip of anorexia. Every bone was visible, her skin stretched so taut, she could hear it creak like leather.

The sight of her heart made her forget the bear.

It beat against her thin flesh, outside her rib cage. As she grew more and more frightened, it pulsed faster and faster, her skin protesting, miniscule tears rupturing across her breastbone.

"What did you do to me?" she asked the bear.

It stood on its hind legs, its head scraping against the ceiling.

When it reached its paw toward her, she watched a black claw extend, resting above her fluttering heart.

"I can do this," the bear said.

The claw punctured her heart, but there was no blood. Just a loud, wet hiss, like when Andrew bled the radiators at the start of winter.

*   *   *

Kate scrambled in the bed, gasping for air. The first breath refused to come. Panic seized her spine. When she thought her lungs had closed for good, they miraculously unlocked. She drew in a great, desperate breath. She sat up with her hand at her throat, but it took her several minutes to settle down.

There'd been a dream. A weird, bad feels kind of dream.

For the life of her, she couldn't remember it.

Maybe that was a good thing.

Just another nightmare log for the dream fire. She could burn down the world with her nightmares.

Goddamn meds, she thought.

It was dark outside.

Andrew was asleep beside her, Buttons by her feet.

Her tablet was on its cradle with a note: "*All ready for your browsing pleasure. Surf responsibly.*"

Swiping the screen, she checked the time. Half past two.

She'd slept through everything.

Again.

Her cheeks burned, hands balled into tight, painful fists. Kate cried silently, angry and disgusted. When she settled down, she propped herself up on the pillows and meditated. She fixed her intention on her nightmares, giving them the form of a black, pulsating blob. She meditated on plucking pieces of the blob away, bit by bit, until it was gone.

The problem was, she was so tired, she kept falling asleep, the blob morphing into strange visions. When she realised she'd dozed off, she tried again, except the blob was bigger. It went like that for a while, until her last attempt at meditation revealed half of the cottage missing, the wood blown outward and splintered.

The nightmare blob was gone, rampaging into the impenetrably dark woods.

CHAPTER TEN

Andrew's bladder ushered him out of bed. The floor was cold on his bare feet, waking him even more. Kate was snoring, but he noticed that the channel had been changed, meaning she'd been up at some point in the night.

He went to the bathroom and stubbed his toe on the cabinet. Cursing under his breath, he emptied his bladder. He had six or seven beers' worth in there, so it took a while. His mouth was tacky. Slipping his head under the faucet, he lapped up cold water just like Buttons would, before heading back to the living room.

There was still an hour until sunrise.

He was wide awake. There was no sense trying to go back to sleep. He'd just toss and turn and wake Kate up.

So what? the voice he did his best to avoid piped up. *You waited hours for her to get up from her nap. She blew you off for dinner. Might as well get her ass up for a very early breakfast.*

He'd had the perfect day all lined up, and once again, it had been trashed. The blame was on him for expecting anything different. Kate never failed to disappoint.

"Shut up, asshole," he whispered in the dark. Great, now he was talking back to himself *out loud*! Could it be that all of the distraction of work and chores back home had kept him from finally losing his mind?

"Nope," he groaned, getting up and changing into sweatpants and a thick sweatshirt.

He might as well run the voice buzzing in his head into submission.

Buttons poked his head up when he opened the door. Andrew hoped he wouldn't bark and wake Kate up. The lazy beagle just went back to sleep.

The sharp air hit his lungs as if it were made of icicles. He bent over coughing, adjusting to the cold, pine-scented air.

Nature's gonna kill me.

The woods were dark. Too dark for him to navigate safely. It took some adjusting, living where there were no streetlights.

He'd have to stick to the semipaved driveway leading to the main road. It wasn't all that long, but if he went up and back a few times, it should be enough to clear his head.

Andrew's feet crunched on the gravel, kicking up rocks in his wake. He didn't bother warming up. Hauling ass as if a starter's pistol had suddenly gone off, Andrew powered down the centre of the drive, guided by the meagre moonglow.

Yes, he'd been disappointed when Kate hadn't woken up. That was normal. Who wouldn't be?

That hour at the dock had knocked her out. It saddened him to see Kate so fragile. When they were dating, she'd loved all kinds of outdoor stuff like rock climbing and taking their bikes on cross-country trails. They'd push their bodies to the limit, come home sweaty, muscles jittering, and make love before and after a shower. The pre-shower sex was always more passionate, wild and reckless. Post-shower sex was tender and loving and would usually knock them out for hours.

Now, sitting on a dock in the sun was enough to wipe her out.

It made him frustrated, sure, but it also made him mad as hell. He was mad at nature for creating pointless diseases that ruined and took lives. He'd been so mad at God, he hadn't been in a church for almost ten years. He used to go every Sunday, even though Kate thought it was silly. Church gave him comfort, made him feel whole.

He realised it was all bullshit. There was no silver lining to Kate's struggles. This was not making her a better person, or them a stronger, more enlightened couple. They were tired and ground to dust on their best days. How the fuck could that be the plan of a Creator they were supposed to look at as their father?

Maybe God was an abusive addict, like so many dads he'd come across. That would explain a hell of a lot.

So yes, Andrew was angry, and he'd argue his right to be so with anyone.

And some days, like today, even if he didn't want to face it, he was angry at Kate. *With* Kate. *For* Kate.

She could have woken up for dinner, bro. Face it, she's addicted to misery. You showed her a good time, and she went back to her addiction. That's what you get for trying.

"Fuck...you!"

Speaking of addiction, you and she both know those pills got her, man. They got her in that death grip.

"If she didn't have them...she'd be out of her mind with pain."

That's what she keeps telling you. The least she could have done was skipped one or two last night so she'd be up with you.

"I said shut the fuck up."

He spit into the dark woods, over and over, as if banishing the forbidden thoughts into the pitch.

Andrew turned when he hit the access road and headed back toward the house, running harder, faster, breath exploding from his lungs in short, hot bursts.

He could stop and take his aggressions out on a tree. Maybe find a branch and whip the holy hell out of the elm by the car. Not that the tree deserved such abuse, but he was pretty sure it wouldn't feel a thing.

And if it was true that all of nature was an extension of God, all the better.

Better take one to my head, he thought. *Maybe if I hit myself hard enough, that'll make it stop for good.*

Or maybe the streak of Catholicism in him wasn't quite as dead as he'd thought, seeking penance for his sinful introspection. Would flagellation be the same if his flesh didn't feel the bite of the branch?

He sprinted up and down the drive two more times, the voice in his head chattering nonstop, making him angrier.

After grabbing the thickest branch he could find in the soft pink glow of sunrise, he ran to the nearest tree and hammered it again and again. He thought of batting practise in high school, nights in cages, swinging at buckets of balls until his hips and shoulders worked in synchronized unity.

Klock! Klock! Klock!

Andrew's fevered pummeling echoed in the still morning air.

It took the branch snapping in half to make him stop. He stumbled backward into the car, flinging the wood into the brush. His legs and arms had gone soft.

Part of him wanted to cry, but he'd never, ever let it have its way. Not over this. He was not going to cry over his own twisted, uncontrolled thoughts. They weren't worth shedding one tear over.

Trying to catch his breath, Andrew turned and leaned his forehead against the car's cool roof.

He felt wasted, obliterated.

But at least the forbidden thoughts were gone.

Klock! Klock! Klock!

Those weren't echoes.

Andrew stiffened.

What the hell was that?

"Great, now you've woken up the neighbours," Andrew said, looking about the shadowy woods.

Something heavy crashed in the distance. It sounded like a medium-size tree falling down.

Or a bull moose making its way toward the house.

He did not want to be out here, exposed, if a moose was near. His legs shook, but he forced them to move. He felt relieved once he was back inside the cottage.

For some reason, he locked the door before sliding onto the floor, ear pressed against the wood, listening.

★   ★   ★

"I am so sorry," Kate said.

"It's no biggie. Buttons and I grabbed some beers and watched porn all night."

Andrew was on the back porch, the door open wide, early summer air filtering into the cottage.

"I didn't realise I was that tired."

Buttons was in bed with her. He'd found a way to get under the covers next to her, his head on the corner of her pillow. He was awake, listening in on their conversation. She rubbed his velvety ear between her thumb and index finger.

"That's what good mountain air will do to you," Andrew said. He had three of his mouldy paperbacks on the table. One of the first Elvis Cole detective novels by Robert Crais was at the top.

"There aren't any mountains."

With a sweep of his hand, he said, "Oh, they're not far. You don't have to see them to enjoy the benefits."

When she lay back against the pillows, Buttons lifted his head and plopped it on her chest.

"You're such a loon," she said.

"By the way, your dog's taste in porn?" Andrew gave an exaggerated shiver. "You might want to rethink having him in bed with you. That's one subversive beagle."

"And you're a dope to boot."

"But a dope who loves you."

"I'm sure that's what you think you do," Kate said, hiding her grin under the sheet.

"Now I take it back, little crip."

"That's more like it."

He made her a lunch of toast with peanut butter and half a protein shake. She gagged on the shake but didn't voice a complaint. Not after standing him up the night before.

"I think I'm ready to do some hiking," she said, moving out of bed and into the soft chair by the doors.

"That moose should be gone by now." Andrew washed their plates and glasses, a towel tossed over one shoulder.

"What moose?"

"I heard a big sucker in the woods by the house this morning. Remind me not to go out for pre-dawn runs."

With all of the time Kate had spent looking out the doors at the woods and lake, she was surprised she hadn't seen a moose yet. Supposedly they were everywhere out here in the boonies. "Did you see it?"

"Hell no. I hauled ass into the house."

"You didn't at least look out the window?"

A curious look came over his face. "No, I didn't. I was so beat up from my run, I just kinda collapsed onto the floor."

"I'm sure that won't be the last moose to come snooping around. I found this moose tour online last night over in New Hampshire. It's just thirty minutes away. They take tour buses to popular moose spots at night."

"That sounds cool." Andrew stretched, his shirt riding up his stomach. She noticed the bit of a pot belly that had grown since their arrival. There were a growing number of empty beer cans in the recycling bin. Maybe she was weird, but she liked the extra meat on her husband. It made her excited, which then led to wondering when her body would allow her to enjoy him properly. Right now, the thought of even the gentlest sex was exhausting.

As much as she wanted to be intimate with Andrew, the pain and pills and constant battering of her will made it almost impossible to get in the mood. A part of her, of the old, vibrant Kate, cried out to tear off their clothes and fuse skin to skin.

"Why don't you take me out for a drive?" she said. It paled in comparison to reliving their days as newlyweds in their dream house, but it was all she could muster at the moment.

He perked up at the suggestion. "You want a tour of the town?"

"Yes. And I want to see what's playing at the drive-in."

"Your wish is, like, the thing I gotta do," he said, taking on a wise-guy voice.

Andrew helped her into the shower, and dried her hair with the blow dryer while she sat on the closed toilet lid. It felt amazing to be clean. Daily showers were hard when she ran fevers or didn't have the energy to get up. Showers were as wonderful as they were tiring.

"I think Buttons needs to check things out too," she said as Andrew took her arm, walking her to the front door.

"You're right. He told me last night he needs more beer anyway. I'll let him pick it out."

Andrew stopped the second they stepped onto the modest porch, staring at the car.

"What is it?" she asked, gripping him by the elbow with both hands.

"Looks like I got away just in time. That moose must have rubbed his antlers or his dirty butt all over the car."

It was then she noticed the streaks of mud on the driver's-side window, hood and roof. Smeared swirls of dirt and grime coated that side of the car.

"That must have been one dirty moose," she said, snickering.

"Good thing they have one of those self car washes in town. Jesus, what a mess."

Buttons sniffed the mud, barked once, tail wagging, and hopped into the back.

As Andrew walked Kate to the passenger side, she took special note of one of the mud smears on the car's hood.

It almost looked like a handprint.

*   *   *

Kate and Buttons stayed in the car while Andrew cleaned it, the powerful hose splattering the caked mud into the rainbowed mist. When he was done, he jogged to a vending machine and came back with a Christmas tree air freshener. He gave it to her.

"Pine scent," she said. "Really? Everything already smells like pine up here."

"Save it for when we go back home. It'll remind us of Maine."

He turned onto the two-lane Main Street, headed toward the quaint town. "I wish I'd grown up here," she said, staring out the window.

They passed an old Victorian house that had a for sale sign on the front lawn. The bay window of the house was filled with very old porcelain dolls.

"Now that's creepy," Kate said. Andrew slowed the car to take a better look.

"Not the best sales ploy," Andrew said. "Unless there's a market for people looking for homes filled with sinister-looking dolls."

Several had red, white, and blue dresses, holding tattered flags in hands missing fingers.

"At least they're patriotic," Kate joked.

"Salute them bye-bye."

Down the block was an ice cream shop advertising the best curly fries in town. Kate wondered how many other places were making and selling curly fries in Bridge Mills. Were curly fries *a thing* in New England? She knew lobster was huge up here. Too bad she refused to eat something that looked like a cockroach from hell.

They drove by a local bank she'd never heard of, a hairdresser's shop with a barber right next door (*I'll bet it's the same owner*, she thought), a thrift shop, a market simply and aptly called Food Mart, a six-booth diner, a deli, and several antique shops. Kate was not one for old stuff. She'd watched enough paranormal shows to worry that the wares in those places were haunted.

It sounded silly, but it was how she felt. Andrew made fun of her all the time. He believed in ghosts about as much as she believed in the fairy tale of alien abductions.

"You want ice cream?" Andrew said, pulling into the second ice cream shop on Main Street.

"They sure love their ice cream up here."

"This one has a Grape-Nuts flavour," he said, getting out and running around to get her door. Buttons scampered over her lap.

"Why would anyone want Grape-Nuts ice cream?" Kate said.

"Because it's good. And it gives the illusion of health."

They were the only ones at the shop. A disinterested teen girl wearing a Korn tour hat took their order. Kate had double chocolate chip.

They sat at a picnic bench, watching the town do its thing, which wasn't much of a thing at all. Only a few cars idled by, with fewer people walking about.

"You wanna try?" he said, angling his cone toward her.

She took a small lick. "It's like licking sandpaper. When did you ever have Grape-Nuts ice cream?"

"A couple of times when I came in for food and stuff. You don't like?"

She crinkled her nose. "Yuck."

"Well, no one will ever make you a food critic. If it's not one of your five surviving taste buds, it's yuck."

She dabbed his face with her ice cream, leaving a stray chocolate chip in the corner of his nose. "And sometimes, it's just plain old yuck."

After they finished, he asked if she wanted to go back to the cottage.

"I'd rather stay in the car if you feel like driving around. At least I'll be able to see the sights."

"If you love trees, this will be a sightseeing orgy of delight."

It didn't take long to leave the town of Bridge Mills in the rearview mirror. Andrew was right: evergreen trees were everywhere. There were scores of others, but Kate was no tree expert. She knew about dogwoods because her grandparents had one in their yard. And pussy willows because they'd sung about them in first grade. That was the extent of her education as an arborist.

She kept the window down, her face turned toward the incoming breeze.

"I'm sleepy," she said when they turned onto a logging road. A huge truck laden with freshly cut timber rumbled ahead of them. "If I take a nap, will you keep driving?"

"Sure." He reached across and caressed her cheek. Andrew loved to drive. She always wondered why he hadn't become a long-distance trucker. He loved that show about the crazy guys who drove big rigs across the ice. Back when they used to travel, he'd worn his trucker hat when he drove, pulling into sketchy trucker stops to get what he called *the true flavour of America*.

Instead, Andrew had settled for an office job he didn't like very much. She often wondered if he did it because of her. After all, office jobs had medical benefits.

Cut the guilt crap, she thought. *Just enjoy the day.*

At the moment, Andrew was happy, and that was all that mattered.

She opened her pill bottle. She stared at the little white pill in her palm. Then she made a fist and closed her eyes. It could wait until they got home. First, a little nap.

When she awoke a short time later with stabbing pains in her chest, struggling to breathe, the idyllic day was officially over. Once again, her spine had turned into the Great Wall of Fire. She flailed in her seat, bolting upright, her eyes bulging out of her head, left hand over the centre of her chest while her right pulled her collar from her throat.

I need air! I need air!

Andrew found a hospital on his GPS, flooring the accelerator, holding her hand and trying to be calm, but failing, while telling her to just breathe.

CHAPTER ELEVEN

The miracle of chest pains was that you never had to waste a single moment in the ER waiting room. Poor Andrew had been stuck filling out forms and going through the litany of her ailments, surgeries, and medications. Luckily, they had created a document that they stored on their phones for emergencies like this, so he didn't have to try to do it all from memory.

Kate was kept overnight in a hospital that would pass for a walk-in clinic back home. Andrew slept in the car with Buttons. They were forty miles from the cottage and he didn't want to leave her. He looked terrible when he came to her room that morning.

"How's Buttons?"

"I fed him a sandwich from the vending machine. He Dutch-ovened me in the car all night. It's safe to say he's feeling more chipper than I am at the moment." He sat on the edge of the bed and took her hands. "More importantly, how are you feeling?"

She was hooked up to a heart monitor, a couple of IVs dripping fluids in her veins. The beeping of the monitor had kept her up most of the night, despite her exhaustion. Hospitals were not a place to get rest. Kate squeezed his hand. "I'm much better."

"No more pains?"

"Not since last night."

She was shocked to learn she hadn't had a fever when she was admitted. The rippling flames in her back made it feel like she'd been thrown into a bonfire. Thankfully, that had calmed down as much as her heart.

He poured her a cup of water. "You want a drink?"

She looked at one of the IV bags. "I'm so full of fluids, I have to pee every fifteen minutes."

"What did the doctor say?"

Dr. Pranjeep had taken care of her in the ER, stopping in at six in the morning to check in on her before he headed out for the day. He'd been extremely kind and thorough. He'd never met someone with Ehlers-Danlos syndrome before, like most doctors, and had a lot of questions once they realised she was not having a heart attack. To his credit, he didn't try to move and dislocate her joints. Kate couldn't count the number of curious doctors who'd sent her into spasms of agony just to satisfy their inquisitiveness. It was one of a host of reasons she didn't care much for the profession, despite needing them to keep her alive.

Being sick was one thing. Being sick and a guinea pig was another, and she was done being a guinea pig and a curiosity.

"He's pretty sure they'll release me early this afternoon. I didn't have a heart attack."

Andrew paled. "Wait. They thought you had a heart attack?"

She patted her pillow so he could lie next to her. They faced one another, noses touching. "When people come in with massive chest pains, yes, that's what they assume. They didn't know me from Eve. Turned out to be exactly what I knew it to be, my good friend lupus. My numbers are really high, and we both know what that does to me."

He kissed the top of her nose. "If you want to know the truth, I thought you were having a heart attack too."

Smiling, she said, "I assumed from the way you drove. Thank God there weren't any cops around."

"They would have had to follow me here."

"Well, the good news is I'm fine. Or my version of fine. They gave me some stuff to calm the swelling, and I have no idea what the nurse slipped me before, but I'm beat."

Andrew ran his fingers through her hair, giving her goose bumps, especially when he grazed the back of her ear. "It has nothing to do with the meds." He gestured to the window. "The sun is out, so all good vampires need to sleep."

"Ha-ha."

It had long been a joke between them that she didn't have lupus but had, in fact, been bitten by a vampire bat. Ever since her illnesses, her internal clock had gone haywire. True, she did tend to sleep more during the day than at night, often wandering around the house in the dark. No matter what she did to change that, forcing herself to stay up when the sun was out, she went right back to the same old pattern.

Maybe Andrew was right. It would be nice for some super vampire powers to kick in.

"I should probably drink some blood to activate them," she said.

Andrew looked at her as if she'd just spoken a foreign language. "What the heck was that?"

She covered her mouth, giggling, "Just thinking out loud."

"I don't even want to know what goes on in your head."

"No, you don't." Patting his chest, she said, "Now, go outside and get Buttons out of that car. Find a place to eat. I'll call you when they come in with my discharge papers, and you can whisk me the hell out of here."

"You sure? I could stay. I'll find a kid or someone to watch Buttons."

"Oh yeah, just offer our dog to any kid that comes along. Get out of here and watch our baby."

He reluctantly got out of the bed.

"Promise you'll call me the second they tell you you're free."

"Cross my heart."

Andrew chuckled. "Pick a more reliable organ."

Kate shrugged. "Sorry, I ain't got one. You'll just have to trust my poor, enlarged, overtaxed ticker."

She hated to see him go, wiping away a few silent tears. But it was going to get too hot for Buttons to stay in the car, and Andrew looked like he needed some sustenance before he ended up in the bed next to her.

After turning up the television to drown out the beeps and chirps of the heart monitor, Kate turned onto her side, wishing she had her Mooshy to cuddle.

*　　*　　*

Kate was groggy but happy to leave the hospital. They were handed a slew of written instructions about following up with her doctor, who was only three hundred miles away. The most important thing was rest.

"That's one thing I do well," Kate said from the wheelchair.

The drive back to the cottage was quiet, Andrew expecting her to say her chest hurt at any moment. Last night had scared him more than he'd let on. It might not have been so bad back home, but up in Maine, where they didn't know the local hospitals or if there even was one where they'd been at that moment, it was terrifying.

He wanted to carry her inside but she refused.

"I'm not that bad...yet," she said.

Getting her comfortable in bed, he asked, "You want me to shut the blinds so you can get some sleep?" The bags that were always under her eyes were nearly purple.

"I'll feel better with them open."

Buttons had his front paws on the bed, sniffing her face.

"I think someone's glad to have you home," Andrew said. "You need something to drink? Something to eat?"

She waved him off. "Just sleep."

He swiped his book from the kitchen table – an old Elmore Leonard gangster novel – and got a beer from the fridge. "I'll be in my spot right outside so I can keep an eye on you."

Holding out her arms to him, she said, "No, stay in here with me until I fall asleep. Please?"

He snuggled beside her with her head on his chest.

"I had a great time yesterday," she said, yawning.

"Me too. And, bonus, I got to drive the car over ninety miles an hour."

"That you did."

He turned on the TV, knowing he was at the right channel when he came upon a black-and-white movie. She loved those black-and-white flicks. It was too bad their lives were muddled in varying shades of grey.

Kate was asleep in minutes, her tiny snores signaling it was safe for him to head to the porch.

The late afternoon sun was obscured by fast-moving clouds. It looked and smelled like rain was heading their way.

Andrew read and drank, trying to calm himself down. For a moment yesterday, he'd thought this was it. The look of pain and terror on her face had nearly sent his heart into palpitations.

I guess I thought by coming up here, we'd escape this shit.

He crushed the can of PBR and went inside for another.

It was foolish to think they could outrun the microscopic killers that lived inside Kate. The rational part of him knew that was impossible.

But was it too much to ask for a tiny break? They only had these three months. After this, he'd be back to the grind and Kate would be on the doctor merry-go-round. There'd be plenty of time for health scares and hospitals.

He'd thought…no, hoped Maine would be different.

Nothing ever was.

Grey clouds scudded overhead, the lake seeming dark and foreboding. The temperature dipped while he drank in frustration. He stared at the dock. The day Kate sat beside him felt as if it had happened years ago.

He'd been so mad at her.

And then he'd worried himself sick that he was going to lose her.

Maybe I should start going back to the shrink when I get home. Jesus, I'm fucked up.

He tried to read but couldn't concentrate. His arms felt heavy, the stress morphed by the beer into exhaustion.

The patter of a light drizzle woke him up, the soggy book on the porch floor, his fifth beer empty. Slicking his hair back, he grabbed the ruined book and went inside.

Andrew ate a tuna fish sandwich and finished the remaining PBR, watching a comedy because he really needed a laugh. All the while, he stole glances at Kate, Buttons sitting vigil beside her, wondering, if they couldn't have some peace here, was there any hope for a normal future?

*   *   *

"Hrrrffff!"

Kate went from dead sleep to wired instantly.

"Buttons, sshhh!" she whispered. It was nighttime, the TV on low, Andrew sleeping beside her. He'd been through the ringer as much as she had and didn't need Buttons waking him up.

The beagle was curled up on the chair, fast asleep.

Must be chasing cats in his sleep.

The steady trickle of rain plinked on the cottage roof. By the flickering light of the TV, she could see water pooled on the back deck. Andrew had left the kitchen windows open a crack, letting in the petrichor of the passing storm.

Petrichor.

It was one of Kate's favourite words.

Kate had discovered it during one of her online searches, looking for the perfect way to describe the smell of rain. Little did she know, someone had already invented the strange-sounding word that fully encapsulated the scent of rain soaking into the earth. She liked to impress people with it whenever it rained.

"*Hoffff.*"

She sat up straighter in bed, glancing at Buttons. That hadn't sounded like him. In fact, it sounded as if it were coming from the small window over the kitchen sink.

What is that?

It was a cross between an old man clearing his throat and an animal grunt.

Andrew had said he heard a moose outside one morning. The evidence had been all over their car.

Kate muted the TV, ear cocked toward the window, listening.

Below that window was the front porch. If something was that close that she could hear it from across the cottage, that meant it had to be standing on the porch. Tensing, she waited for the creak of the old boards as whatever was out there moved about.

Stillness.

Her heart *whu-thump*ed, but there was no pain.

Stop getting yourself all wound up. It's just an animal.

The porch was too narrow for a moose, or so she thought, but there was plenty of room for a bear. Were there bears out here? What about some big cat, like a mountain lion? She made a mental note to do some research on the local wildlife.

Not that it was helping her now.

If there *was* an animal, Buttons would be awake. He might be old and lazy, but he loved giving at least a half-hearted growl to critters great and small.

The beagle hadn't moved a muscle.

One hand barely touching Andrew's shoulder, she held her breath, searching for a sign that they had an intruder on their porch.

Scritch.

It was almost as if someone had picked at the wooden windowsill with the edge of their nail. Or the sound of wood settling. Or her imagination.

It could have been anything, really.

Bad feels, she thought.

She'd woken up with a case of the bad feels, and she was bound to misinterpret any strange sounds. Plus, there was that new sedative the doctor had given her as a parting gift. It could be messing with her.

It didn't matter.

The bad feels were the bad feels. She lay silently, not daring to so much as shift her weight, eyes darting around the cottage. It was a small relief not to see a shadow peeking at her from some dark corner.

Of course the shadow's not in here. That's because it's out there.

After waiting five long minutes, Kate felt she could get out of bed and check. Shadow or bear or whatever, she refused to lie there worrying, her ignorance making things worse.

She knelt beside Buttons and woke him up. He licked her face, his eyes sleepy.

"Let's go see the bear, But-But."

He followed her into the kitchen.

Before looking out the window, she steeled herself.

Was this really what she needed right now? Her chest was beginning to tighten, but not so much as to alarm her. But if she did peek out that window and come face-to-face with a bear, how would it feel then?

A bear is better than what you think is around when you get the bad feels. And at least there's a whole house between you and it.

Regardless, being this tense, if she went into some kind of cardiac arrest, how was Andrew supposed to get her past the bear and into the car?

Buttons.

He could scout it out for her.

"Up you go."

It was a struggle, lifting him onto the counter. The old dog was far heavier than he looked. Her wrists and elbows were not happy with her plan, the abused joints aching terribly.

"What's outside?" she said, pointing at the window. Buttons sniffed her hand, his nose pressing against the screen. He simply panted, as usual, tail wagging.

I bet he wants to go outside now, you dummy.

Edging him aside, Kate inched closer to the window.

She sagged with relief when she saw nothing but the trees and their car. The porch was mercifully empty.

Feeling sorry for putting Buttons in harm's way – though in retrospect, there was no harm in it at all – she gave him a few treats and let him come up into the bed with her and get under the covers.

"Did I dream that something was out there?" she whispered in his flaccid ear.

First I think there are shadow men in my house, now phantom bears outside the cottage. I don't even know what to believe.

She remained awake until first light, wondering what she could trust about herself anymore.

CHAPTER TWELVE

"Look for scat on the porch when you leave."

Andrew stared at Kate with his shirt in his hand. He was getting ready for a nice run, just enough to flush the niggling hangover from his system.

"Scat?"

"I thought I heard a bear on the front porch last night."

"So, you want me to look for bear scat."

She looked up from her tablet. "It's not like you'll really have to look. If it's there, you'll see it right away. I've been reading up on bears, and Maine only has black bears."

Tugging his shirt over his head, Andrew said, "Is that good or bad? I always forget which one is worse."

"Good. Brown bears are nasty, bordering on evil. They eat their own cubs, for crying out loud. No, black bears are smaller, shyer, and tamer."

He had to take his sneaker from Buttons, the old beagle resting his head on it. Back in the day, the dog would have chewed it to tatters, slobbering all over it.

"So I don't need to worry about bears when I'm running around."

"Not the black bears. There hasn't been a fatal bear attack in Maine since the 1800s. If something's going to hurt you, it's either a moose or a tick."

Andrew took a cold water from the fridge, swallowing down his vitamin. "Well, I'm not going to run screaming from a tick."

Kate looked at him seriously. "You should. They have Lyme disease up here now. Go put your big boy pants on and cover those hairy legs. We can't afford to have us both sick."

Rather than argue with her, he quickly changed, knowing he was going to be wearing shorts no matter what once things heated up. They'd been through so much, he figure he was owed not coming down with Lyme disease.

"How do I look?" He did a little dance by the bed. She pinched his ass.

"Sexy. Before you go, can you please get me a drink so I can take my meds like a good patient?"

He gave her a soda, her morning beverage of choice, and half a protein shake. She made a face at the shake. With one look, he got her to drink the shake with grim acceptance. Kate looked awful today, despite her chipper mood. It was obvious she'd been up all night. He'd felt her tossing and turning and had almost asked her to turn down the TV a few times.

She unscrewed the cap of her mason jar and fished out a handful of pills.

"Scat patrol is in effect," he said, opening the door.

Thankfully, the porch was poop-free.

"No bear, hon," he said. "Or at least if there was a bear, he or she didn't have to go potty."

He paused when he saw four gouge marks on the wooden railing. Had they always been there? He'd spent very little time on the front porch. They looked like claw marks, or they could just as easily have been saw marks if someone had tried to do a little handiwork, using the porch rail to rest something against.

Maybe it was Kate's bear. It didn't have to poop, but it left its mark anyway.

Since there was no way for him to be sure, he was not going to tell her and get her all riled up. Knowing Kate, she'd make him stop running for fear of him being mauled or eaten by Gentle Ben. Andrew needed to run more than Kate needed to wonder if there were actually bears around.

"You feel better now?" he said to her.

"Yes. Much. Run free. I'll see you when you get back."

"You have no choice."

No driveway for him today. The sun was out and the path was calling. It was easier going now, muscle memory helping him to avoid some of the worst dips and obstacles in his way.

In fact, he was able to do his usual reckless-abandon scurry, knees rising so high with each stride, they nearly touched his pumping elbows. It only took a few minutes to get his heart rate in full gallop, sweat starting to pour down the sides of his face and small of his back. The ground was still wet, squishing under his feet, mud flecking his pants.

For once, he was running out of habit rather than anger. The beer last night had really helped to settle him down, dulling all the sharp edges that usually troubled his days and nights.

His shoulder nearly clipped a tree. Spinning away, he stepped into a clump of wiry brush. It took some effort to extricate his legs.

Good thing Kate made me wear long pants.

Lungs burning, he checked his watch. He'd been running for twenty minutes.

A hole had ripped open in his pants leg. No matter, he was done running for the day. His head felt clearer, the aches in his bones replaced by the hum of endorphins.

Walking back to the cottage, he decided he'd stop in town and get more beer. Maybe he'd even buy a bottle of Dewar's. His dad had been a connoisseur of cheap whisky. Andrew always thought his father looked so grown up, so cool, so in command of all he surveyed, when he had a highball glass of the amber whisky in his hand. He'd tried Dewar's himself several times but couldn't get over the burn. His own tastes were on the pricier, smoother side.

Now was as good a time as any to try again. He wasn't feeling very much in command of all he surveyed, so a little mimicking of his father couldn't hurt.

In a rare break in the trees, he was afforded a narrow view of the lake. It was still as glass today. The old kayakers were nowhere to be seen. Sometimes up here, he felt like the only person left in the world. The silence and solitude could be overwhelming. Right now, they felt just about right.

A kayak. I really should rent one from that place by the barbershop. It'll be nice to get on the water. I'm pretty sure I can strap it to the roof of the car.

Lost in his thoughts, he didn't notice the little homemade shelter until his wrist banged off one of the support branches.

"What the heck is this?"

He wasn't sure how he'd missed it when he first set out on his run. Not far from the cottage, someone had gathered fallen branches and fashioned them into a kind of makeshift tepee, the triangular opening revealing a bed of leaves and pine needles inside. Heavily leafed branches were woven between the supports to keep out the elements.

Crouching down, he found a stick and poked around the floor of the tepee. It smelled damp and mossy with a hint of old shit.

It smelled wretched, but an animal hadn't done this.

Andrew looked above the structure and could just see the cottage through the low-hanging branches.

Is someone spying on us?

It could be kids. It looked wide enough inside to fit up to three preteens comfortably. He hadn't seen a single soul in these woods since they settled in weeks ago. If there were kids about, he would have at least heard them. The cottage and surrounding acreage were so quiet, so far removed from the regular white noise of civilization, he joked to Kate they could hear a frog fart from a hundred yards away.

And when was this little hut away from home erected? He was pretty sure it hadn't been here a couple of days ago. On the other hand, when he ran, he noticed very little. Maybe the people who'd rented the cabin before them had creative kids who watched a lot of *Survivor*.

It could be some homeless person erecting a shelter to keep out of the storm. There didn't seem to be anything left behind, no sign of food or scraps of clothing. Maybe whoever built it had just needed a place to stay for a night and had moved on.

It could be a bunch of things, and all of them bugged Andrew. Maybe if it were deeper in the woods, he wouldn't mind. But he could see their cottage from here. Why build it so close, unless it was to keep an eye on them?

"You're being paranoid."

Yes, he was, and he wasn't going to make any apologies for it. Where he and Kate had grown up, paranoia kept you safe.

He jogged to the house, saw that Kate was asleep.

"C'mere, Buttons," he whispered. The beagle came scampering over. Andrew clipped the leash to his collar and walked him to the tepee. "Go on, sniff around."

Buttons went inside, tail wagging to beat the band, sneezing when the pine needles tickled his snout.

Now, the old dog was no bloodhound, but he was a dog just the same with a heightened sense of smell. Maybe he could at least point in the direction where their mystery neighbour had gone.

Inside the tepee, Buttons flopped onto the ground.

"What are you doing? No sleeping on the job. Get up."

His tail thumped the bedding, eyes drooping closed.

"Look, I know you're old as the hills, but you can't be that tired. Show me who made this."

He tugged on the leash, but Buttons wasn't having it. The beagle closed his rheumy eyes.

"You're unbelievable."

Could dogs sniff out intent? If someone had been crouching in there with a head full of bad things, would Buttons – or any dog, for that matter – pick up on it, even if they were long gone? Was there a scent to evil? Would it linger like a ghost, an emotional spectre?

How have you jumped all the way to evil?

On the plus side, Buttons didn't seem the least bit concerned.

"Okay, let's go inside and see Mommy."

That got Buttons on his paws. Mommy was everything to him. Even a comfy tepee couldn't keep him away from her for long.

By the time Andrew showered and changed and ran to town for some supplies, all thoughts of the sinister tepee had vanished. He had no idea why it had disquieted him so much. The more he thought about it, the more ridiculous he felt, until it was best to forget about it.

The Dewar's and ice-cold craft beer chasers helped.

*　　*　　*

"You want to come out on the porch?"

Andrew's tongue had gone soft at the end, *porch* coming out *porsh*. They'd watched a Coen brothers movie together, laughing at the madcap absurdity, a bowl of popcorn on the bed between them. It was a hot day. He'd found a standing fan in the supply closet and set it to oscillate, keeping it by the open sliding door to suck in the fresh air.

She didn't know how many beers he'd had, but sometime during the middle of the movie, he'd poured himself a glass of Dewar's whisky over ice. When she'd looked at the drink with surprise, he'd said, "You always said I'm a carbon copy of my dad."

"I thought you hate Dewar's."

"Hate is a strong word. I'm beginning to see why my dad liked it so much."

It was actually good to see him relaxing. He needed it before he popped a blood vessel in his brain. Or someone in the face.

She laughed when he winced with each sip, forcing the alcohol down.

"Smooth," he said, winking.

The sun was just starting to set when the credits rolled.

"I'll be happy to go to the *porsh*," she said.

"Here, let me help you."

"I've got it. Why don't you get me a soda?"

She shuffled past the fan and clicked it off. This was the time of day for the loons to come out, and she didn't want to miss them. There was something so tranquilizing about their musical ululations. When dusk came, she'd mute the television and listen for them, falling asleep for her nighttime nap to their lullaby cries.

Andrew came out with a soda for her and a refill on his whisky.

"So, you're becoming a hardcore drinker now, huh?"

He tipped his glass. "I'm at least going to give it the old college try." He looked wary, as if he expected her to scold him like a child.

"Well, you've earned it." She kissed his cheek. A loon sang out and she smiled.

It was frustrating for her to feel so shaky inside when all she'd done was walk a few feet onto the porch. Her hips and shoulders ached especially badly today. What made her pause before sitting down was that microwave feeling that ran up her spine. It came and went in seconds.

What the fuck? I hate my body.

Normally, this was when she'd vocalise how much she wished she could trade her body in for a new one. Andrew would sympathize with her, or if it had been a bad day, give a small nod, absorbing her litany of complaints and desire to do some body snatching. It wasn't until they'd come up here and gotten away from her comfort zone of discomfort that she realised how often she complained. People around them marvelled at how she took each setback like a marine, but only Andrew knew the real Kate and how she was handling her illness.

Bravery was appropriate for her public face. But when she was home and it was just them, she felt she could collapse, gripe, cry, bitch, bemoan, and lash out.

Not to say that he took it all with aplomb. They'd had some hellacious fights over the years. Andrew never said he was tired of hearing her complain. When they fought, it was usually over something stupid like *Where's the remote?* or *I told you not to do the dishes; the doctor said you have to stay off your feet.*

Andrew was a passionate man, just as she was a passionate woman, and their squabbles could be the stuff of legend.

They argued less and less with each passing year. For some people, it was a sign of maturity, of coming into their own as calm, rational adults. Kate worried that her illness was bleeding them of that sometimes wild, reckless fervor. And Lord knew, passion of any kind had been in short supply the past few years.

"Look, there he is," Kate said, leaning forward and pointing at the loon in the middle of the lake.

"Wonder where his mate is."

"Can't be far."

Another warble, and up popped the loon's mate from under the water. Seconds later, they both dove, searching for dinner.

"You know," Andrew said, "we're turning into that old couple from *On Golden Pond*. Should I be alarmed?"

"Only if you don't wanna suck some face."

He kissed her softly, the sharp bite of whisky deliciously rolling around her tongue. When they'd met, Kate had been the one to drink Andrew and all their friends under the table.

Ever since she'd been put on the cocktail of meds, she'd had to give up drinking altogether. A good, stiff drink was one of many things she missed.

Kissing Andrew now reminded her just how much.

What I wouldn't give for a nice cocktail and a roll in the hay. Scratch that, a few cocktails and a good old-fashioned fucking.

A sharp pain in her hip from leaning to kiss Andrew forced her to break away.

"You kiss way better than Henry Fonda," she said.

Andrew sat back and took a sip of whisky, his face puckering for a moment. "You're good, but that Kate Hepburn, she was a hellcat. It's why I married you. She got me addicted to Kates."

She punched his arm, hurting her fingers in the process. "You wish Katharine Hepburn gave you the time of day. Even when she was in *On Golden Pond*."

"Hell yeah. She'd be my sugar momma and we'd be rich. This would be our permanent home, not just a summer escape."

Kate was about to punch him again when something snapped in the woods. It sounded like someone taking a dry branch and cracking it over their knee.

It was loud, and it was close.

Andrew jumped up, spilling his drink on the crotch of his shorts.

"Whoa," Kate said, giggling at his soaked crotch. "You're too drunk to be wound so tight."

He ignored her, going to the railing and looking around.

"Hey, I was only kidding," she said.

What had him so excited? It was probably just a branch falling. They were surrounded by trees, and not all of them were healthy.

Andrew shushed her, which raised her dander just a bit. Her mother had been a world-champion shusher. Nothing got under Kate's skin quicker than a shush.

After a few moments, he said, "You hear anything?"

She raised an eyebrow at him. "Yes, my husband freaking out over a tree limb."

"Hold on. I'll be right back."

He leaped over the rail, hitting the dirt hard and disappearing around the side of the cottage.

"Andrew, where are you going?"

The Adirondack chair was built on an angle that made it hard for Kate to get up on her own, but she managed. Buttons was on his feet too, nose between the wood slats, staring at where Andrew had gone. Unlike her husband, the dog didn't seem all that concerned.

"Andrew!"

She noticed someone in a canoe. When they heard her, they stopped paddling and waved. She couldn't see them well enough to tell if it was a man or woman, young or old. Waving back, she gripped the railing and leaned as far as she could without losing her balance, hoping to see where Andrew had run off to. His footsteps were unmistakable, fading with each passing second.

"I think your daddy needs to be cut off," she said.

How the hell could a snapping branch get him so riled up? She made her way to the front of the house, standing on the porch, her hips crying out for her to get off her feet and lie down.

Cupping her hands around her mouth, she called his name.

When he didn't reply, she started to get worried.

Thrashing sounds close by didn't help matters much.

Buttons whizzed past her feet, bounding down the steps and into the woods.

"Buttons! Stop!"

The dog that had to be coerced to leave her side didn't even break his stride as he too slipped into the woods.

"What the heck's going on?"

Her heart started to race, and with that came the pain. Her left hand massaged her chest while her right held on to the doorframe.

"Andrew! Buttons!"

"Where's Buttons?" Andrew startled her, popping out from behind a tree as if he'd been hiding there the whole time.

"I think he went looking for you. Why did you run off like that?"

He looked in her eyes, and she saw the shine of panic wash over his face.

"Oh my God, I didn't mean to upset you." He ran onto the porch, wrapping her in his arms.

"Really? You jump off the porch, dash into the woods, ignore my calls and you didn't think that would freak me out?"

"I wasn't thinking."

"No, you were thinking, but about what?"

"First, let me get you inside and I'll go find Buttons."

Kate looked over his shoulder and saw the beagle trotting toward them with a big, broken stick in his mouth. It was a wonder he'd been able to get his jaws around it, much less carry it.

"I think Buttons found the source of your panic," she said, not believing it. How could Buttons know that was the branch out of all the branches lying about that had startled Andrew?

She took it from him, and Andrew took it from her. The splintered ends looked fresh. But that was impossible.

After they went back into the cottage, Kate said, "Okay, spill it. Why did you get all weird?"

He told her about the shelter he'd found, and how it was within sight of the cottage. If it had been built by some kids, he and Kate would have heard them playing. Andrew, being a wary Jersey boy, had been worried that they had some strange-o lurking about, keeping tabs on them. When he heard the branch snap, he'd thought maybe he could catch the person.

Kate shivered. She didn't like the thought of being peeped on when they were basically out here all alone.

"Did you see anything?"

"No," Andrew said, pouring himself a glass of water. "Shelter's still there, but it's empty. I kicked it apart for good measure. Now they know I know, and hopefully they'll move along."

"Should we call the police?"

"And what? Tell them I found a little shelter in the woods? They'd think I was nuts."

"Not if we explain what it could mean."

He propped her pillows up behind her. "Even I think I'm overreacting. Imagine how they'll look at a pair of out-of-towners. Look, it's nothing. This is what happens to your brain on low-grade whisky. I'll stick to beer from here on."

Kate said, "Do you think an animal could have built it? It could have been a bear den or something."

Andrew ran his hands over his face. "What's with you and bears? The only bear we're going to see out here is Yogi Bear if you find an old cartoon show."

"I did hear that animal outside."

"Which was probably a passing moose. And neither animal knows how to build a wooden shelter that looks like a tepee. That I can guarantee you."

Now that he had relaxed and they'd talked it out, the balloon of anxiety in Kate's gut started to deflate. Andrew wasn't the most observant person, especially on his runs. He didn't know that she sometimes watched him, nervous that he'd hurt himself with the way he recklessly sprinted around the neighbourhood. That little shelter could have been there for weeks, months even.

"Promise me one thing," she said, taking a blood pressure pill and her prescription iron supplement.

"Yeeessss," he said, cautiously.

"Next time, before you run off into the woods, tell me what the deal is before you leave."

He smoothed her hair from her forehead. "I promise."

"Oh, and one more thing."

"What's that?"

"Change your shorts."

CHAPTER THIRTEEN

Andrew had been true to his word and hadn't drunk any more whisky. But he did have a couple of beers before calling it a night. He was snoring like a lumberjack with sleep apnea, his guttural wheezing loud enough to beat the band and their roadies.

Needless to say, Kate couldn't sleep. She'd nodded off and slept through dinner, which from what she saw in the kitchen sink had been soup and a sandwich. The few hours of rest had taken the edge off her exhaustion. Now, between Andrew's snoring and the pain in her shoulders, there was no way she was going to be able to close her eyes.

Sometime before morning, she'd be wiped out and would finally zone out, just in time for the day to start.

Maybe Andrew was right and she was a vampire.

As impossible as it seemed, she was getting less sleep in Maine than she had back home. At first she'd thought it was because she needed to get used to the new surroundings, but that wasn't it. No, everything was off with her. That damn treatment was wreaking havoc with her system. If she wasn't burning up, she was weaker than normal and feeling strange. Being in chronic pain had made her hyperaware of her body. She couldn't describe the way she'd been feeling. It was if her body had been replaced by another damaged, worn-out model that was completely unfamiliar to her.

There was no way she was going to tell Andrew. What could he do about it anyway? She just had to hope it passed and she could get on with enjoying their magical summer.

She watched Cary Grant in *Topper* and sucked on some candy to help her nausea. When the pain got this bad, it always turned her stomach sour. Candy didn't make it all better, but it helped, sometimes more than medication.

A chilly breeze floated through the open windows. Kate snuggled under the blankets. Buttons lay on his side by her feet, snoring as well.

When she was a kid, Kate had been terrified of the dark. To make matters worse, she'd been plagued by night terrors between the ages of five and seven. Not only were there boogeymen in her closet, child-munching beasts waiting for her foot to slip out of the tuck at the end of the bed, and red-eyed creatures floating outside her window, but even her dreams, her only means of escape, were to be feared. Telling her it was time to go to bed was like informing an inmate that old Sparky was waiting for him to take that long walk.

She'd spent many a night frozen with fear in her bed, mouth open wide but no sound coming out, praying to God that her mother and father would somehow sense her distress and come to her rescue. The mere thought of walking down the hall to their bedroom in the dead of night gripped her with incalculable fear.

She wasn't afraid now.

The irony was not lost on her that the dead of night had become her 'me time'.

Now the dark was about candy and old movies.

And sometimes bad feels and shadows.

With the onslaught of the microwave feels she was getting up here, she almost missed the familiar bad feels.

Almost.

She checked her tablet, saw it was time for a pain pill. Swallowing it down, she nestled her feet under a snoozing Buttons so he could warm them up.

A gusting wind was kicking up small waves breaking on the shore. The crickets, perhaps agitated by the wind, were chirping louder than a Metallica concert. Kate was tempted to turn the TV up and drown it all out, but she didn't want to wake Andrew.

Better close the windows, she thought.

Leaving the comfort of the bed (not that she was ever truly comfortable), she slipped on some socks and padded in the dark to the kitchen. Buttons woke up and joined her. She gave him a doggie treat, thanking him for the company.

Still thinking about her old night terrors, perhaps because she'd had quite a few reminiscent episodes as of late, she cringed remembering how some of the kids used to call her Katie the Coon. She was the only kid in third grade with dark circles under her eyes.

Kate often wondered if those years spent walking around in a fog – two crucial, formative years at that – had permanently altered her body chemistry. The nightmares ate away at her psyche and health, and when they left, her body needed something to replace them. So, rather than wait for her to become exposed to a strange disease (and who knew how long that could take), it decided to rebel against itself.

Her mother thought her 'little theory' was ridiculous, but her father, well, it gave him pause.

"It could be all those night terrors were the broken cells growing in your body," he'd said to her one night over pumpkin pie and coffee. Her mother had been in the kitchen, cleaning up. Dad hadn't looked so good himself. He'd been talking of early retirement a lot, though Mom pooh-poohed it, telling him he still had a lot of earning to do if they were going to have golden years, not bronze years.

Kate had just been diagnosed with lupus, and she was terrified. Her father's hand felt cold, clasped over hers. "The mind is the most complex and mysterious organism in the universe," he'd said. "There are parts of it that know more than it will ever let on. Maybe it does that to protect us. It could be that those night terrors were created to shield you from the truth. The autoimmune diseases wanted to be heard. But something in your mind, the Wizard behind the curtain, since you loved Dorothy so much, refused to let them. Now, it couldn't silence them entirely, but it could mask what they were trying to say. By not knowing what was going to come for you as you got older, you were able to live a more carefree life. You were a real spitfire, you know that? The unstoppable Kate. I don't think you would have been the unstoppable Kate if you'd known this was always waiting for you. You wouldn't have had all those wonderful experiences, and maybe not even Andrew." He sipped from his coffee and stared at his pie. "Funny to think that we should be grateful for those night terrors. Life is like that. Funny. Even when you think it's serious as a five-alarm fire."

Kate had had to use two napkins to soak up her tears. She'd loved her father more than she ever thought possible at that moment.

Less than a year later, he was gone after a quick but ignoble dance with pancreatic cancer. He never did get to retire, those last days neither golden nor bronze nor tin. He went from the office to the hospital to the hospice, all within the span of five weeks. Death had given him a fast pass, but he'd suffered so much those last two weeks. The phrase *white-hot agony* hadn't even put a dent into what he went through, at least until hospice took over.

She missed him so much. More so now that it felt as if she'd also lost her mother. Their relationship had never been the best, but without her father to mediate, it was a disaster.

Buttons nudged her calf, banging his tail against the cabinet.

"You want to close the windows for me?" she said softly.

Buttons put his paws on her thighs, waiting for his ears to be scratched.

"Yeah, I guess you're too short anyway."

She leaned over the sink and grabbed the lip of the window, pausing. Kate looked through the screen, the darkness so complete, she couldn't even see the car parked in front of the house just fifteen feet away.

No bears. No moose.

No shadows. It was too dark for shadows.

Andrew let out a whopper of a snore.

"Someone's going to have a sore throat in the morning," she said to the beagle.

Closing the other window by the dining area, which was just an extension of the living room, she paused again, enjoying the cessation of jagged cricket legs.

She was just about to go back to bed when a high, piercing scream cut through the closed windows as if they were made of onionskin paper.

Kate reflexively flinched, hunching her shoulders as if something had flown into the house and was circling around her head.

She tottered into one of the dining room chairs, heart doing a madman's samba.

What could have made such a noise?

It sounded as if it had come from both outside and within the cottage, like it was everywhere at once, the blaring of Revelation's trumpets.

Kate's back flared and her knees turned to water. She had to pull the chair out from under the table and sit before she fell down. The fiery sensation went all the way to the top of her head. She grabbed at her hair, expecting it to come away in clumps from having been burned from her scalp.

Hands shaking, she looked over at Andrew, who was still snoring.

How could he sleep through that? It sounded like someone was being killed.

I have to get my phone.

She saw it across the room, the divide stretching out before her like taffy.

I have to wake Andrew up and call the police. Whoever made that noise is hurt, if not dead by now.

Kate sat and listened for it to come again, knowing if it did, she might pee herself. Taking slow, steady breaths, she concentrated on expelling the heat within her body outward with each exhalation. She pictured Ryker beside her, his hand on her shoulder, encouraging her. After a minute or so, she started to feel more in control of herself.

There was another screech, but this one not as loud, not nearly as close. It sounded as if whatever had made it was heading away from the cottage.

And it was most definitely not *in* the cottage.

She should have been relieved at that, but she wasn't.

Buttons looked up at her, breath huffing from his open mouth, as if nothing had happened. Andrew rolled over on the bed, still very much asleep.

Did I imagine that?

It was so, so loud. Buttons barks at cats when they meow by our windows at home. He didn't even react.

Andrew might have been sleeping off a day and night of drinking, but even that wouldn't explain how he could not even stir after that first scream. She could still hear it, reverberating in her brain, an echo from the cauldron room in hell.

What disturbed her most was her inability to figure out if it was a person or an animal. Something about it made her think it was both. But that was impossible.

She prayed it was an animal. Because if a woman had made that noise – that fading, horrid scream – someone had done terrible things to her, carrying her into the night.

Rubbing her arms to chase the chill away, Kate got up, her body demanding she sit back down. Biting her bottom lip, she stutter-stepped into the living room and collapsed on the bed.

Andrew snapped awake.

"What happened? Are you okay?"

His voice was gruff, strained, made raw by the booze and snoring.

"Shhh," Kate said, hand over his mouth.

"What are you doing?" he mumbled.

Whispering, she said, "I need you to open that window."

"Why did you close it?"

He slipped out from under her hand, rubbing his eyes.

"Please, just do it. And try not to make any noise."

Andrew looked at her, confused, but did as she asked.

"A little more," she said.

He opened the window all the way, visibly shivering.

"You want to freeze me out?"

"Shhh. Just listen. Do you hear anything?"

He paused, listened, scratched his head.

"No."

Neither did she.

"You mind telling me what this is all about?"

Feeling like a fool, she sighed and said, "I...I thought I heard someone screaming."

"When?"

"A couple of minutes ago. I can't believe it didn't wake you."

He got a bottle of water from the refrigerator, taking a long draw. "You sure it was a person?"

"Yes. No. It was loud and it scared the shit out of me."

Kate pulled the covers up to her chest, a thin fabric shield against the things that went shriek in the night. Buttons jumped up on the bed.

Andrew looked at the dog and said, "Man, I must have really been out if Buttons didn't wake me up."

Smoothing the covers, suddenly nervous to look Andrew in the eye, she said, "Buttons didn't bark."

"But you said you heard someone screaming. I can't imagine Buttons keeping his big mouth shut."

Kate ruffled his fur. "I know it's weird, but he didn't react at all."

The mattress shifted when Andrew settled in. The look he gave her now made her feel like a world-class ass, not to mention angry.

"Didn't you put a new fentanyl patch on before we went to bed?" he said.

Her blood immediately went to full boil. "I'm not some addict having hallucinations."

Putting his hand on her leg, he said, "Come on, you've had episodes in the past. It's not your fault. Those are powerful drugs they have you on."

Through gritted teeth, she said, "Do I look and sound like I'm out of it?"

Yes, there had been times when she imagined all sorts of things. But it was very obvious when the medication had her in its grip. Those times, she didn't even recognise her husband or surroundings. She recalled tattered bits of those moments, Andrew filling in the rest. It always made her uncomfortable, face in her hands, exclaiming, "Did I really say that?"

This wasn't one of those moments.

Andrew deflated. "No, you look fine. Maybe you were sleepwalking."

"I couldn't have been sleepwalking because I've been up for hours."

Oh Lord, she wanted to slap him. It was as if he were accusing her of some mighty wrongdoing, which she knew was irrational. The past few minutes had her on an emotional roller coaster, and she needed her husband to settle her down, not send her on the next loop-de-loop.

When he leaned over to hug her, she pulled away.

"Look, I'm sorry. Wouldn't you rather it be a hallucination or dream than some poor person screaming for their life out there?"

She went to say something, but bit her tongue instead. Tonight was the first time she'd put on a new patch in tandem with the new light sedative she'd been given. Maybe, just maybe, they didn't play well together.

And she really didn't want that to be some poor, hurt, terrified woman out there in the woods.

Staring at Buttons, who had grown bored and closed his eyes, she said, "I hate it when you're right."

She leaned into him and he held her, his stale beer breath something powerful.

"Yeah, me too. It's not easy being right so much of the time. Heavy is the head that wears the crown."

Kate pinched him, eliciting a sharp yowl.

"Now you get to stay up with me until I can fall asleep."

Propping up their pillows, he said, "Fine, but no black-and-white movies. I need something in colour with action. Naked boobs if we can swing it."

"I married a child."

"Action and nudity keep me young."

She laughed, and it felt amazing to release the pressure that had built up inside her. "Then you're going to grow old real fast with me around."

Andrew clicked around, settling for a Vin Diesel movie.

She had just started to believe that maybe she had been kind of sleepwalking when the penetrating scream happened again, this time sounding as if it were right outside their window.

CHAPTER FOURTEEN

"Did you find anything?"

Andrew was in the kitchen, buttering up some toast for her. He had a plate for himself heaped with scrambled eggs and sausage links.

Neither of them had been able to go back to sleep. Here they were, eating breakfast at the ass crack of dawn, Kate tapping and swiping away on her tablet.

"Yes, but he's thirty miles away," she said.

The pink-and-yellow sun did wonders to calm their nerves. As did having a task to concentrate on.

"Thirty miles is nothing up here. It's the equivalent of the corner store back home," he said, handing her a plate of toast and glass of orange juice. She nibbled on a corner.

He hoped she hadn't noticed him checking the lock on the door as he walked past it.

"Not many ratings, though. I don't know," she said, brow furrowed.

"I don't think people up here give a crap about Yelp and all that nonsense."

Andrew tucked into his eggs, slathering them with hot sauce.

"Well, it's either this guy or a vet in New Hampshire. It looks like a county clinic. The drive would take about an hour."

"I'll stick to the one in Maine," he said.

Buttons sat by the bed, looking up at them, waiting for scraps.

"Want some sausage?" Andrew said, barely above a whisper.

The dog waddled to his side of the bed.

"He heard that," he said.

"Something has to be off with his hearing," Kate said. She took a birdlike sip of her juice. "There's no way he heard that last night and just decided not to react."

Andrew gave Buttons a sausage and patted his head.

"No, you're right. That was so loud, it was like someone had pressed their mouth against the screen and was shouting at us."

What he didn't want to say was that the sudden, shrill cry had frightened him so much, his balls had shriveled to raisins and still hadn't gone back to normal. How had he not heard it the first time? Maybe he should get his hearing checked while he was out with Buttons.

Hearing issues aside, it had been terrifying. He'd snapped the lights on and they'd waited, holding one another, wondering when the next shriek would come. When he went to check the window, she'd pulled him back onto the bed. A very big part of him was grateful. It was a moment when he was supposed to be alpha male macho, but he wasn't sure he wanted to see what was on the other side of the window.

So they'd sat quietly, minutes turning into an hour, finally allowing themselves to unclench, just a little. As dawn broke, Kate became fixated on the dog's hearing and had been looking up places to take him ever since. She could get like that – obsessed with something to take her mind off what was really bugging her. Like the way she obsessed over those old movies.

"I'll call when their office opens at nine," Kate said. She set the toast aside and dove back into her tablet.

Andrew had decided he was going to skip his morning run today. Dashing around in the woods alone had lost a lot of its appeal.

"What are you looking for now?" he asked.

"Scary animal sounds."

The three-word search returned over a million possibilities.

"All I want are the videos," she said, opening the first link. The title was 'Ten Most Chilling Animal Sounds'.

She turned the volume on her tablet all the way up.

The room was filled with a lion's roar. Buttons went on high alert, barking like mad.

"Calm down, buddy," Andrew said, hooking his finger under the dog's collar and keeping him close. He'd heard that as well. Maybe he didn't need to go to the vet at all.

"It definitely wasn't a lion," Kate said.

"I don't think we needed a video to prove that. At least we know Buttons will give it right back to a lion."

His joke fell flat as the lion faded away, a crocodile's warning rumble emanating from the small speakers. All ten animal recordings were of big animals found in Africa and Asia.

"Next," Kate said, clicking her way through audio compilations of all sorts of animal cries.

Nothing sounded familiar until they heard a fox screaming. Andrew's flesh prickled. It sounded very human, almost like a small child screaming at the top of their lungs.

"That's pretty close," he said.

Kate frowned, playing the audio three more times. Poor Buttons was starting to get antsy, his tail tucked between his legs.

"Maybe we should use headphones," Andrew said.

Kate looked at Buttons and her face softened. "Poor baby. I'm so sorry, But-But. Mommy got a little…"

"Obsessed," Andrew finished for her, getting the headphones and adapter from the bedroom so they could both be plugged in. They used it often to watch something on her tablet that they couldn't get on their old, pre-smart television back home.

After feeding Buttons her toast as a small act of apology, Kate put her headphones on and replayed the chilling fox noise.

Andrew shook his head. "I don't think that's it."

"Me neither. Let me refine this a little."

This time, she typed in 'scary north American animal sounds'.

They sat listening to more foxes, badgers, bears, and bobcats. They were all unnerving, but not what had been outside their window.

When Kate clicked on a screeching deer, they both stiffened.

"I didn't know deer could make a sound like that. It's awful, like a child being beaten," Andrew said, heart beating just a little faster.

Kate shivered. "Did we really just freak ourselves out all night over a deer?"

Andrew had to laugh. "If we didn't know we were dumb city folk before, we do now. Did you know deer made any kind of sounds? I thought they were all mute, except for Bambi."

Kate smiled for the first time that morning. "Let's just listen to a few more."

Andrew had no desire, knowing that it was definitely a deer they'd heard. For it to make a sound like that, something had either spooked it or hurt it.

He didn't pay much attention until she opened a file for an owl.

They looked at one another.

"Okay," Andrew said, "it could have been an owl too."

Tapping the screen, Kate verified that there were a dozen species of owl in Maine.

"Or maybe a deer battling an owl," she said.

He took the tablet from her, turned it off, and set it on the end table.

"You need to get some sleep. You look terrible," he said.

She nodded. "I am so tired. You should too."

"You know me. Maybe I'll take a nap later. Once I'm up, I'm up."

He tucked the sheets around her.

"We are a pair of world-class chickenshits," he said, kissing her.

"I'm sorry I woke you up."

"Don't be. I'd hate to think that I would sleep through all of that and leave you alone and wigged out all night, even if it was just over a deer or owl."

"Or both!"

"Right. Or both." He gave her her morning medication and she was asleep before he had the dishes washed.

Lucky, he thought.

Now that their ridiculous fears had been assuaged, he had to go for a run just to prove to himself that he had some bit of testosterone left. Buttons followed him into the bedroom as he got changed.

"You want to come, old man?" he said.

He made an executive decision not to bother with the vet. From everything he could see, Buttons could hear just fine. Just why the beagle hadn't reacted to the deer/owl was a mystery, but not one that Andrew would lose any sleep over.

Maybe he could dial things down a bit today. The old anger was nowhere to be found. There was nothing to pound into submission. He was too damn tired to be upset.

His run was actually an amble, Buttons not sniffing around so much but going at his own leisurely pace. The air smelled extra sweet this morning.

"God's bakery," Andrew said.

They trudged through the litter of leaves and needles, the lake peeking between the trees. He saw the elderly kayakers out for their morning exercise.

Buttons barked, tugging on the leash. Andrew's shoulder snapped, and he had to hurry to keep up.

The dog dove under a pile of brambles, front paws scratching at the dirt. When his furry head emerged, he had a squirrel in his mouth.

Andrew cringed. "Put that thing down, Buttons."

He opened his mouth, the top half of the squirrel thumping on the ground. Its grey coat was splattered with what looked like fresh blood.

"Where's the other half?"

Buttons wagged his tail, tongue dripping drool and squirrel blood. Toeing the area where the beagle had found the squirrel, Andrew was unable to locate the missing chunk.

"Glad I already ate breakfast. Come on, buddy."

They walked for twenty minutes and Buttons didn't find any more severed critters, much to Andrew's relief.

He let the dog back inside, Kate fast asleep, and took a thorough tour around the cottage. Tracking was not one of his specialties, but that deer had been so close, it had to have left some sign of its presence. The ground beneath the window on the side of the house where it had made its last pained cry was lush with grass. He didn't see any small depressions anywhere.

"Check for scat," he mumbled, remembering Kate's request the day she'd thought a bear had been on the porch.

For the first time, Andrew wondered if he should have found a place a little closer to civilization. Maybe with more people around, there'd be less wildlife to scare the piss out of them. There were occasional bears that went pool hopping in New Jersey, and he'd once spotted a deer in their backyard, but those were rare instances. At least the Jersey beasts had the common courtesy to be quiet when they lurked about.

Not so with the fauna of Maine.

Andrew and Kate were the interlopers here.

Finding nothing, he ended up on the dock, dipping his feet in the water. With the sun on his face and the lake so still, it was perfect for napping.

If it was an owl, I'm not climbing trees to look for evidence.

He couldn't get that sound out of his head, nor the one he'd heard that early morning. Every time he started to doze off, the screeches returned, raising the hackles on the back of his neck, even though he knew damn well they were just the weird cries of some harmless animals. Animals hidden by the dark of night, just out of sight.

Looking back at the cottage, he could almost see inside the glass doors to their bed.

A strange thought floated through his brain.

We can't see them.

But they can see us.

CHAPTER FIFTEEN

"You're burning up," Andrew said. "And we ran out of Tylenol. I'll have to go to town to get some. You need or want anything else?"

Kate had kicked all of the sheets off, her skin feeling as if it were being pricked by live wires. Her muscles ached, joints swollen so much, she feared they would crack like old walnuts. It was a very bad day.

"How are we on soda?"

Andrew checked the fridge and the cabinet where they stored their drinks. "I'll get more. You want a magazine or something? Maybe the paper?"

She shook her head. "I don't think I could concentrate enough to read a full sentence."

"I could get you *USA Today*. I don't think they write in full sentences."

"How about some English muffins? For some reason, I have a craving."

Andrew scribbled on a scrap of paper. "Officially on the list. You going to be all right? I was thinking of renting a kayak while I'm out."

She was happy to hear that. She'd noticed him looking wistfully at the lake more and more. He'd taken a few quick dips, but she could tell he really wanted to explore it beyond the dock. She wished she could join him, but there was no way her arms could paddle a kayak. Her shoulders would dislocate on the first stroke.

"I'll be fine. You have to leave for work every day, and I feel like crap nine times out of ten. Go forth and get your toy. You deserve it. Take your time. I have a couple of Tylenol in my backup pill case."

Aside from her mason jar of pills, she had an old Altoids tin she usually stowed in the car for emergencies. One of every medication was in the tin.

He smiled and kissed her forehead, covering it with a cool washcloth.

"Be back soon."

Buttons followed him to the door and whined after he closed it. Since Andrew had been around day and night, the beagle had grown more attached to him.

"Don't be a traitor, But-But."

He happily bounded to the bed.

He was still very much her baby. Kate petted him until even that made her tired.

She'd been more tired than usual. Ever since *the night of the shrieking deer*, as Andrew had nicknamed it as if it were a B horror movie, she'd found it hard to sleep when it was dark out. Well, harder than usual. Her senses were on high alert from sundown to sunup, which in turn was wearing on what was left of her immune system.

Today's fever came without that microwave feeling. Even so, she waited for her back to feel like someone had sprayed lighter fluid on it and flicked a match her way.

Despite being weak and clammy, she started to get antsy. Perhaps it was having the threat of her secret microwave feels hanging over her, or the niggling feeling that something about this place wasn't what it appeared to be. Strange noises aside, other aspects of their vacation home were bugging her more and more.

Like, why really had it been available at the last minute? And not just for a week or two, but the whole summer? Kate was starting to doubt the realtor's story about the previous renters having a death in the family.

Also, where the hell were their neighbours? Andrew said he still hadn't seen another home on his runs. She hardly saw anyone ever on the lake. Were people avoiding this place for a reason?

Or was all of this just nonsense, another aftereffect of her treatment, her mind spinning on overdrive?

A ball of nervous energy in her gut grew and grew until she couldn't sit still anymore. She had to get up and do something, no matter how much she hurt or her body begged to get back under the sheet.

She forced herself to get out of bed. The day was a little overcast, threatening rain. The increased humidity only made her joints feel worse.

You're going to hurt like hell whether you stay in bed or get up off your ass and do something.

Andrew's housekeeping had gone a little sideways since they got to Maine. And why not? They were on vacation, after all. There were clothes in and around the hamper, socks scattered on the floor, dishes in the kitchen sink. And the bathroom could stand a little bleach cleaner.

If you can't properly christen the house with Andrew, this will have to do.

Kate groaned whenever she bent down to pick up clothes or get the cleaner from the lower cabinets. Buttons followed her around the house. She tossed a load of laundry into the washer, which was kept in a closet near the kitchen. She'd at first thought the closet was a pantry, but it contained a small washer with a top-mounted dryer instead. Leaning against the sink, she washed the dishes slowly, meticulously. She had to take a break before tackling the bathroom, sitting down to catch her breath and dispel the dizziness in her brain.

Days like today, when she was sick to death of being sick, sexually frustrated – hell, frustrated in general – and harbouring a low buzz of being freaked out, she pushed herself to restore a modicum of order around her. It wasn't much, but it gave her some sense of control back. It always ended in tears and blinding pain and sometimes worse, but once she started, she couldn't stop herself.

Andrew was going to be mad. They'd danced this dance so many times, she knew the lines of both sides of the argument by heart. He worried about her and got furious when she pushed herself to the brink. To him, tidying up the house was an absurdity. There was no sense in her doing it, knowing she'd flatten herself out. He'd yell at her out of anger and fear and exasperation.

She'd fight right back, angry that he couldn't understand, no matter how many times she explained it to him. Sometimes she just needed to feel useful, needed. It wasn't like sitting around was making her any better.

Shaking off the blowup resounding in her head, she and Buttons went to the bathroom. A little Ajax in the sink and liquid gel in the toilet had it smelling spring fresh. She swept up the hairs – pubic and otherwise – and flushed them. The shower was too much for her to tackle. Bending over the lip of the tub to scrub it clean seemed a physical impossibility. Instead, she sprayed it down with tile and tub cleaner and rinsed it with steamy water.

Once that was done, she decided to sweep the living room. The dust bunnies were growing in number and had been clinging to Buttons like burrs lately. She put on her headphones and listened to music while she worked, upping the volume to drown out the escalating pain in her bones and dull ache in her chest.

Sweeping led to rearranging the clothes in the bedroom and organising their drawers. It was by far the most she had done since they'd gotten here, and she could feel the price she would pay coming on.

Fuck it. All that wood and old newspapers by the fireplace need to be tidied up. Once you do that, you can take some pills and lie down.

She didn't remember finishing that and moving on to sweep the back deck. Lost in her music, she screamed when a hand touched her shoulder.

"You nearly gave me a heart attack," she said, tearing off her headphones.

"What the hell are you doing?"

Andrew had dropped a couple of plastic shopping bags on the floor by the bed and must have rushed outside when he saw her on the back porch. The front door was wide open, letting in who knew how many bugs.

"I just wanted to straighten some things up."

He put a hand to her forehead. "You're burning up. Have you lost your mind?"

A massive wave of spins sent her tottering against the porch rail. Now that the music had stopped, her forward momentum halted, she realised her fever had returned with a vengeance. A fledgling fire sputtered at the small of her back. She tensed with despairing anticipation.

"There's nothing wrong with me helping out."

Andrew ushered her into the living room, his grip on her arm a little tight. "Actually, there is. You're sick, Kate. Who the hell cares about the dishes and the porch?"

She pulled out of his grasp, sitting on the bed even though she desperately wanted to stand on her own two feet.

"Yes, I'm sick. It's not like it's going to get worse."

Andrew closed his eyes and shook his head. "Of course it can get worse! It can always get worse!"

Kate refused to tell him how much her chest hurt. That would only make him right, and she couldn't allow that. Not at this moment.

"It's not like I did a crazy amount of work around the house," she said.

His eyes widened. "I was gone for three hours. From what I can see, there isn't anything in this place you haven't touched and straightened. Christ, why do you insist on doing dumb shit like this?"

Tears sprang to her eyes and she looked away, quickly wiping them with the back of her hand. "Because I can help too. You don't have to do everything."

"Actually, I do."

A fat worm of anger twisted in her gut. "Fuck you, Andrew."

"I wish you would."

He grabbed the bags and stormed to the kitchen, slamming the front door shut. Through it all, Buttons had found a chair to settle on, eyes flicking back and forth between them, bored with having to be subjected to the same old clash of two overstressed people.

It always happened like this. They went along fine; then something would have them both exploding way out of proportion to the core of their disagreement.

They didn't argue as much as they used to, but when they did, it was always a no-holds-barred affair.

Andrew bringing up the very sore subject of sex was a button neither of them liked to push.

She thought she'd smelled beer on his breath.

"Are you driving drunk now?" she asked as he slammed cans and boxes onto the counter.

"What?"

"You smell like a brewery. I hope you didn't hit anyone on your way home."

She knew he wasn't drunk. So what if he had a beer or two with his lunch? But she also knew that it was the right button to push.

"You're ridiculous," he said. "Maybe if I could be on the pills you take, I wouldn't need a beer to relax every now and then."

Another low blow. Kate wanted to spit at him.

"So now you're saying I'm a junkie?"

When he didn't respond, only giving her a cutting glance, she wanted to do more than spit at him. Yes, he was scared and worried for her, but why was he being such a monster? Moments like this, Kate thought it was a good thing she was disabled, because if she weren't, it might come to blows. Then again, if she weren't, they wouldn't be having these arguments.

She lay back against the pillows, trying to shut out the sound of him clunking around the cottage and slamming doors.

He finally settled in the bedroom. Neither of them spoke for an hour. Sometime during their argument, he'd put a new bottle of Tylenol on the table next to her along with a glass of water.

Seeing the pills and water, she was torn between wanting to launch the glass at the wall or cry. Even throughout them being awful to one another, he cared enough to make sure she had what she needed.

"You're two very passionate people," her mother had told her in a rare moment of sincerity. This was back when she was first diagnosed with Ehlers-Danlos syndrome. Putting name to it was scary, but at least it explained why her shoulders and wrists kept dislocating, and her increasing fatigue. "This isn't going to be easy because neither of you like to back down. You're gonna fight, you're gonna cry. But that's because you love each other. Love and anger, they're all the same thing. The day you don't fight is the day you worry."

Kate recalled that conversation often.

Well, she and Andrew must really still love one another.

She dozed off, waking when she felt someone staring at her. Andrew was in the chair across from the bed, a magazine on his lap, his eyes locked on her.

She wanted to say she was sorry, but pulled back. How could she be sorry for doing something that made her feel more whole?

"You know what gets me?" he said, his voice much softer, all of the feverish anger bled from his tone.

She met his stare.

"All of that energy you expended today could have been used to do something good and fun."

"Oh, like have sex with you? Is that why you got so mad? I could have been blowing you, but instead I cleaned the house?"

Andrew visibly sagged.

"First, you say having sex with me like it's a horrible thing. Of course I want to have sex with you. You're my wife." Flipping the magazine aside, he took a deep breath and rubbed his face. "So yes, sex would be nice. Or we could go to the dock. Or have a barbecue and sit beside the fire pit. Watch the sunrise on the beach. Or a million other things that are a billion times better than scrubbing a toilet. And your excuse is always, 'it's not like it can get worse'. But it can. We've seen it get worse. You get this amnesia when you go manic like this. The problem is, my brain won't let me forget."

She didn't know what to say. He was so calm, so resigned. Her husband looked like a beaten man.

Normally, after a big dustup, they would apologise and move on, neither wanting to dwell on the negative. They had enough of that to deal with.

Andrew rose from the chair. "What hurts me most is…you choose that stuff…over me."

Kate felt the hot tears cascade down her cheeks.

"I'll sleep in the bedroom tonight," Andrew said.

He walked slump-shouldered out of the living room.

He'd even left her a cheese sandwich on a plate covered in plastic wrap on the end table.

Her pride kept her rooted to the bed. He might have been honest, but that didn't make him right. She hadn't chosen cleaning a house over being with him.

She hadn't.

Then what the hell had she been doing?

No sooner had he left than her body ignited. She grabbed fistfuls of the sheet and tugged. Her blood boiled. Her heart went out of rhythm. Kate's vision wavered, and for a moment, she thought she was going to throw up.

She lay back and closed her eyes, concentrating on making the flames go away.

Please, dear God, leave me. I can't take it!

She tried to picture being on the ice planet Hoth, the chill winds and snow dousing the blaze in her body, Luke Skywalker doing his best to bring down her body temperature. The image didn't last long. It was easily replaced with a vision of crackling flames.

When she was at the brink and about to cry out (for relief or merciful death, she wasn't sure), the cottage went sideways and she nearly blacked out.

The pain had crested and, just like flipping a switch, was gone.

Kate buried her head in Mooshy and sobbed, wanting Andrew desperately and not wanting him just the same.

CHAPTER SIXTEEN

She'd refused to eat the sandwich earlier. Now that she was up once again in the dead of night, she was hungry. Kate didn't remember taking the plastic wrap off the sandwich. The bread was hard as a rock.

Every muscle in her body was killing her. Looking over at the kitchen, she thought she might as well have been gazing at the shores of Ireland. There was no way she could will her bones to get out of the bed and into the kitchen to make something to eat. Her foray into housekeeping had done a number on her, as it always did. So why was she still surprised?

Stomach grumbling, she settled for chewing on her nail.

It was her first night alone in bed since they'd come to Maine.

Andrew had told her a week ago that there was a small island, not much more than a pile of rocks and dirt with one lone, skinny tree jutting from the random clod of earth, smack in the middle of the lake. It couldn't be seen from the cottage. He'd spotted it on one of his runs.

Kate felt like she was on that island, removed, alone, and uneasy.

"But–But?"

Even the dog was nowhere to be seen.

Probably in the bedroom with Andrew. I'll bet he bribed him with treats to get him away from me.

She made a fist, digging her nails into her palm.

You know he didn't do that. He wasn't even mad before. He just looked, I don't know, sad.

Shifting in bed to find the remote was agony. Bones popped and nerves shouted at her to stop.

Tomorrow would be a bad feels day. She really had overdone it. The bad feels would sit on her chest like a demon for more than just a day. They would leer at her from dark corners. Wait for her when she stumbled into the bathroom at night. Whisper terrifying words in her ear just as she was about to fall asleep.

Why can't I find a middle ground? Why does it always have to be all or nothing?

A cool breeze wafted through the living room, making her shiver. She wiped her brow and her hand came away damp.

Her fever was back to boot. Of course it was. But at least it wasn't that goddamn microwave feeling. That was a fever of an entirely different order.

She popped a couple of Tylenol with a nerve-blocker chaser. Her fentanyl patch was due to be changed tomorrow. There was never much left in it by this point in the cycle, which helped the pain waltz right in, front and centre.

There was no harm in slapping on a new one a day early, but the patches were in the bedroom.

She could call out for Andrew and he'd be up in a flash. He'd get her a new patch and fix her something to eat. Yesterday's argument would be forgotten while he took care of her. Just by saying his name loud enough to be heard one room away, she could be fed and in less pain, comfortable enough to fall back to sleep.

So why wasn't she doing it?

Because you're a stubborn bitch. It might not be your finest quality in Andrew's eyes, but it's the one trait that's kept you going this long.

It would be the thing that would keep her from having to undergo chemo.

How many doctors had told them her will alone had gotten her through several life-threatening situations? Enough for her to believe it, which was why she kept her stubborn streak honed to a fine, sharp edge. It was her last defence against the thing she didn't care to think about.

Lost in her thoughts, she barely heard the first *plink* on the roof of the house. It was so light, so benign, she just assumed it was a falling pine cone.

The second was louder, loud enough to get her full attention. It sounded as if something had hit the roof directly over her head.

Could be a bird. Maybe it dropped a little something on the way to its nest.

She was looking for something to watch when a snatch of a lesson from the sixth grade came crawling from the depths of her memory.

Birds don't fly at night.

Wait, was that true?

Kate looked at the ceiling, the slotted boards and light fixture washed out by the grey-and-white glow from the television. Her aching muscles tensed, waiting for something else to fall on the roof.

Grabbing her tablet, she did a quick search to see if her school lesson was correct (or her memory, for that matter).

There were actually plenty of birds that were nocturnal, including owls, the potential culprit of the flesh-crawling scream they'd heard that night.

Jesus, people talked about big cities never sleeping. Whoever had coined that phrase had never lived in the woods. The noise and hustle and bustle were markedly different from Times Square, but there was a whole world in constant motion up here.

There was a harder tap, this time on the side of the house. Kate pulled the covers up to her chest. She knew it was ridiculous, but the thin sheet was all she had to cower behind. Sudden sounds in the night were damn good reason to cower.

"*Hooooooohhhhh!*"

The scream was so sharp and resounding, she heard Andrew stumbling out of bed. Kate released a sharp yelp in answer to the cry in the night.

"What was that?" Andrew said, sliding on the bare floor in his socks.

"It came from out there," she said, pointing to the open kitchen window.

"It sounded like a monkey or something," Andrew said. He'd fallen asleep in his clothes. Cautiously walking to the kitchen, he cocked his ear to the window.

"Andrew...don't," she pleaded. She did not want him near that window. Whatever was out there sounded big. Andrew had said it was like a monkey, but to her, it was more like a larger primate. An orangutan or gorilla. No, that had to be wrong. It couldn't be either.

But it was an animal. No person could make a sound like that.

It was real and it was alive and it was right outside their cottage. The nearest help was miles away, and all they had to defend themselves were some feeble locks on the doors and a scattering of steak knives.

"You hear anything?" she whispered.

She jumped at the *tick-tick* of Buttons waddling into the room. He stood between her and Andrew as if unsure which way to go.

"I think I hear something moving in the woods," Andrew said.

"Just close the window and come here."

He held up a hand to silence her.

Then she heard it too. The steady crunch of leaves.

So, so close.

Andrew pointed at the window, his body turning, finger following the progression of the footsteps. Kate watched with growing dread as whatever was outside walked along the side of the house, making its way to the backyard.

The backyard, where all that separated them was a pair of flimsy sliding-glass doors. She threw the covers back, swinging her legs over the side of the bed. Her hips strained, the cold floor feeling like fire on the soles of her feet.

Andrew bolted to the doors.

"Quick, lock them," she said.

Instead, he grabbed her tablet, swiping crazily at the screen.

"What are you doing?"

"Doesn't this thing have a flashlight app?"

Before she could answer, a blinding beam of hot, white light burst from the tiny square at the back of the tablet. He went to open the door.

"Don't!" Kate exclaimed.

"If it's an animal, the light should scare it off."

With a half turn of his wrist, the lock disengaged. He paused to look back at her, his face betraying the certainty in his voice.

What she wanted to say was, "What if it isn't?"

"Please," she said instead, but there was no stopping him.

Andrew pulled the door back, the night sounds invading the cottage. A tangy smell of earth and something else, something old and rancid, made her cover her nose. It was a fleeting thing, a pocket of trapped gas waiting for release. But it resided on her tongue, trapped in the hairs of her nose.

Cri-crack. Cri-crack.

Whatever it was, it was lead-footed, unconcerned with stealth. Almost as if it wanted them to hear it.

Andrew stepped onto the porch, holding the tablet before him like Moses with the stone tablets. The light didn't penetrate deep into the woods. Kate struggled to her feet and stood, holding the edge of the door. The night air was cold and damp. When she spoke, her breath swirled in a heady mist.

"Maybe we should go back inside."

She laid a hand on Andrew's taut shoulder. He swept the light beam around the yard. They could barely see the fire pit, and that was only ten or so yards from the porch.

Something was still walking out there.

Cri-crack. Cri-crack.

"I can't see anything," Andrew said.

It has to be right in front of us!

The crunching of leaves and twigs never stopped, always just out of the light's reach, circling them like a shark.

"We need to go back inside, right now," Kate said, digging her nails into his arm.

"Who's out there?" Andrew shouted.

The walking stopped.

As did all of the night sounds. It was if a voice from on high had said, "Shush," silencing every cricket and critter mid-raucous.

"Whoa," Andrew whispered, the tendrils of his breath spiraling into the black.

Kate's heart plummeted into her stomach. The flesh at the back of her neck bunched up and felt alive with creepy-crawlies.

Andrew kept the light pointed at a particular spot, as if he was awaiting whatever was out there to step into the spotlight.

"Andrew."

She tugged on his sleeve, but he didn't budge. He stood there, frozen, waiting, barely breathing.

"Andrew!"

This time she wasn't taking no for an answer. She pulled Andrew with all her might back into the living room. The force of her yank on his shirt seemed to snap him out of the strange spell that had come over him. Slipping one arm around her waist, he slid the door shut so hard, she was afraid the glass would shatter. The lock snapped back in place with a satisfying *click*.

Feeling naked and exposed, Kate pulled the chain to close the blinds on the door.

Kate's heart hurt. The pain radiated to her shoulders, stabbing her temples with pincers. She had to calm down.

The thing out there had stopped when Andrew spoke.

Like it understood him.

Which meant it wasn't an *it*, but a *who*.

"Did you see anything?" she asked Andrew breathlessly.

"No. The flashlight on this thing sucks."

He helped her sit in the chair and moved it, and her, away from the doors.

Kate felt as if she were going to shake apart. It was hard to catch her breath. "What do we do?"

Andrew's eyes darted around the cottage. He ran to the kitchen and yanked the window closed. He then double-checked the lock on the front door before disappearing into the bedroom, where she heard another window bang shut.

When he came back to the living room, he was holding an axe handle.

"Where did you find that?"

"In the supply closet. It's missing the most important part, but it's the best we have."

He was about to sit on the bed next to her when there was a tremendous crash, the impact on the house so brutal that the framed picture of a bowl of fruit sailed off the wall in the dining room.

They both jumped, yowling. Kate instinctively grabbed him, pulling him closer. Andrew gripped the axe handle so hard, the tops of his knuckles were a deathly white.

Buttons scampered to the dining room and began to howl, a long, wistful note that chilled Kate to her core. He'd never made a noise even remotely like it before. He should have been barking, wanting to get at whatever was outside the cottage.

Instead, he almost sounded...mournful.

"Fuck," Andrew hissed.

She knew he wanted to run out into the dark and confront their unseen stalker. But he also wasn't going to leave her side. He never did.

"What did they do, hurl a goddamn boulder at the house?" he said, the cords on his neck standing out.

Kate tried to settle him down, though she felt she'd need five Valium to calm down herself. "Maybe...maybe they're leaving. That was their last attempt at freaking us out."

"Well, it worked."

Because they had sealed themselves within the house, they couldn't hear if there was still anyone out there, walking the perimeter of the cottage, looking for things to throw at it. The not knowing was almost worse.

Buttons stopped his howling, finishing with a wet chomp and a sneeze. He came back to the living room, turned twice, and then lay down beside the bed.

Kate and Andrew waited for an interminable amount of time, afraid to move, not daring to speak, waiting for the next crash to sound.

None came, and sometime after three, Andrew put the axe handle down and plucked her out of the chair and settled her onto the bed. He got them each a glass of water and lay down next to her.

"What do you think that was?" Kate asked, her stomach gurgling loudly.

"I don't freaking know." His jaw muscles were flexing nonstop. "Maybe some hillbilly asshole wanting to mess with us."

She nestled into him. "But that first scream. That…that couldn't come from a person, could it?"

"I don't know, but as soon as it's light out, I'm going to check."

His body felt as hard as stone. Kate could almost smell the sour burn of adrenaline and anger seeping out of his pores.

If it was a person and they were anywhere near the cottage come dawn, Kate almost felt sorry for them.

CHAPTER SEVENTEEN

Somehow, they had both managed to doze off, Kate's head on Andrew's chest. Her drool had soaked his shirt, her cold hand on his face. He carefully extricated himself, clasping her hand to warm it up without waking her. Kate's circulation was so bad in her arms, she had a perpetual case of what he called 'ice lady hands'.

It was almost seven. He opened the blinds on the doors and peered out at slate skies, the countryside dulled by a solid mattress of low clouds.

He slipped on his sneakers, woke Buttons up, and grabbed the axe handle.

Last night he'd been conflicted, terror and anger jockeying for post position. Now, in the grey light of day, he was still angry and also curious. Kate had thought it was an animal and they had been overreacting... again. She'd said this over and over while they watched TV, trying to convince herself, a steady cadence of self-hypnosis. He went along with her because she needed to settle her nerves. He saw her wince and grab for her chest a couple of times. The last thing he wanted was to have to rush her to the hospital in the dead of night.

That wasn't an animal.

He'd been asleep when the scream erupted, so he didn't have a full sense of the noise it made – animal, human, or otherwise. Catching the tail end, his brain still gauzy from sleep, he'd only known that someone was shouting.

"Come on, bud," he said, opening the door. Buttons preceded him onto the porch, sniffing furiously, tail as still as the nonexistent wind.

Andrew walked off the porch, but Buttons continued to sniff around as if latching on to a brand-new scent.

"Man, I wish you could talk."

Buttons surprised him by looking up and giving a quick, friendly bark.

"I stand corrected. I wish I understood dog."

The first thing he wanted to see was the side of the house where the picture had fallen off the wall. Hours ago, he had worried that it was the start of worse to come. Would rocks through the windows be next? Was there more than one person out there? Once whoever was out there had access to the house, nothing was off the table. Maybe he'd seen too many home invasion movies, but he wasn't naive enough to believe that just because he and Kate were up in Maine, crime didn't exist. Or murder.

At the moment, he was concerned about damage to the house and losing his deposit. If that happened, he would find the person responsible and get the money from them one way or another.

"Come on, Buttons. We don't care about the porch."

The dog dutifully followed him, showing he could understand Andrew. There was a chance that dogs were smarter than man.

The kayak was still secured to the roof of the car. He'd meant to take it down to the lake yesterday, but then he'd come home and seen the state Kate was in after doing her mad maid routine again, and he'd seen red.

As he turned the corner of the cottage, it was plain to see what had been thrown at it. A rock the size of Andrew's chest lay on the ground, the wood of the house splintered from the impact.

"Shit."

It had hit the side of the house about ten feet up from the ground. Andrew lifted the stone. Christ, it was heavy. Someone would have to be a world-class shot-putter to get it up that high. Or just enormously strong.

Buttons got on his hind legs to sniff the rock.

"Go ahead, buddy, and remember that smell. Next time, you warn us when he's coming."

He wasn't going to leave this rock nearby as ammo if the bastard came again. Andrew walked it down to the lake, huffing and puffing with every step. He went to the end of the dock and dropped it in the water with a tremendous splash. He'd like to have thrown it farther out, but he wasn't Superman.

The silence draped over the lake was unsettling. Even the birds weren't out, the overcast skies keeping them asleep in their nests.

Buttons walked around the cold, unused fire pit. Andrew kept an eye on him. He didn't want their city beagle running off into the woods. God knew, the humans weren't faring so well out of their element.

Andrew heard the rhythmic splashing of the kayak paddles before he saw the old couple. Out here today, he wouldn't be surprised if they could hear his heartbeat riding along the surface of the lake.

Their kayaks, one green, one yellow, made the turn around the small spit of land that lent a degree of privacy to the cottage. Hugging close to the shoreline, wearing helmets and life jackets, the man and woman paddled with serene intensity.

Seeing them up close for the first time, Andrew was struck by how old they actually looked. His father used to call octogenarians *wrinklies*. That always made Andrew laugh as a kid, for shit sure he would never be a wrinklie. Old age, the kind of old age that made you look like a walking, talking mummy, was the kind of thing that happened to other people. *Old* people. Andrew would never get old, and even if he did, he'd never look like that.

"Hi," Andrew said, waving.

The pair of wrinklies, white hair peeking out from beneath their yellow helmets, dipped their paddles in the water and brought their kayaks to a stop five feet from the dock.

"Good morning," the man said with surprising gusto. Andrew was expecting a shaky voice, timbre thin as a moth's wings.

"Enjoying this beautiful sunrise?" the woman asked, her smile bright enough to make up for the dingy clouds. Andrew had a feeling she smelled like fresh-baked pie and strawberry preserves. It was a weird thing to pop into his head, but there it was, just the same.

"At least it's not raining," he said.

"It will later today," she said. "All into the night. But they say sunny skies tomorrow."

"Getting in your morning exercise before the storm?"

The man laughed. "It could be teeming and we'd be paddling along. The only things that keep us away are lightning and the cold. It's cold a long, long time up here, so we make sure to get as much in as we can when things heat up. I'm Henry, by the way. This is my wife, Ida."

"Pleased to meet you. I've watched you for weeks. In fact, you inspired me to rent my own kayak."

Ida looked around the dock and shore. "Oh dear, did you sink it?"

"It's still strapped to my car. I was going to bring it down today."

"Do you kayak often?" Henry asked.

Andrew shrugged. "A few times. I won a kayak race in camp when I was a kid."

Ida tapped her life vest. "Invest in one of these. I know you kids think you're invincible. Better safe than sorry."

He chuckled. He hadn't been called a kid since, well, since he was a kid. Hell, he was pushing forty. Though to them, he must seem like a newborn. They couldn't be younger than ninety, which made their jaunts in the kayaks all the more remarkable.

One good thing talking to them was doing was bleeding the anger from his system. Andrew felt the tension in his shoulders and jaw start to ease.

"I'll keep that in mind."

She narrowed her eyes at him, knowing he was not going to get himself a life vest.

"How do you like the house?" Henry asked.

"It's beautiful. Everything is beautiful up here. So peaceful."

"Where you from?"

"New Jersey."

"The Garden State," Ida exclaimed. "Do you have a garden?"

"I tried growing tomatoes a couple of times. My wife and I have black thumbs."

Ida clucked at him. "There are no black thumbs. It's just a matter of chemistry and attention."

"Ida grows world-class rose bushes. People come from miles to see them. We used to host a party every year in our garden, but parties are a little much for us these days. We're content to let people wander the front yard and admire them."

They talked for several minutes, Henry and Ida asking him questions about his job, if he had a wife (*Oh, where is your Kate? The poor dear. You please tell her we said hello and can't wait to meet her when she's feeling better*), what made him come to Maine, how long were they staying, and so on.

He sat on the end of the dock so he wasn't standing over them like a benevolent giant. They might be wrinklies on the outside, but there was still a spark of vitality to them. It warmed his heart to see, but was also painful. He realised this would never be him and Kate. If the doctors were right, Kate would achieve young Andrew's wish and never become a wrinklie.

"Where do you live?" Andrew asked.

Henry pointed behind them. "A ways back. There aren't many houses on this lake, and all of us are full-timers. The winters are rough, but we have people to help with the shoveling and plowing. These days, I'm happy to shovel my spoon into my mouth without spilling half of it on my lap. Your cottage is the only rental. It used to belong to Fred Windham."

Ida interjected, "No, Fred owned it before. Remember? He was Abe's son, but he didn't like the cold. Or our wet springs for that matter. He sold it to that couple from outside Boston. What were their names?"

Henry tapped the handle of his paddle, thinking. "Yes, Ides, you're right. That was the Harrelsons. Uh-huh. The Harrelsons bought it from Fred, but they only stayed a year. His job transferred him somewhere and the commute was just too much. They've been renting it out ever since."

It looked like they wanted to go, Ida resting a paddle in the water, but Andrew had one last thing he wanted to ask.

"Are there any kids living around here? Like teenagers?"

Ida shook her head. "No kids that I know of. You and your wife are the youngest people out here right about now. Of course, there may be grandchildren popping in for a visit."

It wasn't the answer he was hoping for.

"Why do you ask?" she said.

"It's nothing. We've been hearing strange noises and someone was throwing rocks at the house last night. I'm sure it's just someone messing with us."

"I don't see how that's possible. Everyone up here pretty much keeps to themselves. I'm sure you've noticed this isn't exactly a hotbed of activity. I can't see the Hensons or D'Angelos harassing you and your wife."

"Who are the Hensons and D'Angelos?"

Henry pointed to the left and right of the property. "Your neighbours, though I doubt you'll see much of them. And I'm sure you've seen how much they've spaced out the parcels of land. Hard to run into someone, unless you catch them up by the main road when they're coming to check the mail or heading out."

Andrew forced a laugh. "My wife thinks it's animals. There was a deer the other night that woke us right up. It was making some awful noises."

Ida smiled. "They will at that, especially if they get scared, which isn't too hard to do to a deer. You'll get used to everything soon enough. It takes some adjusting. Trust me, when Henry and I moved here from Connecticut forty-three years ago, we jumped at every sound. Ours was only the second house built on the lake. We felt like Mother Nature wanted us out."

That made Andrew feel better. It was almost as if she knew exactly what he needed to hear and was delighted to give him comfort. Maybe Kate was right.

Never question the wisdom and kindness of the wrinklies.

"I won't hold you up anymore," Andrew said. "It was very nice meeting you. Hopefully when my wife is feeling up to it, we can have you over for lunch."

"I never turn down a free meal," Henry said.

"Take care of your Kate. We want to see her real soon," Ida said, and the pair paddled away.

"Let 'er rip, Ides," Henry said, chuckling as his paddle skipped the water's surface.

Andrew watched them sail away, Henry raising his hand in a final farewell.

When he looked down into the water, he could see the rock. Ida had said the sun would be out tomorrow (thank you, *Annie*). He'd go for a swim and carry the rock to where he couldn't see it. An animal hadn't thrown *that* rock.

He'd brought them here to relax and recharge before Kate's next round of hellacious treatment. Andrew joked that he and Kate must have been child killers in a previous life. Their current incarnations were just a long step toward penance. Well, it appeared that penance involved spoiling his Hail Mary pass at peace.

Spending their nights with one ear open was not the way he wanted to wile away the rest of the summer. That wouldn't do. He was not going to cower like a child or be run off. He'd be damned if he let that happen.

There was a way to fix that.

CHAPTER EIGHTEEN

Days later, Kate's fever had come back and refused to be broken, leaving her feeling worse than ever. She'd called her doctor in the morning (the connection giving out several times, driving Kate to the brink of madness) and it was as she'd expected. The mélange of chemicals they'd injected into her body two months ago were still doing their thing. Like an acid trip (her analogy, not his), it could come back and hit her hard at any time. Right now, it was going full MMA on her, and there was nothing to do but grit her teeth and ride it out.

The problem was, the pain was so bad, even her teeth hurt, so gritting them was out of the question.

Andrew had taken the kayak out after she insisted she didn't want him lurking around the cottage. There was no sense having them both trapped in there.

Kate sighed.

Trapped.

That was the last thing she'd expected to feel in her dream lake cottage.

Yet here she was, truly and madly trapped in more ways that one.

She called and left a message for Ryker. She kept playing phone tag with her brother while he was going from speaking engagement to speaking engagement. She in turn slept through his return calls. Kate missed him so much. Since his career had taken off, she'd seen less and less of him. Ryker would know how to set her at ease. Quick text messages wouldn't do. She needed to hear his voice and tell him about the vibe the cottage was giving her, along with the strange new microwave feels she'd been suffering through. He was the one who'd coined *bad feels days*. He'd get a kick out of the microwave feels.

"Instead, I get Mr. Floppy Ears," she said, rubbing Buttons' head.

The past few nights had been mercifully quiet, but she was still having trouble sleeping after dark. That was why she wanted to watch *Two for the Road* and take a nice, long nap.

She checked her tablet and saw it was time to dip a hand into the mason jar. After fishing a few pills out, she swallowed them down with a meagre sip of water and settled into Mooshy, which contoured itself around her head. From her vantage point, looking out at the lake, she couldn't see the sun, but its reflection on the water burned a horizontal line right to the back porch. There was nothing more she wanted in this world than to be out there with Andrew. Knowing her, she'd challenge him to a race, the stakes typically being something he'd been wanting to do in the bedroom. Before everything had gone to shit, she'd been strong and fast and highly competitive. Even a kayak race (she'd only been in a kayak twice in her life) would net her at least 50/50 odds of winning.

If sex was on the line, there really were no losers, except that time Andrew had whipped her in miniature golf and she had to let him film them doing it in the shower. They'd watched it once after that, Kate viewing the whole thing through the slits between her fingers. Andrew had loved it, his tent-poled shorts attesting to that, but she'd hated it. The angles were all wrong, the lighting less than flattering.

Is that really the face I make when I come? Oh, no, don't spread my cheeks for all the world to see. We look like we're in pain.

She'd made him delete the video, and she never wagered on miniature golf again.

And here she was reminiscing about things that would never be, missing her life with her husband even though they were still together, more so now than ever.

Kate watched Audrey Hepburn and Albert Finney snipe at one another in an airport diner, her eyelids getting heavy.

When the back door slid open, she practically levitated off the bed.

Andrew walked in, no longer wearing the bathing suit and his black Ramones T-shirt he'd had on when he left to go kayaking.

"Whoa, it's only me," he said.

Kate's heart pulsed against the back of her tongue.

"I think I nodded off for a second. You scared me."

"If by 'a second', you mean three hours, yeah, you definitely nodded off."

He had a beer in one hand, the paper in the other. He tossed the paper by the growing pile in front of the fireplace. They hadn't lit a fire yet because Kate was paranoid about burning the house down. But when they finally did, they'd have enough fuel in newspapers and magazines alone to keep it going for a week.

She frowned, looking at the television. There was a commercial for a water park on the Maine coast.

"Great, and I missed *Two for the Road*. How was the kayaking?"

He went to the kitchen to get another beer. "Great. The lake is a lot bigger than I thought. You can see a few houses tucked away, but most of them are hidden by the trees. The only way to know anyone lives nearby is by their docks. No big boats, though. Just little Sunfish and rowboats."

Kate looked outside. The afternoon sun cast narrow shadows on the porch. The sheet felt like razor blades sliding over her flesh. Her left hand was so numb, it didn't feel as if it were attached to her. There was a fresh bruise by her wrist. She'd most likely been sleeping on it for a while. She bruised like old fruit.

Shaking her hand, the feeling coming back in painful pins and needles, she said, "Did you meet anyone?"

Andrew settled into the chair opposite the bed. "I thought I spotted a guy walking away from his dock. Old Henry and Ida are the only people I've seen up close. Other than that, it's like having our own private lake."

Not so private, Kate thought, hearing those sounds outside their window as if they had happened seconds ago.

Andrew touched her cheeks with the back of his hand, tucking her hair behind her ears. "I can cook pancakes on your skin."

"The phrase is *fry an egg*."

He shrugged. "It's still in the breakfast realm. I like pancakes a lot more than eggs. No matter what, you're still *en fuego*. You know what? My agenda is clear for the day. How about I slip into my pyjamas and we watch movies until our eyes get crossed?"

Kate thrilled at the idea. It was one of the few things she could do with her husband. Andrew existed in a restless state. Sitting for one movie was usually his limit; then he had to get up and do something. Those nights when they cuddled and went on a movie marathon were her favourites.

"I think nothing would make me happier," she said.

Andrew stripped right there and then.

"We'll need snacks and drinks," he said, turning to give her a wonderful view of his buns. They weren't as tight as they used to be, but they were hers and she loved them as much as she missed holding them.

"Come here."

He stood beside the bed, his soft cock inches from her face. There had been a time when it wouldn't stay soft for long. He'd loved the fact that she was not a big foreplay person. She went right for what she wanted, ready or not.

"Now turn around," she said.

Andrew smirked, then gave a slight turn.

She reached out and gave his ass a light pinch, then smacked it.

"Hey, I charge extra for the rough stuff."

"Now get me some pretzels and a soda."

He gave an exaggerated bow. "I live to serve."

God, she wanted him. But every nerve ending was raw and agitated, her skin ultra sensitive. Even the playful slap had sent ripples of sharp pain up her arms. She could try to have sex with him, but she'd be in tears in no time. The last thing she wanted to do was get him excited and let him down. It was better she live with the frustration. She'd become a world-class expert at sexual repression.

He covered the bed with bowls of junk food, got her a soda and a beer for himself, and then went into the bedroom to put on boxer shorts and a sleeveless shirt.

"Kiss me," she said as he settled in next to her.

"You have any movies in particular you want to watch?" he said, putting his arm around her.

She handed him her tablet. "You pick. I bequeath control to you."

He chuckled. "Get ready for some brainless entertainment."

"I expect nothing less."

They munched (well, mostly Andrew) and watched a trio of action movies, each more outlandish and brash than the last. She hadn't even realised he'd fallen asleep during the third movie until it was almost over.

By then, night had crept over the lake, and Kate's pain pills lulled her to a numb nothing, her home away from home.

★　　★　　★

The view from the top of the swaying evergreen tree was dizzying.

Kate looked down at the roof of the cottage. The chimney remained cold and empty. She would have loved the sweet smell of woodsmoke up here.

Day turned preternaturally fast into night, the chirping of the birds on the branches beneath her fading into stillness. From this height, Kate thought she could touch the moon, but she didn't dare take her hand off the crown of the tree for fear of falling.

The night air caressed her body, kissed her face, melded into hungry hands that probed her most tender parts. She leaned into the wind, nerves shuddering with each whispery touch.

A crash from below pulled her from her ecstasies.

Dark shapes had surrounded the cabin.

Andrew!

She screamed to get his attention but no sound escaped from her constricted throat.

They're going to get him! Dear God, they're going to get him.

Kate tried to climb down the tree. Her hands were coated with thick sap, sticking her to the narrow trunk like flypaper.

The shadows ran round and round the cottage until they were a solid grey blur. When the door opened, light spilling onto the front porch, she nearly wept.

Her husband stood in the doorway, staring at the spinning shadows.

He stepped onto the porch.

No, Andrew! Go back inside!

The top porch step creaked under his weight.

The second silently supported his advance.

The oscillating wall of shadows spun faster and faster.

Please, look up! I'm here! Can you see me? Don't go near them. Go back inside. Please, Andrew, look at me!

He squared his shoulders and ran into the wall.

A dull concussion rocked the roots of the tree. The trunk groaned as it began to crack in half.

Andrew lay stunned on the porch, his legs and arms bent into bizarre angles.

Kate pleaded with the tree to let her go. She could feel its terror through the palms of her trapped hands.

It was dying. The moon canted as the tree started to fall.

Now a scream ripped free as Kate tumbled down, down, down.

Heading toward Andrew.

The sap snapped and she broke free, flailing in the night sky.

She didn't remember hitting the ground. She lay within the shadow wall.

Every bone should be broken, but she'd never felt better, stronger, healthier.

Her hand brushed against the wall. It was like touching the backs of bees in a hive, the kinetic energy of Mother Nature's joy buzzer.

Kate laughed.

She was hungry.

Andrew lay broken and unconscious.

Why was he always running at things?

Running from things?

Her stomach grumbled.

The fading pulse at his neck looked so delicious.

No! I won't do it!

An impossibly large shadow stepped into the doorway within the cottage. This wasn't a shadow. This was real. She couldn't discern a shape or any features, but she knew it was real.

And it was watching her.

Waiting for her to feed.

To heal.

Kate found herself on her knees beside Andrew, weeping. Hot saliva dripped from her mouth. She touched her lips to the savoury pliancy of his neck. It would be so easy to bite down, to rip and tear and eat.

"Noooooooooo!"

She jerked away. The shadow thing in the cottage gave a warning grunt.

"Go to hell," *she whimpered, pulling Andrew's lifeless, crooked arm over her body. He breathed his last breath against her neck. She nestled into his corpse, the little spoon cradled by the big spoon, willing herself to ignore the escalating cries of the shadow thing as it stormed out of the cottage.*

*   *   *

It felt like someone had ripped the flesh from her side, exposing her steaming meat and sinew to the jaggedly cold night air. Kate awoke breathless, dizzy, utterly disoriented by the fiery agony.

Forcing herself to calm down, she looked down to see Andrew had his arm draped over her. The weight of his arm had sent her nerves into a frenzy.

Grabbing him by the wrist, she whisked Andrew's arm away. It hit the mattress with a dull *plop*. He didn't even break a snore.

It hurts, it hurts, it hurts so much.

Rubbing her side only made it worse.

Kate shifted farther from Andrew, sweat dampening her hairline even though it had gotten quite chilly in the darkened cottage. Her tablet lay between them, the television off for a rare instant.

Plit. Plit. Plit. Plit.

The patter of tiny rocks bouncing off the roof instantly made her forget her pain.

Buttons, who was down by her feet, heard it as well and gave the ceiling a casual glance.

The droning chirp of crickets seemed louder than ever, as if they had been tasked with masking the movements of the rock thrower. Kate looked over at the kitchen and saw the window had been left open. Andrew had fallen asleep and forgotten to close it.

She felt exposed, the partially open window wide enough to allow all of her nightmares into the cottage. She and Andrew might as well have been on the porch, the door locked behind them, left out for the dark things.

Dark things?

You're getting a little carried away with yourself.

Things were far better to consider than people. Nothing was more terrifying that people gone bad, their brains rotting like spoiled meat in the sun. Of all the atrocities Kate had been witness to during her life, all of them had been perpetrated by people, not monsters. The boogeyman didn't shoot up schools or drive trucks into crowds of people. Ghosts didn't hijack planes or murder families in their sleep.

People, bad people, did all of those things.

Was one of those bad people out there now?

Ka-thump!

That one got Kate to hop out of bed, heart racing.

"Andrew," she whispered.

He stirred, turning away from her.

"Andrew," she said, sharply this time.

"*Ahoo. Ahoo.*"

Andrew bolted upright. "What was that?"

"They're back," Kate said, trembling. "You left the window open." She heard the accusation in her voice. When they'd gone to bed with the window closed, their nights had passed uneventfully. But Andrew had forgotten to put their talisman in place, and now their stalker was back.

It was utterly irrational, but Kate didn't give a great goddamn.

More rocks hit the roof, sounding larger now. And then there was that "*Ahoo.*" Over and over, that strange cry. It rose and fell in volume, as if the maker of the bizarre hoot was circling the cottage.

"Close the window," Kate hissed.

Andrew ran to the kitchen and paused with his hands on the window. What the hell was he waiting for?

Whap!

A monster of a rock crashed into the house, this time sounding as if it was coming from the bedroom.

Kate couldn't see Andrew well in the darkness, but she could discern his shape leaning into the window. She turned a light on.

"No lights," Andrew hissed.

She quickly snapped it off. "Did you see anything?" she said, back to whispering.

"No. Not yet."

She could plainly hear someone walking outside. A branch cracked and Kate slapped her hand over her mouth.

That was followed by something hitting into the sliding doors. Andrew had remembered to draw the curtains, so she couldn't see what it had been. The temptation to open the blinds a crack and see was overwhelmed by her fear.

"What are they doing?" she said, on the verge of tears.

Andrew's voice sounded cold and heavy, coming out of the darkness.

"They want to scare us."

Rocks and other things continued to bounce off the house, Kate flinching every time. Her shoulders felt like they were going to break, her heart banging in against her chest.

"*Ahoo!*"

It was loud this time. So loud, she was sure the sound caromed off the still lake, slipping into the bedrooms of the houses nestled in the woods. To Kate, that yelp didn't sound entirely human. Nor did it sound like any of the animals they'd listened to. It was something entirely...other.

"That's it," Andrew said. His footsteps thumped on the hardwood floor as he ran to the bedroom. "They're fucking with the wrong guy."

"Andrew? What are you doing?" Buttons started barking. She so wanted to turn a light on. The dark felt tangible, cloying. She heard Andrew open the closet door, boxes being thrown aside.

The rocks continued to pelt the house, that gut-churning *Ahoo!* on steady repeat.

"Shut up! Shut up! Shut up!" Kate shouted, feeling like her heart was going to burst. She was feeding off her husband's rage. Enough was enough.

Andrew strode into the living room, fully dressed and holding a huge flashlight. When he flicked it on, keeping it pointed at the floor, the entire cottage lit up.

Shielding her eyes, she said, "Where did you find that?"

Before he could answer, she saw the rifle in his other hand.

A rifle?

His breathing was ragged.

"No, you are not going out there. Where the hell did you get a gun?"

He tucked the flashlight under his armpit and grabbed hold of the doorknob to the front door.

"We'll discuss this later," he said. His eyes were flat and cold with fury.

"I don't want you going out there with a gun, Andrew. Have you ever fired one before?"

What worried her more was her belief that brandishing a gun led to the other person taking out theirs. So far, their night stalker had been content to pitch rocks and make a lot of weird noises. Neither was going to hurt them.

What if they saw Andrew with his rifle and, sensing the stakes had risen dramatically, decided in a flash of anger to have the final word?

Kate could tell there was no stopping him. The moment he opened the door, Buttons rushed into the night.

"Buttons, get back here," Andrew snapped.

He followed the beagle, slamming the door behind him.

The rain of rocks suddenly stopped.

Kate sat alone in the darkness, the salt of her tears stinging her lips. She no longer cared about the stalker. She was worried about Andrew and Buttons.

She heard walking, but it could have been Andrew. Buttons had stopped barking. She thought of the old dog running recklessly into the woods and getting lost – or even worse, stumbling across the stalker and being hurt.

From off in the distance, there came another "*Ahoo.*"

The crickets silenced.

The night went perfectly still.

The only sound in the cottage was Kate's soft sobs.

There came a pointed *click*, the sound of metal against metal.

Kate held her breath.

The explosion of gunfire sounded like the end of the world.

CHAPTER NINETEEN

Andrew sat in a hardback chair in the tiny dining room, the new Remington 783 on the table. Dawn had finally come, but he didn't feel as if he could exhale just yet.

"I'm so sorry, honey," he said.

Kate was on the bed, heavily sedated. After he'd come back into the house with Buttons, the pallor of her skin and look in her eyes had rocked him to his core. She'd refused to go to the hospital, insisting she just needed to make sure he was okay and to take a sedative to calm down. She had a scrip for anti-anxiety pills (if anyone had reason for anxiety, it was Kate) that she didn't use very much. He found a pill after dumping the mason jar on the bedspread. She'd been pretty zonked out ever since.

"Huh?"

Her eyes were only half-open, the corner of her mouth slack. Thank God, she'd gotten some colour back in her cheeks, though kissing her forehead a few minutes ago had told him most of that colour was coming from the returning fever.

Andrew didn't bother her, watching her eyes slowly close all the way.

Once it was light enough to see well, he was going outside...without the rifle.

Firing it last night had scared the hell out of him. He hoped that if he wasn't now a murderer, it had frightened off the lunatic who had been harassing them for good. He'd been so goddamn angry, the whole thing was just a big, black blur. Maybe it wasn't such a good idea to give a firearm to a guy with anger issues.

He hadn't thought of getting the rifle until he spotted the firearms case at the sporting goods store the next town over. He'd stopped by to pick up a small life vest, realising that if he drowned, there was no one left to properly care for Kate. Ida would have been proud of his very grown-up decision.

And then he'd gone and done something to erase that pride.

Perhaps he was being overly paranoid, but he couldn't shake the feeling that their stalker was indeed a man and quite possibly nuttier than a pecan pie. Once he found out how easy it was to get a rifle (a few hundred dollars and a background check that took all of fifteen minutes), he figured the small investment was worth some peace of mind. The burly man running the rifle department took the time to show him how to load it, carefully going over all the bells and whistles (including a lot on the attached scope, something he was pretty sure he'd never use) and advising him to learn the owner's manual by heart. Andrew guessed it was easy to see he was no experienced hunter. The man never questioned his reason for buying the rifle, something he'd worried about the entire time.

Little had he known he'd be firing it less than twelve hours later.

He knew Kate wanted to give him holy hell about it, but that would have to come later. He'd nearly scared her to death when he fired off a warning shot.

"Please don't tell me you shot someone," she'd said when he came back inside, his hands shaking uncontrollably.

"No. No. I just wanted him to know I wasn't messing around anymore. I shot it into the air."

The truth was, the more he thought about it, the less certain he was that he'd pointed the muzzle straight up into the sky. He'd been so amped up, he thought he might have shot straight into the woods. There was no reason to tell Kate that. He'd already done enough damage.

All I wanted to do was save her from all this anxiety, and I just made it worse. Why the hell did I shoot? The guy even said never to fire the rifle unless you clearly see what you're shooting at. I didn't see shit.

He looked out the window at the brightening sky, and then at the front door.

The moment you walk out there, our entire lives may be changed…and not for the better.

He was sick to his stomach, the knot of dread so enormous it physically pained him.

There was a chance whoever it was had run away the moment he and Buttons went outside. That was when all of the chanting and rock throwing had ceased. Buttons hadn't strayed far from the porch, hadn't gone off barking. Could it be there had been no one nearby for him to chase?

"Not that you're very reliable lately," he said to the dog, who lay on the floor with his head on his front paws.

Andrew's vision wavered, and he realised he was crying. To think he might have destroyed their lives in one single, stupid moment. He wanted to rush outside to prove to himself that his fears were overblown, but he was in turn terrified to see them justified. The front door both beckoned and repulsed him.

Wiping his tears, he muttered, "Fuck it."

When he tried to turn the knob, it slipped in his grasp. His palm was slick with sweat. He had to rub it on his pants in order to just open the door.

Keep it together. It's going to be okay.

His legs went wobbly as a newborn deer when he stepped onto the porch. Buttons nearly knocked him down as he bounded out the door, heading straight for his favourite pissing tree.

Tiny rocks littered the narrow porch.

Leaning on the rail, Andrew looked into the woods, temporarily relieved there wasn't a body rotting on the ground, chest splayed open from the gunshot.

Which way did I shoot?

It had been in the direction of where their car was parked; that much he was sure of. He felt guilty at his happiness that he hadn't blown out the windshield or buried a bullet through the hood into the engine.

Slowly, he stepped off the porch, Buttons uttering a quick yap and coming to his side. For the dog, it was a fun moment to be outside. Andrew wished for the dog's ignorance and innocence. Andrew offered up prayers to a God he no longer believed in, making promises he knew he'd never be able to fulfil in return for not finding a body.

Enough early morning light was penetrating the tree canopy for him to see well beyond the cottage. He held his breath as he walked around, waiting to see his worst nightmare come true at any moment. He kept his eyes on the ground, looking for spatters of blood.

Oh God, if there's a blood trail I have to follow, I don't think I can do it.

His heart fluttered as he explored, Buttons scampering about. Only when he'd been at it for a full half hour did he allow himself to finally exhale, leaning against a tree because he wasn't sure his legs could hold him up anymore.

Buttons kept looking back at the cottage.

"Yeah, I know you wanna go back inside, bud."

He hadn't shot anyone. He wasn't going to jail. He wasn't going to have to leave Kate.

Andrew sank to the ground, the exhaustion of the past night flooding his system. He'd be perfectly happy going right to sleep out here, the rough bark for a pillow, bugs crawling all over his body. He was just so damn tired.

From his vantage point, he could see the side of the cottage. The roof was filled with rocks big and small.

"Son of a bitch."

Whoever had been out here had had a field day using the house as target practise.

He'd shown them he wasn't going to take it lying down anymore (despite the fact he was lying down at the moment). That *had* to scare them off. Look how terrified he'd been just being on the safe end of the rifle.

Buttons barked, eager to get back inside. Andrew had to grip the tree to pull himself up.

Should he go up on the roof later and sweep those rocks off? He remembered seeing a ladder on the other side of the house. The roof was slanted, but it wasn't high up. If he left the rocks up there, they'd roll into the gutter and there'd be issues when the next storm came rolling in.

Tomorrow. I don't trust my legs to go up there today.

All he wanted to do was shower, get comfortable, and slide into bed next to Kate.

He saw the rabbit just as he was reaching down to pet Buttons.

It had been bent in half, its hind legs tangled up in its ears. There was no blood other than a slight stain at its mouth.

Why the fuck would someone do that?

Buttons spotted the rabbit too, and darted over to sniff it.

"Get away from there."

He crouched down to get a better look. It was white with black spots and lean, not like the kind people kept as pets. He'd have to bury it before Buttons used it as a chew toy or Kate saw it. She loved animals, and the sight of the folded bunny would set her to tears. That meant he'd have to look for a shovel. If he couldn't find one, he'd head to the hardware store in town.

For now, it would have to be left to the elements. If he was lucky, a scavenger would cart it off and save him the trouble.

Dusting off his jeans, he noticed the rabbit was not alone. Ten feet away, by the tree line, was a pile of dead squirrels crammed into the hollow of a dead, gnarled tree, the top half of it sheered off a considerable time ago. There had to be at least a dozen squirrels in there, their broken bodies jammed into the small opening.

An animal didn't do that. Animals didn't stockpile their kills. Not like that.

Holding Buttons by the collar so he wouldn't tear into the squirrels, Andrew felt his gorge rise when he saw they were all missing their heads.

He was suddenly very glad he'd bought the rifle.

Even more so that the sick son of a bitch who'd done this knew he had it.

*　　*　　*

Kate's fever didn't break for three more days. The painful, burning microwave feels ebbed and flowed. A few times, Kate thought for sure her spine was going to break…or melt. It usually got bad at night, when her husband was fast asleep. Even though he didn't have work in the morning, she still didn't want to wake him up. There was nothing he could do about it anyway. Dr. K had said there'd be miserable days ahead for her.

Andrew never left the cabin, other than to walk Buttons. He'd mentioned going back home more than a few times. At first, Kate was game, but she was far too sick to travel.

Then, as the nights went back to normal, they both began to relax.

Andrew was up to reading a pulp paperback a day, sitting on the porch with his beer, always looking in to make sure she was okay. She wanted him to use the kayak, go explore, but she also loved the comfort of having him close by.

"At the rate you're reading, you're going to have to get another bag of books," she said when he came in to make them lunch.

He tapped his temple. "I'm feeling smarter every day."

He'd been very quiet the past few days. She knew something was on his mind, but expressing his feelings had never been one of his strong points. After the relief of knowing he hadn't accidentally shot anyone, Kate had called 3-1-1. She and Andrew agreed there was no need to tell anyone that he'd fired his rifle. A very nice, middle-aged sheriff's deputy had come by and taken their statements. Kate had watched them from the window as Andrew showed him the rocks on the roof and porch.

When they came back inside, Kate said, "Do you think it's just kids messing around?"

The deputy, by the name of Jerry Miles, smiled, as if this kind of thing happened every day. "I'm sure of it. You may have realised that there isn't all that much to do out here. Kids, they get restless, do stupid things. You're the new people, and trust me, news travels fast in town. I have a couple of locals in mind that are capable of doing this. They're harmless potheads who watch too many horror movies. On Halloween, they like to dress up as Jason or Freddy and scare the little kids. Morons of the highest order. I think I'll pay them a visit after this. They usually hang around the woods behind the park. I guarantee, they won't be back."

There was something about his confidence that soothed her. She'd been expecting Barney Fife and they had instead gotten Danny Reagan from that show *Blue Bloods*. It was wrong of her to assume the authorities would be slack-jawed locals with a badge. She'd never been so happy to be so wrong in her life.

"Thank you so much."

His leather belt creaked as he fished out a card and handed it to Andrew. "You call me if it happens again. But like I said, this should be the end of it. Feel better."

He'd been true to his word. No more rocks. No more strange noises.

"You want half or a whole cheese sandwich?" Andrew said.

"Half, with lots of Miracle Whip, please."

Andrew made their sandwiches and put her plate, napkin, small bag of chips, protein drink, and soda on a flat piece of wood he'd fashioned into a bed tray.

"For the queen," he said.

"I don't feel very royal today."

He kissed her forehead. "You also no longer feel like the Human Torch, so that's a step in the right direction."

She took a bite of her sandwich and said, "You know, you can go out and do something today. There's no reason to be cooped up in here when you don't have to be."

He devoured half his sandwich in two bites. "Don't you worry about me. I'm happy right where I am."

"But I do worry about you. When we're home, I don't want you to look back at this summer with regret. Why don't you try some fishing? You said you used to love to go fishing with your grandpa when you were a kid."

He smiled at the memory. "Yeah, that man loved to fish. Unfortunately, he handled everything and I was so young and dumb, I never bothered to pay attention. I wouldn't even know how to tie a line or set up a reel."

"Then go out for a drive and find a better pizza place. I just don't want you stuck in here with me every day. It's bad enough one of us is glued to the bed. I give you permission to find a bar and drink with the locals."

"The only bars around are VFW halls. I don't think I qualify for membership. The closest I got to the military was playing *Call of Duty*."

Kate took another bite of her sandwich and was done. She wasn't feeling very hungry today, though she knew her appetite could be revived by a slice of Milano's pizza. She'd have to wait until September for that.

See you in September.

Now she understood the longing and promise in the old song her father used to sing around the house. It figured that for her, it would be over pizza and not a boy.

Andrew got up to put his plate in the sink. "Besides, I have work to do on the house."

Kate looked around the mostly spotless living room. The only real mess was the pile of papers by the fireplace.

"What kind of work?"

"Tomorrow's the Fourth of July. Gotta make the place spiffy for the holiday. The bathroom floor needs a good mopping, and I have to get all those rocks off the roof. Plus, I have to move some furniture around."

"What on earth are you talking about? The furniture is just fine where it is."

He stood over her with his hands on his hips, a mischievous smile on his face. "Not if we're going to have company."

Kate eyed him suspiciously. "Company? I know you want to have that old couple over, but I don't feel up to it."

"Oh, I'm sure Henry and Ida already have big plans. Probably organising the fireworks display as we speak and getting the DJ booth set up."

"Har-har."

"Nope, instead of the Keepers of the Golden Pond, I invited your brother and Nikki to come up for a long weekend."

At first, Kate wasn't sure she'd heard correctly. She stared at him, mouth hanging open.

"You know. Ryker and Nicola. We were at their wedding. I believe he made you eat a worm when you were four."

An enormous grin spread across her face. "Are you kidding me? I thought they were going away to San Diego."

Ryker had met Nicola, Nikki to them, on a visit to London, where he was conducting a three-day seminar on unlocking your career potential. Nikki said it was love at first sight. Ryker didn't disagree. They'd married after a three-month courtship and had been inseparable ever since. It should have made Kate jealous, her little brother living such an amazing life, so full of energy and the entire world wide open for him. All she ever felt when he recounted his latest adventure was pride.

She guessed that was exactly the way big sisters should look at their baby brothers.

Andrew could no longer hold back his own wide smile. "Nope. I called him and said we had a spare bedroom and could use the company. He cancelled San Diego and booked a flight to Portland that afternoon."

Kate felt the tears spring in her eyes. "Come here." She pulled him in for as much of a crushing hug as she could muster. "Thank you so much. Every time I think I love you as much as I possibly can, you go and do something that makes me love you more."

"Don't love me too much. I'm fragile."

CHAPTER TWENTY

Andrew had spent the entire previous day cleaning the cottage, both inside and out. Kate kept trying to help, and he had to keep insisting she get her butt to bed and enjoy her time as a passive observer. She was as stubborn as a mule. Every time he left the living room to tackle something, he'd rush back in to find her washing dishes or attempting to order his kindling pile. He'd command her to return to her spot on the bed and get back to work. The bouncing back and forth was exhausting, Kate never realising that her attempts to help actually made things more difficult.

But she was clearly happier than he'd seen her since the day he'd carried her over the cottage's threshold. There was no way he was going to harsh that mellow.

When Kate called the cops a few days ago, he'd rushed outside to dispose of the dead rabbit and cover up the squirrels. His fear was they would talk about it in front of Kate and how much more that would upset her. If having the deputy approach the teens he thought were harassing them didn't work, Andrew could always reveal it to him later.

For once, good fortune was on their side. The night visitations had stopped, and Andrew had bought a shovel from town and buried the bodies, feeling like he was in some kind of horror movie, the day of the burial dark and gloomy, with thunder rolling on the horizon.

So now he sat in his car outside Portland International Jetport, waiting for Ryker and Nikki to arrive. Before he left for Portland, he'd gone to the market and stocked up on enough food and drinks to last a week. He'd even bought a portable grill, the old kind his father used to take with them on picnics when Andrew was a kid. It had been a long time since he'd cooked with charcoal and lighter fluid. When he'd bought a gas grill for his own house, his father had remarked, "Food won't taste as good. Everyone knows proper barbecue needs a hint of that lighter fluid flavour."

He'd even found what looked like a little pop-up store two towns over that sold fireworks. As it turned out, you could buy and use fireworks in the majority of towns in Maine, Bridge Mills being one of them. He'd spent a hundred dollars on some colourful rockets. He wasn't a fan of the big-explosions ordinance, like M-80s and cherry bombs. Neither was Kate. It would be nice to set a few rockets off by the dock, the sparkles illuminating the darkened lake.

Listening to a rock station (*Why don't they have stations this good in New York, the biggest radio audience in the country?*) Andrew checked his work email on his phone for the first time since leaving Jersey. His inbox had over a thousand messages.

A thousand.

What would it be like when he got back?

The knock on his window nearly made him drop his phone.

Ryker had his face pressed against the glass, distorting his features.

"Didn't mean to wake you," he said, laughing.

Andrew got out and gave him a hug. Ryker had let his hair grow, his thick black shag slicked back and tied in a bun. His overly large, perfect teeth were so white, they were blinding, even in the midday sun. It was a smile meant to dazzle, and dazzle it did. People paid good money for that smile, a smile that said anything was possible if you set your intentions right.

What Andrew called psychobabble for the masses, Ryker called success.

"You are a sight for sore eyes," Andrew said. "I see you've hitched your waggon to the man-bun craze. I thought you were a leader, not a follower."

Ryker's eyes rolled upward. "Totally Nikki's idea. She likes it. I'm not crazy about it, but if I avoid mirrors, out of sight, out of mind."

"Speaking of Nikki, where is she?"

People were streaming out of the arrivals gates, lugging bags on wheels.

"She had to make a quick pit stop to the loo, as her people say."

Andrew stowed their luggage in the trunk. He clapped Ryker on the shoulder. "Her people will be your people once you start having babies."

"Don't rush me, big guy. We're having too much fun right now."

Kate and her mother were eagerly waiting for grandchildren, nieces, and nephews. All of the pressure was on Ryker and Nikki, but you'd never know it when you spoke to them about it. Andrew liked to kid him because he knew how much guff Ryker got for not getting to work on the next generation.

Ryker waved his arms. "Over here!"

Nikki emerged, looking as if she'd just stepped off the hair-and-makeup chair on a movie set. She was as stunning as ever, her long red hair flowing over her shoulders, piercing green eyes taking in what passed for the hustle and bustle of Portland, which was a far cry from the airports in New York, where they lived.

She saw Andrew, broke into a run, and leaped into his arms.

"Andy, how have you been?" she exclaimed, planting a kiss on his cheek.

"I've been. Have a nice flight?"

He opened the door for her and she slipped into the backseat. "It was, once I got a few vodka tonics in me. Flying is absolute shite these days. I keep telling Ryker he needs to book more gigs so we can buy a private plane."

They all settled into the car.

Ryker said, "And I tell her the day I spend all my money on a private plane is the day you have me committed."

"Oh, pooh," Nicola said, playfully slapping the back of Ryker's seat.

Andrew pulled away from the airport and merged onto I-95. They made small talk, Nicola's sense of humour as salty as ever. It was what had attracted her to Ryker in the first place. A smart, good-looking woman who could make a sailor blush was a dream come true for his brother-in-law.

Hopping off the highway and making their way to Route 302, Ryker got serious and asked, "So tell me, how is she? Whenever I talk to her, she says she's fine, but she doesn't sound fine. I think she won't use Skype because she doesn't want me to see her. Easier to keep up the lie that way."

Nikki sat forward, her head between them. She said, "I long ago gave up asking their mum about her. It's like talking to the fucking old Berlin Wall. I know she dotes on Ryker, but she can be a real prig when it comes to Katy."

Katy.

Ryker and Nikki were the only people in the world she allowed to call her that.

Andrew drew in a deep, tired breath. He'd known they were going to have this conversation before they got to the cabin. Being the bearer of bad news was never fun.

"She's not good," he said.

Nikki covered her mouth, eyes wide. Ryker sat up straighter in his seat.

"How bad?" Ryker asked.

"Look, it's not life and death now. Not like before. But she's been real sick. Her immune system is shot to hell. I'm not sure she even has one. The new treatment is a horror show. She had it almost two months ago and she's still suffering from the aftereffects. The doctors are giving her the summer for her body to kind of recharge and recover. But when we get back in September, she has to go through it all again."

Ryker asked what was involved in the treatments, and Andrew told him about the needles, each one large and filled with what was essentially poison. His brother-in-law's permanent smile turned into the very rarest of frowns.

Andrew said, "I guess the one good thing you can say about it is that it's not chemo."

The word hung over them like a suspended nuclear warhead. They all had been through Kate's struggles and knew what chemo meant. It meant last chances, organ transplants, and so much worse.

"How is she holding up mentally?" Nicola said. "The poor girl. She's already been through so much. It has to be wearing her down. Wearing you both down."

She gave his shoulder a gentle squeeze.

"She's as good as you can expect anyone in her situation to be. Better than most."

Ryker said, "I'm always on the lookout for doctors that are making huge strides in treating autoimmune diseases. I sent Katy over a few to look at a couple months ago, but she never got back to me. I didn't want to push and upset her."

Andrew chuckled, breaking some of the tension. "That's your sister. Stubborn to a fault. She never even told me about them, which means she has no desire to see more doctors."

"Even if they can help?" Nicola said.

"In her mind, they all just look at her as a lab rat. They poke and prod and sometimes hurt her, and then declare there's nothing they can do for her. Trust me, we've had this conversation before, and she's just done with them."

Ryker shook his head, a fist tapping his knee. "Maybe for now, but I'll break her down."

"Good luck. Hopefully your powers of persuasion are better than mine."

"Hey, it's what I'm paid for."

They moved on to lighter subjects. Nikki marvelled at the quaint small towns they passed along the way. Then she started telling dirty jokes, and Ryker filled the car with raucous laughter.

Andrew just smiled. They were exactly what Kate needed now. He hoped their positive energy would completely dispel the strange air around the cottage and lift Kate's spirits so they could really get down to enjoying their summer together.

* * *

Kate might have felt like sleeping, but she'd forced herself to shower, put on a nice sundress (that she didn't remember packing), and break out her makeup bag. She was excited to see Ryker and Nicola. Even Buttons seemed less lethargic.

Andrew had done an amazing job on the house. It was spotless, champagne chilling in a tall popcorn bowl he'd found under the sink. Once she had herself all made up, there was nothing to do but wait for them to arrive.

And don't even think of taking a nap.

She knew if she did, she'd be dead to the world and looking like a hot mess when they got here. It was hard enough being in a room with Nikki on her best days, wondering if Andrew thought he'd drawn the short straw.

He loves you and would never think that. And Nikki is the sweetest sister-in-law I could have asked for. It's not her fault she looks like a freaking Victoria's Secret model.

No, it wasn't, and it was unfair to even think that way. Kate laughed. She could always blame it on the meds.

At a little after one, she heard the key slip into the lock on the front door. Andrew had been keeping all of the doors locked since the rock-throwing night. Kate got up from the chair, legs a little unsteady, heart racing – but for once it was because she was excited and happy.

The door swung open and Ryker burst into the cottage, followed by a smiling Nikki, with Andrew bringing up the rear, bags in tow (like Jimmy Stewart in *Mr. Hobbs Takes a Vacation*, she thought, giggling).

"Katy!"

Buttons went for Ryker, hopping excitedly around his legs.

Ryker swept her off her feet, his strong arms wrapped around her waist.

"I can't believe you're here," she said.

"Once Andrew called and invited us, there was no way we were going anywhere else." He put her down but she was immediately bowled over by Nikki.

"My sister from another mister," Nikki cooed. "You look great, Katy."

"I wish. I love your earrings."

Nikki flicked the dangling jewels. "These are a make-up gift from your brother for forgetting our anniversary."

Ryker, who had gone out the sliding door and was admiring the lake from the porch, said, "I didn't forget. I was at that seminar in Denver, and by the time I got back to my room, it was too late to call."

Arching a perfectly sculpted eyebrow, Nikki said, "Like I said, he forgot. If he hadn't, I would have gotten my usual roses and gold bracelet. The price tag is in direct proportion to the guilt."

Kate said, "I wish Andrew would forget our anniversary every now and then."

He came over and kissed her cheek. "Oh, I'll get you earrings then, but I don't think they'll exactly measure up." Grabbing the dripping bottle of champagne, he said, "Shall we start things off right?"

After popping the cork, he poured champagne into four water glasses. The cottage hadn't come equipped with champagne flutes. Ryker and Nicola might have money and be world travellers, but they didn't give a fig about stuffy propriety. They clinked glasses.

"To an awesome Independence Day with my favourite sister," Ryker said.

"I'm your only sister."

He added, "Who never needed to work hard to be my favourite."

They all laughed and drank. Even Kate had a small sip of champagne. Their laughter sounded so strange in the cottage. Strange and welcome and invigorating. Pained joints, tired bones and overtaxed organs couldn't keep Kate from smiling.

*   *   *

"Come here, big sis," Ryker said, pulling her into the bedroom. His and Nikki's suitcases had been stacked beside the dresser. The room smelled of Nikki's perfume – something French and floral.

They sat on the bed, her brother tenderly holding her hands in his. Nikki and Andrew were in the dining room, having a drink and talking about some British TV show that he'd found recently and loved.

"Nice man bun," Kate said with a roll of her eyes.

"Happy wife, happy life," he said, looking like he hated it as much as she did. "How are you feeling?" Before she could answer, he held up a hand. "And don't tell me fine. I can see you're not fine. Be honest with me. I can take it."

She sighed, feeling the defences she put up on a daily basis start to weaken.

"I've been better," she said.

"Andy says the doctor talked about chemo."

She bristled. Even hearing the word made her anxious and scared. "It won't come to that."

Ryker rubbed her hand. "I'll pray every day it doesn't. So, what are the mad doctors doing to get you better?"

She told him about the treatment and the shots in and around her spine. He winced.

"Jesus, I'm sorry you had to go through that. That must have hurt like hell."

"That's putting it mildly. And naturally it's experimental because nothing about me is ever close to normal."

His fist thumped the mattress. "I really wish I could take all of this on for you. It's totally unfair that you have to get every damn genetic disorder our dysfunctional family can muster, and I can't even catch a cold."

She smiled. "That's what older siblings do. We protect the young and weak."

They shared a quiet laugh.

"Are you at least still meditating?" he asked.

That made her remember the first time she'd tried to meditate in the cottage and the weird feeling that had come over her.

"As a matter of fact, I think even you will find this kinda trippy."

She recounted the entire session to him – how she conjured the word *fever* and chipped away at it, willing it to depart from her body. The raging fire that had erupted within her, coalescing into a hot ball of agony in her gut before bursting from her, leaving her spent and cold.

When she was done, his brow was furrowed and he was lost in thought.

"Oh, and I have a new kind of feel. I call them microwave feels," she said.

"Microwave feels?"

"Whatever they put into my spine surfaces every now and again, and it feels like I'm being cooked from the inside out. Hence…"

"Microwave feels."

"Yep. They feel way worse than bad feels, but without the lingering shadow man."

Ryker shook his head. "You still see the shadows?"

True, she'd never told Andrew about the shadows, but she had been very open with Ryker about them. He never flinched or said she was crazy or high, even if he thought it. She felt guilty about hiding it from her husband, but wives had to have some secrets. She'd been so overexposed to him and a bevy of doctors and nurses, it made her feel less like an outsider to keep a few things from him, like every other married woman she knew.

"Not up here, which is a good thing. No, instead of shadows, I get a funky vibe off this place. You feel anything?"

"Just concern for you. Even if there was some weird energy here, I don't think it could cut through my apprehension."

"You need to stop worrying about me."

"I will when you're all better."

She gave him a hug, so grateful to Andrew that he'd brought Ryker here. She didn't know what she'd do without the two most important men in her life.

Ryker rubbed her shoulders and said, "Now, back to that weird meditation. Has it happened to you since that first time?"

"To be honest, I've kinda stayed away from meditating. It really freaked me out."

He nodded. "Understandable. That would flip me out too. You're going through a lot. I think where you may have gone wrong was focusing on a negative. We can both agree a fever is a negative, right?"

"It sure as hell is."

"Which means you gathered this negative energy around you. I don't know what the heck that burning sensation was. It's probably a coincidence that that stuff the doctors put in you reared its head at that moment. Whatever, the combo was powerful. So powerful, you may have attracted negative energy in the process."

Kate sighed. "So I brought whatever strangeness on myself?"

"Not intentionally," he was quick to add. "But if there's something out there or in here that's a tad on the dark side of things, your meditation may have called it over like a dinner bell."

She wasn't crazy about the dinner bell analogy, but she was feeling lighter just talking to him. "So, I've somehow attracted this bad juju, whether it be in the form of a person, place, or thing. Right?"

Ryker shrugged. "It's possible. I've told you, we can attract and manifest anything we put our minds to. With you being a little, off..."

"Way off."

He grinned. "Way, way off, you managed to pull in some bad vibes that have been lingering around. Who knows, maybe this is where some pioneers were attacked by wild animals in the 1700s, and you're latching on to their anger at having their lives cut short."

"Very dramatic," Kate said.

"And most likely completely wrong, but you get the gist."

Chewing on a fingernail, Kate|said, "Is there a way to reverse it?"

He grabbed her elbows and helped her stand up. "Yes. By having fun with Nikki and me this weekend. We'll make you forget all that weird stuff and leave you positively glowing."

Kate smirked. "This isn't one of your seminars, you know."

"Which is why I won't send you and Andy a bill. Now, what's for dinner? I'm starving."

*   *   *

Andrew barbecued steaks on the little collapsible grill, almost knocking it over twice. Kate and Nikki watched the boys from the Adirondack chairs on the back porch. Her sister-in-law had consumed a bottle of wine all by herself and was working on her second. So far, the alcohol didn't appear to have any effect on her.

"Do all Brits have hollow legs?" Kate asked. "I mean, where do you put it?"

Nikki was five-eight and all of a hundred and twenty pounds. Kate didn't know where the woman put anything, much less liters of alcohol.

"It's born of necessity. You ever see a cooking show about strictly English food? Ugh. We drink to survive."

Kate tapped her can of soda against Nikki's glass.

The boys were drinking beer and talking, but she couldn't hear them. Kate kept recalling the look in Ryker's eyes when he'd first walked in. He'd tried to mask his shock, but she'd caught that glimmer of trepidation. They hadn't seen each other in almost three months, with him travelling every week. She'd lost some weight since then, and she knew her makeup couldn't hide the bags under her eyes or the greying tone of her flesh. It made her realise how much worse things had gotten when Mr. Positivity couldn't put on his happy face…at least in that moment.

"Are you chaps just about done?" Nikki called out to them.

"Five more minutes," Andrew said. "Give or take."

Ryker shook his can. "As soon as the beer's done, the steaks will be, too."

"Good. I'll set the table."

Kate struggled to get up, her arms weak and wobbly. "I've got it."

Nikki put a hand on her shoulder. "At best, I'll allow you to watch me. You can tell me where things are. Come on, up you go."

Kate felt like a child, needing Nikki's help to get up and into the cottage. Nikki directed her to a chair at the dining room table, and then poured herself a fresh glass of wine.

With Kate's direction, she found everything to set the table, warmed up pre-made bowls of creamed spinach and mashed potatoes (Kate cringed at that, but Nikki and Ryker were also not the slightest but picky when it came to food. As she'd heard Nikki say more than once, *Today's food is nothing but tomorrow's shite*), and managed to down her wine seconds before Ryker and Andrew came in with the platter of steaming steaks.

As good as the steaks were, Kate's appetite wasn't up to eating much. She nibbled on the potatoes, just enjoying the company. Andrew looked happier than he'd been in a long time. He'd always been a social person, and she realised he needed this as much as she did.

After dinner, Ryker, of all people, cleaned the dishes.

"I see you've domesticated him," she said to Nikki.

"I'll be able to confirm that if I ever see it happen at home." When she broke into a fit of giggles that left her gasping, Kate knew the wine had hit home.

They sat around the living room, Andrew finally lighting that fire at Nikki's insistence. He looked like a pyromaniac who'd been handed matches for the first time in a decade. Kate swallowed her fear and had to admit it made the cottage cosy and smell this side of heavenly.

When night fell, Andrew said, "I have a surprise."

"Should I be nervous?" Kate said, feeling so drowsy but, for once, very content.

He thought for a moment, the glow of an entire day and night of drinking having put some pink in his cheeks. Swaying slightly on his feet, he said, "Possibly." He went out to the car, and for a brief moment, Kate almost told him not to go outside, *not in the dark*. Ryker and Nikki's laughter stopped her admonition. Andrew came back inside holding two huge plastic bags.

"Anyone want to light some rockets?"

Ryker jumped up and grabbed a bag. "I haven't done fireworks in forever. Let's go!" At that moment, he looked and sounded like he had when he was ten. Kate remembered them lighting penny rockets at their uncle's beach house, Ryker insisting he hold the stick and letting them go at the last possible moment.

Nikki opened the sliding door. "Ooh, a proper Independence Day. I may just pledge my allegiance to the flag."

Kate was happy to see everyone so excited, but her energy was seriously on the wane.

"You guys go. I'll watch them from in here."

Ryker handed the bag to Andrew. "Not a chance. Come on, I've got you."

Her protests fell on deaf ears as her brother knelt before her and got her on his back.

"See, all you have to do is sit. I'll take care of the rest. Remember when Dad used to give us pony rides?"

"Every day as soon as he walked in the door from work," she said, smiling at the memory.

He carried her all the way to the dock, while Nikki brought a chair for her to sit on.

It was so calm out here. Even the loons were silent, tucked away for the night. Kate was more appreciative for her brother than she could express.

For the next half hour, Ryker and Andrew lit the sky with sparkling greens, whites, reds, and golds. Nothing was loud, just bright and beautiful. Kate pulled Andrew in for a kiss.

"Thank you," she whispered in his ear.

"You know I love you, right?" he replied, his tongue thick and clumsy.

"I always do."

When the fireworks were done, they sat for a while longer talking, their voices skating across the lake's dark surface. Kate hoped their neighbours, wherever they were, weren't upset by the loud interlopers.

And so what if they are? We're allowed to have some fun on a holiday!

While everyone talked in drunk speak, Kate kept peering into the woods, unable to shake the feeling they were being watched. There had been no signs of their night visitor since Andrew fired the warning shot, but that didn't mean he – or they – weren't out there.

So why did the back of her neck tingle?

When Andrew carried her inside, she clung to his neck, eyes adjusted to the dark, seeking any dark shapes that didn't belong. But the woods were nothing but shadows, and the only things that didn't belong were themselves.

CHAPTER TWENTY-ONE

"You up for a run?" Andrew asked Ryker. His brother-in-law sat on the back porch, drinking a coffee. The man bun was gone, and it was obvious he was nursing a bitch of a hangover.

"I'm barely up for a crawl, man. You still run like the devil is chasing you?"

Andrew snickered. "Yep."

"Then I'll really pass. You're gonna hurt yourself one day."

"I do it to make sure I don't hurt other people."

The sun sparkled on the lake like spilled diamonds. Maine had decided to forego its usually chilly, damp start and had gone straight to warm and bright. Andrew looked back and saw Kate still out, lying on her side, her arm draped over Mooshy. Yesterday had been a long day for her, and he knew how much she'd pushed herself. Today was going to be a complete washout for her.

Ryker said, "I don't blame you for being angry. I get angry when I think of what Katy's going through, but I don't have to live with it twenty-four-seven. It's just sometimes, I'm not even sure what I'm angry at. Maybe it's a lot of things. Some days, it's just this fuzzy, all-encompassing hate, you know? And sometimes, it's hating myself for not being here more or doing more to take care of you both."

Andrew clapped him on the shoulder. He didn't know what to say, but he was sure that if he opened his mouth, it would come out wrong. Heart-to-hearts with anyone but Kate didn't come naturally. Hell, they were even difficult with her.

Instead he said, "It's not easy for any of us. But I'm not going to let Kate or me go down easy."

"I know you won't." He took a sip of coffee and suddenly snapped his fingers. "I just remembered this dream I had about Katy a little while back."

"Is that the one you called her about?"

"Yeah. But then I got tied up with all these conferences. Spring is my busy season for some reason. I never got to talk to her about it."

Andrew hated dream interpretations, but he asked just the same. "What was it about?"

Now Ryker tilted his head, thinking. "I can't recall all of it, but I remember shadows. A lot of shadows around her. Well, not around her, but coming out of her."

"Shadows coming out of her?"

Ryker clucked his tongue and said, "I know, it's weird. The thing is, it felt very real, like one of those lucid dreams. I don't have them very often, so it stuck with me. I looked up a few books on dreams, and shadows can mean a whole lot of stuff. Basically, it's like negative feelings, aspects, or emotions that you've bottled up or things about yourself you're afraid to look at."

Andrew desperately wanted to run, but he also wanted to hear more. "But wouldn't that then mean the dream was really about you and your feelings?"

"I think if they were coming out of me, sure. But I dreamed about them coming out of Katy. Look, I have no idea what it's about, but I did wake up concerned and wanted to just talk to her. With everything she's gone through, it's no surprise that she'd have an endless bundle of dark emotions."

"There's a lot going on inside that head of hers, but she doesn't talk about it much. She does meditate from time to time, though. I always hope it helps."

Ryker nodded. "Well, I'll see what I can drag out of her. Unlike you, I'm a bull in a china shop when it comes to her."

Andrew smiled. "And I'm grateful for that. You can get away with so much more than me. You've got that sibling thing working for you."

As Andrew was turning to go back in the house, Ryker snagged his arm. "Hey, what kind of wildlife do you have up in these parts?"

"Most of what you'd think would be roaming around. Nothing too wild and exotic."

"I guess there's a lot of moose up here."

Stretching, Andrew said, "That's what they say, though I've yet to see one. I thought I heard one once. Word is, you don't want to come across them. They're huge and cranky and dangerous. Why do you ask?"

FLAME TREE PRESS
FICTION WITHOUT FRONTIERS
Award-Winning Authors & Original Voices

Flame Tree Press is the trade fiction imprint of Flame Tree Publishing, focusing on excellent writing in horror and the supernatural, crime and mystery, science fiction and fantasy. Our aim is to explore beyond the boundaries of the everyday, with tales from both award-winners and original voices.

•

Other titles available include:

Thirteen Days by Sunset Beach by Ramsey Campbell
Think Yourself Lucky by Ramsey Campbell
The House by the Cemetery by John Everson
The Toy Thief by D.W. Gillespie
The Siren and the Spectre by Jonathan Janz
The Sorrows by Jonathan Janz
Kosmos by Adrian Laing
The Sky Woman by J.D. Moyer
The Bad Neighbour by David Tallerman
Ten Thousand Thunders by Brian Trent
Night Shift by Robin Triggs
The Mouth of the Dark by Tim Waggoner

•

Join our mailing list for free short stories, new release details, news about our authors and special promotions:

flametreepress.com